Buster
and the
Magic Star

A Cat and Dog Adventure Story

Robert Chadwick

Pursuant to sections 49 and 53 of the Copyright Act of Canada Copyright issued on October 29, 2013 by the Canadian Intellectual Property Office, Ottawa, Canada
Buster and the Magic Star
© Copyright 2014 Robert Chadwick and
Les Éditions Champ Fleury

ISBN 978-0-9696710-2-2

Les Éditions Champ Fleury
Estrie, Québec
CANADA
Printed by Create Space

Library and Archives Canada Cataloguing in Publication

Chadwick, Robert, 1941-, author
      Buster and the magic star : a cat and dog adventure story
/ Robert Chadwick.

ISBN 978-0-9696710-2-2 (pbk.)

      I. Title.

PS8605.H325B88 2014   C813'.6   C2014-907531-6

Find us online at:
www.EditionsChampFleury.com
info@EditionsChampFleury.com

Cover design and text layout by
Tim Doherty of VisImage,
Sherbrooke, Quebec

Prologue

When the first light broke over the horizon a great ocean covered the land while vast chunks of the planet slid about on the earth's molten core. Rock and earth heaved up from the ocean floor and the waters mixed with the soil, then broke free, and gushed towards the west cutting hydraulic canyons into the limestone sea bottom. For a thousand millennia torrents of water poured from the volcanic highlands through terra-gouges filling the deep basin that would become the Great Salt Sea. When the waters stopped flowing, the land dried; flowers and grasses grew out of the earth, and near-humans carrying wooden spears and stone hand axes came up from Africa to hunt and scavenge the iron-red land. A thousand generations later their descendants had walked all the way to China while the ones who stayed behind changed their species and became humans. As the millennia spun away in the backwash of the earth's cycle, the humans crafted the bow and arrow, a tool that allowed them to kill at a distance, away from biting teeth, trampling hooves, and ramming horns. The taut-strung bow and its killing arrows turned the people living along the Wadi Shabaktu into proficient hunters: they called themselves the 'Redland Wanderers.'

Book I

The Redland Wanderers
East of the Great Salt Sea: 10,000 Years Ago

"Mama, Mama!" yelled the young woman standing outside her family's stone hut overlooking the Wadi Shabaktu. "Grab some beating sticks and come quick! The ground-crawlers are pissing and shitting in our seed bin and they'll ruin our food if we don't get rid of them!"

Nadu heard her mother's feet pounding the earth as she came around the corner of their neighbour's hut brandishing two olivewood sticks half her height in her left hand. Previously, the sticks had been used to beat wild goats, vicious camp dogs, and disobedient children. Now they would be put to work killing mice. Negotiating the turn, the older woman pitched one of the sticks in her daughter's direction, which the girl caught in mid-air. Sticks in hand, the two women turned, and headed towards a chest-high cubicle that served as their grain bin which contained enough wild grass seeds to feed their family for months. Winter was coming; hunting wasn't good, and the seeds she and her mother had harvested were the family's only hope of surviving until next spring.

Standing on each side of the bin they ripped the thatched cover off the top of the stone structure, letting it fall to the ground, and set to work flailing at the undulating forms burrowing about in the seeds. With hard-landing blows they struck at the seed pile and its population of ground-crawlers drawn to the bonanza of human-collected grain. But the girl and her mother were poor predators and they did not kill any of them. Their noises and stick flailings only scattered the ground-crawlers sending them running to the safety of their burrows. Even though on occasion they did kill some of them, their numbers continued to increase with every new basket of seeds dumped into the bin. At one time the ground-crawlers stayed in the fields and were easy food for birds, foxes and Desert

Cats. But since the Redland Wanderers had begun to depend on grain for their food, the furry pests came in droves to eat the seeds the humans had shaken and beaten from the heads of the grain stalks.

"We didn't kill a single one, did we?" said her mother after they had worked up a rodent-beating sweat.

"No," said her daughter wiping her brow, "but we did manage to drive them away from our food. That's something isn't it?"

Watching from a short distance away, several old hunters sitting in the dirt with their backs leaning against one of the huts laughed through their toothless mouths at the mother and daughter.

"Why don't you beat your children or your dogs? Why do you pick on the stone huts that have no legs to run away and no arms to protect themselves?"

Embarrassed, Nadu and her mother turned away, as they leaned their sticks against the side of their hut.

"What can we say to them?" Nadu asked.

"Nothing daughter; nothing at all."

As the days and weeks passed, they knew there was little chance they could keep the rodents from their grain supply.

"What good does it do to store piles of seeds if the ground-crawlers get them?"

§

A steady wind blew from the west, the temperature was mild, and the hot season had not yet begun to parch the earth.

"Nadu, pass me another handful of those stalks," her mother called. The older woman was bent over, her rough hands touching the ground, while her head looked sideways at her daughter of 13 years. Like most unmarried girls, Nadu wore a dress made of woven flax tied with a cord at the waist. Threadbare and patched, the dress began at her neckline and extended well below her knees. Like all of the Redland Wanderers, Nadu had walked on her horn-hard, bare feet ever since she had taken her first steps.

"Here," Nadu said.

Her mother took the bundle with both hands, raised it over her head, and brought it down hard against a large rock lying flat on the ground. The impact released a shower of golden seeds that scattered in front of her. The seed-headed stalks had blown wild in the wind since forever and were the staple food of the ungulates that had once roamed the plateaus and steep banks of the wadis in great numbers. Watered with the winter rains, by spring the meadows blossomed, and the seed-eaters; gazelles, sheep and goats, filled their stomachs with the grasses.

There was a time when Nadu's ancestors never stooped to liberate seeds from stalks. But the Redland Wanderers had learned that in hard times, when game was scarce and people were hungry, the grasses could be pulled out of the ground by the handfuls and their seeds beaten out of them. Swept up in handfuls and chewed, the seeds became a sweet gob in their mouths. If the seeds were put into a container of boiling salt water they made a nutritious gruel, and if they ground the seeds into powder and mixed them with water the mishmash formed a paste that could be cooked on hot stones until it turned into a tasty flatbread. Eaten with salt, olives, or goat cheese, the thin bread was delicious; almost as good as red meat.

§

"Don't you want to take a break?" said Nadu. "We've been working since sunrise and you look very tired. Let's take a rest and drink some water."

Her mother nodded and slowly stood upright, placing her hands on her hips, twisting to the left and then the right, re-aligning her body parts as she straightened herself. They sat down with the wind at their backs and drank long gulps of water from a soft-skinned sheep's bladder. While they rested they ate pieces of thin bread and an angular chunk of cheese that was so hard it made their gums bleed. In the good years they would have thrown the rock-cheese to the dogs. This year they threw nothing away.

"Do you think we will have enough to eat this year?"

"Well," said her mother, "the rains were good this spring and the ground has not dried out yet, so there will be lots of golden seeds and if we can harvest enough of them, there will be bread for everyone. What worries me is storing the grain for the winter. Snakes, and most of all those cursed little ground-crawlers, come all the time and destroy our food. If only they were bigger we could kill them and eat them, but they are small, and there is no meat on them. They just disappear into the ground."

She continued:

"But yes, I think we will make out well this year. I am worried about some of the others: those who have eaten all of their meat and have only a little grain stored. They will have a hard time, but for our family things will be better, and despite the ground-crawlers our grain bin is full." She paused, and then changed the subject saying:

"I don't know why the men have to be out hunting at a time like this," she said as she stared out across the Wadi Shabaktu.

"Why are they hunting now when we need them here to help us with this hard work? They are not blind. They know there are no animals to hunt, yet they are not with us, they are not helping us with this back-hurting task."

They took one last drink, plugged the flask, and returned to their tasks.

§

"Brother," Nadu called out, "was the hunting good while you were away? Did you and your father kill anything? Did you bring home some meat?"

His answer did not come quickly, and she knew that when they reached their huts there would be no gazelle or sheep hanging from the game tripod that stood unused in the centre of the camp. No one had hung a kill from it for nearly a month.

"No sister," he answered, "we killed nothing and we saw little except other hunters. Like us they had not killed anything either. We did see some lions, and had to keep our distance, and stay close to our fires at night or they would have eaten us. We are not the only ones desperate for food. All the hunting animals are desperate like us."

Then he stopped, and turned towards Nadu looking deep into her face.

"Sister, I will tell you the truth. The animals are gone and father and the other men can't understand why. So beware, all the men are downhearted tonight. It is the third time in as many weeks that we have hunted and killed nothing. We saw only intruders who do not belong here; people from somewhere else, who have captured wild sheep and brought them to eat the grass on the lands of our ancestors. Be careful Nadu how you speak to our father tonight. He fears for our people, and says he does not know what will become of the Redland Wanderers."

"Brother, I am only an unmarried girl and do not understand the ways of men who are hunters, but even I know that the food animals are gone. We have only the seeds to eat, and if we wish to stay in the Redland we must become seed-eaters and bread-makers, not hunters."

"No sister, listen to me. Our father is a hunter, and all of his fathers before him were hunters too. He knows no other way in the world. He makes arrows and bows and spears. He cuts wood for bows and works the fine flint of the Redland until it makes points that can puncture the hide of every animal that roams the Wadi Shabaktu. Our father knows no other life. He cannot be a seed-beater like you and our mother. A hunter does not beat seeds to make a life for his family".

"You're right. What dignity is there for hunters in beating seeds against stones?"

§

At night the elders told stories about the Redland Wanderers. Their faces lit by firelight, they spoke of a time when everyone in the Redland hunted gazelle or wild sheep and goats. During the warm months they ate beans and roots from the ground, and from the trees wild pistachio nuts, olives and birds' eggs cooked over fires on thin shards of slate. But according to the old stories, no one ever broke their backs collecting piles of seeds. Eating the grains of the fields was what people did when they were starving; when they became like the hunted animals and got down on all fours and grazed as if their arms and legs had suddenly become cloven and hard-hooved.

"What has happened to our lives?" they would ask as they stared into the burning embers of the night fire.

"We are the Redland Wanderers; brothers of the hunt who roam the Wadi Shabaktu, killing great meat animals and taking their red flesh back to our wives and children. We will not be prisoners shackled to fields of dirt in search of tiny, windblown seeds."

As the rodents tunneled their way into the mounds of seeds they relieved themselves, and their urine dripped down into the depths of the grain piles, turning them into inedible waste. There were those who claimed that the black kernels of faeces could be picked out and thrown away and the smell and taste of rodent urine washed away making the grain edible. But sometimes eating spoiled grain could be fatal.

"Old Magadha died during the night from the vomits and the shits," Nadu's mother told her one morning. "She shouldn't have eaten the seeds, but she did and now she is gone. Some people say she is better off dead. Life with food spoiled by ground-crawlers is not worth living."

§

That night, Nadu awoke to some sounds she did not recognise:

What's that noise? she asked the darkness, raising herself on one elbow.

"Mama," she hissed. "Listen! I hear something outside near the bins, but I don't think it's the ground-crawlers. It's not our dogs either. I think it might be the Desert Cats."

"Desert Cats?" said her mother. "We hardly ever even see them around here, what would they be doing here?"

"I think they have come because there are so many ground-crawlers. Desert Cats eat little things, and I think that's why they're here." They moved to the door of their hut, pushed back the gazelle skin flap, and peered out into the darkness.

"You're right, they're Desert Cats for sure, and if they are here for the ground-crawlers that is very good. Ah! I see one just there," her mother whispered, as she spied a feline with a rodent in its mouth.

"I see him too," Nadu whispered; "right there at the base of the grain bin. Oh, and look, there's another one over there!"

"Desert Cats," said her mother. "This is good, this is very good! They will eat the ground-crawlers, and maybe there will be some seeds left for us."

§

By the time Nadu and her mother heard the feline noises that night, Desert Cats had been living in the region for several million years; long before the seed-gathering humans had set foot in the Redland. Because the small Desert Cats evolved as solitary creatures keeping their distance from humans, it was difficult for them to come into the settlement and hunt among the huts and grain bins with people and dogs everywhere, even in the dark of night. As more people saw how useful they were for protecting their grain supply one village woman suggested that they should capture some of the cats and keep them inside the grain bins where they could catch the mice and rats.

"Don't be silly," argued another villager. "If we put them inside the bins how will they relieve themselves? They will spoil the grain just like the ground-crawlers." Everyone was against the idea.

"I have a better idea", said another woman. "Let's put a rope collar around their necks and tie them up outside the grain bins where they can wait for the ground-crawlers, but they won't spoil the grain." Tying up Desert Cats outside the grain bins never worked. Confused and frightened, the cats stopped catching the rodents altogether. Instead, they howled their discontent driving the people to distraction and soon they were released.

"I have another idea," said Nadu's younger brother. "We do not need to tie them up. I will use the spirit-ways of the ancestors, and make an image of a cat attached with a rope near the grain bins. When the ground crawlers see the image they will think it is a real Desert Cat and stay away from the grain bins."

"Yes, let us use the ways of the ancestors to kill the ground-crawlers," they agreed.

For several days the young man pecked and pounded at the door post of his family's hut until a beige-coloured petroglyph of a Desert Cat tied with a rope to a grain bin, stood out clearly against the reddish background of the upright mass of limestone. The cat image was clear and they thought it would work. The hunters laughed at such attempts to keep cats in the village.

"Desert Cats are useless," they claimed.

One hunter stood up on the speaking stone before the entire village and announced:

"My best dog kills ground-crawlers all the time." Some of the people murmured that if that was the case why hadn't anyone seen it happen? Another man added,

"We don't need those Desert Cats coming into our village. We have enough mouths to feed. If we let those Desert Cats in they will just want our food."

How stupid some adults are, thought Nadu.

Despite that, after a few weeks of watching the ground-crawlers decimate their grain stores, more and more people were beginning to realise that the Desert Cats would be important for their survival, especially during the coming winter months.

§

Nadu was not tall, and she could not lift heavy things, but she had the ability to see things clearly, and so one fall afternoon she stood up on the speaking stone, the place where normally only grown men stood when they wanted to say something important.

"Please listen, everyone," she called out in her thin voice that could barely be heard past the first row of huts. A few people close by turned their heads to see what was going on. Most wondered why such a young girl should be allowed to stand on the speaking stone and address the people.

"Listen, everyone, please, she repeated. "You all know that our seed-food is diminishing because of the ground-crawlers." There was a muttering of agreement among the crowd, and someone called out:

"Everybody knows that girl. You don't need to stand on the speaking stone to tell us that. Tell us something we don't know or else get down!"

She was sweating with fright, and knew she shouldn't be standing on the speaking stone. But she had to speak to the people before all their food was either eaten or spoiled. Breathing deeply and trying not to lose her courage, she continued.

"Nothing can stop the ground-crawlers except the Desert Cats, so we must make it easy for them to come into the village and do their work." Some in the gathering crowd muttered their approval, while others grumbled against the girl and her defence of Desert Cats. Knowing she had a little support and doing her best to ignore the unkind comments, she continued.

"The dogs are hungry and have no meat. Like some of you, I have even seen the dogs chase the Desert Cats away. But it is the cats that protect our seed food. Not the dogs. The dogs protect our sheep, although we have only two of them left, and the dogs guard our settlement from the outsiders. Everyone knows this to be true. But it is the Desert Cats that kill the ground-crawlers, not the dogs."

To the girl's relief, her mother came forward, jumped up on the speaking stone, and standing beside her, put her arm around Nadu's waist.

"My daughter is right," she yelled out with a voice that carried to the edge of the village. "I have seen with my own eyes, and so have you, how the Desert Cats protect our seeds from ground-crawlers." Her words received approval from many of the village women, but most of the men were reluctant to show their support, even those who agreed. Then, one man rose and walked in their direction and stood up on the crowded speaking stone next to the two women. He did not dare push them, but he glared angrily at them hoping to make them step down. Nadu started to step away, but her mother tightened her hold on her daughter's waist, and the two women stood fast: they did not get down.

"The daughter of Manu is wrong," said the man turning his face to the crowd that had gathered around.

"Desert Cats do not help us. Where are they when we go out to hunt? Can a Desert Cat run down a gazelle? Can a Desert Cat herd sheep? The answer is no! Who do you think herds the sheep and goats? Who runs the gazelles to exhaustion, circles them, and then waits for us to come? Only dogs do that. Only dogs bring food back to camp.

Giving Nadu a mean look he said, "Your problem is you speak from a young mouth that knows nothing; you do not know the ways of men. Your father should be ashamed that he has allowed you to speak before the Redland Wanderers."

Nadu's father knew that his daughter was too young to stand and speak from the speaking stone, but he knew she was right about the Desert Cats; he had seen them kill ground-crawlers with his own eyes. He also knew that the hunter was a mouth-talker, that his words were wind and meant nothing, so he decided to put things right. He walked across the open space to the speaking stone and in one step he was up on it, and he struck the man in the face with his closed fist, causing his mouth to bleed copiously. The man stopped talking and bent over. The people cheered, for they knew the man was a mouth-talker and seldom brought back any meat for his family. Holding his face, he staggered down and away from the speaking stone leaving Nadu and her parents standing on it together, surrounded by their fellow Redland Wanderers.

§

Winter was hard that year. Old people died before their time. Babies and little children cried for food and then went silent. As temperatures fell and food ran out the weak and sick slipped away quietly into the emptiness of hunger. For some it wasn't so hard to die since death put an end to their hunger. By a month past the winter solstice the people had eaten their last sheep. Now they had only salt-gruel and flat bread left. There was no food for the dogs, and what gruel the canines could sneak from an unguarded bowl wasn't enough to keep them going. The people knew they had to make the choice between feeding their children or their dogs. One of them finally gathered up the courage to say what no one wanted to say:

"We have to eat one of the dogs, and it would be best to start with an old one whose time is near. We may end up eating all of them before we have any seeds to eat in the spring." The others nodded their skinny heads in agreement.

"Soon the dogs' corpses will lie rotting on the ground, and their deaths will have benefitted no one. Let us eat them now while they can give us nourishment otherwise they will die for no reason."

In that saddest of all winters the Redland Wanderers ate their dogs with long teeth. Every fatless, stringy bite of dog meat left the taste of guilt in their mouths, a taste that did not go away until long after they had swallowed it. The people learned that in the face of starvation hunger is a cruel master, and of the two organs, the stomach was more powerful than the heart.

Unlike the dogs, the Desert Cats had never depended on humans for food, so while the dogs dreamt of meat and bread, and then perished, the felines feasted on the mice in the grain bins. As the number of dogs diminished the number of felines increased and before long there were fewer and fewer ground-crawlers.

By late spring almost every dog in the settlement had been eaten, and yet famine continued to stalk the collection of huts and grain bins that overlooked the Wadi Shabaktu. Hunger would stay with them until the seeds could finally be turned into bread and gruel. Yet, despite their pitiful, hungry condition, outside their huts the days grew longer and warmer. There were red and yellow flowers everywhere; tender leaves poked out from tree branches, and the maturing wheat and barley grasses grew higher every day. Many were so hungry they went to the fields and bent over on their hands and knees like herd animals, and munched the unripe grass shoots with teeth and mouths not made for such tasks. Though the tender green shoots looked good, their hunger was not much assuaged by uncooked seeds meant for ungulates, and often they evacuated their stomach contents in bouts of diarrhoea that left them emptier than before. Despite the harsh conditions, Nadu and her family had managed to survive the winter, and weren't as badly off as some of the others. The seeds would be ripening soon; it was just a question of weeks now, and people knew that if they could just hang on a little while longer there would be food in abundance for everyone.

§

While her father and brothers slept, Nadu's mother said, "Let's go outside and see what's going on with those Desert Cats. Let's see if they are still protecting what little food we have left in our grain bin." Outside in the cool night air they watched the felines as they moved about hunting their prey.

"It looks like there are fewer ground-crawlers around here than before, so they seem to be doing their work," said Nadu.

Then she changed the subject and said, "You know Mama, I think most of the people who survived so far are going to make it through the next few weeks until harvest begins, even though there are some people who don't have enough, and are in real trouble."

"Yes, a few of them are. In our family we still have enough grain for one bowl of salt-gruel a day so we will be alright if no one gets sick. As for the others, we will share as much as we can with them, and with the ancestors' help we can only hope they make it."

While the cats went about doing their work, Nadu looked up to the heavens and noticed the Great Cat, the familiar lion-shaped constellation that leapt across the spring and summer skies every year. While watching the starry beast's form her eyes fell on something else; something she had not seen before. She tugged her mother's arm and pointed to the sky.

"Mama look! Look up! What's that? Do you see it, that big, sickle-shaped moon with the bright star right next to it? They're so close together they're practically bumping in to each other, and they're so bright tonight I think I can almost reach out and touch them. What is that?"

"Ah, I know what that is," said her mother. "That's the Magic Star. It happens when the crescent-shaped moon and a bright star appear close together." She kept her gaze towards the heavens as she continued her commentary, "it's a good sign and I think it means that the time of hunger is coming to an end, and that soon we will all have enough to eat." Then she added.

"Ever since the time of the ancestors the Magic Star has been a sign of good things to come. The elders will be very happy when I tell them about it in the morning."

Nadu looked up again and realised that she was witnessing something very profound. After their terrible winter it was a very welcome sight. Then her mother turned to her in the dark and said,

"The Magic Star not only means that the famine is over, it means that we will have new goats and sheep, and new dogs to protect them, and everything will grow in abundance.

"And you know what else?" she said once again looking at her daughter. "The elders also tell us that the moon is a young man, and the star is a young woman. They are night lovers meeting in the heavens after all the Redland Wanderers have gone to sleep so they cannot watch their lovemaking."

"Night lovers?" repeated her daughter. That sounds wonderful."

"Yes, it is, and it is a good sign for a young girl like you who is about to be married."

Even though it was dark and her mother could not see her face, Nadu felt herself blush, and she said:

"Should we wake the others and tell them about it? They might want to see something as important as that."

"Yes, I think we should. In fact, I think it is time to celebrate!"

News of the Magic Star spread quickly through the settlement. Soon people were coming out of their huts covered with blankets and animal skins, and looking up at the sign in the heavens. Someone began drumming and was soon accompanied by a flute, then by more flutes and drums; then a stringed instrument was added to the night orchestra. As they danced and chanted they put more wood on the fire and soon it was burning brightly. Some women brought out a big bowl of salt-gruel, warmed it on the fire and everyone ate from it. The nourishment gave the hungry people the strength to sing and dance through the night, and release the burden of hardship from their hungry bodies and their famished spirits. They only returned to their huts just as the sun began to push the lid off the top of the darkness and peek into the daylight.

For a long time, Nadu and her mother stood in silence and watched the Magic Star until it disappeared. On the ground around them the Desert Cats patrolled the grain bins protecting their dwindling food supply. That night they knew they were going to live.

§

Finally, the tiny seeds began to turn from green to brown, and soon the harvest was in full swing. The men stayed and helped their wives and children cut and gather the sheaves of grain and beat and shake the seeds from the gathered stalks. They talked less about hunting, and concentrated on how to prepare the fields for planting, and how to grow more grain. When they discussed spears and bows and arrows, they spoke little about using them to hunt animals for food: instead, they spoke about using their bows and arrows to kill any outsiders who wanted to take their land.

§

Just before the end of the famine Nadu received a handsome young Desert Cat as a gift from her brother. He had taken the kitten from its mother when it no longer needed her milk and brought him back to the settlement. Nadu named the cat Mushi, which in the people's language meant 'Black like the night.' Mushi looked different from the other Desert Cats; his coat was bitumen-black with a white patch on his chest instead of the usual camouflage colours of the desert. He was friendlier than the other Desert Cats and he liked being around humans. In his first year Mushi grew into a strong hunter and ate many ground-crawlers. Although sometimes he would disappear into the wild, he always came back to the settlement. Everyone liked Mushi and knew he was Nadu's cat.

§

After the spring harvest and the end of the winter of the great famine, Nadu was married to the strong and handsome Zakutu. She left her father's house and moved in with her husband into the house he had built a stone's throw away. She took Mushi with her and he was also welcomed into their new home. A year later Nadu gave birth to one of several children. Although some of them died, in the years that followed, a few of her babies lived, and like the other village children, as they grew from toddlers to children they played with the black Desert Cat and taught him the ways of humans. In his new home Mushi learned to play with Zakutu's new born dogs, and by the time they were grown they got on well. From then on the dogs guarded the flocks and the Desert Cats ate the ground-crawlers. As the years passed, and Nadu's family grew in size, more Desert Cats came to the settlement to hunt and live among the people. Harvests were good for many years, and starvation did not return. The flocks of sheep and goats multiplied, and every year their grain bins were filled to the top until the seeds spilled over the sides onto the ground.

"The ground-crawlers can have those if they want, but it makes no difference because the cats will eat them anyway," Nadu and her mother laughed as they admired their grain bin filled to overflowing.

§

Despite the good harvests and plenty of food, Nadu was never strong and some years later she fell ill. She coughed and twisted, but after struggling for several days and nights she closed her eyes forever. When her body turned cold, her husband did not want to bury her the way the people had done in the past. Everyone knew that Nadu and her Desert Cats had saved the people's food and they wanted to give her a new kind of burial, so Zakutu spoke to the people, saying she should be buried inside her husband's house so she could be with those she helped feed and save. The people agreed and her body was brought to the house where she had lived with her husband and her children. Then Nadu's father, the old hunter now resigned to the life of a seed-beater, opened his sparsely-toothed mouth and spoke to the people.

"Redland People, the daughter of the womb of my wife was as wise as any of the elders because she stood before the people and spoke the truth to them, though she was not yet a woman. She said with a strong voice that we should have Desert Cats, and as you all know, she was right to speak that way. Now because we honour her and because we want her spirit to stay among us in our settlement, we will dig a hole under her husband's house and lay her there to be close to us. Because she made the Desert Cats come to us we will honour her memory and lay with her the black cat, Mushi, who is old now and wants only to stay by her side. We will do this so they may sleep together in the red earth."

And so on that day the men and women went into the house of Nadu's husband, as many as could squeeze in and be part of her burial. They sang and they chanted while her husband and her children removed the flat stones on the floor and scooped out baskets of dirt and carried them outside. When the hole was deep enough her husband picked up his dead wife, and laid her in the freshly dug cavity. Then the women who had watched over Nadu during her illness handed to her father her black cat, Mushi, who could no longer hunt ground-crawlers, the old black cat whose eyes were cloudy, whose teeth were broken, and who drank only goat's milk in his last days. The people said that Mushi's time was near and that he belonged with Nadu. He was her cat and it was best that they should go into the land of the ancestors together. So her father took Mushi, in his gnarled hands, and with the skill of an old hunter he held the cat in front of him, he placed his thumbs on the cat's neck, and in one swift move he pushed inwards and broke the bony connection between the cat's head and his body. Mushi let out a slight gurgling sound as his life escaped out of his mouth, and his lifeless head fell limp in the old man's hands. Then they placed Mushi in Nadu's arms, and before they put dirt over them, they laid a pot filled with ripe seeds, and sealed tightly with bitumen, next to them. With their tears dripping into the dirt the people carried baskets of earth back into the house and filled the pit where Nadu lay with Mushi in her arms, his whiskered face on her breast.

As soon as her resting place was filled with dirt they replaced the floor-stones, and afterwards the people walked outside into the sunshine and went back to their fields and to their flocks and their lives. As the centuries blew away like chaff from the golden seeds, Nadu and Mushi slept beneath the flat stones for one hundred centuries until one day some humans from a foreign land came and dug up the ancient huts of the Redland Wanderers. To their surprise, on the door post of one of the dwellings, they uncovered a petroglyph of a cat tethered to the ground and wondered what it could mean. When they dug deeper under the floor of the long-abandoned structure they found Nadu and the Desert Cat she held between her fleshless arm bones. So they took them away and put them on display in a brightly lit glass case in a great and famous museum somewhere in the world.

Book II

Rainbow Farm
10,000 Years Later: Woodbridge County, Eastern Townships, Quebec

The interior of the old garage was oven-hot and the air hung thick between the water-stained rafters and the wooden work bench that had lain unused for the better part of a decade. On this mid-August afternoon there was not a whisper of a breeze as the uninsulated walls and corrugated tin roof absorbed the wavy heat of the sun and held it fast long after dark, until the coolness of night returned in the early morning hours. In this breathless enclosure, Nameless, a mother cat with a half-empty milk sac and a litter of five kittens, did her best to find a comfortable position on the oil-spotted blanket that served as her bed. While she stirred about trying to find a more comfortable position, a clowder of mewling kittens kneaded her stomach and bobbed their heads into her damp fur in search of warm milk. In the weeks immediately after she gave birth her own nourishment had not always been sufficient to ensure that her kittens received adequate nutrition.

Nameless was a feral cat; she had no home, and except for some recent handouts, she had no one to take care of her. She wandered the neighbourhood streets and the nearby wooded areas with other feral cats looking for food and coming in and out of heat on a schedule that was more reliable than the timing of her next meal. Like most unsterilized female cats, on an regular basis she gave birth to a litter of kittens, most of which died before they reached maturity. Although the local animal protection society did its best to control the cat population through adoption and sterilisation, Nameless had never benefitted from any of their initiatives. That summer she gave birth to her third litter in as many years in a tired old garage that leaned up against a white clapboard house like a drunk against a lamp-post. Few, if any, of the kittens born to her had ever had names given to them by humans; they were just mewling little creatures pushed up against their mother's stomach searching for whatever nourishment they could find. In the weeks to come several of the kittens would die while the others would grow to maturity only to live out the short lives typical of homeless street cats.

Nameless would not survive to see any of the kittens in this litter grow to adulthood. She would be dead by mid-winter from a neck wound that refused to heal and turned septic. Exacerbated by the hard winter, her infection would slow her down and she would no longer be able to hunt or scavenge sufficient food to feed herself. Other than a few of the local cats no one would notice her death or even know about it until the spring thaw when the village street sweeping machine and its accompanying road crew would find her desiccated remains on the side of the road. With one flick of a shovel a street worker would dispose of her corpse along with the discarded beer cans and fast food containers the road crew swept from the sides of the road during the municipality's annual cleanup campaign. Like the rest of the roadside garbage, her corpse would be disposed of before the tourist season began in the summer.

But for the moment, while wasps buzzed in the rafters, like mother cats everywhere, she nursed her brood with patience and forbearance. As her kittens drew their meagre rations from her body she fixed her eyes vacantly in one corner of the garage panting a few gulps of fresh air through her open mouth. Between breaths Nameless listened for the now welcome sound of dry cat food being poured into an old aluminum cooking pot somewhere close by.

Across the narrow alleyway, a widowed pensioner-lady in her early eighties living out her final years alone in a white clapboard row house tore the cardboard lid off a small box of dry cat food and poured it out. As the pellets of ground fish scraps and grain meal struck the bottom of the pan they made a tinny, metallic sound that had come to signify welcome nourishment for the mother cat. For some time Madame Gauthier had been putting out small quantities of food on her back porch for the too many cats that wandered the neighbourhood, and on more than one occasion her neighbours had politely reminded her that as long as she fed the cats they would only continue to multiply, creating an ever-increasing number of hungry, feral animals that nobody wanted and nobody cared for. Nameless was just the kind of cat her neighbours cautioned her about.

Not true, she thought to herself. *I love them all and would take care of every one of them if I were a little younger.*

She responded to her neighbours' comments by smiling politely, but she kept on buying food and fed as many cats as she could. She had loved cats as a child on the nearby farm where she grew up, but after she married her husband refused to allow cats or dogs into the house so she had passed nearly fifty years without any pets at all. Since her husband died she finally had the chance to have some part-time cats of her own; she fed them when she could and enjoyed seeing them eat and hearing them purr with contentment. Despite her love of cats, after so many years without them and remembering her husband's strict warnings about how dirty and disease-ridden they were, she never took any of them into her house.

It was several weeks earlier that the elderly woman had heard faint mewling sounds as she walked by the garage and realised that a cat had given birth to a litter of kittens.

Since I have cats in my own garage I better start feeding them, she thought, and it was then she began leaving small quantities of dry food and a little milk on the back porch to help the mother feed her kittens. But on this hot afternoon as the cicadas sang in the maple trees and the kittens tugged and nuzzled their mother's teats, Madame Gauthier opened the side door of the garage and placed the metal food bowl on the cement floor. Ignoring her usual cautious measures around humans, as the bowl hit the floor Nameless jumped up, scattering her brood on the old blanket, and headed for the food. As the old woman stood outside the doorway peering into the semi-darkness of the garage the cat consumed the dry food hungrily with the knowledge that she and her kittens would eat their fill today and sleep the sleep of caloric contentment well into the night.

§

Madame Gauthier's house had been built sometime around 1900, a few decades before she was born. The original occupants of the house were an accountant and his family in the employ of the Dominion Cloth and Leather Company, manufacturers of buggy whips, harnesses and corsets; artifacts of another century. But because automobiles didn't need to be whipped and corsets went out of style, the company switched to making munitions for the 1914-1918 war. They switched again for the 1939-1945 war, then again for the war in Korea. For a long time after that Canada stopped going to war and started sending its soldiers all over the world as peacekeepers until, like the buggy whips and corsets, peace went out of style too. For most of the twentieth century a variety of managers and foremen occupied the modest house, spending as much as a decade in it, making and raising their families before moving through promotions or demotions to somewhere else. One after the other tenants of the white house lived through economic hard times and saw young men march off to a succession of wars, their numbers diminished every time they returned home. Residents saw hemlines go up and down; they saw men throw away their hats and cut their hair close to their scalps, only to let it grow long again decades later. After the second great war of the twentieth century factories in the region began to close down and people had no choice but to move to Montreal or Ontario or British Columbia to find work.

By the early seventies the smart ones with job skills and diplomas had moved on, leaving mostly the poor and unskilled in the town. In place of prosperous employment the people who remained adopted the social-assistance and minimum-wage lifestyle that had sustained most of them for the last two generations. In place of the good factory jobs came a cycle of menial labour for low wages, secondary school dropouts, and much like the feral cats of the neighbourhood, numerous unplanned and unwanted offspring. These conditions served to create an employment dead zone on a street, aptly named 'la rue de la fortune,' where the children and grand-children of the long-gone factory workers now lived and where Madame Gauthier passed her waning years. Living on her husband's small pension, she hadn't made any improvements on the house, leaving it and the garage in their current shabby condition. The last time the garage had been locked was back in the eighties, and now one of its two big swinging doors that had once welcomed buggies and Model T Fords dangled by a single upper hinge, causing the door to hang crooked, and leaving a crack at the bottom which made an inviting entryway for mice, birds and cats who used the garage for nesting and nurturing their young. During its early years the structure had been swept clean and painted on a regular basis and was once the home of shiny carriages, followed by a succession of Fords, Dodges and Chevrolets. Now it stood empty except for Nameless and her litter of kittens, accompanied by a few wasps buzzing and bumping against fly-spotted window panes.

§

For 60 years a covered wooden bridge spanned the Tomifobia River as it flowed through the centre of Woodbridge, and then in 1927 a rush of flood waters broke the back of the old structure and washed its oak beams and maple roadway planks downstream, scattering them for a kilometre among the trees and bushes that lined the banks of the river. After the flood the bridge was replaced by a steel and concrete structure that in some incarnation was still standing. The wooden bridge was long gone, but the name Woodbridge escaped the flood waters and remains to this day.

A century earlier Woodbridge had been a thriving community like many others in the region, with water- and steam-driven mills and a dozen small manufacturing companies. Its main street was paved and had electric lights. The town boasted three hotels, and the Grand Trunk Railway ran two trains through the town every day except Sunday: one passenger and one freight between Portland, Maine and Montreal. The village was surrounded by nearly one hundred family-owned farms where people worked from dawn to dusk and lived hard but good lives. Then the world changed. The mills closed, and in the new economic order family farms became unviable and people moved to the big cities where the manufacturing jobs were to be found. Much of the once prosperous area went into economic decline, and several generations later the inheritors of these changes struggled on trying to make ends meet, many helped along by government assistance of one sort or another.

§

They were a group of twelve- and thirteen-year-old boys always in search of action, always on the lookout for something to do. Perhaps because they were too young to pursue sexual interests, they ambled around the village looking for ways to get into trouble. Every once in a while they would pass by the garage at Madame Gauthier's and hassle any kids hanging around there, or any animals unlucky enough to be inside when they showed up. If there weren't any kids to push around there might be someone's pet they could terrorise, or a nest of birds up in the rafters they could destroy. Today they were in luck for in one corner of the garage lay Nameless, quietly nursing her kittens. She was a perfect target. As the boys yelled and poked at the mother cat, one of her kittens, a grey cat with a white belly and paws, managed to flee the nest and hide while the boys did their bully-work. Although frightened, the tiny cat escaped their jabs and kicks, and when the boys left, he returned to his mother and her warmth. In the foray, two of her kittens had been thrown out of the garage, and had not returned. Later on she would go looking for them, but they were never seen again. No doubt they wandered about until they succumbed to starvation. Despite their demise, their deaths were a good sign for the three surviving kittens because now there was enough milk to go around.

The boys were back a few weeks later, and once again Nameless tried in vain to defend her kittens. They poked at her with sticks and kicked at her with scuffed shoes. She hissed and arched her back and did her best to protect her brood, but she was no match for them, and was forced to take cover leaving her kittens exposed. This time the boys singled out the grey and white kitten and began tossing him through the air. The six-week-old kitten shrieked in terror as he was hurled from one pair of outstretched hands to another. When they grew tired of throwing the spitting and hissing little mass to each other they opted for throwing him high up in the air, and letting him drop to the floor. He landed with such force that every time he hit ground his minute legs buckled under him and a tiny puff of air was expelled from his lungs. Wishing to refine their cruelty, they realised that if they threw him with enough force he would strike the rafters. They laughed and carried on as his little body struck against the wooden joists before falling back to the floor. It seemed they were intent on killing him.

Then they stopped.

In unison, their eyes moved from the kitten to the garage door where the silhouette of a large German shepherd filled the back-lit doorway. The big dog fixed his eyes on the adolescents, and cut short their antics. He made a low growling noise, and raised his lips exposing the pair of big canines in the front of his maw with two rows of carnassial meat-slicing teeth directly behind them. As if emitting some paralysing force from his eyes, the boys were held fast by the dog's predatory gaze. In the presence of the shepherd they had forgotten about the kitten who had disappeared into a corner someplace.

As it turned out the boys were making too much racket for the dog's taste. He lived with quiet adults and hated raucous children, so when he heard the child-noise billowing out of the open garage door like a cloud of smoke, he had to put a stop to it. One growl had silenced them and now he had their undivided attention.

§

German shepherds look like wolves, and to most people they conjure up images of primordial forest creatures, like the ones who befriended our club-wielding ancestors during the last Ice Age. Given their appearance, it's easy to imagine these creatures lurking around cave entrances illuminated by the campfires of prehistory. Despite their antique façade, the breed only appeared at the end of the nineteenth century. Powerful and intelligent, shepherds gained legendary status as message carriers, cable layers and mine sniffers during the Great War of 1914–1918, at a time when many animals, horses and dogs in particular, saw military service. Many were horribly wounded, and they died by the tens of thousands in the service of their respective countries, much the same way their human counterparts gave up their lives for King and Country.

When a shepherd is nearby making killer noises, most humans melt with fear, and that's just what happened to the ill-mannered boys as they stood with their eyes riveted on the wolf-beast. None of them had ever seen the dog before, so they knew he wasn't from anywhere in the neighbourhood. As they looked at the dark creature outlined against the light of the garage door opening, one of them, unable to disguise the sound of fear in his voice, whispered:

"Do you think he'll bite?" No one answered.

"How can we get out of here?" asked another. The boys remained stone-still fearing that if they made the slightest sound or move the dog would instantly rush in and maul them. Unlike their experience with the nursing mother cat and her litter, their machismo didn't apply to large wolf-dogs, so none of the boys attempted to kick or poke the big canine the way they had the mother cat.

A whistle shrieked from down the alleyway somewhere outside. To the boys' surprise someone actually controlled this beast, and was calling him right now! The shepherd recognised the sound, put away his fangs and shifted his attention from the boys to his master's call. He hesitated briefly, then turned in the direction of the whistle and was gone. As the wolf-dog vanished from the garage door, long held breaths gushed from constricted lungs, and smiles returned to reddened faces. They were safe!

The dog's timely appearance at the garage was a stroke of luck for the kittens, but only one of them understood that it was the dog that had unintentionally come to their rescue. When the grey and white cat first saw the dog he was barely conscious from being thrown about. In reaction to the dog he wanted to make his hair stand on end, and his arch his back, but he only managed to let out a tiny hiss as he picked himself up and crawled away. His instincts warned him that the dog was dangerous, but he was pretty certain it was the dog that had scared the boys away and saved him. He never forgot that.

A week later the bullies were back. This time checking the garage to make sure the shepherd wasn't there before going inside. Once again, they found Nameless and her litter. They were intent on catching the grey and white cat again, but this time the little cat was determined to get away. He ran for cover, first one direction then another, nearly escaping his tormentors, but his short little legs wouldn't carry him fast enough to outrun the boys as they yelled and kicked at his little form. Despite their blows and grasping hands he made a break for the outside. He ran hard, and reached the door, but no sooner was he outside than an unseen hand shot out of nowhere and snatched him off the ground.

§

Jeff Walker recognised their voices, and saw they were terrorising a mother cat and her kittens. When the little feline broke free and ran towards him, he deftly reached down and scooped him up off the pavement, and immediately clutched him hard against his chest. The boy knew that in a situation of fear and panic, cats will scratch friend and foe alike, so as soon as he had the cat in his grip he crushed him tightly against his chest to minimise claw damage, and the tactic worked pretty well.

The boys went to the same school, and Jeff knew their reputation, but unlike some of his classmates, he was not afraid of them. Jeff Walker did not run from bullies. He played football and hockey, sports where you got roughed up a bit, and he knew how to stand up for himself. Jeff realised that the instant he took the bully-boys' plaything away from them he would have a fight on his hands, but he hated animal abusers, and was determined not to let them get the little cat again. To keep possession Jeff clutched the kitten against his chest in his right hand, parried the incoming blows with his left, and stood his ground.

How am I going to get out of this mess? he wondered, as he backed up against the garage wall. *I can't hold these guys off for very long with only one hand.*

Jeff was a lefty and his counter blows came from the opposite side of his opponents. That gave him a slight advantage, plus, he had the schoolyard confidence of the big and the strong, and he knew the boys confronting him were not good fighters; they were just common runt intimidators. The first time he took a swing at one of them he landed a solid punch on a big skinny kid, sending him staggering across the pavement with blood on his face. Over the next few minutes Jeff took a few hits, but managed to dodge most of the blows. As one mean-looking fat boy wound up to take a swing at him he skilfully moved out of the way like he did when a slap shot was coming his way.

This fat boy's fist isn't any faster than a puck, he thought, as he stepped to one side and watched it go by.

Then he heard the fist strike the side of the garage with a pulpy thud followed by a howl of pain that brought the fighting to a stop. The swinger bent over in the middle of the alleyway cradling his hand. His buddies gathered around him and administered tough-guy comments as a form of first-aid. One of the boys turned towards Jeff and announced:

"Don't worry Marc; we'll get him for you! Double that!"

Jeff ignored the comment.

Hey, despite being outnumbered I'm doing pretty well, he thought, as he looked down at the kitten against his chest. *So far these guys haven't really gotten to me, and I've managed to knock two of them out of the fight.*

§

Madame Gauthier looked up from her housework and saw the commotion behind her house. As hands were raised and arms waved about in the melee of fists and swearing, she knew she had to help the boy holding the kitten. It would be futile to call the *Sûreté du Québec* and report a case of kitty abuse in progress. She needed to call people who could do something right away, and that's when she remembered the dog and cat people from the local animal shelter. She had just read about them in the newspaper, and was sure they would be able to handle things much quicker if they knew what was happening. The paper was still on her kitchen table, and in an instant she found the right page with the shelter phone number and dialed it. When someone answered she explained the situation in a few brief words, telling the man on the other end of the line she needed help at once. As she spoke into the telephone she looked out her back window and saw that things had intensified in the alleyway, which gave a sense of urgency to her plea for help. The animal shelter man told her that he was just down the road and would come over right away.

"Create a diversion if you can," he advised. "Go outside and yell at them. Tell them you're going to call the cops. No wait. Tell them you have called the cops and they are on their way. Just hang on as best you can and I'll be right over. I'm only a couple of minutes away."

While talking on the phone her eyes were fixed on the action outside her back window. She shuddered as she saw the boys pushing and shoving Jeff against the garage, and saw one boy take a big wide swing at Jeff only to see his aggressor go down, holding his hand and writhing in pain.

Hey, good one! That boy deserved that.

Not having a gun or a sword, and with her eyes still on the action outside, she put down the phone, and grabbed the weapon of choice of hearth protectors since ancient times: her broom. Armed and feeling a sense of power, Madame Gauthier stepped out onto her porch, and opened her mouth to yell at the boys as loudly as possible. But her octogenarian voice box made a noise that was anything but intimidating. It sounded more like a raven hoarking up a gob of undigested food than a warning to cease and desist. She had hoped for something a little more authoritative, but instead of scaring anyone she just embarrassed herself. Despite that, she did get the boys' attention and they turned to see what kind of creature could possibly have made such a disgusting noise. The rough sounds she made were confusing, and initially the bullies thought the old lady was having a heart attack. They didn't know if they should run to help her, call 9-1-1, or run away before she fell over dead. They stood in silence until one of them realised that it was only old-lady Gauthier. The boy laughed at her laryngeal noises, and immediately the others joined in. They certainly were not about to be frightened by an old lady!

Despite the undignified sound she had made, she had succeeded in creating a diversion, so she put on the meanest expression she could, and banged her broom on the clapboard siding.

Hey, maybe this worked? Maybe it will buy enough time until the shelter people get here?

It wasn't long before the neighbours came out, and began yelling at the boys and threatening to call the cops. Big deal, the boys thought. They knew from experience that the cops never came for such things. Besides, Madame Gauthier was just an old lady and the rest of them were either pensioners or young stay-at-home moms holding diapered babies, or toddlers clutching the legs of their sweat pants. Mothers with children could in no way intimidate young warriors, intent on abusing a kitten! One young woman holding a baby on her hip threatened to tell the boys' parents if they didn't stop harassing Jeff.

"Hey lady, why don't you come over here and save this sissy and his pussy?" one of them yelled back.

The boys laughed at this taunt, and they mocked the would-be kitten saviours, but their noisy ridicule turned out to be a mistake since it woke one particular man from his afternoon nap. When Guillaume Leblanc stepped out on the porch of his modest, two-storey house next door, the tenor of the confrontation changed, and the boys' bully demeanour vanished. Leblanc was a retired man who wasn't afraid of the boys, and didn't need the safety of his back porch for protection. He proceeded into the alley and walked with confidence towards the boys; now they were the ones in trouble. Guillaume Leblanc was known in the village as 'Le Gros Guillaume'—Big Guillaume—with 'tough' implied in the name.

He did not tolerate bullies. Monsieur Leblanc was a well-liked and respected man who had worked as a stone cutter in the granite quarries of Woodbridge all his life. In his younger days he had earned a reputation as an enforcer at the quarry. Although now in his late sixties, he was still strong and tough, and a gang of boys were no threat to him. The closer he came, the more they realised they were in for it.

Still holding on to the grey and white cat, Jeff breathed a sigh of relief when he saw the big man start walking towards them. Jeff knew Monsieur Leblanc quite well, and knew he would read the situation and put things right. As the boys backtracked, deprived of their fun, they promised they would beat Jeff senseless the next time they ran into him. But Le Gros Guillaume immediately made it clear that if they attacked Jeff he would personally beat each one to a pulpy lump even their parents would not be able to recognise. That seemed to do the trick, except one boy stood his ground.

"Hey old man," the boy snarled at Guillaume. "At school our teachers are always telling us to report bullies so I'm reporting you to the cops and to my dad. You hear? Yeah! I'm telling my dad that you bullied me and my friends, and he's going to come down here after work today and kick your old geezer ass! You got that?" Laughing in the boy's face, Guillaume bore down on him.

"Listen, snot-face Johnny, you tell your dad to come over. I'm sure he remembers the last time we met up and I kicked his skinny, ass all over the quarry. You be sure and remind him of that, OK?"

Recalling now that some time back his tough-guy dad had come home with a swollen jaw and bruises, it dawned on the boy that this old man might be the guy who had redecorated his dad's face. Connecting the dots, the boy continued to withdraw until the big man drew within arm's reach. Then he turned and ran. As the bully boys exited the premises, heads down, and mumbling the empty words of the defeated, Guillaume walked up to Jeff, and said:

"Seems like you and your friends were having a little party. Why didn't you send me an invitation young man?"

"Monsieur, I guess my mom forgot to send it, or maybe it got lost in the mail? Anyway, I'm glad you decided to crash it." They both laughed, and as the tension diminished, Jeff lightened his grip on the little cat and had a look at him. Even though his heart was still beating rapidly the kitten seemed to know that the giant human was not going to harm him. Relieved, instead of meowing, the cat began to make chirping sounds as he looked up into Jeff's face.

"Hey," said Jeff looking over at Le Gros. "Do you hear this little guy? He's a real singer, isn't he?"

"He sure is," said the older man. Then he added: "Sounds to me like he's singing country stuff, doesn't it?"

"Yeah," said Jeff. "He is singing country alright, and he sounds like that guy over in Coaticook, you know, what's his name?

"Yeah, I know who you mean", said Le Gros. "He's on the radio all the time these days. Arlie 'what's-'is name,' the guy with the really funny name?"

"Yeah, Arlie Trogsworthy, right?" said Jeff.

"That's the one", Arlie Trogs... whatever."

"Maybe we should call this cat 'Trogsworthy,'" Jeff suggested.

"Maybe we should," said Leblanc laughing.

"Trogsworthy; now that's a name for a singing cat."

§

With the situation under control the porch-bound neighbours exchanged a few comments about the pitiful state of young people these days as they cuddled their babies and one mother wiped a well-crusted mucus flake from her toddler's nose with the end of her shirt. They then gathered up their charges, and as quick as it had started the episode was over. The cat was saved, the mean boys had been vanquished and everyone returned to their homes and apartments. Seeing the situation had been diffused, Madame Gauthier noticed that some leaves had blown on to her porch and she began using her broom for its intended sweeping purpose instead of as a noise-maker. As she passed her broom across the white painted planks she noticed that her throat had a slight roughness to it.

Perhaps it's a good time to go inside and make myself a big cup of tea, she thought.

§

The animal shelter people arrived just after Guillaume Leblanc had saved the day. An unshaven man with salt and pepper hair drawn back in a ponytail named André, dressed in workman's overalls, stepped out on the driver's side of a beat up old van with a sliding door on one side. The van served as the animal shelter's main vehicle for pickups and errands and doubled as an ambulance. In back there were several animal cages of different sizes. Francine, a middle-aged woman dressed like a farmhand, stepped out on the passenger side of the van. It was known all over Woodbridge that Francine and André had the thankless task of running the animal shelter on a tiny budget of undernourished municipal grants and contributions from community groups and a few generous individuals. They were the ones who did the job no one else in the community wanted; rounding up strays, providing them shelter, feeding them, attending to their medical needs and finding them homes.

The two of them walked towards Jeff and Guillaume Leblanc, and letting out a sigh of relief Jeff handed the frightened kitten over to André who looked the cat over for any visible injuries. Back at the shelter they would do a more thorough physical examination. As he gave him a quick once-over checking for sores, parasites or open wounds the kitten chirped and meowed in a melodious fashion.

It almost sounds like this little guy is singing, André thought.

When he had determined that there was nothing wrong, he put the little grey and white cat in a cage in the back of the van along with one of his littermates Francine had spotted in the back of the garage. Their mother had disappeared and when she returned in a few hours she would find her little family gone. Francine looked at André with knowing eyes that said they had seen this sort of thing all too often before.

"The mother's hiding somewhere around here and the rest of the litter has scattered to who knows where. One of us can swing by later and look for survivors, but it'll be a miracle if we find any more of them." André nodded and they headed for the truck.

"Hey Francine," said André as he grabbed the door handle and got into the truck. "Did you hear that little grey and white kitten?"

"I did," she said. "He's a real little Pavarotti isn't he?"

"A real what?" asked André, whose musical tastes did not match those of Francine.

"I mean he's a real opera singer. You know 'opera singing'?"

"No I don't know nothin' about stuff like that Francine. You know that. But I do know singing, and it sounds to me like this little guy has a voice like some kind of singer. Maybe country and western, you know?"

"Right," she said as the van pulled out of the alley way and headed for the shelter.

§

At the shelter the grey and white cat's life changed for the better. He had more food, he was secure from predators and bullies, and he had more companionship than ever before. Lost and truant animals were kept in an old barn up a country road several kilometres outside of town that had been converted into a kind of animal rooming house. They were kept there until someone came to either retrieve them or give them a home. The staff consisted of Francine and André along with several local volunteers and two secondary school students who were planning to go to the veterinary school in Saint-Hyacinthe once they had graduated. On weekends, concerned and curious pet lovers came to make the rounds of cages and pens and sympathise with Francine and André and their brood of cats and dogs. As prospective adopters moved through the barn some people found dogs or cats they liked and gave them homes. Others, unhappy with the choices, departed, leaving a collection of long faces looking out from cages and common rooms – their hopes for adoption dashed.

Maybe we'll have better luck next time, they thought.

Older dogs and cats and the ones who weren't handsome or beautiful had been there for a long time. They were the ones rarely chosen and the shelter was now their only home. No animal was ever euthanized at the Woodbridge Animal Shelter, and some of its residents would live out their entire lives there. The conditions were crowded, the food was bulk-cheap and monotonous, and although they might not have the homes they wished for, at least they had a home, and could stay there as long as needed. Most of the 'lifers' had accepted their situation, happy not to be out on the streets somewhere cruising the garbage cans and dumpsters for a few scraps of food and an uncertain future.

The grey and white cat loved the food at the shelter; he had never had so much food in his short life, and ate his fill as often as he could. It may have been monotonous for some, but he ate it with gusto. He did have some difficulty adjusting to his new surroundings. Other than the brief instant when the German shepherd stuck his head in the garage door at Madam Gauthier's, he had never been around so many dogs before. During his time at the shelter he encountered many cats and dogs and saw many new and interesting things. He made friends, got into fights, and began to notice that female cats were different and desirable. The shelter was noisy with the constant barking and rough-housing of the dogs and their fights which sometimes had to be broken up by the caretakers. The cat was not overly aggressive and tried to avoid fights, but in an area shared by thirty cats it was difficult. He was still young and small, just out of kitten-hood, so he was usually the victim when the bigger cats felt aggressive. He missed his mother, his three sisters and his little brother, the runt of the litter who disappeared without a trace, and he longed for a calmer environment. In Madame Gauthier's garage they had very little food and there was always the threat of bully boys, but despite the hardships, they were a close-knit family and his mother had done her best to feed and care for them. He longed to be with them again.

§

"My name is Lebeau. That's what all the other cats call me because they say I'm beautiful. Do you think I'm beautiful?"

The grey and white cat looked at Lebeau and had to agree: he was indeed beautiful—beautiful to the point that he felt inferior.

"Yes, I do," he said. "You are very beautiful. I wish I were as beautiful as you."

Like the grey and white cat, Lebeau too had a grey and white coat, but his was mixed with beige highlights, and the two cats did not look alike at all. Lebeau was long-haired, and had a narrow head and a streamlined body. His markings made him look as if he were dressed like an ancient human king from Egypt. He had natural black *wedjat* markings around his eyes as if some feline cosmetologist had made him up while he was still in the womb. The black streaks started at his eye sockets and wove their way through his grey and white facial fur sweeping over his head, steaming down the back of his neck, and clothing him with an Eighteenth Dynasty *nemes* head scarf before the dark lines became lost in a wavy sea of luxurious grey, white and beige fur.

The grey and white cat looked at him and said once again, "Yes, I do think you are beautiful. I guess that's what your name means in the mouth noises those tall, two-legged creatures make, eh?"

"Yes it does, but I don't know how much good being beautiful will do me. I'm not as big as some of the other cats around here so I have to run from them when they get in the mood to fight, and I'm no good with the lady cats anymore so they think I'm useless. That is until they are sterilised too. Then it's a different story and we will all be the same."

In a very short time Lebeau and the grey and white cat became close friends.

§

With lots of food the grey and white cat grew rapidly, and despite his rough and deprived kitten-hood it was clear that when he was fully grown he would be a big cat, much bigger than Lebeau and most of the other cats at the shelter. Although quite ordinary, and certainly no beauty, the grey and white cat was solid-looking as he stood on his four white paws. He was covered in short, thick fur that gave him the demeanor of a robust yet friendly feline. The snout portion of his muzzle was splattered with short, white fur, as if he hadn't had the time to lick the milk from his face before the colour set. He had a large body, yellow eyes, and a bib of white fur that extended from under his chin, down his neck, and across his stomach all the way to his tail.

"Do you have a name, or are you one of the un-named who live here?"

"I don't have a name other than the mouth noises my mother and siblings made when they wanted to get my attention. Is that what you mean by a name?" he asked.

"Not exactly, no. A 'name' is something humans, those big two-legged creatures we see around here, give you when they adopt you and let you live with them."

"Really, so a name is something those giants give us when they take us to live with them?"

"Yes," replied Lebeau.

The grey and white cat had never even thought about being named by creatures who were not cats, and to his surprise he was a little embarrassed that he did not have a name. He was also curious why a cat who had once been adopted was now living in the shelter, especially a beautiful cat like Lebeau.

"Wait," he said. "If you have a name then that means you were adopted, right? So you actually got out of this place, but now you're back in. What happened? I mean if you have a name you shouldn't be here, no?"

"You're right, I was adopted when I was a kitten, but then they threw me away and I came here. I don't actually know how I got here. One day not long ago, some big creature, just like the ones here, came by and scooped me up off the street and brought me here. I've been here since."

"So the giants adopted you and gave you a name?" The grey and white cat asked again trying to better understand.

"Yes," said Lebeau. "Incidentally, 'those giants' are actually called 'hu-mans,' in case you're interested."

"Hu-mans", the grey and white cat said as he formed the sounds around his cat lips with some difficulty, "it sounds so odd, doesn't it?"

"Yes," said Lebeau. "They are odd creatures and often difficult to understand. Sometimes they love us cats and want to care for us. Like the two humans who brought us to this big place and give us food and do not harm us. Then there are others who do bad things to us, even kill us. I do not understand their behaviour. They are an odd kind of animal, unlike any others I have encountered in my life,"

"I agree with you Lebeau. I am young and know so little of the world of cats and these two-legged creatures who call themselves 'hu-mans.' I know some mean ones harmed me before I came here, and yet another saved me from my attackers; both of them were these 'hu-mans,' as you call them. I find it difficult to understand their nature, that's for sure."

Lebeau changed the subject. "Do you want to take a nap together?"

"Yes, I would like that, and we can groom each other, too, OK?"

Some cats are loners while others can bond with each other and become good friends. Such was the case with Lebeau and the grey and white cat. From that day on they tumbled and groomed, and played with each other for hours at a time; then they would curl up for one of their frequent naps. Soon they felt as close as brothers, but they both dreaded the day they would be separated and taken to different homes and, in Lebeau's case, given a new name once again.

Lebeau had been sterilised and was not as aggressive as some of the other unneutered males. To control aggression and overpopulation Francine and André neutered all their animals before putting them up for adoption. So, one morning when he was about six months old, the grey and white cat, and several of his shelter-mates were taken to a veterinary clinic in the town of Coaticook where the veterinarians and other staff members donated their time and skills and neutered the animals from the Woodbridge Animal Shelter. That evening the grey and white cat came back to his shelter-home a different creature.

Lebeau remarked that when would-be adopters came around to view the animals, the cute, cuddly dogs and cats were the ones they took home with them. Some of the 'lifers' had given up all hope of ever being rescued. That worried the grey and white cat. After all, he was just a young cat hardly out of kitten-hood with pointy ears sticking straight up out of his head, and a face punctuated by two big yellow-green eyes: nothing unique about that look.

Will I spend the rest of my days here and become a 'lifer' like them? he worried. There's nothing special about me, and I'm certainly not beautiful like Lebeau. I would really like a home with a dog and Lebeau and some nice hu-mans, but I don't think my chances are very good.

§

Once a year, animal lovers in the area held a benefit soirée at a local restaurant to raise money for the Woodbridge Animal Shelter. Musicians and dancers performed as people helped themselves to platefuls of buffet-style food. It was between a Blue Grass band from Vermont and a troupe of folk dancers from Saint-Herménégilde that Francine explained to a middle-aged man and woman that two young cats had just been brought in to the shelter and were in need of a good home. In years past the couple had rescued two homeless dogs from the shelter and now they were looking for a cat to replace the legendary Kiku, a female mouser who had been 'cat in residence' at their farm for eighteen years. She had died earlier that spring and had been laid to rest in the family animal cemetery.

The next day the couple stopped by the shelter to have a look at the cats. The first cat they looked at was the handsome, long-haired male, Lebeau. Francine informed them that the cat's name had been changed by one of the staff volunteers and he was now officially called 'Buddy Lebeau,' and that was his name when he was presented to the couple for adoption.

"Of course you can name him whatever name you want once you take him, but we really like his name."

The man and woman thought Buddy Lebeau was a nice name for a cat, and from then on that was his name, although at times it would be shortened to Buddy or Lebeau or just plain 'Beau-Beau.' It was easy for the man to understand why the cat was so-named. Buddy Lebeau was a beautiful cat, and when the man picked him up Lebeau folded into his arms and purred. It was clear that he was an affectionate cat with a calm and gentle personality. The man would learn later that this soft, docile cat was also an excellent hunter and a natural athlete who would have a very long and happy life with the people who adopted him. Buddy Lebeau's story was unknown to the shelter people. He had been found wondering around one day a few streets away from Madame Gauthier's house and the people who found him took him to Francine at the shelter.

Like his mother, Nameless, the other cat up for adoption had no human-given name. The people at the animal shelter just called him 'the grey and white cat.'

"I think he's had a rough start in life, but he's going to grow up to be a good-sized cat," Francine explained to Tillman Charbonneau and his wife Annie Perrault. He was a fairly ordinary-looking cat, with plain yellow-green eyes like millions of others cats: not the blues of a Siamese or the alternating blues and yellows of Lake Van cats, nor the emerald greens of Persians. But when the man and woman looked him over and held him they both agreed that he was a fine, healthy-looking cat. When the man suggested that he looked like a 'Buster type' the volunteer staffers all nodded yes even though no one knew exactly what a 'Buster type' was. As they discussed his appearance they all agreed that he looked like a handsome young cat dressed in a grey tuxedo over a white shirt and wearing white socks. He wasn't too cute, but he looked strong, and full of life and vitality, and he gave the impression that he was ready to 'bust out' from his past to start a new life.

There was a deeper etymology behind his name that passed unnoticed by just about everyone except his wife. Tillman Charbonneau knew that the name Buster was the diminutive form of the Latin, *robustus*—robust or solid—and the newly-named Buster was certainly all of those things. The cat didn't know that in the ancient city of Rome the name his adoptive parents had chosen for him had been given to generations of favoured animals and household pets. But whether he was called Robustus or Buster, to the couple he looked like a keeper. He would fit right in at their place and be a good companion to the other animals. He also looked like he would be a good mouser and could help keep the rodent population under control. When Francine and André explained how Buster had been mistreated by some of the local bullies the man and woman were practically moved to tears. That settled it.

"We'll take both," said the woman as her husband nodded in agreement.

"Yes, we can use two cats at our place, and we have lots of room. No problem."

Other than the occasional visit to the garage by Madame Gauthier, the mean boys and Francine and André, Buster had not been around humans much so he didn't understand any of the sounds they made, and found their mouth noises incomprehensible. But Buddy Lebeau did recognize human sounds, and he knew what they were saying, and explained to Buster in excited meows and teeth-chatters that they were both going to the same home with the two nice-looking humans.

"Grey and white cat, listen to me, this is important. 'Buster,' that's your new hu-man name. Do you understand?"

"I'm not quite sure what you're saying Lebeau."

"Right now it doesn't matter," he answered. "You'll understand later. What's important is we're not going to be separated, isn't that good news? We're going to live together with those two hu-mans standing over there. They're taking both of us home with them and we're going to live together someplace where they have lots of land and other animals. We're going to be together! Isn't that wonderful news?"

Buster's eyes grew large and yellow-green.

"Wow! That *is* good news," he exclaimed. "That's the best news I've ever heard in my life!"

§

As the pickup truck with Annie and Tillman in front and the two cats in cages in the back seat drove up the long gravel driveway they were being watched attentively by a dog named Mecki. Mecki was the name of the mutt-breed 'Head Watchdog' at Rainbow Farm, and Rainbow Farm was the name of the adopted cat's new home. Mecki was a handsome-looking specimen with the dark brown and black colouring of a German shepherd, but Mecki's main blood line was Akita, as his ample folds of collar ruff and a semicircular tail that arched over his back and rather shamelessly exposed his rear end demonstrated. This mixture gave Mecki a muscular, big-chested stance. Annie Perrault had named him after a famous sailor, '*Mecki der Seemann*,' from a German top-forty song that was popular back in the 1950s. Mecki was a natural watchdog, and after Sam, the previous First Dog at the farm had died several years earlier, Mecki took over the head dog position and handled the task with great expertise. He dealt with all security matters on the fifty hectares of land, everything from trespassers and errant deer to itinerant salesmen and pesky, tract-bearing preachers. He was a responsible dog, and despite his gentle demeanour Mecki had a fierce, no-nonsense look about him. When he put on his mean face he scared people, and even some of their close friends would not come to Rainbow Farm if either Tillman or Annie were not there to handle him. Mecki frightened most people just by raising his hackles and showing his teeth. Although Mecki never bit anyone, delivery and service people were always reluctant to exit their vehicles when they reached to top of the long road that led to the farm house. Who could blame them? The dog looked scary.

Mecki was an affectionate and loving dog. When he grew to adulthood he was determined never to be pushed around by anyone, and once Annie and Tillman brought him home, no human ever bothered him again for the rest of his life. During his years as head dog, he faced down bears, held his own against a wandering moose trying to get into the garage, and at least once a week he chased packs of coyotes off the big meadow or into the woods behind the house.

One of Mecki's most memorable guard dog episodes occurred when a vanload of errant evangelicals came up to Quebec from one of the northern border towns in Vermont. They cruised around like bait anglers in a fishing boat trolling the back roads for converts. Apparently everyone in Vermont had been saved, and wishing to expand their operations, they ventured north and scouted out the English names on the mailboxes that dotted the dirt roads in the region. Their task was made more difficult by the fact that most people in the region were Francophones, and couldn't understand a word the 'Sanctified Disciples of Christ' said to them. But despite their special standing with Jesus, they had no divine protection against dogs, and they only came up the long road to Rainbow Farm once. Why they stopped at all was puzzling since the family names on the mailbox, Charbonneau and Perrault, were not English. Perhaps they mistook one of the names on the mailbox for something else or maybe they were just eager to do God's work among the heathen French who were now ripe for conversion, since most of them had abandoned their Catholic roots *en masse* decades earlier.

Mecki enjoyed his job so much that on occasion he could be a bit of a rascal. Sometimes, as he watched a vehicle coming up the driveway, he would go down a ways to determine if they were friendly visitors or intruders. If they looked acceptable he would bark them into the parking area in much the same way ground personnel with a pair of orange batons in their upraised hands, guided incoming aircraft to their gates at the airport. At other times he would hold back and wait, giving the visitors the impression that there was no watchdog on the premises. Then, just as they stepped out of their vehicles, he would roar out from the behind the chicken house emitting frightening mouth-blasts of barks and growls. With a kind of perverse doggy humour he loved to watch the expression on people's faces as they suddenly came to the realisation that this peaceful country setting was the home of a mean-looking canine. It was just such a greeting strategy he used to welcome the missionaries on one occasion, and it worked very effectively. When the pious proselytisers, in their dark suits and white shirts, took their first steps out of their hallowed Dodge van they were met with the ungodly sight of a be-hackled, barrel-chested, creature that was about the closest thing to the devil they had ever seen. Their feet had barely touched the ground when they froze in their tracks, several of them wielding their King James' like shields for protection that the Almighty didn't seem to be providing them. It took only seconds for the head evangelist to determine that God's will meant for them to remain in their van and look elsewhere for converts. As a result of Mecki's unfriendly welcome they decided that no matter how much these people needed to be saved, the occupants of this particular farm would not be offered salvation. In fact, given the demeanour of their accursed watchdog, they deserved to go to hell anyway.

§

Mecki's raison d'être was to guard Rainbow Farm and all those within it, and to that end, his duties there constituted the length and breadth of his existence. There was not a hint of existential angst in his dog mind; he knew exactly why he was on earth. There were no pressing philosophical thoughts that weighed on his mind like some of the cynics (κυνίκοί), dog philosophers who carried on the ancient Greek tradition of canine philosophical introspection in the salons of old Quebec City and Montreal. Between bouts of eating and dreaming, they would lounge about under fancy dinner tables discussing the nature of good and evil, or the old pre-Socratic saw, the problem of the one and the many, while just over their heads, their humans feasted away on sumptuous candle-lit food. Most were well groomed pure-breeds who pretended to be the inheritors of some great philosophical tradition. There were no homeless street dogs among their interlocutors.

Nonsense! Mecki grumbled to himself when he thought about them. *Not one of them could chase a herd of deer off the meadow or rid the chicken house of 'racks' without getting their hinders bitten off!*

Unlike Sparky, his companion dog at the farm, he did not play with human toys. He considered it frivolous to waste his time chasing balls or catching Frisbees. Mecki thought chasing round things or sticks thrown across the lawn was counterproductive, and when he saw Sparky tearing across the great expanse of grass in front of the house chasing a ball or a stick or some other human-propelled object, he would ask himself:

How could a dog do that sort of thing and still maintain a watchful eye on the place?

It was equally difficult for him to understand the behaviour of his humans who batted, swatted and flung all manner of missiles, balls and sticks across the lawn, into the meadow and even into the icy waters of the pond just so Sparky could retrieve them. As intelligent as they sometimes appeared to be, they never succeeded in convincing Sparky that he had retrieved enough objects. Sparky seemed stricken with an insatiable chasing mania which could never be satisfied even after he dropped breathless from exhaustion.

Maybe it's his age, Mecki reflected, *something to do with youth? Naw. Gotta' be something else. I was never like that when I was young.*

Despite his disdain for games and frivolous chasing activities there was one exception to his contempt for playful activity: Mecki loved to play ice hockey!

§

Mecki had a terrible puppy-hood. He was a rescue dog from a puppy-mill litter that had ended up in the small town of Smith's Landing south of Sherbrooke. His original owner was a vicious man who had been arrested on domestic violence charges. The judge had given him a suspended sentence for beating his pregnant girlfriend and told the man to find other ways to channel his violence. The man decided if he couldn't beat his partner without getting in trouble (they had no children so he couldn't beat them), he would get a dog he could abuse and maybe avoid doing jail time when his anger management problems got the best of him. So he paid five dollars at a garage sale for a cuddly little puppy eager to please and be loved. Dogs were not allowed inside the apartment building, which suited the man fine, so he tied him up outside and provided a small, cardboard structure for him to live in. Occasionally he fed the dog. It was winter and at night the temperature often fell to minus 20° C or even minus 25° C. When the dog whined and barked the man went outside and beat and kicked him until he was quiet. He enjoyed beating the little dog and during the first few weeks he listened intently waiting to hear the dog so he would have an excuse to go outside and inflict pain on him. He named the dog 'You-little-son-of a-bitch,' and the puppy soon learned that if he made any noises he received only pain and beatings. He became a very quiet dog. After successive nights of boot-kicked ribs and a punched and swollen muzzle, he suffered and shivered through the cold nights in silence. Even with the fear of additional beatings sometimes he couldn't help himself and he cried into the darkness for help. None came. Though he was not yet three months old, his joints and bones hurt from the relentless cold. His carton box received little warming sunlight during the daytime, and in the dead of winter the freezing nights came all too quickly. By mid-February he rarely made a sound or even opened his eyes. He was seriously malnourished, and quietly freezing and starving to death.

Jeanne Ferland knew the dog was suffering and needed help. She also knew that the man was mean and she did not dare say anything to him about the way he treated the dog. She was afraid to draw attention to herself for fear the man would beat her like he did his girlfriend and the little puppy. On several occasions the man had seen her in the hallway or in the parking lot getting into her car. He leered at her and she knew instinctively that not only was he mean but was a sexual predator as well. If she had any contact with him she ran the risk of being beaten and raped.

Jeanne was unemployed, which was nothing new for her. She had lived in or near poverty all of her life, drifting from one waitress or factory job to the next. For a number of years she had cleaned hotel rooms until illegals from somewhere were brought in and she had been replaced. After that she got a job in a factory assembling vacuum cleaners. While it lasted, her assembly-line job had given her a level of financial freedom she had never experienced before. But the factory closed last December, and the only Christmas gift she received this year was moving into the dump she currently called home. Her best chances were working as a waitress, and earlier that day she had been promised a job in one of the touristy restaurants on the Rue des Cantons, a place frequented by tourists and locals. The winter months were a little slow, and tips weren't going to be as good as in the summer, but at least she had something. She would start work on the following Tuesday, but for now she was nearly broke with only two twenty-dollar bills to her name. In the previous weeks of job hunting, she had cut herself to peanut butter and cracker meals, stopped driving her car, and stayed in at night. Her entertainment was watching welfare TV, which she did by adjusting the rickety set of rabbit ears perched on top of the small screen television set that came with the place. It would have been nice if she could go out at night and mix with people so she wouldn't have to sit alone and listen to the puppy huddled in on itself in a cardboard box outside in the cold. Every evening for the past few weeks she had turned up the volume and concentrated on whatever was on that night to take her mind and her ears off the little dog. Despite the volume, almost every night she heard the unmistakable crying of the puppy.

Be strong, she told herself, *people everywhere suffer far worse things than that little dog. Get a hold of yourself,* she scolded, trying to harden herself against the sounds of hunger and cold.

I can't do anything about it, the guy is a criminal and I'm afraid of him. I hate it that the dog suffers, but I don't want the guy to beat me up and rape me. She turned the volume up even louder until she was sure the neighbours would begin banging on the walls, and did her best to ignore the crying. As the blur on the TV screen danced nonsensically in front of her eyes she kept saying to herself:

I'm a coward! I'm a coward!

§

Jeanne was not alone. Other people in the building had asked why the man did not care for the dog and see to its needs. His response was the same one he always used when confronted about something: he got mean and made the veins in his neck stand out like ropes of bloody anger running between his head, and his body telling them in very threatening terms to mind their own business. There was no one in the building who could physically challenge him, and empathy has never been an option for bullies: so the abuse continued. By mid-February the man had left the dog outside for more than a month.

Finally, she couldn't stand it anymore, so when the dog abuser wasn't around Jeanne would sneak down and feed and comfort the dog. Some of the other occupants encouraged her; a few made noises about calling the authorities; none did. Some gave her food for the dog. Although intimidated, people were doing something, and while still undernourished, and abused, at least he wasn't starving. Jeanne called the puppy-abuser the 'monster man' and when he was not around she considered taking the little dog into her apartment so he could warm up, but given the circumstances kindness was risky and might get both of them into more trouble than she could handle. She thought about calling the police, but she knew they paid no attention to animals. While discussing the plight of the dog with a woman she met waiting for her job interview she learned about Francine and André and the Woodbridge Animal Shelter. Jeanne realised that if anything was going to get done she would have to do it herself. She couldn't keep the dog in her apartment, but if she could take him to the shelter it would be far enough away that monster man would not be able to find him. Once there someone might even adopt him and give him a good home.

Even if someone just gave him a not-so-good home it would be better than what he has now, she thought.

§

On that Saturday evening in February, the sun had already set hours before and the darkness and cold had moved in for the long winter's night. It was still too early to retire to bed so she rose from her chair once more and twisted and rotated the rabbit ears on the TV. When the picture came in she turned up the volume so she could watch whatever was on. It was the evening news. This was not something she normally did, but she had the evening to kill so she might as well see what was going on in the world. Jeanne was smart, but, uneducated. She didn't read the newspapers, not even the sleazy tabloids, and her language skills were only good enough to be a waitress; good enough to misspell customer orders for meals and drinks, written so she could remember them. Reading a newspaper article was at best boring, and she understood little about the world around her; the world of people she considered to be rich and fancy. For her, anyone who had a steady job in a factory or with the government was either well off or just plain rich. The kind of people who were so well off they would never have to fill out a request form for social assistance, would never stand in the line-ups at the employment office, and would never be hungry enough to visit a community soup kitchen. Her circle of friends consisted of people who had grown up in poverty, and had dropped out of school long before completing their Secondary V to do as their parents had done before them: go to work so they had enough money to buy their own cigarettes, beer, and if there was anything left over, maybe a few condoms, just in case they got lucky.

It was eight p.m. and the newscast came from Montreal. As the announcer moved from one news item to the next, a combination of voices and video clips of talking heads appeared on the screen showing overturned cars in Ontario, and the smoke and fire of a conflict from somewhere in a part of the world she had never heard of. Despite her limited knowledge of politics she knew that there were wars in some parts of the world, but she had no idea where places like Somalia and Afghanistan were, let alone why anyone from Canada would want to go there and fight with the locals. Jeanne tried her best to concentrate on the TV images, but after a few minutes she gave a deep sigh and resigned herself to her world, the world of the dingy apartment, the lack of money and a suffering dog. That was her world, not the one on the television. She may not have understood what was going on outside in the big world of rich and fancy people who drove new cars and took winter vacations in Cuba or Mexico, she may not have understood the machinations of the politicians as they tricked and obfuscated their way through another day in Parliament, but there was one thing that she did understand. She understood that down a flight of stairs outside her apartment there was a little dog suffering in the cold who needed her help. She understood that video clip of reality all too well. That was her newscast, not the one on the television, and it was gnawing at her mind while her sense of well-being was being eaten away every minute that passed knowing that a defenceless creature was suffering, even perishing, in the cold not twenty metres away.

When a string of commercial announcements interrupted the newscast she reduced the volume and once again heard the crying her heart sank to the floor.

That's it, she thought, *tonight things will be different.* She jumped up and headed for the kitchen pantry where she found the half empty container of peanut butter. She would take some peanut butter and bread to the puppy, and then bring him inside for the night, get him warmed up, and then take him to the animal shelter in the morning. It was Saturday night, and chances were good monster man would come home too drunk to notice his little dog was missing, and she could take him to the shelter early in the morning and be back before he woke up.

He'll probably be hung over anyway and won't know what's going on until sometime around noon or later, she thought. *If he says anything I'll just play dumb and say I don't know anything.*

With the folded piece of peanut-butter-smeared bread stuffed into her coat pocket she peered out into the parking lot and checked to make sure the monster man's car was not in its usual parking place. It wasn't. The coast was clear. She walked down the dimly lit back stairs and peered out into the snow covered parking lot. She could see the cardboard box stuck up against one corner of the building with its chain attached to the wall and leading to a small clump of fur huddled inside.

I better do this quickly and get it over with. I hope he's out tonight, but you never know. He may come back early, she thought.

She knew the dog would be frightened, so she whispered a few comforting words as she drew near his huddled form. The little ball of frozen fur stood up shakily when he saw her approaching. Cold, lonely and hungry, he was so weak he could barely wag his tail. He hoped the woman might have some food for him, or at least wouldn't beat him. He desperately wanted food and relief from the cold, and tonight he was in luck.

Jeanne broke off a piece of the sandwich and he swallowed it in one gulp. Three pieces later and the sandwich was gone.

"Not to worry," she said comfortingly to him as she patted his head and rubbed his frigid coat.

"There's more where that came from my little friend. As soon as I get you inside my apartment I'll feed you all you can eat."

She knelt down, picked the puppy up and drew him to her. He immediately snuggled into her arms and chest desperately searching for warmth. He found it with Jeanne. Still holding on to him she reached down and undid the clasp that attached him to the chain and let it fall to the ground. As she stood up cradling the dog in her arms he suddenly became agitated and tried to break free. Fearing he would run away before she could help him she said with her soft voice,

"Easy does it little guy, you're safe with me." But there was a very good reason why the puppy was so agitated.

§

"What do you think you're doing with my dog lady?" a voice demanded. She turned quickly, almost dropping the dog as she saw the sinister-grin face of monster man less than a metre away. She could smell liquor on his breath.

"Oh!" she stammered. "You frightened me! I didn't see you," she said, desperately trying to remain calm.

"I'll bet you were hoping not to see me at all weren't you?" he said, still with his scary smile. He was right on. She was terrified of him, but kept telling herself to remain calm and maybe she could get out of this. She had most certainly been hoping not to see him, and she looked back at him with a flat expression on her face and didn't say anything. He was the last person on earth she wanted to see, but he had surprised her and caught her with his dog in her arms. She held on tightly to the dog as she realised that they were both shaking, and it wasn't from the cold.

"I didn't hear you coming," she said, hoping to take the conversation away from being caught in the act of stealing his dog, but the ploy didn't work. Even in the dim light his psycho-blue eyes stared holes of terror right through her face. She had to say something.

"I was just trying to help, that's all," she said with a nervous little laugh. "He was hungry and I gave him something to eat," she said looking down at the dog as if she were having a conversation with him.

"Didn't I boy, eh? Good dog. Good dog." She repeated desperately.

Still trying to move the conversation in a different direction she asked nonchalantly,

"Cute little guy isn't he? What's his name?" She said forcing a smile that cracked her face into two distinct pieces.

"Lady, his name is 'You-little-son-of-a bitch,'" he said as he self-righteously puffed himself up, as if he were the good guy who had just saved a child from a house fire. Inside her jacket sweat oozed from her armpits and dampened the sides of her blouse. Outside she was still trembling.

"And y'ere trying to steal him ain't ya?"

It was true, he had caught her red-handed and she really didn't know what to do except take a very cautious step backwards. But in spite her attempt to put some distance between them the monster man took up the slack and drew closer, casting his shadow of intimidation over her. With the sly, fear-provoking grin of a predator who knows his prey is helpless, he said,

"What were you planning to do with my dog? Were you just going to steal him? People go to jail for stealing, don't you know that? Or are you so fancy that you're better than the law and you think you can just get away with it?"

She caught her breath. In the middle of what was probably the most dangerous situation she had ever been in her life, her train of thought was suddenly derailed in the cold night and the fragments of her fear fell in a pile around her feet.

Fancy, she thought? *He thinks I'm 'fancy'?*

No one had ever referred to her as fancy. They usually called her "common" or "tacky," and although she fought against those words, and had even come to barroom blows over them, deep inside she feared that she probably was both, common and tacky. She knew she was unsophisticated; she knew that her tastes were on a level with the unemployed who, on a good payday shopped at Wal-Mart, or else were relegated to bargain basements and soup kitchen meals at the end of the month. But somehow, tonight, she knew she was better than that. Tonight she knew that despite her social status she had something that this man and so many others lacked: she knew she was decent. She knew she was not mean, that she had never stolen, she had never hurt other people, and she had never harmed defenceless creatures. Now she was about to become a victim of somebody who was all of those things if she didn't do some quick thinking. So, from out of nowhere, as if she was on a roll of good luck at a reservation casino, an idea came to her: an idea that could help diffuse the situation and maybe save both her and the dog. She blurted out in monster man's face:

"I'll give you twenty bucks for your dog mister." Monster-man was now the one whose thoughts were derailed. He didn't know how to respond. The only thing he could think of to say was,

"You want to buy that little mutt, lady?"

"Yes, I'll buy him right now," then she added as an afterthought.

"Sell him to me and you'll be rid of him, you won't have to worry about him anymore. He won't bother you at night."

He grinned and said,

"He's worth more than twenty bucks honey; he's worth double that at least!"

"Yeah, I know he is, but I'm not working right now and that's all I've got". She couldn't believe her luck! Her idea had changed the tenor of the conversation and the guy was actually negotiating with her.

He must need the money, she thought.

She was about to continue the conversation when a female voice called out to him from the second-floor balcony.

"Yves honey, it's getting late and I'm making a nice big hamburger for you. You want to come in now and eat?"

Saints preserve us! sighed Jeanne from deep inside her backsliding Catholic heart.

It's his girlfriend. She's probably been watching the whole time he's been talking to me.

"Hold your horses," he replied impolitely." I'm makin' a deal with this lady to sell my dog."

He wants to sell! He wants to sell! I might get out of this yet!

Then, almost as an afterthought, he turned his head in the direction of the balcony and yelled up at the woman.

"Don't burn my burger, you hear?" he said in his usual threatening manner. The woman replied:

"Then you better come in soon, honey," she said sweetly, as if she were speaking to the kindest, gentlest man in the world, "It's almost done."

Monster-man wanted to go out drinking with friends that evening, but he was broke. Selling his dog to Jeanne was just what he needed to get some cash. But twenty bucks wasn't enough.

"Give me thirty and he's yours," he countered, thinking that thirty dollars was enough to buy him an extra beer at the bar later on.

"OK," she said quickly, thinking that if she could get out of this situation for only ten bucks more it was worth it. If she bought the dog for thirty dollars she would still have a ten left to get her through the weekend. Not much, but it would have to do. It would mean more peanut butter and the old TV, but for the extra money she would have peace of mind and might avoid ending up in the battered women's section of the local hospital.

I'll just pay it and get by over the weekend on my last ten bucks. Anyway, I'll have tip money on Tuesday, she thought.

So while she held the puppy with one arm she reached into her coat and retrieved her wallet. With some difficulty she managed to get her wallet out with one shaking hand while the dog was tucked under her other arm. As her open wallet dangled in front of her monster-man noticed that it contained not one twenty dollar bill, but two. His asking price was right there in front of him!

"Hey, that's my price right there," he glared down at her. "You were lying to me, bitch, and I don't like liars," he said towering over her, his masculine form blocking out the bright lights in the parking lot behind him.

With one quick gesture his hand shot out and he grabbed her wallet.

"Gimme that!" he commanded as he seized the two twenties from the money pouch, and slapped the empty wallet back into her hand. She fumbled around trying not to drop it and still hang on to the dog. By the time she looked up again he was walking off across the snowy parking lot folding the two bills into his jeans pocket, contemplating a juicy hamburger and a night out. As his lean and muscular form moved away Jeanne closed her eyes and breathed a sigh of relief. She had rescued the dog and stood up to monster-man. The gnawing burden of puppy abuse had been lifted. As she heard him open and close the door to his second floor apartment, she clutched the puppy close and walked as quietly as she could up the back stairs, hoping no one would see her.

She and the puppy slept soundly that night and the following morning the sun shone brightly through the heavily frosted windows. After a breakfast of milk and cereal, Jeanne took the puppy on a leash and walked down the back steps to her car. She hadn't started it in a week and in this cold weather the battery was bound to be low. She hoped it wouldn't give her any trouble. She knew that she might get away with keeping the dog in her apartment for a day or two, but eventually the concierge would see him and she might be kicked out or have to pay an extra charge for invented damages the dog had caused. In fact, the puppy was perfect. He didn't make a sound and she took him out early in the morning to pee, he didn't have enough food in his system to poop so there was no mess to clean up. Once in the parking lot she furtively opened the car door and slipped the puppy into the front seat on the passenger side. The car windows were covered with a heavy layer of frost and the inside of the old Chevy was more like an upholstered meat freezer than a means of transportation. She slid in behind the wheel, put the key in the ignition, and after a few torturous groans the motor came to life. While the car warmed up she scraped visibility patches in the windows, and within minutes she was heading down a side street before turning out on the asphalt road going south. Thirty minutes later she pulled up in front of the Woodbridge Animal Shelter. After explaining the puppy's situation to Francine the dog was made to feel at home, given a bowl of food and a warm place to sleep. Not long after, Francine was on the phone with Annie Perrault. She knew that Annie and Tillman were looking for a young companion dog for their old dog Sam, and she was sure she had just the dog for them. One week after Jeanne had purchased him from Monster-man, the puppy, once named 'You-little-son-of-a-bitch,' had been renamed 'Mecki' and was living in a warm house with plenty of food and kind people to take care of him.

§

Tillman Charbonneau and Annie Perrault lived at a place called Rainbow Farm. Their ancestors were not French-Canadians, but like many people in Quebec, Tillman Charbonneau's name was a *mélange* of French and English family names and surnames. Although predominantly French, throughout its history Quebec had served as a refuge for immigrants, many of them non-Francophones: the British of course because they were the conquerors; then in the 18th century a few Jewish immigrants were allowed in, and during the Irish potato famine in the 1840s and 50s, people with names like Blackburn, Ryan or Johnson came by the boatload to what was then called Lower Canada. Although from far away, many grew up in a French milieu, were educated in French, married into Francophone families, and despite their non-French names, their first language was French.

Evidence of ethnic mixtures and hybrid marriages was sprinkled about in the pages of telephone directories and voting lists, leaving traces of crossbreed monikers that in some cases approached the level of onomastic haikus. Mixed-marriage names produced astonishing amalgams such as the German-French Helmut Tremblay or the French-English, Didier Smith. Reflecting the recent increase in immigration from the Middle East, one of the most ethnically unique cross-cultural names in the Smith's Landing phone book was the Arabic-French, Mohamed Lévesque.

Tillman Charbonneau's forbearer was Tillman Fletcher, a press-gang sailor who came from England as part of the invasion force that conquered La Nouvelle France in 1759. For the next two centuries the sons and daughters of Fletchers married and buried a succession of wives, husbands, children and grandchildren and intermarried with diverse families of French-Canadian settlers in the region that would later become the city of Sherbrooke.

Annie Perrault took the family name of her adopted father, Jean Perrault, when she and her mother immigrated to Canada from Germany after the Second World War. Both Tillman and Annie were multi-lingual professionals. Tillman Charbonneau was an academic and had studied at the Université de Montréal. Annie Perrault was a McGill University graduate who had worked as a translator. After their two children were educated and well established, the couple purchased a 50-hectare piece of land with an abandoned house and some dilapidated out-buildings on it, and became part of the *nouveaux campagnards*, or 'new country people,' phenomenon. The view from the recently renovated house looked across a wide hayfield and a rolling valley that stretched out for seven kilometres to the east. When they first purchased the land and its collection of 19th century wooden structures they didn't know what to call it until one day after a late afternoon shower they saw a chromatic arc of multi-coloured bands of light that in true fairy-tale style, touched down in the centre of their meadow. Several days later Tillman Charbonneau hung out a sign above the mail box proclaiming the place to be *La ferme arc-en-ciel*. Some of their friends called it 'Rainbow Farm.'

The large green house was situated on the summit of a gentle knoll, surrounded by rolling hills and green meadows dotted with black and white dairy cattle and collections of beige and reddish-brown beef cattle put there by local farmers to fill in the spaces between the meadows and the stands of maple and spruce trees. Over a ten-year period they renovated the old house, fixed up the out buildings, planted flower and vegetable gardens, and cleaned up the dead trees and fallen branches in the nearby forest. The rejuvenated forest had a stream and small lake, connected by footpaths that resembled a provincial park. Instead of populating Rainbow Farm with big animals they brought it back to life with a collection geese and ducks, some laying hens, and a few Sunday-dinner chickens complimented with an assortment of rescue cats and dogs.

Kofi: Cat of Wisdom

The cat walked with a purpose in his steps. He had some place to go, even though he wasn't quite sure where that someplace was, but he was certain he would know it when he found it. Earlier that evening a thunderstorm had blown in from the west, booming and soaking everything. At one point he caught the pheromone love scents of a female somewhere out there in the night, but he did not respond. He had more important things to do.

Forgive me the unpardonable crime of not answering nature's love call, oh beautiful one, he thought, *but I've got to get where I'm going and I just can't respond right now.*

He paused, shook his rain-soaked coat, and looking around in the darkness contemplated his situation; should he stop and wait out the storm until morning or keep going? The steady rain was punctuated by vertical high-speed flashes of light that water-coloured the few details he could make out.

I'd better find some shelter and settle in for the night; doesn't look like this is going to clear up anytime soon.

He was about to hunker down under some low-hanging fir tree branches when a sustained series of lightning flashes lit up the area, and in strobe-light details he could make out the silhouettes of some buildings far off the road. It was hard to tell what they were, but a second flash confirmed his sighting.

It looks like some big structures on that knoll up there. Better to find a human shelter than stay under these branches and risk getting soaked. It doesn't look too far so I think I'll head up, and see if I can find a place to get dry and sleep for a while. I can hunt later, since even the mice are staying inside tonight.

He worked his way through the bushes and trees that bordered the long driveway as he approached the cluster of buildings.

It's the middle of the night and I'm sure all the humans who live here will be sleeping. I'll just go into the first open door I see and look for a dry place where I can sleep for a while. I sure hope there aren't any mean dogs on the prowl.

Just then he saw a light go on in one of the dormer windows on the second floor.

What do you know? Someone in that big house is awake. Maybe I can get them to open the door and let me in?

The light in the upstairs room was still on when he walked by the outbuildings and past the sleeping chickens. No dogs barked and even Figaro, the watch-goose, didn't stir. Unknown to the cat there was a very good watchdog on the premises, but he was currently cowering in storm-fear in the upstairs bathroom.

There are all kinds of possibilities here, he thought as he looked around, *and I think it might just be what I'm looking for. I better let them know I'm here.*

He headed straight for the front door and began meowing as loud as he could.

§

Long after the sun had set the night-time air clung like a hot soggy blanket over the meadow, and Annie and Tillman had finally managed to fall asleep wrapped and twisted in their damp summer sheets. After midnight a vertical wall of rain began to pour out of the sky and the night was shattered by lightning and thunder. They woke with a collective start as the sky filled with white-hot light and thunder claps exploded close by shaking the house. Ever since they had first come to Rainbow Farm one of their great summer excitements had been watching the meteorological spectacles that the Estrie region provided. In years past they had looked out from the second floor dormer window and watched the electric lines of light fall from the sky and then counted the seconds until the thunder clapped to estimate how far away they were.

"One-thousand-one; one-thousand-two; one-thousand-three," they would count after a big flash, waiting for the boom. "Is that supposed to mean feet, metres or miles? I never can remember, can you?"

"You got me there, I can't remember either."

After a while they went back to bed and it wasn't long before Tillman began to snore. Annie couldn't sleep, and as she lay in bed listening to the crack and crackle of the storm as it moved east towards Lac Megantic, she thought she heard another kind of sound outside. It sounded like some kind of animal.

No, she thought, *it couldn't be, not in the midst of a storm like this!*

But there it was again; and this time it sounded like a cat meowing just outside the house. No, actually howling was more like it. By the tone and intensity of its meows it sounded as if the cat were not just some rain-soaked stray seeking asylum. It sounded like a very important cat that had been left outside in the elements by mistake, as if the butler had overlooked the master's favourite cat and in error had left him outside to face the meteorological perils of the night. Her curiosity piqued, Annie rose from the bed, knowing it was her duty as the *Chatelaine* to come down immediately and let the misplaced creature back in. Surely someone would pay for such an oversight!

She picked up the flashlight from the night table and made her way down the stairs. By the time she had reached the front door she could see that the midnight howler was sitting just outside on the porch. She glanced down and through the raindrops reflected back by the light of the torch, she saw the outline of a cat pressed against the glass panes of the door. Amid the thunder and flashes Annie gasped.

"A Siamese cat!"

Of all cats, why would a Siamese cat be out on a night like this, in the middle of a thunderstorm no less?

To country people Siamese cats were fancy cats that people tended to associate with the city and the big stone houses in Westmount or Outremont. No one could remember a Siamese barn cat; such an animal simply didn't exist. Farm cats had been dragged through the gene pool so many times they all turned out pretty much the same. But this mid-night visitor was different.

This is no ordinary cat. I better let him in, she thought as she moved to open the screen door, feeling the spatter of raindrops on her arms and feet.

The door was barely ajar before the good-sized cat marched straight into the house, tail held high and dripping water on to the old hardwood floor. As he stepped over the doorsill he gave a big meow of thanks to the doorkeeper, as if she should have been expecting him.

"Tillman!" she yelled towards the upstairs bedroom,

"What now?" he moaned into his pillow.

"You're not going to believe this but we have a visitor, a Siamese cat! You better come down and see this guy!"

As she waited for her husband to make his way down the stairs, Annie noticed what she would refer to from that day onward as the Siamese cat's 'landing gear'; the two, chocolate brown testicles that stood out against the lighter beige colour of his hind quarters. Judging by their size, she concluded the cat was an un-neutered male.

That would explain why he was out on such a night, she thought.

The siren calls of queens in heat had been sending tomcats out on rainy nights in quest of copulation for millions of years, and the ability of members of the class Mammalia to reproduce had depended on hormone warriors like him since they first emerged in Mesozoic antiquity. With the demise of the egg-laying dinosaurs, mammals like this one had deftly employed their newfangled reproductive appendages to outbreed other land species. Little did she know that reproduction was not the reason this cat was out tonight.

§

The Siamese was slim, sleek and handsome, and centuries earlier in Thailand people kept beige-coloured, short-haired cats like him to patrol the rice paddies for mice and rats. They were called *wichien maat*—'moon diamonds'—and long ago Buddhist monks wrote about them in a venerable book entitled, *Tamra Maew*, 'The Cat-Book of Poems'. It was from these origins that this cat had received his exposure to the feline brand of Buddhism. The earliest Siamese cats to arrive in Europe were shown at the first officially-recognised cat show held in the Crystal Palace in London in the 1885. At the time the breed was referred to as the 'Royal Cats of Siam' and was highly prized by cat fanciers. Breeding was strictly controlled, and like adherents of the eugenics movement so popular at the time, there was to be no marrying outside of the family. Sometime later, some of his Siamese relatives made their way to Ottawa in the company of Sir Winfield Hornbostel early in the 20th century. Eventually a few Siamese cats ended up in Quebec City in the 1950s, and were the ancestors of the Siamese who now found himself at Rainbow Farm. Apart from that, much of the story of this midnight intruder would remain a mystery.

Perhaps, thought Annie one cold winter's day while watching him sleep in front of the big wood stove, *it's better that way.*

The Siamese was unique, particularly since no one had gone to the animal shelter to rescue him and bring him to Rainbow Farm. Instead he found Rainbow Farm. When Annie opened the door that stormy night the cat simply walked in, gave a meow of thanks, and showed her his big blue eyes as a way of introduction. After such a display Annie couldn't resist: she immediately fell in love with him.

I hope whoever owns this cat never comes looking for him, she thought. Then she caught herself. *How selfish of me! Of course Tillman and I will make every effort to find his owner.*

And in the weeks and months that followed they did just that. They knew all too well what it was like to lose a beloved animal and could imagine the worry and the pain of whoever had lost this beautiful creature. Once inside the house, having charmed the *Chatelaine* the cat asked her for some food, since he had worked up a *grand appétit* while making his way through the countryside. When he arrived that rainy night, temporarily there were no cats living at Rainbow Farm, so there was no cat food for him. Improvising, Annie took him to the unused cat feeding station and gave him a handful of dog food which he ate greedily. But once satiated, he looked around and noticed that there was something unusual about the feeding arrangements. While bent over the food bowl eating, he looked up and saw a watercolour painting of a Tibetan cat monk looking down on him. The painting was attached to the wall just above the feeding area. He was taken aback by the strange spectacle, and stared at it for a while noting its details.

Now there is a familiar face, and a welcome one at that, he thought.

He was amazed that something so oriental was to be found so far from the Orient, here in the countryside of eastern Canada.

I had a good feeling about this place when I saw it from the road in lightning light, but I never imagined that I would ever see a creature from the Tamra Maew *staring down on me here. This surely must be the sign I have been looking for. And now that I have seen it I know that at last I have found my true home.*

As he contemplated the watercolour he thought: *I wonder how these farmer folk got a hold of a painting like this?*

§

By the time the Siamese arrived the Buddhist monk-cat watercolour had been overlooking the cat feeding station in the back room for at least a decade. Annie and Tillman named it the '*Buddha-cat,*' though neither of them knew where it came from, or how it made its way to Rainbow Farm. However, the cat knew the instant he saw it that it was an illustration from a very old and famous cat manuscript that he had seen some years back, and he also knew that the likelihood that any house in Canada would have such a painting was extremely rare. It was a sign, and when he saw it the Siamese believed it meant the people here were good and this house was his new home. He was right; the people were good and he would live the rest of his long life at Rainbow Farm.

As for the two humans, Annie assumed the painting came from one of Tillman's ancestors who picked it up during the time of British colonialism a hundred years ago. Tillman thought it came from one of Annie's ancestors. Neither of them was right. The painting had been picked up during the Boer War by a now long-dead relative of the original owners of the farm, and the water colour rendering had been in the house for over a century, long before the couple purchased it, and long before the place became known as Rainbow Farm.

Once his hunger was satiated the cat went upstairs and found a comfortable place in Annie's clothes closet amongst her softest cashmere sweaters. As he curled up in their softness he thought,

I'm home. Yes, at last, I'm home, and I'm going to love it here. He slept till late morning the following day.

The Siamese was not a pampered, declawed condo-cat who had lived life inside the confines of a house or apartment. He was an independent hunting cat, and though he liked human box food, he was capable of catching enough food to feed himself comfortably without anyone feeding him. He was long, lean, shorthaired, and had the markings of a typical seal point of his breed. He had deep blue, slightly crossed eyes, and claws and teeth that seemed longer and bigger than those of most other domestic cats. He was so good at climbing trees that he typically found his inner catness by going out on long branches high above the ground and walking to their very end like a four-legged *Cirque du soleil* tight-rope walker. In the days that followed his arrival he made himself indispensable by ridding the house of the mice and chipmunks that since the demise of the previous cat, had become a nuisance, pooping here and there and storing cashes of seeds in clothing drawers and in the big oak desk where the couple kept their important papers. He was particularly useful in the chicken house, where he went on 24-hour rodent *jihad*, decimating the population of mice and chipmunks and eliminating a family of egg-eating snakes.

Tillman and Annie were immediately besotted with the affectionate cat, but despite that, they knew they would have to make a serious effort to find the cat's owner. They agreed that if after a month they had been unsuccessful they could start thinking about keeping him as their own. To that end they put up notices in the local grocery and hardware stores in nearby Abenaki Falls, and in several convenience stores and gas stations over in Smith's Falls and Coaticook. Annie could just imagine that whoever had lost the Siamese cat must be worried for his safety and would be heart-broken over losing him. They checked with Francine at the Woodbridge Animal Shelter and went as far as Sherbrooke with their inquiries. Despite the announcements and flyers, after a month no one had come forth to claim him so from then on they considered him their cat. Perhaps more importantly, the cat considered them to be his new parent-humans and Rainbow Farm to be his new home. Once they decided they had made an honest effort to find his owner, Annie looked at her husband and said,

"Let's give him a name, OK? but something special, like the name of a good person, not some celebrity type." Her husband concurred, and they discussed what he should be called. Ordinary names were not even considered. He would not be a Spot or a Puff or a Buzz, and names like Ghandi or Ho Chi Min didn't seem right either.

"I hate some of the names people give their pets. I mean whoever came up with Sputnik for a cat or Zamboni for a Dachshund? It's downright silly, and the poor animal is stuck for the rest of its life with a dumb name some human gave them. I want him to have a special name so let's call him Kofi, what do you think, Tillman?"

"Well, it's sure better than Sputnik or Zamboni so why not?"

From that day on Kofi was his name.

Kofi's human-given name was one he bore with pride, but he didn't flaunt the fact around the nameless barn cats he encountered over in Abenaki Falls. Domestic cats do best when they live with humans, as they have done ever since they threw in their lot with the tall bipeds long ago. Kofi was aware that most homeless cats were very sensitive about not having human homes or human names, and those without them were the cats with no one to care for them. Like vagabonds and homeless people, they lived short, tough lives hunting for their food in the wild, while spending much of their time on the lookout for animals who considered them a food source. By the age of one or two years, most barn and forest cats gave up ever being adopted or having a real home with a human family. The more fortunate found shelter in an out-building on a farm somewhere, the rest were on their own in the woods and fields.

§

Buster and Buddy Lebeau knew that humans gave their cats and dogs all kinds of strange and unusual names, so they weren't too astonished by the name Kofi. They learned that the name Kofi meant 'Friday' in some collection of human noises from a land far away. But they were unaware that a number of Felinologists maintained that the modern form Kofi was originally derived from the name of the Fourth Dynasty Egyptian King, *Khufu*, the builder of the largest and most impressive of all the pyramids of Egypt, the big one situated to the west of the Nile River near Cairo. Buddy Lebeau and Buster knew nothing about such etymologies, but it didn't take long for them to discover that Kofi had a very philosophical nature and was the only cat in the Tomifobia Valley who was a practicing Buddhist. Neither Buster nor Buddy Lebeau had any idea what a Buddhist was or what it meant to be one. The closest they ever came to anything connected to philosophy or religion was when they heard some of the local children refer to cats as *Catolics* and dogs as Protestants. The two of them were just young cats, and neither of them had any idea what it meant to be a Protestant or a *Catolic*. To them such things were just children's chatter, the kind of incomprehensible mouth noises young humans made when riding their bikes or playing games. Cats don't have anything like religion nor do they have cat gurus or cat popes living in big buildings somewhere. Cats only have survival strategies. Although they don't have religion, cats do have a very strong sense of feline unity (*Felinia universalis*), a sense that every cat, large or small, wild or domestic, is part of the great family of domestic and wild cats and share a feeling of reverence for the notable ancestral cats who preceded them. They also share certain attitudes about nature and food and about how to best maintain their 'inner catness,' the feeling of well-being cats get when they are in harmony with their environment. Later on, Kofi would instruct Buster and Buddy Lebeau that such harmony was exactly what the *Buddha-cat,* a notable cat thinker from a far-off land, taught his fellow felines long ago.

§

Since ancient times humans have considered cats to be spiritual creatures, to be either venerated or feared. In the past cats were everything from major deities in pharaonic Egypt to witches' familiars in medieval Europe. But the very concept of the supernatural was always foreign to cats, and there have never been any reported cases of cats who believed in ghosts or spirits, or what seems to felines to be that most irrational of all human beliefs: post-mortem existence. Even the generations of cats who lived through multiple dynasties of Egyptian history did not believe that any part of them would live on after death. Yet for twenty centuries the ancient Egyptians mummified millions of cats, placing their desiccated remains in shrines and tombs from one end of the Nile River Valley to the other. As Egyptians prayed to their cats while alive and wrapped them in long bands of river flax when dead, the cats inside those cloth prisons didn't share the eschatological beliefs of their mummy makers. Cats didn't mummify each other, only humans did that. Just being a cat was always good enough for them, and the very idea of dead cats living in a dark tomb with dead humans was universally unappealing. The cats of Egypt were amused by the idea that humans worshipped them, and grateful for the favoured treatment that divine status bestowed upon them. But at death they had seen what happened to the corpses of dead cats and dead humans, and they knew that no one survived the maggots.

Most cats never thought about such things, although some of the more philosophical ones did reflect on being one with all cats as a way to deepen their sense of inner catness. Kofi was just such a cat. In contrast, Buster and Buddy Lebeau came from modest backgrounds; and although they were intelligent and quick-witted, they had never been exposed to a sophisticated and thoughtful cat like Kofi. They were just young garage cats of humble origins and lucky to be alive. Not so with Kofi, who carried himself with abundant confidence and an air of philosophical nobility.

§

Along with their human-given names pets may also have titles given to them by their humans. Mecki's title was 'Head Dog of Rainbow Farm,' a label which carried some weight with other dogs in the area, particularly with unfortunate dogs that were tied up all the time and lived out their lives immobilised on the end of a chain. Mecki was never tied up. He ran free from one end of Rainbow Farm to the other, rarely trespassing on to the adjoining farm properties except for a brief patrol-sweep to chase off unwanted intruders. He was not a herding dog like collies or sheep dogs so he had no innate desire to herd other animals, and he learned early on never to bother any of their neighbours' livestock. His main task was to keep the Virginia Whitetails from eating the plants and flowers and to make sure the coyotes and racoons kept their distance from the chicken house.

The other dog at Rainbow Farm had only recently been rescued just a few months before Buster and Buddy Lebeau arrived. His name was Sparky. He was young and inexperienced, and looked up to Mecki and learned everything he could from him so he could help take good care of Rainbow Farm. Because Sparky was the apprentice dog his title was less prestigious. He was known as 'Number Two Dog' or 'Monday Dog' as opposed to Mecki's other unofficial title, which was 'Sunday Dog.'

Dedication to his watchdog vocation was Mecki's raison d'être. He spent most of his time looking out across the big meadow towards the tree lines that ran east down each side of the property to the gravel and dirt road. As he scanned the meadow he saw every hawk in the air, every raven that strutted through the grass scavenging for rodents, and every quadruped on the ground. Deer were easy to see, and even at a distance of two hundred metres from the house, if Mecki thought they were getting too close, he would leap up and take off after them. Mecki never actually caught any of the deer, even though he was fast enough to do so, and he never had any intention of harming them. To Mecki, deer were sport, not food, and it was part of his job to chase all large animals off the meadow.

"A clean meadow is a safe meadow," he always said.

Mecki could run all out for about two hundred metres and then he ran out of air. The deer on the other hand were distance runners and could keep going long after Mecki stopped to watch them disappear into the next field. In late May and early June the female deer often came to the big meadow to give birth in the long grass that provided good cover for their young and nourishment for the mother does. Over the years Tillman and Annie had seen deer mothers drop their fawns into the deep green grass, so when it was birthing time they made certain that the dogs stayed close to the house and did not bother the females or their fawns during the first critical days of their lives.

Mecki was especially angered by raccoons and considered them little more than mammalian bandits. On summer nights when they attempted to dig their way into the chicken house for egg and chick snacks, Mecki became particularly incensed, but he had to be careful. He learned the hard way from bites and scratches that racoons could hold their own against dogs. When confronting groups of 'racks,' Mecki emphasised barking and growling techniques and limited his charges towards three or more of them, keeping a safe distance.

Mecki was very well liked by the local dogs in the nearby village of Abenaki Falls and he enjoyed socialising with them. But other than his occasional social visits he rarely left his post for more than a few minutes. About the only time he had dog company was when he went to play hockey with the village dogs and the human children they seemed to attract. Noticing his lack of companionship, Tillman and Annie decided he needed a dog friend. So they went back to Francine and André at the shelter looking for a dog that would make a suitable companion for him. It didn't take long before they chose a young, fairly large, white-haired mutt to be the new 'rookie dog in residence' at Rainbow Farm.

§

"We should call him Ragamuffin if you ask me," said Annie, as she stared at the big, white dog.

"The way he looks with that long, unkempt coat, I think maybe Tramp would be better," observed Tillman.

Before making a decision they considered 'Vagabond,' 'Hobo' and 'Rascal' as well; any of those would have fit his personality and demeanor, but they finally settled on Sparky.

When they first brought the young dog home Sparky was excitable and nervous, and he did not know anything about proper dog etiquette in the company of humans. He stuck his nose in women's crotches, he leg-humped the village children and he sniffed people's behinds without shame. It took months to socialise him properly, but eventually he learned some basic manners. Within weeks of arriving at Rainbow Farm Mecki took Sparky on his first visit to meet some of his dog buddies over in Abenaki Falls. When Mecki presented him to the other dogs there was the usual sniffing of undercarriages and hackle displays mixed with a few snaps and growls. But, other than one domination incident between Sparky and a Boxer named Boxcar, they all got along. The dogs hung out for a while and communicated in growls and barks about the upcoming hockey season and how soon they could meet down on Tomifobia pond for a few games. They were all looking forward to another season. Seeing that Sparky's introduction had gone well, Mecki signaled it was time to go and the two Rainbow Farm dogs started back home.

§

Across the road from the wooden grain silo were several old frame houses that formed the central core of the village. It was late November and there was still no snow on the ground, but one citizen, Wendell Pendergast, was doing his best to get people into the Christmas spirit by displaying a 'loving-hands-in-the-workshop' version of the nativity scene on his front lawn. The centrepiece of the jig-saw crafted crèche was an open stable structure surrounded by two fiberboard camels and a trio of plywood shepherds tending their freshly cut and painted sheep. The entire ensemble gazed in awe at the little wooden Christ Child lying in the manger in the company of a beatific Mary and a strong, carpenterish-looking Joseph. The Three Wise Men from the East stood just behind them.

Buoyed by the success of his introduction, Sparky felt the need to leave his mark somewhere in the village. He looked around for a good spot to urinate and when he spied the crèche he thought it would make an excellent back-splash.

Perfect, he thought as he headed across the road towards the wooden figures. Seconds later, and in front of half the population of the village, Sparky formally introduced himself to everyone in Abenaki Falls by urinating on the cut and painted likeness of the saintly Joseph. In midstream, several adults witnessing the event gasped and shouted with indignation.

"Oh no, get that dog out of there! Shoo! Shoo!" cried one woman. "This is disgraceful!" called another. The village children looked on at the spectacle and laughed.

"Hey! Look at that white dog!" said one boy pointing towards Sparky. "He's pissing on one of the Three Wise Guys!" The other children roared with laughter. But one of the older children, who had attended Sunday school, tried to put them right.

"It's not one of the 'Three Wise Guys' you dummy, it's Jesus!" But another youngster saw his error and jumped in to correct him.

"It's not Jesus; he's the little wooden baby in the box on the ground. It's Jesus's dad!"

"Jesus's dad?" said one incredulous local resident to no one in particular as he walked out of the co-op store with a bag of supplies under his arm. "Don't they know that Jesus's 'dad' was called Joseph?"

He had heard the commotion as he stepped out of the store, and as he turned and looked across the road he realised that he was just in time to see the final few seconds of the canine bladder spectacle.

"Jesus's dad," he repeated shaking his head. "Kids these days don't know shit from shoe polish. They don't even know the characters from the Bible story. Oh well," he sighed, "there's nothing I can do about it. They don't teach them anything these days," he lamented as he got into his pickup and turned the key.

The man who had jig-sawn the crèche-set into existence came running out of his house, cursing Sparky with some of his own doggerel, and with complete disregard for the seasonal notion of 'peace on earth, goodwill towards men,' yelled out,

"You four-legged-son-of-a-bitch, get off my lawn!"

Thinking the man was trying to be friendly, Sparky gave him a big doggy grin and wagged his tail, but Mecki sensed right away that was something wrong, so he barked out a sharp, no-nonsense order to the white dog.

"Sparky! Come on it's time to get out of here!" With that the two of them ran past the last few houses of the village and off into the fields towards Rainbow Farm. Later that day Sparky thanked Mecki for taking him to town. He said he enjoyed meeting everyone and he especially liked the part just before they left, when the kids were yelling and the whole town was carrying on because they were so happy to meet him.

"Think nothing of it kid," Mecki answered, "I'm glad you had a good time today." Mecki wasn't exactly sure why everyone started yelling at Sparky, but he was pretty sure it had something to do with Sparky peeing in the wrong place. Normally when a dog urinates, as long as he's not doing it on the floor or on somebody's shoes or an article of clothing, humans didn't seem to mind. But he had been around long enough to know that sometimes humans react in strange ways when dogs do certain things, and in those circumstances it was best to just get out of town.

§

Later that day Annie received a phone call from one of the village residents who complained about the incident.

"That damned white dog of yours had the nerve to desecrate the birth of Our Lord right in front of the whole village!" he barked. "I worked long and hard to bring that scene here to our little village so people could enjoy it and get into the feeling of Christmas, and your dog ruined it," he growled into the receiver.

Knowing that Sparky was just a mutt-dog who had never attended Sunday school, and did not know the Christmas story, Annie was sure Sparky had done no wrong. The caller (she couldn't identify him) was doing his best to make her feel guilty, but he chose the wrong person for that tactic.

"He's just a dog," she told him, "and he doesn't really know anything about 'Your Lord' or anybody else's lord for that matter and," she tried to explain speaking calmly into the black holes of the phone, "if you want to keep people's dogs from peeing on 'Your Lord' then I suggest you build a fence around him." The caller hung up grumbling his discontent. Later she told Tillman about the call and asked,

"Do you know who in the village made that thing?"

"Yeah I know who it is. It's that self-righteous, blowhard, Wendell Pendergast".

Afterwards Annie was upset. She liked to get along with people in the community and didn't want any hard feelings with her neighbours so she and Tillman decided not to let Sparky go to the village again until Christmas was over.

The new dog had lived an unhappy and neglected puppy-hood, but he had not been the victim of physical abuse. By the time he had been rescued and taken up residence at Rainbow Farm, the year-old dog showed no signs of any behavioural problems that might have been caused by human abuse or neglect. Although no one beat him, he did go without food and proper shelter for periods of time, but he had never suffered the kind of cruelty Mecki had. If there had been some bad moments in the past, Sparky's jovial personality was strong enough to smooth them over. Despite his puppy-hood he was a good natured dog who just wanted to be loved. He was young, energetic and always ready to play, and by the end of his first summer at Rainbow Farm Sparky was Mecki's main helper.

Like the two new cats, Sparky was delighted to be at Rainbow Farm and was an eager 'Second Dog.' He loved playing; he loved wrestling with Mecki, and most of all he loved chasing sticks and balls or whatever object anyone would throw for him. He cherished the forest walks with the whole family and quickly learned to sit down on demand and wait for a treat just like Mecki and the cats.

Buster immediately loved the big white dog and it wasn't long before he was sniffing and rubbing against him trying to discover what he was made of. The cautious feelings of the first day or two didn't last long for the other cats either, and in no time they were all friends. Sparky knew nothing about cats, and because of his size he had to learn to adjust to the smaller creatures and not to be too rough with them. It wasn't long before he was licking and tumbling them when they played and they responded by batting his wagging tail or bumping against him. They even groomed him. Buster was besotted with Sparky and they would run around on the vast lawn in front of the house playing tag or hide and seek among the flowers and bushes. Buster didn't mind if Sparky got a little clumsy and clopped him with one of his big paws. He was just happy to have a big dog buddy. Ever since his episode with the mean boys in Woodbridge and his memory of how the bullies had turned into cowards before the German shepherd, Buster knew he wanted a dog friend. So much so that he was certain that Tillman and Annie had specifically gone out and found a suitable pet dog just for him.

How lucky I am, Buster thought, *I am just like the children in the village who have their very own pet dogs to play with.*

Ideally, Buster would have preferred a puppy, but a fully-grown dog was good too. It wasn't long before Sparky even came to him when Buster gave one of his special chirping meows.

How many cats can do that? Buster thought with a sense of pride.

The following spring, as the days began to warm up, Buster and Sparky would lie together on the lawn while Sparky practiced his meadow scanning skills that Mecki was teaching him. Buster knew that if any mean boys came along Sparky would chase them away. He was right about that, the big dog would never let any harm come to Buster or the other cats. While he played with the cats Sparky also learned to be a good watch dog. Mecki taught him how to jump up and be at full speed in three steps so he could chase deer and coyotes off the meadow.

"You gotta' be fast if ya' wanna' to take care of this place, you know what I mean number two dog?"

Right. I got it, Meck." It wasn't long before Sparky was a first rate watchdog.

§

Before Europeans came to this part of the world, the Abenaki lived and hunted in the area that had always been known as 'The Waterfall of the Abenakis.' In the 17th century the Abenakis became allies of the French fur traders and for centuries they used one of the gentle bends in the river as a seasonal campsite. Further downstream the grey slate bed of the Tomifobia River dropped five metres, creating a roaring waterfall which forced *les voyageurs* to disembark and *portage* their birch-bark canoes around the falls before continuing downstream. After the American war against the British, white settlers coming into the area from the south used the same bend for their campsites and eventually settlers from England came to the region and established farms and businesses. By the 1840s, they had installed a large water wheel on one side of the falls and used it to power a saw mill and grain mill. The site that became the hamlet of Abenaki Falls (later changed to Indian Falls and then Johnson's Falls, before changing back to its original name late in the 20th century) had seen its heyday a century earlier, and what remained consisted of a handful of century-old farmhouses scattered along the river's banks a twenty-minute walk through the fields and forests behind Rainbow Farm.

The one structure in Abenaki Falls that stood taller than any of the others was the wooden grain silo whose vertical slats were held together with corroded iron rings that wrapped all the way around the sides of the 100-year-old structure. The silo sat adjacent to the farmer's co-op store next door. Wherever there is grain there will be mice and rats to eat the grain, and cats to eat the mice and rats, so it made sense the cats would congregate at the silo and entertain themselves on hot summer afternoons or moonlit nights. Gathered at its circular base the cats would purr and growl at each other and flirt and fight. As long as it had existed, the silo had served as the official *centre culturel*, as the mostly French-accented cats referred to it in their mouth noises. Kofi went there once or twice a week and after the new cats had arrived he would take Buster and Buddy Lebeau with him. In the village Kofi showed another side of his multifarious personality. It came as somewhat of a shock to Buddy and Buster that although he was called Kofi at home, in the hamlet of Abenaki Falls, particularly before Annic had him neutered, he was known among the female cats as 'Tomifobia Slim.'

The felines who gathered at the silo were mostly tough, un-neutered farm cats with scarred faces and torn ears from their territorial and copulatory encounters with other cats, and although they could be very pretty, the lady cats were tough, no-nonsense queens and about as dangerous as the males. Country cats can fight anytime they want, but since he was different, most of the cats just wanted to make cat noises with Kofi, knowing he had seen the world beyond the farms and forests of the Tomifobia River Valley. There was one fearsome-looking cat named Goliath, the most intimidating of all the cats of Abenaki Falls. Goliath looked like an escaped convict from cat prison, and at eight kilograms, the other cats kept their distance. His big frame was covered with a beat-up orange coat that looked as if the moths had eaten it and his face and ears were in tatters and so scarred it appeared that someone had bolted a section of a latticed fence to his face. Goliath was crude, rough and jealous of the handsome and wise Kofi, and sometimes he tried to attack Kofi, but the fast and agile Siamese could outrun and out-climb the bigger cat. In his inner catness, Goliath thought Kofi was very cool and secretly admired him, but, having been cast in the role of the village tough guy, Goliath couldn't change his persona halfway through the cabaret of life and start showing respect to another cat. They never got along very well until they were both very old cats many years later.

§

During their first year at Rainbow Farm Buddy Lebeau was still a young cat and Buster was just past kitten-hood when they first arrived. Like all of their animals, from the ducks and geese and chickens to the pond turtles, Tillman and Annie were kept an eye out the young cats and made sure they never got lost. They loved their animals and the whole family, especially the dogs and the cats, took daily walks in the woods while the human couple dispensed treats for them. Soon the cats worked out little routines where they jumped on old tree stumps or piles of stones and waited until Tillman or Annie came by to give them tidbits of food. It didn't take long before the cats knew each stone, stump and fallen tree along the forest path and knew exactly where to stop and perch for the next treat. The two dogs received plenty of treats as well but they didn't have to jump up on tree stumps to get them. They just ran about chasing squirrels up the trees and ground hogs into their holes, or sniffing deer scat on the leafy forest floor.

As the spring turned into summer Buddy Lebeau learned to hunt mice and birds just like Kofi, and the two of them spent time hunting every day along the edges of the fields and deep in the forests behind the barn. The Rainbow Farm cats spent most nights outside for most of the year, but in the really cold months of the winter they stayed in the house. Safe inside the warm house, the animals would hear the mystical howls of winter coyotes as they celebrated their kills of forest game in the darkness. Buster was the happiest grey and white cat in the world his first spring and early summer at Rainbow Farm. He learned that the forest was full of deer and moose, and once he even saw a bear in the deep woods. Having grown into a young adult cat, he passed much of his time outdoors chasing butterflies and grasshoppers and lying quietly by the small fish pond inside the rose garden surrounded by a cedar hedge where Annie worked for hours every summer day weeding and talking to her roses. Buster spent afternoons staring into the deep, clear water, watching the orange-coloured fish swim among the water lilies and occasionally he would dip his paw into the waters in an attempt to catch the green frogs that lived amongst the aquatic plants. Happy and content, Buster hunted every day, but unlike Kofi and Buddy Lebeau who ventured much farther from the house, he only took short jaunts on the other side of the split-rail fence into the nearby woods. While Lebeau and Kofi were bringing birds and squirrels and mice to the back porch to eat, Buster stayed closer to the garden and the chickens and Annie.

§

Although nature provides cats with the instinct to hunt, to be good at it young cats must practice and develop their skills. At his young age the only hunting title Buster could claim was 'mouser,' the lowest skill level hunting cats would admit to. There were lower-level hunting titles but young cats never spoke openly about them; they were too embarrassed to acknowledge them. Before they learned to hunt seriously, kittens and immature cats chased all manner of buzzing and crawling insects, plus dirt toads and tree frogs. When they caught them they usually ate them, although the amphibian residents of the Tomifobia Valley secreted a mild toxin which made them edible, but unpalatable. Once they tasted frog juice most cats left them alone.

Unofficial titles such as 'insector' and 'frogger' were given condescendingly to young cats by the older ones, and once they grew up the younger hunting cats did not like to be reminded of the naïveté of their youth and rarely mentioned such things in the company of cats their own age. Only older cats who were confident with their hunting abilities felt secure enough to reminisce about their first attempts to catch fast-moving life forms that were neither noble nor tasty. Older cats would smile and laugh about how proud they felt as kittens when they caught leaves or snowflakes or brought down grasshoppers or butterflies. Although they didn't garner much respect from their fellow cats such exercises were valuable and helped them learn to judge distances and track their prey. They all admitted that, frogs, and particularly grasshoppers, tasted awful, the equivalent to a ten-year-old human boy eating a plug of chewing tobacco and then getting sick from it. Cats were unanimous in stating that in their youth they rarely ate bees or wasps more than once.

At the age of one, Buddy Lebeau was a very good hunter and would remain the best hunter at Rainbow Farm throughout his long life. Before he was a year old he had acquired the titles of 'mouser' and a few months later, 'chipmunker.' Although they are much faster than mice, chipmunks live in the ground and are fairly easy prey. Mice are the easiest prey of all. Mice are slow and have little in the way of natural defences against cats. Once spotted in the open grass, unless they can make it to a hole in the ground, mice are a cat meal. With their short legs and tiny teeth and claws, mice really aren't equipped to defend themselves against the bigger teeth and claws of cats. What makes them even more vulnerable is that mice communicate with each other at sound frequencies which are inaudible to humans, but are easily picked up by cats. With their sharp sense of hearing cats use mouse communications to locate them and hunt them down. Like Mounties wiretapping the phones of criminals, cats are constantly spying on mouse conversations as they squeak back and forth to each other. Against predators like cats, snakes, hawks and foxes, the only reason mice survive at all is because they are prolific breeders producing billions of offspring every year. If it were not for predators like cats, the surface of the planet would be overrun with mice.

On the other hand, rats are not always an easy catch. Older cat-ratters claim that a cat has to develop a taste for rat meat since it is gamier and not as sweet as mouse meat. Early in his second year Buddy Lebeau had picked up the much more prestigious title of 'ratter,' a feat that required a much higher skill level than killing mice, birds or chipmunks. Rats are bigger, faster and equipped with beaver-like incisors that can inflict nasty bite wounds. Rat teeth never stop growing, so rats must chew and gnaw all their lives until they fall over dead. Cats avoid confronting more than one or two rats at a time, because in numbers, rats can quickly turn the tables and become cat killers. Cat lore is full of frightful stories where lone cats are set upon and torn to pieces by gangs of rats. Muskrats are even more difficult and dangerous for cats to bring down and they are rarely hunted. Even old and sick muskrats could go to ground or swim to safety if they needed to escape a cat. Nevertheless, it was generally agreed that when the fearsome Goliath from *La ferme de l'Est* said that he had caught a muskrat and ate it, the story was no doubt true.

"He's so big and strong I'll bet that Goliath could bring down a small deer," said a farm cat one night when a bunch of them were hanging out down at the grain silo. There was nothing to do except tell stories since the males were all scratched up from fighting and none of the females were in heat.

"No, better than that," said another, "I'll bet he could bring down a small moose!"

Such a comment was greeted by gales of cat laughter, but it did not diminish the fact that Goliath was a real bruiser.

Cats avoid larger rodents such as beavers. Beavers are huge compared to cats and are never on the menu. They also keep their distance from skunks, for obvious reasons, as well as porcupines and marmots. Birds are a different story. Cats normally don't attempt to catch birds high up in trees unless they are immobile nestlings or young birds that have fallen to the ground with insufficient flying skills to regain the safety of a tree branch. Late May and most of June were good times for catching nestlings just learning to fly, as they flapped out on their own and fell to the ground. It must be a terrible and frightening time for young birds to be obliged to leave the nest knowing that on the ground there were hunting cats waiting to make a meal of them. Buddy Lebeau didn't need to wait until nesting time to catch birds. At one year old his hunting skills and athleticism were so good he could simply leap up from the ground and catch low-flying birds on the wing. This gained him the much-coveted title of 'flying birder.' It was a title only a few cats ever attained despite the innate athleticism of the species. For cats it was the equivalent of an Olympic gold medal in some high-performance sport. Buddy Lebeau's method consisted of positioning himself flat on the ground near trees frequented by low flying birds. When one flew by, Buddy simply jumped straight up off the ground, often well over a metre, and caught the unsuspecting creature with a single paw swipe. When Annie and Tillman saw Buddy's bird catching skills they made sure there were no low-hanging branches in the back yard or in any of the gardens so Buddy wouldn't have an unfair advantage over the birds. They even moved all the bird feeders to higher locations, out of Buddy's reach. These precautions reduced the number of kills he made, but Buddy could still occasionally snatch an unsuspecting bird out of the air as he walked through the forest.

That summer Buster was most certainly a 'frogger' and an 'insector' as he fearlessly chased down the green frogs on the lawn or the brown ones who lived in the trees, plus he honed his hunting skills by snatching butterflies from the air as they flew from flower to flower. Although he ate them they were not his favourite food. By June he had captured and eaten his first mouse, a milestone in the life of a young cat. For all cats soloing a mouse was an unforgettable rite of passage surpassed only by making kittens. Before he ate the mouse he discovered, like countless generations of cats before him, that he loved playing with it. When he began eating it, he first bit into the head and felt the full joy of crunching the thin, crisp shell of mouse cranium between his teeth. Since cats cannot produce large amounts of fat in their bodies they must get it from the animals they eat, and mammal brains consist almost entirely of fat. This is why cats almost always eat the head first. In the world of carnivores fat is what matters most, so as Buster bit down on the cranium of his first mouse kill the fat-rich brain exploded in his mouth and flooded his taste buds with the flavours of warm, freshly-killed mouse brain. From that moment on Buster knew his reason for being alive: cats eat mice!

§

10,000 years ago, both cats and humans numbered only a few million. Now there are nearly a billion cats on the planet, and more than seven billion humans; since the two joined forces, both species have done exceptionally well. Cats are both the essence of cuteness, and creatures from our fear-induced nightmares, either as nocturnal nuisances hissing, howling and procreating, or as charming lovable companions. In the media cats are calendar creatures rolling balls of knitting yarn off Grandma's table, or snow-white kitten TV actors with hairdryer-blown coats chasing rolls of errant toilet paper around bathroom floors before caressing the bottoms of stylish and sophisticated defecators. Some fear cats or find them mysterious to the point of being creepy; black cats with their yellow eyes in particular, conjure up images of familiars and witchcraft. Unlike round-eyed humans, cat's eyes open vertically like arrow slits in a medieval fortress which some think enables cats to shoot out rays of light against their enemies. But there is nothing supernatural about cat eyes; they just have a layer behind the retina that reflects light like a roadside highway sign. The ancient Egyptians had a different take on cat eyes: they interpreted their expansion and contraction as a reflection of the waxing and waning of the moon.

Cats were sacred to the Egyptian goddess Isis and were often pictured with her. Later on, during the Roman Empire, cat worship grew in popularity, and eventually the goddess Isis and her cats were worshipped as far north as Germany and England. Unlike today, where people have trouble giving away surplus cats, the 10th century AD law code of the Welsh King Howel Dada reveals that cats were so valuable people bought and sold them. A newborn kitten sold for a penny (a sizable sum in the day), an inexperienced youngster for two pence, and you could get four pence for a cat that had killed a mouse. The fine for killing a cat from the chef's pantry, where of course large amounts of food were kept, was either a sheep or a lamb. Other penalties for killing a cat included enough grain to cover the dead cat when held by its tail with its nose touching the ground. Cats found much favour in the Middle East and Africa as well, and it is recorded that the prophet Muhammad loved them and Beybars, the Sultan of Cairo, established charitable organisations to feed and shelter homeless cats.

Like many ethnic groups of humans throughout the saga of cat-human history, cats too have known periods of respect and even deification, while at other times they have endured torture, persecution, and 'felinicide.' By the 13th century AD, cats were admired as pets in much of Europe, especially by women still worshipping the cat-loving goddesses Artemis and Diana, two spiritual leftovers from earlier Greco-Roman times. Fearing competition from more popular deities, Church authorities expended much effort in the bloody commerce of putting cat worship out of business. They found that nothing was more efficient for getting rid of pesky heretics than straight forward mass extermination. So, as human cat worshippers were rounded up and burned in church yards and city squares across Europe, so were their cats. In 1233, Pope Gregory IX issued the *Vox in Rama,* a papal decree that identified black cats with Lucifer, and condemned all cats to death. Church-generated cat hatred continued and many sources claim that in the 15th century Pope Innocent VIII went so far as to excommunicate cats from the Church.

This came as quite a shock to the cats, since they didn't even know they were church members to begin with. There are no records indicating how the cat population reacted to being excommunicated, but it appears that most of them didn't seem to mind too much when they heard the news.

"How could they kick us out? We weren't even baptised!" said one cat philosopher.

§

Usually when humans hear cats caterwauling at night they tend to think they are just copulating. But, contrary to popular belief, nocturnal cat noises often come from cats recounting myths and stories to other cats. Unknown to humans, there is a great and venerable tradition of cat myths and stories that were known already in the Early Bronze Age, and which have been passed down through subsequent generations of cats now living in many parts of the world. Some nights, when the neighbourhood cats met at the grain silo, the older cats would share the stories they had learned in their youth. In many stories rats represented the forces of chaos and destruction and were the villains in numerous cat epics. The main theme in these classics emphasised how cats saved their species by eating ruthless and barbaric rats who threatened the existence of all life forms on earth. But given the sometimes difficult relations between cats and dogs, canines were also cast as the villains in a number of 'cat versus dog' stories. The most notable of these was *Les chiens de la Bastille,* a story that first appeared in Paris at the time of the French Revolution. As cats tell the story, when the Bastille prison was liberated, along with the human prisoners large numbers of companion dogs were released as well. Once free, the dogs carried out brutal attacks against nobles loyal to King Louis XVI and their many pampered and over-fed cats who lived in luxury, while their feline *sans culottes* cousins languished in poverty. Such events brought about *le règne de terreur des chiens*, a period little known and poorly understood by human historians, during which cats were hunted down and killed by dogs. In some instances royal cats were even guillotined by the revolutionaries along with their human masters.

Among felines, two of the best known cat epics are the Burmese classic, *The Rats of Rangoon*, and another south-east Asian thriller, *The Cats of Krakatowah*. Both have similar story lines except a volcano gets worked into the Krakatowah version. The better known of the two, *The Rats of Rangoon,* is a gripping tale about a family of ancestral cats caught in a primeval forest on the edge of the earth where evil rats eat cats like humans eat chicken wings at happy hour. In the story, a gang of fearsome *Rattus rattus* under the leadership of a Teutonic rat named *Dunkel Fleischfresser*—The Dark Flesh-devourer—relentlessly stalks a pair of heroic proto-cats through the depths of the forest, threatening to exterminate the original mother and father of all cats. Only through a series of spine-tingling events are the feline primogenitors, Ur-cat and his true love Ur-kit, able to vanquish the forces of rat-darkness and produce the first family of domestic farm cats. One of the favourite episodes of the epic, at least for the Abenaki Falls crowd, was when a rat demonesse taking the name Meow-Meow, disguises herself as a beautiful cat and tries to tempt Ur-cat with her charms. Meanwhile, his mate, the beautiful Ur-kit, is helpless to come to his rescue because she is caught in a great net carried about by flying snakes. For cats, the story is both riveting and frightening and on dark nights skilled cat storytellers can go on for hours using gestures and pantomimes to audibly and visually act out the story's episodes. The local Abenaki Falls cats believe the stories to be about real events, and like other locals, the cats from Rainbow Farm were firm believers in the cat lore expressed on dark nights at the foot of the old grain silo.

§

In the autumn and early winter of Buster's first year, the pond that lay sunken into the brown farmland behind Rainbow Farm began to take on the done-in and weary look of the late fall season. Once September came the children were off to school and the pond returned to its rightful owners: the animals. Gone were the boys and girls of summer with their little wooden boats, their fishing poles, their worms freshly dug from compost piles and their hidden packs of cigarettes hastily smoked downwind of younger brothers or sisters, who might divulge their yellow-fingered secrets to disapproving parents. Between mid-October and mid-December the pond had few human visitors except the occasional duck hunter. But while the days shortened and the leaves fell, and the humans gathered fire wood and tightened storm windows, the pond's beavers and muskrats prepared for the winter months. The deer came to drink in the early morning light followed by coyotes sniffing their spoor, and a dark brown female moose (Annie called her 'mousse au chocolat'), followed closely by her calf, came for a weekly visit to feast on the fading water plants.

Tomifobia Pond was home to ducks, Canada geese, and from spring to fall was a busy stop for migrating birds transiting from breeding to feeding grounds. Pairs of red-wing blackbirds, king fishers and sand pipers stayed through the summer, bringing their young into the world on the modest-sized body of water and its surrounding marshes and wetlands. The pond's winged visitors had been hunted by indigenous peoples, then settlers and more recently by the locals. By December the waterfowl were gone, the hunters' guns were silent, and an icy quiet fell over the pond. When the last of the autumn leaves had fallen and cattail fur blew in the wind, the surface of the pond began to freeze over as the nights grew colder, only to melt to clear water under the midday sun. Then, one morning just before Christmas the temperature fell sharply and overnight the surface was covered with a slick sheet of ice. It was too thin to support anyone's weight, but after a few more minus 20° C nights, by New Year's Day it had become rock-solid.

The silence was broken when the pond froze over and came to life again to the most recognisable sound of winter activity in Canada: the sound of boys and girls, and their dogs, skating across the Zamboni-free ice, their shouts punctuated by the sounds of gliding skates, hockey sticks pounding against the frozen surface, and pucks being slapped around on the ice. By the Christmas school-break boys and girls from the local farms searched basements and garages for sticks, gloves, helmets and collapsible goalie nets. As the ice thickened, they sharpened their skates, gathered up their gear and headed out for the best little hockey-surface this side of Woodbridge: Tomifobia Pond.

"As-tu vu ça, là? J'ai compté un but, moi!"—"Hey, did you see that? I scored a goal!" Such were the unmistakable sounds of kids playing hockey.

One cold Saturday morning Kofi and Mecki recognised the sounds of the local kids playing hockey. And if the kids were playing then so were their dogs and that meant there would be lots of fun! But first, Mecki had to get things organised. Sparky and the new cats had never seen a game before, so he called them together in front of the chicken house and explained that they were going to see their first hockey game.

"OK you cats, listen up," he said looking at Buddy and Buster, his under-slung jaw pushed forward. "Cats don't play hockey OK? Hockey is a dog's game, and me and the dogs over in Abenaki Falls let some of the farm kids' play along with us. So you guys just watch, eh?"

The two new cats nodded their understanding, but really, they had no idea what he was talking about. However, Kofi knew what to do. He would take Buster and Buddy to a clump of fallen trees a stone's throw from the pond, and they would watch the game from there and not draw anybody's attention. Kofi ushered the new cats into the space under the trees where they could peer out between the old tumbled tree trunks and catch all the action. Once the cats were ensconced they looked out from their cover and saw a bunch of children and dogs sliding about on the ice, but their actions were completely incomprehensible to the two new cats who just turned and looked at each other with puzzled expressions on their faces.

Mecki and Sparky headed for the ice and were welcomed with pats on the head and back slaps by the village kids who knew Mecki quite well. They were delighted to have Sparky with them and welcomed him as a new member of their hockey gang. Right from the start Sparky felt honoured and a little intimidated to be accepted into the group, given that he had never even set foot on the ice before. Sparky's first tentative steps on the unfamiliar surface brought some snickers and comments from the half-dozen local ice-dogs, but after the customary orifice and genital inspections and some hackle raising, the dogs settled down and got ready for the game.

Kofi told Buster and Buddy that the dogs from the adjoining *Ferme de l'Est*, just up the road, were telling Mecki and Sparky that they were going to 'kick the buttocks' of the Abenaki Falls' kids in the game. Down on the ice, Mecki just snorted at the suggestion, gave the kids a "we'll see whose butts get kicked" look, and headed for his end of the ice. The young cats didn't understand the idiomatic sense of the phrase and asked why farm kids would want to expend the energy to kick a few farm dogs in their butts. Apparently it was a dumb question and Kofi let it go unanswered. The older kids made sure the nets were in their right places, and got things organised for the opening faceoff. Just before the game started several other cats from one of the neighbouring farms showed up. They exchanged the usual feline neutral ground pleasantries as they found places inside the woodpile. Now there were five of them peering out from their wooden bunker at a bunch of kids and dogs skating around on a frozen surface. Once settled they waited for the game to begin.

All of the dogs except Sparky were veteran hockey players who knew the game and had no trouble following along. To ensure things went well Mecki told Sparky that,

"It takes a few games to get the hang of things, so just stay on the outside and run along with my team for a while. Understand? Just stay on the outside and watch me, OK?"

"Right," said Sparky obediently. The white dog's heart was pounding with excitement. He didn't know what to expect, but he had learned many things from the older dog and he was more than willing to do as he said.

The puck was thrown down and the game started. As the youngsters skated about jockeying for their positions and trying to take control of the puck, the dogs got right in on the action. Like the children, the dogs raced around on the ice, sliding and slipping and doing their best to avoid the slap shots and the fast passes that whizzed from one side of the ice to the other.

What in the name of Cerberus is going on here? Sparky wondered.

The two new cats were simply dumbfounded by what they saw. To begin, Buddy Lebeau couldn't figure out why no one fell through the ice. He knew that a short time ago it would have been impossible to walk on the water.

"How can they do that?" Buddy kept asking Kofi.

"It's because of the cold Buddy," he answered, distracted from the action by Buddy's question.

"This is crazy," said Buster. He was amazed that humans and dogs could go on the slick ice and thrash about like angry wasps while swinging clubs at each other. Reflecting on the humans' and dogs' preoccupation with chasing around a little round black thing on the frozen surface of a pond, Buddy Lebeau wondered what it was all for.

"Does someone give them food for doing this?" he asked Kofi again.

"For them, Buddy," he said, "it's like playing with a mouse before you eat it. You know that feeling you get?"

"Ah, OK, I get it," he said.

As the afternoon continued the new cats agreed that this was the craziest and yet most wonderful thing they had ever seen. They loved it! And even though they did not know anything about hockey, after the game got going they began to catch on to some of the basics, and by the end of the afternoon they could more or less follow the action. They knew that somehow you had to put the little black thing in the cage-like contraption at each end of the ice. They also observed that to prevent one group from putting the round thing in the cage contraption it was OK to use their sticks like hooks to trip up their opponents.

"Did you see that? They hit each other with those sticks and then they use them to manipulate the little black thing into that cage," Buddy Lebeau recounted to Buster.

"Yeah I see," said Buster, his eyes glued to the action. Then he commented: "They sure like hitting each other with those sticks, don't they!"

"Yeah, do they ever!"

In the opening minutes the two teams managed to get the puck from one end of the ice to the other with passes zipping across the ice only to be batted down by a stick or blocked by a skate, and no one even took a shot at the nets as the scrums of sticks and skates coalesced, and then broke apart when one player managed to get the puck and move it down the ice. Both defenses were good, and though there were a few shots on goal, nobody scored. Then Big Joey Tremblay scored in the upper right corner of the net over the left shoulder of the Abenaki Falls *Prédateur* goalie, and the players and their dogs went wild. *La Ferme de l'Est* kids jumped up and down, scratching grooves in the ice with their skate blades while their dogs barked, made hackle displays, and charged the opposing dogs while their humans cheered.

Peering out from their shelter the new cats were dumbfounded.

"May the Great Cat protect us!" said Buddy Lebeau. "What's going on? What was that?" he exclaimed looking towards the other cats huddled in their wooden hockey bunker.

On the ice the kids from Abenaki Falls remained undaunted; they had been down a goal or two before and were not inclined to panic. The game started up once again as a boy wearing a Montreal Canadiens sweater centered the puck and a great big dog named 'Muttface' seized it in his teeth, spun around and headed for the other goal. As good-natured as the dogs were, when their hockey blood was up, the kids didn't dare put their hands close to the mouth of any dog holding a puck. But the Abenaki Falls kids knew how to get the puck out of Muttface's mouth. He hated having his tail pulled so, as soon as he picked up the puck, one boy skated over and grabbed the big dog's tail. Muttface immediately dropped the puck, spun around, and tried to bite the offending hand. In an instant, Mecki darted in, grabbed the puck and made a fast break-away towards the net at the opposite end of the pond. Before he could get to the opponent's net, two players caught up with him and he was surrounded. With a crowd standing between him and the net, Mecki did something few other dogs, or kids, could do. He performed his famous move known to all Tomifobia Pond hockey players, dogs, children, and even a few cat hockey fans. He executed a difficult manoeuvre known as the 'Hound Around'. This was where Mecki made a wide, sweeping move to his left on the outside of the net drawing everyone in that direction. Once the opposing team bought into the fake, Mecki did a 180-degree *volte face* by digging his powerful claws into the ice like figure skaters do when they perform spins or *pirouettes*. He promptly came to a dead stop while the right side of the pond was wide open with nobody to defend it. For an instant, as everyone tried to reverse their directions, Mecki had a clear path to the net and only the goalie could prevent him from scoring. Having seen this move before, one boy dropped his stick and lifted both hands to form a megaphone-mouth:

"Watch out! Watch out! It's the Hound Around! He's doing the Hound Around! Cover the right side!" In a heartbeat a chorus of children lung-hollered the alert, transforming it into an a cappella ice chant.

"It's the Hound Around, the Hound Around! Stop him. Stop him!"

But it was too late. By the time they realised what had happened Mecki went in and faked a pass to an alert eleven-year-old who sold the pass to the opponents by taking a slap shot on goal. For an instant the *La Ferme d l'Est* kids took their eyes off Mecki and looked to see if the puck had gone in. It had not—not yet, because Mecki still had it between his teeth. When the goalie moved left to block the fake shot Mecki charged the open right side, and with a snap of his head, he flung the *rondelle* right into the open net. The puck went between the bars with enough force to push the netting out the back. The Abenaki Falls kids raised their sticks and roared in unison.

"He scored! He scored! Mecki scored!" they shouted.

"Did you see that? Did you see that?" They rejoiced, slapping and hugging each other while waving their sticks in the air. "The greatest hockey dog in all of Canada!" they yelled again and again. With the thrill of victory in his heart, Mecki turned and ran back into the crowd where his teammates fell on him, hugging him and pulling on his tail and patting him; cheering loudly and telling him what a good dog he was. Then his teammates began chanting:

"Mec-ki! Mec-ki! Mec-ki!"

And so on this sunny winter day, the one-time abused puppy-dog that Jeanne, the waitress from Smith's Landing had saved from Monster-man, and now the Head Dog of Rainbow Farm had just scored the most beautiful goal imaginable and was the hero of a bunch of kids and dogs and a few cats watching from nearby on Tomifobia Pond. That day Mecki was a very happy dog and as he took his victory lap around the pond he thought,

It sure beats being tied up outside that dingy apartment. An unmistakable smile appeared on his face as he ran through the crowd.

Inside their hockey bunker, under their collection of logs and branches, the cats had been following the play with keen interest, and when Mecki scored they jumped up, bumping their heads on the low-hanging logs.

"Did you see that play?" one old tabby who fancied himself a bit of an expert was heard to say to a younger, first-time village cat.

"That was what ya' call a perfect 'Hound Around.' Yes sir, and only Mecki, the famous hockey dog from Rainbow Farm, can do it right, eh?" The younger cat duly nodded his head in reverential acknowledgement.

The cats knew that Mecki had done something special, that he was a hero, and even though cats didn't play team sports, in that moment both Buster and Buddy Lebeau wanted to be like Mecki. They were so proud of him and so proud to be the cats from Rainbow Farm where Mecki, the famous hockey dog, also known as 'The First Dog of Rainbow Farm', lived.

Wow, thought Buddy, as he and Buster exchanged glances, *what an honour for all of us!*

§

The cats looked out between the logs for the next two hours as the feeble winter sun moved from mid-heavens to the west, while children and dogs skated, passed and shot until they dropped on the ice from exhaustion. No longer able to skate, they dragged themselves to the edges of the pond where they slumped into the banks of shovelled snow. Worn out from their efforts, they reluctantly removed their skates, put on their civi-boots and headed for home.

Later, as the cats followed Mecki and Sparky back home they reflected about how good their lives were.

"Doesn't get much better than this, eh Buster?" said Buddy Lebeau.

"No, Buddy, it certainly doesn't get any better than this. I'm so glad we came here Buddy. I'm so happy here."

§

Once abandoned, the pond returned to its millennial owners, the frogs and muskrats hibernating beneath the water in the dark, frozen soil while comatose fish languished in the dark waters beneath the skate-scarred surface. The resident family of beavers, led by a big male the local kids had named 'Justin,' was snug in its stick and mud house not far from where all the action had taken place. Around midnight, as a gibbous moon rose in the east, some deer came to the edge of the pond and paused for a moment, puzzled by the skate marks. Then they walked across the frozen white surface where only hours before cats had marvelled at the icy spectacle of children and dogs playing hockey on Tomifobia Pond.

§

Except to go out every day to hunt mice in the garage or the chicken house, during the winter months the cats spent much less time outside. The three of them passed most of their time indoors playing kitty-tag with each other and with the dogs, or sleeping in front of the big wood-burning stove as it radiated a soft orange light through smoke-coloured glass doors. Growing more and more secure in their new environment, their old lives slipped into the past and they thought more about the present than about the hard times they had lived through earlier in their lives. By time the sap began to flow out of the maple trees and into the long metal buckets that hung like deciduous Christmas tree decorations across the Tomifobia River Valley, Buddy Lebeau had grown to become a beautiful, athletic hunting cat, Kofi was as wise as ever, and Buster was growing into a big strong cat.

Bedlam Barn

Buster and the other animals knew something was afoot when their humans hauled out the cat cages, gathered up the dog beds, and the containers of dog and cat food, and loaded them all into the truck. As all the animals stood around watching Tillman and Annie, Mecki told Sparky and the three cats that he had experienced this sort of thing before and that something big was going to happen. Around noon the couple went around the house shutting windows and locking doors. Once the house was secured, they attached Mecki and Sparky to their leashes and put each one of the cats in a wire cage, and loaded them all in the back of the truck. Buster had never left Rainbow Farm, and he did not like the look of things. Tillman drove them a few kilometres up Chemin de Bellevue to a place called *La maison des petits animaux,* the dog and cat kennel. From the minute they turned into the driveway, Buster didn't like the place; it reminded him of the animal shelter, of being a kitty-orphan.

The kennel was a large barn where lots of other cats and dogs were staying. To Buster the place was ominous, an animal prison where dogs and cats were sent when their humans didn't want them anymore. Buster thought he was being abandoned, but the other cats and dogs said their humans would come back soon and take them home.

Come back for them? Buster had never heard of anything so ridiculous. *Why would humans leave their animals in the first place only to come back for them later?* He doubted such a thing was possible.

Why didn't they just keep them at home and not waste a trip bringing them here to begin with?

That made no sense and he did not believe the humans would ever come back for any of them.

This is the end of Rainbow Farm and everything I love, he decided. *I can't understand why Kofi and the dogs aren't more upset. We've been abandoned and they seem OK with that. What's going on anyway?*

He was sure they had all been put back in a shelter again to wait for adoption by another family. Within minutes of their arrival he was depressed and panicky. Despite the way he felt, the dogs seemed happy, and like dogs always do they wagged their tails and barked their heads off. When Tillman put Buster's cage on the ground the young cat looked up at him, his eyes pleading not to be abandoned. He chirped and meowed desperately to be taken back home, but his cries for help fell on deaf ears. Tillman, the man who had come to the shelter and rescued him, was now abandoning him. He would have to find a new home with new people. He and his cat and dog brothers would never see Rainbow Farm again.

Why are they doing this to us?

Just like Tillman, Annie was excited about their trip and was not paying any attention to him or any of the other animals. She was busy talking to the kennel lady and giving her bags of food for the animals.

I wonder how long that food will last, Buster asked himself. *Once it's gone we will be in trouble. We might starve.*

Instead of understanding how frightened he was his beloved humans just got in their truck, waved goodbye, and left.

They dumped us. We don't mean anything to them. Another wave of depression washed over Buster. *How could they just leave us like that?* His heart sank to the ground.

He looked at Buddy Lebeau and Kofi in desperation and asked where they would find another home and who would come and take them. Buddy wasn't sure, and didn't know what to make of things, but Kofi said not to worry so Lebeau didn't.

"They will come back and get us Buster, so don't be concerned," said Kofi. Despite his great respect for Kofi, Buster didn't believe his humans would ever come back.

"But I *am* worried, Kofi. I'm worried they will never come back for us."

"Of course they will," said the older cat. "They'll only be gone a few days and then they'll come back. You'll see."

Despite Kofi's assurances terrible thoughts raced through the grey and white cat's mind. He couldn't fathom being separated from Buddy Lebeau and Kofi and never seeing them again. He would never have his own dog again, and Sparky would probably go live somewhere else.

I will probably be a 'lifer,' and have to spend the rest of my life in this horrible place.

He wasn't the only one who was upset. As he looked around he saw other abandoned cats peering down from the scratching posts and cat perches that lined the walls of the incarceration room. One look told him that they were not happy either.

No wonder, he thought, *they probably miss their homes just like I do. I wonder how long some of these guys have been here? Maybe they're 'lifers' like the ones at the other shelter I was in.*

The atmosphere in the cat room was tense and the cats already in there were on edge and cranky. They did not interact with each other or play cat games like Buster and his cat brothers did when they were home. Several of them openly meowed their discontent. One cat stood in the corner and howled while the rest of them just silently hunkered down in their misery.

As soon as the Rainbow Farm cats were released from their cages and entered the room one particular cat caught Buster's attention. It was white, covered with long hair, and had an ugly, flat face. The unfortunate animal was very upset. It hissed and growled and carried on in a very unfriendly manner.

Poor thing, Buster thought sympathetically, *he must have been in some kind of horrible accident that left him with a smashed-in face and a nasty disposition. I'd be nasty too if I looked like him.* When the animal warden came into the cat room, 'flat face' hissed and tried to scratch her. Kofi said it was because they could hear the dogs in the next big room.

"No," Buster insisted, "it's because they have been abandoned, and they know they will have to find new homes."

"No, that is not the reason Buster so stop saying that and take it easy OK?" Kofi said trying to calm his cat brother, "things will be alright. You'll see."

Despite Kofi's attempts to calm Buster the grey and white cat remained convinced the kennel was a kind of pet prison or mental institution for cats who had lost their inner catness; cats who were suddenly homeless and adrift in an unfamiliar place with a population of barking dogs close by.

"This is not *La maison des petits animaux,* Buster reasoned; *this is the cat crazy-house. This is 'Bedlam Barn.'*

Every time the dogs barked and started carrying on in the next room the cats hunkered down closer to the floor expecting them to break in and attack. Buster felt sorry for the cats who did not live around dogs, or who did not have dog friends. They were not accustomed to dog sounds and their manners.

In one part of Bedlam Barn there were more than a dozen dogs of all sizes and colours. They were all together in a large common room barking, growling, yapping and wrestling. Even Mecki and Sparky were joining in and making noises and throwing other dogs to the floor or being thrown about themselves. Some dogs even took turns humping each other.

May the Great Cat preserve us! Buster sighed as he peered through the big glass window that separated the two rooms, *they look absolutely disgusting!*

Buster couldn't ever remember having the urge to leg hump another cat or worse, one of the humans, but that was what Sparky was attempting with the kennel warden until she booted him in the chest and he un-humped her leg. Buster and Buddy weren't surprised when Sparky began playing and rough housing with the other dogs; he was always like that. Sometimes Sparky drove Mecki crazy because he constantly wanted to play and wrestle.

When Mecki had enough he would grab Sparky by the scruff of his neck and throw him to the ground, and 'chew him out,' so he could do his job. But at the kennel Buster was frankly disappointed with the usually serious, no-nonsense Mecki. In the company of other dogs, he suddenly lost his composure, and within minutes of their arrival, he threw himself into the rowdy play with a mob of spaniels, collies and retrievers. They looked like a bunch of canine spastics in a cage match.

How can they be enjoying themselves? he asked. *Don't they know they could be here forever?*

Buster didn't know it, but Mecki and Sparky had been here before and for them the kennel was a kind of doggy summer camp. Unlike the cats, the dogs were not unhappy to be there, and in the company of his dog buddies Mecki had a big, goofy grin plastered across his face. Clearly he and Sparky were having a good time. As Buster observed the dog spectacle through the window there was one dog in particular who repulsed Buster more than the others. The dog was a hulk, a canine sumo wrestler, who slobbered long strings of white mouth slime all over the furniture, the floor, the food bowls, and the other dogs. Buster looked at Kofi and Buddy Lebeau and exclaimed:

"That thing is absolutely disgusting!" The other two nodded their heads in agreement. Buddy Lebeau said that in his entire life he had only seen one other animal that slobbered like that: cows.

"Yes, you're absolutely right," said Buster. Cows were walking slobber machines. They drooled and dripped great strings of slime and spittle mixed with partially chewed vegetation as their jaws moved back and forth grinding away on cow food.

"This dog must have cows for parents!" exclaimed Buddy Lebeau.

Buster was pretty cool about most things. Even when they had taken him to the veterinarian where the vet-woman jabbed and poked various parts of his body and pricked him with needles and stuck instruments with tiny lights and gauges on them into his orifices, he had remained calm. But Bedlam Barn was different: he had to escape and go back home. He would have to find Annie and Tillman and try to explain to them that he hated the place and wanted to live with them at Rainbow Farm.

They will just have to take me back; that's all. Even if I have to stay in the chicken house for the rest of my life, it will be better than this place.

§

The night was hot, the windows were open, and a thin screen separated Buster from the cool night air outside. For several hours Buster been pulling and tugging on the screen tearing a hole in it with his claws. The other cats told him to stop but he refused, and through the night-time hours the opening in the screen grew larger. By the time most of the dark hours were past, the hole was big enough for him to slip through.

Cats can jump or fall from great heights and land without injuries. At four metres above the ground the second floor of the barn wasn't a serious barrier to his escape. Buster was young, strong, and knew his way around trees, but in his naïveté he had not realised that the real danger of an escape was not hitting the ground, it was what would happen after he was on the ground. He had no idea where Rainbow Farm was or which way to turn when he reached the road, provided he could find it. He had never negotiated unfamiliar fields and forests and did not realise that even if he knew the right direction, it would take at least four days of steady walking to get home. He was lost before he hit the ground. Despite that, sometime long after midnight he slipped through the hole in the screen, placed his front paws on the narrow window ledge, and moved outside. The air was cool and refreshing. He took a deep breath and thought,

This was the right thing to do. I feel better already. Now I'll get Buddy Lebeau and Kofi, and we'll head for home and then we'll come back and get the dogs. Everyone will be free and back home by the morning. Good plan.

The metal window ledge was narrow and slippery and when he looked around he did not recognise anything, and it suddenly struck him that he had no idea where he was.

Maybe I'd better go back inside and ask Kofi which way to go and how far it is to Rainbow Farm before I jump.

He reversed direction and stepped backwards towards the opening in the screen.

I think I should make some plans before I jump, he thought. *Kofi will know what to do. I'll just back up until I reach...*

His claws made a scraping sound on the galvanised metal as he went over the edge, looking up he saw the star-dotted sky as he fell backwards through the air. Then, in a split second his feline gyroscope whirred into action, flipping his head and body around as he righted himself and with all four legs and paws extended, he struck the ground. Thunk!

Great! Now what do I do? Where am I anyway?

Standing in the bright light of the big exterior lamp hanging high above him he looked from side to side, but saw nothing that was familiar.

Alright, maybe I'll have to change my plans.

He looked up towards the torn window and called for Kofi and Buddy Lebeau, and it wasn't long before they stuck their heads out through the hole in the screen and looked down.

"We heard the scraping noises when you fell," said Buddy.

"Stay calm Buster," said Kofi. "The best thing is to hide nearby until morning until the kennel warden comes. She'll let you back in."

"Right. Sounds like a good idea. I'll hide nearby and see you guys in the morning," he repeated.

From inside the torn window screen Kofi and Buddy Lebeau gave each other worried looks.

"I hope he's alright and he gets back in tomorrow morning," said Buddy.

"I think he'll be fine if he just stays close by," said Kofi.

No problem, thought Buster. He had spent many nights outside at Rainbow Farm, and apart from a few minor brushes with coyotes and foxes, he had never had a problem. But Buster had never been far from home. Even in the old garage with Nameless and his siblings, he may have been hungry, scared and abused, but he always knew where he was. The same at Rainbow Farm; he always knew where everything was and he could find his way through the forests and fields with no problem. It was different here; nothing was familiar.

I'll just stay close by, he thought. I'll just find a place close by where I can hide, and wait till morning. If anything happens I can take care of myself. I am a cat, and I can see in the dark. I have sharp claws and I can climb trees. I'll be fine, he encouraged himself.

Book III

Surviving Wild Nature

It had been hot in the cat room and he needed a cool drink so he made his way towards the sound of a small stream gurgling close by. After a few paces down a gentle stream bank he placed his paws in the damp mud, leaned forward, and lapped tongue-fulls cool water. The kennel light behind him was shining through the trees so he knew where he was, and it would be just a short walk back to the barn.

He was not alone! There was another animal nearby just to his left on the same side of the stream. What was it? Whatever it was, it was close by. He froze, drawing his legs underneath his body forming himself into a tightly-coiled biological spring preparing to flee. Then he recognised its smell. A skunk! Buster had seen them before and he knew they could be a real menace. If one sprayed him he'd be miserable for days and no one would get near him.

I should have detected him! What if it had been a fox or coyote? I must pay more attention, I'm being too reckless.

He retraced his steps back up the stream bank in reverse, but now it seemed much higher and steeper than when he came down to drink. When he reached the top of the bank, he turned around to head back to the barn. But something wasn't right because now he found himself on a flat gravel surface. He remembered thinking that it was odd that the stream waters had disappeared into a metal culvert below him that he hadn't seen before.

Hey, how did I get here? I think I'm on a road or something.

He didn't recognise anything.

Which way was the kennel? Then he saw the glow of the big light shining some distance away.

Ah, there it is, he thought with a sense of relief. He didn't remember it being so far away when he went down to the stream, but then maybe he hadn't been paying close attention. All he had to do now was walk in the direction of the light and he would be there in no time. He started to take a step towards the edge of the road, but something powerful held on to his feet; he couldn't move them.

What's going on?

§

They were coming at him! Two yellow eyes set in a swirl of dust thundering down the hill straight towards him. He wanted to run. He had to run, he had to escape, but he could not make his paws move. He was held in place by two high-beam science fiction rays that paralysed him as an ominous mechanical terror descended upon him. Mortal danger!

I have to run! I have to run! Why can't I lift my paws? What's the matter? Why can't I move? May the Great Cat save me! I have to run!

Thunder-junkers were a great danger to country animals. They came out of nowhere, crippling and killing as they roared about the countryside. Unlike other predators, they killed for no reason and they never ate the prey they left dead on the road or those they threw in broken heaps into roadside ditches. There was no season for them and no way to tell when they would appear. They struck, maimed, killed and moved on. They did not even slow down to see who their victims were. Kofi had told the younger cats about wild animals, skunks, coyotes and deer that had been struck by them, and it was from Kofi that Buster had first heard the terrifying term 'Thunder-junker': machines that the humans had fashioned from earth and fire as only humans can. Machines that made roaring noises, expelled noxious odours, and killed their prey. To cats, it was inconceivable how humans seemed to love their animal-killing Thunder-junkers more than they loved anything else in the world.

How is that possible? he asked himself. Like many humans, Tillman and Annie had a special house where their Thunder-junker lived. They even had a name for the monster: 'Rosebud.' When they got inside it and it began roaring and expelling harmful fumes, the cats ran for cover.

Panic-stricken, he snapped his head one way then the other looking for a way out, a way to escape as the machine moved towards him on a luminous cloud of dust. As it drew closer he could hear the gravel projectiles it fired from its wheels to kill anything standing by the road it didn't strike head-on. Was it the eyes? Was it the noise? Why couldn't he get out of the way? What power did it have over him that made him freeze on the spot? He had to make his legs work. He crouched down low to make himself small so it would not see him. But it had seen him and he could not hide from it. It was so close now he could see the painted parts of the fenders, the iron pipes underneath, and the black wheels spinning beneath it as it rolled closer. If he didn't move in the space of a heartbeat his life would be knocked from his body.

"Move! Move! Do something, do anything!" he yelled at himself. At the last instant the hammer of his own terror struck down on the road surface and broke the shackles of the death ray lights, and he leapt for the side of the road.

With his ears laid back against his mammalian skull, the roar of the junker was surpassed only by the cat-scream that exited his mouth. The predator blasted by in a Doppler of honking sounds, roaring out that it was angry it had not struck its prey. He flew through the air in a tumble of legs, paws and ears landing upside-down in a clump of bushes at the bottom of an embankment. While struggling to right himself he could hear the humans inside the machine making the kinds of rhythmic noises they liked so much. Expressing their anger for having missed their target, someone heaved a metal object out of the window.

Great Cats! He thought. *They must have been desperate for a kill if they even threw stuff at me. I am truly lucky to be alive!*

Eventually he shook off his fear and came back to the realisation that he had to think again and figure out his situation.

I'd better get out of this ditch and find my way back to Bedlam Barn. It's just behind those trees over there.

The sun was coming up now so he couldn't use the big barn light to guide him back to the kennel. But that really didn't matter because he recognised the terrain so he started walking in the right direction. He knew that as morning came the warden lady would be out tending to the animals and she would let him back in. He had decided to abandon his plan to walk back to Rainbow Farm. He would just have to trust Kofi's assessment of things and hope Annie and Tillman came back for them.

I should be there by now, he said to himself. *The kennel wasn't that far away earlier. I'll just keep walking. I know it's close by just over there somewhere.*

He walked for a while longer but he still did not see the big barn. Since he could not see over the top of the gravel road he kept looking to the left of the road for signs of the kennel; but the kennel was on the right, hidden on the other side of the road embankment. He considered going up the embankment to the gravel road to get a better look, but after what he had just been through he was not going to risk another encounter with a Thunder-junker.

This is really strange. I was sure the big barn was just over there, but I don't see it now. I sure don't want to get lost out here. I better find it soon.

He walked for a while longer, thinking he was heading in the right direction, but now the terrain that had seemed familiar a short time before wasn't familiar at all. He climbed a tree and looked about but saw nothing recognizable. He was getting hungry, but his food bowl was nowhere to be found. He continued walking on the wrong side of the road and in the wrong direction until the sun cleared the tree tops. He saw nothing familiar as he walked up a hill and through a large field he didn't recognise.

While I look for the kennel and the warden lady I'll just catch something to eat, he thought.

He felt better after he caught a mouse and ate it, but he was still hungry. He couldn't find any more mice so he caught a few grasshoppers and choked them down. They were a tempting target when they were hopping about, but once swallowed they made him sick and he vomited them up.

What was I thinking? These things taste awful!

The grasshoppers made Buster think of old farmer Lachance who chewed a brown substance he somehow got from the grasshoppers and then put in his mouth. Then he expelled the grasshopper juice on to the ground when the taste became intolerable. Whenever he dropped by to talk to Tillman and Annie he periodically spat slime geysers on to the ground. He was the only human the cats had ever seen who ate grasshoppers.

"I don't think Annie likes him," Buster said to Kofi and Buddy one time during one of the spit-farmer's visits. The two other cats nodded in agreement as they watched farmer Lachance. Tillman felt sorry for him and tolerated his occasional but unwelcome visits. Since they never saw him with insects in his mouth the cats always wondered how he managed to get the brown juice out of the grasshoppers.

"Do you think he catches them and just squeezes the stuff out of them and then sticks it into his mouth?" asked Buddy Lebeau.

"Beats me," said Kofi. "I've seen a lot of strange human behaviour in my day but this one is beyond me."

Buster was glad Annie and Tillman didn't spit up brown grasshopper stuff. But at this moment Buster was doing exactly that. Once he had expelled the grasshopper juice he could concentrate on mouse hunting again. He crouched down by the edge of the field and began picking up the sounds of the mice as they moved through the grass. It wasn't long before he had a meal. Mouse hunting was an exhilarating experience and he felt great after he ate another big one. By noon he was hot and tired, and beginning to suspect he was lost. He was also thirsty, so he decided he would backtrack to the stream for a drink. He spent a good part of the afternoon looking for the stream before he finally found it and drank his fill. He did not realise that it was not the same stream where he had seen the skunk the night before. In the course of that day he had wandered away from the kennel and had come to a second stream some distance to the north. He found a rock ledge in a nearby clump of trees and closed his eyes. When he opened them again it was dark.

I better find the kennel soon, he thought. *I could use some cat food and I don't want to spend another night out here.*

§

That morning Buddy Lebeau and Kofi waited for Buster to return. When the kennel warden opened the door they didn't see Buster anywhere, and gave each other puzzled looks. Where was Buster? He had only been a few paces away from the barn last night. How could he not be there now? Buster never got lost at night at Rainbow Farm, so what had happened to him?

"What have you done with Buster?" mouthed Kofi in cat noises.

"Where's our cat brother?" meowed Buddy Lebeau.

The kennel lady did not answer; she didn't even know that Buster was missing, and couldn't understand why the two cats were carrying on so. She just assumed they were hungry, gave them some food which they didn't eat, and moved on doing her morning rounds, feeding and cleaning up after the two dozen animals housed at *La maison des petits animaux.*

Buddy looked at Kofi and said, "Humans never seem to understand what we're saying, wise cat brother. Do you think she understood anything we said?"

"No, she didn't understand a thing," said Kofi, "and you know, Buddy, cat sounds are not very important to them so humans don't pay much attention to them. They only pay attention to their own noises,"

Later that morning, when the kennel lady discovered the ripped screen in the second floor window, and couldn't account for the grey and white cat, she realised that Buster was missing. She had to find him right away. She knew Tillman and Annie would be furious if she lost him. If she had listened to her husband and installed heavy gauge screens on all the windows she could have avoided such an incident. Now she would have to go out and find him.

He can't be too far away, she assured herself, *and after all, where would he go? There's nothing out there. Nothing except forests and fields, and.... well, nothing but plenty of places to get lost!* Oh, mon dieu, mon dieu! *I've got to find him!*

By mid-morning she had been out for two hours searching the grounds and walking both sides of the road heading south in the direction of Rainbow Farm, thinking the grey and white cat would be heading for home. Five days later she still had seen no trace of him. Tillman and Annie were horrified when she told them Buster had disappeared. They refused to pay their bill until she returned him. They took the other animals home and immediately started taking turns driving around, looking in fields and ditches and calling his name. They thought that once he heard their voices calling him he would run to them and throw himself into their waiting arms just like he always did. But he was nowhere to be seen. The next day the man took Sparky and together they walked the gravel road between Rainbow Farm and the kennel. All along the way he called for Buster, but he saw nothing and heard nothing. That night Annie and Tillman worried and fretted and took turns driving around, shining their flashlights in ditches and culverts and calling Buster's name: nothing. They continued looking in the days that followed, but they heard none of the little chirping sounds Buster made when he was happy to see them and came running out of the woods as fast as his paws would carry him, heading straight for the back room and the feeding station overseen by the omnipresent *Buddha-cat*. After a week they were very discouraged.

§

Buster walked past a few houses and cabins but saw nothing that looked familiar to him. They were too close to the road so he knew they weren't Rainbow Farm, plus they smelled of dogs and he didn't want to risk a confrontation. If he did encounter any dogs, Buster was a stranger, and they would no doubt chase him. As much as he loved dogs, he knew it was best to keep a safe distance from unfamiliar watch dogs who wouldn't recognise him. To them he would be just another stay cat they could chase off. He walked through the night, hunting and looking. As he came to the edge of a big open field he could hear the mice moving through the grass and in their shallow tunnels. Buster knew he was going to catch his fill and eat well tonight. He moved into the deep grass, located the sounds, and pounced and ate mouse brain. Mice were so much better than the food in the cat-food bowl anyway.

One more of these little fellas and I think I will be full for a while. Then I'll have a night-nap, he thought.

He heard another mouse moving in the grass between the tufts of clover and again he crouched and prepared to pounce. Just before he sprang, he thought he detected something, but when he looked around in the grass he didn't see anything unusual. Then… he exhaled involuntarily as all the air was crushed out of his chest when a great weight fell on his back like a chunk of iron. He moved his legs trying to run, but they just flailed in the air. He was no longer on the ground moving through the tall grass where he had been hunting only seconds ago, before his face had been smashed flat into the grass and the wind had been compressed from his lungs.

"Great thundering cats! I'm off the ground," he howled as he felt multiple avian claws dig deep into his back. It was then Buster realised he was going to be the next meal of a Great Horned Owl!

§

The Great Horned Owl was in his prime, with a decade of hunting experience under his wings. He was a big specimen with a two-metre wingspan that allowed him to lift heavy prey. He had been watching Buster from the top of a long-dead spruce tree, but had mistaken him for a rabbit, moving about out in the open field at night. To the owl it was obvious his prey was inexperienced and had made a major error by leaving the safety of the tree line. He would be an easy mark, and the owl's two fledglings would eat their fill tonight. He and his mate would eat some too. Owls have a unique skeletal architecture which makes them an evolutionary marvel. Both eyes face forward, which gives them the same kind of precise binocular vision found in primates like apes and humans, and enables them to judge distances with pinpoint accuracy as they swoop out of the sky and pounce on their quarry. Hunting owls have another anatomical feature that makes them particularly dangerous to ground-creatures: the outer edges of their wings are equipped with serrated edges which act as silencers, suppressing any noise caused by the swishing or flapping of wings. As they plummet from the sky their victims cannot hear them coming, just as Buster did not hear the owl descending on him.

The owl leapt from the high branch and glided downwards towards his target, positioning himself directly behind the grey animal, and then fell on him, sinking his claws into Buster's flesh. Buster shrieked in pain as the claws sank deep into his back, penetrating through the layers of skin and muscle, sliding between several ribs, abrading the right front scapula and cutting muscles before clamping shut in a power grip. But despite his keen vision and years of experience, the owl had underestimated the cat's weight. Because of his grey coat the owl thought his prey was a rabbit, and because domestic felines tend to weigh more than rabbits, Buster turned out to be much heavier than the owl's pre-attack estimates. With his prey locked between his claws, the owl flapped furiously trying to lift the cat off the ground and gain speed, but was having problems getting into the air. He beat his wings with all his might, their tips nearly touching the ground, but he only managed to get about a metre of altitude.

Despite struggling with his load, one thing was working in his favour: he had grabbed Buster at the summit of a knoll, and the land dropped off beneath him as a gently sloping field of grain. The more he flew horizontally the more distance there was between him and the ground, but in real terms he had not gained any altitude. As he struggled with his charge the owl was nearing a line of century-old maples and birches that rose out of the ground like a great wooden fence. As he drew closer the owl realised he would not make it over the trees, and was forced to make a left turn to avoid crashing. This manoeuvre caused him to lose altitude and he came very close to hitting the upper branches of the trees.

Shrieking in pain and terror, Buster could feel the air gusts from the owl's wings as the bird flapped and pumped in desperation trying to stay airborne. Despite everything, Buster sensed the owl was in trouble. His time in the air had allowed him to catch a few gulps of air even with the sharp talons embedded deep in his skin. As the tips of the owl's wings brushed the tree tops, Buster's face and chest were slapped with whip force by upper tree branches, and in wild-eyed panic Buster reached out trying to grab one, in hopes he could tear himself free. Then as quickly as it began it was over, and the round-eyed night-bird released his prey to avoid a collision and risk a crippling injury. Amidst a swirl of leaves and branches the big owl retracted his claws and his prey fell away. Instantly, the big bird shot over the tops of the trees. He had lost the food for his nestlings, but he would live to hunt again.

Buster felt the talons withdraw from his back, and instantly he was in free-fall, banging and bouncing from one branch to another. As he fell, he was smacked and slapped from all directions. It was going to be a difficult landing.

Domestic felines are notorious for surviving falls from great heights. There are accounts of cats jumping or falling from balconies and roof tops, landing on tarmacs or in parking lots, and living to tell about it. Humans and dogs certainly would not survive such falls, and any animal that can survive a seven-storey balcony dive either has divine protection or a surplus of lives to burn up. If he hadn't been injured by the owl's claws Buster might have walked away unharmed from the 15-metre drop to earth. But most cat-fall survivors are not owl-attack victims punched full of holes. Buster landed on top of a row of stones piled along the tree line at the edge of the field, not in the soft grasses of a stand of wheat or the gentle earth of a farmer's pasture. Unlike his fall from the kennel window ledge two nights earlier, because he was injured, he was unable to right himself properly, and landed on his hind legs first and then fell forward in an awkward and twisted position. It was painful, and once down he could not move his hind legs. The holes in his back had not started to burn yet, but over the next few hours, it would feel as if some kind of gnawing animal had embedded itself inside his rib cage and right front shoulder. He lay breathless, stretched out flat on his deflated stomach. He was in shock, gasping for air, and immobile on a hard, bumpy surface.

Where am I? he thought groggily. *Am I still alive?*

He wasn't sure until he caught his breath he could hear a thumping sound which he took to be his heart beating.

Yes, I think I am still alive.

Sometime later he twisted his head to one side and could make out that he was lying on a pile of stones. His only other sensation was pain, which grew more severe as the night-time hours passed in a swirl of stars overhead. His brain had been turned upside-down, and his protective instincts had spilled out of his head all over the stone pile. Now he was completely defenceless, but it did not matter. It did not matter to the barely conscious cat that he was broken and lying in the open, totally exposed to predators.

§

To create farms and till the land, 200 years earlier settlers had cut down the vast forests, removed the tree stumps, picked up the stones scattered about, and plowed the earth. They used the stones to make fences between their fields. Once the fields were prepared, as long as they were ploughed and planted every year, no trees would grow back and they could be maintained indefinitely. But even if the fields were cleared and ploughed year after year, the stones kept reappearing. Like perennial geological fruit every spring the stones would poke and shove their sedimentary heads through the dirt, waiting to be harvested. With no discernible source for them it appeared to farmers that the stones grew as a non-organic crop. The stones required no planting and no fertilizer, and they never failed to produce a good crop. Despite their lack of nourishment they grew to be big, healthy specimens without the farmers ever lifting a hand to care or nurture them. Regardless of the amount of rainfall, whether the summers were dry or wet or warm or cold, year in and year out the stones grew in great numbers, and only sweaty, back-breaking labour could remove them before spring planting could begin. Generations of farmers had collected fieldstones and piled them in rows along the edges of their fields where they served as solid fences following the lay of the land. With the arrival of barbed wire, stone fences gradually fell into disuse, and over the decades the rocky lines crumbled into linear piles of sedimentary and metamorphic geology whose only visible purpose after their billion-year-long evolution was to serve as stony platforms for lichen and nesting places for ground squirrels and chipmunks. This ancient, stony matrix had provided the brutally hard landing spot for the claw-punctured cat, and he was easy prey for any predator that happened to wander by. Luckily that night none did, and Buster fell into a deep, shock-induced sleep. The next morning he could hear the sound of the big machines like those that came to cut the hay at Rainbow Farm. But he knew he was not in familiar territory. There was no Rainbow Farm, no familiar forest, no friendly dogs, and no cat brothers. There was no Kofi to explain things, and no Buddy Lebeau preening and bragging about his hunting exploits. He had been separated from his mother and his siblings as a kitten, and now he was estranged from his Rainbow Farm family: Kofi and Lebeau, the two dogs and the man and woman, the best family any cat could ever have, and he missed them very much. Now his only family was pain: the pain in his legs, his back and his shoulders. He didn't even realise he was hungry.

§

Several kilometres away, Tillman and Annie were out once again walking the roads and ditches of the region looking for their grey and white cat. They looked for several hours that day and each day thereafter for the next week. They called his name from the side of the road; they peered into clumps of bushes looking for a grey lump of fur, perhaps injured but still alive, or perhaps dead. They put on their rubber boots and slogged through marshes; they stopped and talked to people along the road. They rang doorbells at farmhouses, and asked farmers and their children if they had seen a lost grey and white cat. No one had seen him. However, like all the decent and well-meaning neighbours in the valley, they promised to keep an eye out for him. Tillman and Annie did not know they were looking in the wrong place: they were looking in the area to the south and west of the kennel, but in his confusion

Buster had turned east and north, and had headed away Rainbow Farm.

§

He needed to stand up. He needed to get up and find shelter. But there was no question of standing. He concentrated hard and tried to force himself to stand. Then he lost consciousness. Hours later he did manage to draw three of his legs under his body and push upwards. His hips were stiff and painful, and with great effort he could only get three of his legs under him. It was his right front shoulder that was weak, the source of so much pain. He hobbled and stagger-walked a few paces before collapsing short of the nearby tree line. Despite his efforts he knew he was still exposed, so with his back legs he pushed himself along the ground, face and stomach in the dirt, until he made it under a bush.

His ribs and his back were particularly sensitive where owl claws had anchored deep in the flesh of his body. His most serious and painful wound was the claw perforation at the upper end of his shoulder blade. The punctures there had been deep, and healing would take a long time; a month, maybe more. Until then he would walk slowly, and with a pronounced limp, like an old cat ready to close its eyes forever. He was not a normal cat anymore. For some time to come he would be unable to climb trees, or move fast enough to escape ground predators. He was totally vulnerable, and if he lasted that long, would have a hard time staying alive until he was well enough to get around. Without food he would weaken, maybe die. But the situation was not totally hopeless. He didn't see any blood on the ground, nor could he feel any broken bones. He craned his head as much as the pain would allow and assessed the damage on his back.

I don't seem to be bleeding from those claw holes. I can't see anything but dried blood on them. And I'm hungry. That must mean my insides are working. Now I just have to lay low and figure out how I'm going to get something to eat.

He lay under the bushes and rested and slept for the rest of the day. It started raining, and soon the rain was heavy. It rained all night. He was cold and wet and needed to find a dry place.

Where can I go? he wondered looking around for some form of shelter. Then he saw exactly what he was looking for.

Sometimes when the wind blows across the fields of the Eastern Townships and the roots of unhealthy trees can no longer hold them vertical, their grip is torn from the soil causing the trees lean to the lee and then crash to the ground. As their roots snap like cables, they tear out large chunks of earth and rock, leaving cavities where they once drew sustenance. It was in just such a cavity that Buster found a secure place that would provide him with shelter from the elements and serve as a hiding place from predators. Buster spent the next three days and nights lying in his root cellar, passing in and out of sleep and occasionally looking out at the grey sky between the dead roots that hung down like wooden prison bars. When the rain became heavy he withdrew deeper into the tree crevice, away from rain drops that dripped off the ends of the dead roots and pooled in the bottom of the root-hole.

For the next few days visions of the Rainbow Farm standing on a windswept hill came to visit his mind, and he remembered the cold months of the past winter when, as night fell, the humans rounded up the three cats and two dogs for their dinner after which they all spent the evening by the wood stove in the dining room. Buster and the other animals were warm and always secure, but now the sounds of coyotes scratching and sniffing in the nearby bushes jolted him awake. He was not dreaming; they were real, and not far away. Soaked to the bone after days of rainfall, he shivered in fear trying to make his heart stop beating so loudly so it wouldn't give him away. Maybe it was the smell of the woody forest dampness that masked the odour of his own fear and saved him from the coyotes.

The next night he was jarred awake by an explosion. From the dark recesses of his root cavern his lightning-illuminated face peered out as the rain water dripped down from the root-ball. For the next hour Buster witnessed sharp lines of fire tear out from between cracks in the heavens and shoot down to the earth. For an electric instant night became day and he could see across the grassy meadows and wheat fields. After the sky-fires went out the heavens would roar like some great cloud animal.

Book IV

The Cats of Babylon

Two nights later Buster could see the crescent moon floating like an ancient white ship in the deep twilight blue just above the hills and mountains west of Lake Memphremagog. The days of steady rain had washed the skies clean of dust and pollen, and the thin crescent moon hung in the western sky as if suspended by invisible strings somewhere behind the curtains of twilight. Buster was glad to see the friendly light of the moon-lantern, and for a moment he forgot about his pain and hunger. As the sky darkened stars appeared, joining the moon on its night-time voyage. When he looked back to the left of the moon he could see a collection of stars that, since the Pleistocene era, felines had called 'The Great Cat.' The Great Cat added a cosmic dimension to who they were: nature's most perfect carnivores. From anywhere on earth felids from lions to African wild cats, could look up and see a celestial image of themselves moving through the heavens. For them the constellation represented feline beauty, hunting skills and their capacity as mighty copulators. Everything they were, everything that was 'felinity,' was projected onto a collection of tiny, blue-white lights strung across the darkness of the celestial vault.

We cats are very special among animals for we have our own star-image in the heavens, thought Buster.

Modern humans can rarely pick out the image of the Great Cat among the stars unless some person knowledgeable in the architecture of the heavens points it out to them. For those able to step away from the neon haloes of the *aurora commercialis,* as hominids did ages ago, and look up into the ancestral heavens, it is still possible to see their own cosmic origins in the form of unpolluted stars and planets. Like our millennial ancestors, once they moved outside the circle of light of their Ur-Alt campfires on the African Savannah or away from the entrance of some painted Ice Age cave, they too would see the Great Cat, a constellation of stars formed by a backwards question mark that comprises the front half of the body of the cat-beast and a right triangle that forms the other. On the right fainter stars form pairs of legs stretching out in front as the creature springs towards the western horizon, while a tail and another pair of starry legs are strung out into the zodiac behind it. Felines everywhere on earth can look deep into their past and conjure up their extinct ancestors, usually one of the great scimitar cats who lived long ago when the earth was shrouded in a mantle of white and the temperature did not rise above freezing for 1000 centuries.

Buster looked up and for the first time in his young cat-life saw himself in sparkling dots of light as the Great Cat leaned into the western horizon. Over the next few weeks he would see the Great Cat move closer and closer to the rim of the earth, its twinkling paws coming into contact with the tops of mountains and trees. By the end of the month, its forepaws would disappear into the twilight followed by its face, then its head, and finally the rest of the starry body until it was consumed in the red glow of the setting sun. As the earth spun on through July and into August, the Great Cat would finally catch the summer sun, its incandescent prey, and disappear for several months before it reappeared in the fall on the other side of the night. As he watched it fade away, Buster wondered where the great beast went after it disappeared from the heavens. Did it stay in the sky and live with the sun, or did it go somewhere else? During that painful, hungry evening, more than ever before Buster understood that even though he was a lost and injured cat far from his home he was still part of something very rich and very ancient.

§

Through the ages the Great Cat had come down from the heavens and stalked its prey on earth. From Africa, across Asia and in the New World, the big cats were the keystone predators: predatory beasts that had both thrilled and terrified humans for a thousand millennia. Before the first kings put on the Red and White Double Crown and established themselves on the throne of Upper and Lower Egypt, lions had been part of the lore and mythology of the tribes of northern Africa. Aha, one of the First Dynasty Egyptian kings, was so impressed with lions he buried several of them in his underground funerary complex 500 years before the first stone was cut for the Great Pyramid of Giza. Centuries later Khafre, equally awestruck with the constellation of the Great Cat, ordered his builders to make a copy of it right in front of the heap of cut stones he had piled up as a monument to his rotting corpse, the place where he imagined his *ka,* his spirit, would live for a million years. The glorification of corpses, so prevalent among humans, and particularly the ancient Egyptians, was something that felines had never understood.

"Why would anyone glorify dead meat?" they asked. "Somebody should be eating them instead of letting them go to waste," one cat philosopher was heard to comment.

Khafre took the creature that roamed the jungles and savannahs on earth, the same one that journeyed nightly across the sky, and turned it into a symbol for his own post-mortem glorification. As his pyramid grew higher and higher, in front of it his masons chiselled an image of the Great Cat that married leonine power and courage to his frail human form. For ages humans had scampered about the savannahs on their skinny legs, their fangless heads bobbling about on top their shoulders. When the humans saw lions they climbed up in trees or hid in caves. Even those brandishing sticks with sharp stones hafted on to them never meant anything more than an easy meal to the great felines. But with Khafre the weaklings dared to graft the power of lions onto the primate body of their king. It was an insult to felines. Instead of representing the Great Cat in its true form, Khafre created a composite monster attaching a chiselled replica of his own head, his very face, to the sculpted limestone body of the greatest hunter that had ever walked the earth. Generations of humans looked on with awe, seeing grandeur in a face that resembled their own. But to the felines the pile of limestone called *Hor Am Akhet,* or the Sphinx, as it was later misnamed by the Greeks, was an unpardonable manifestation of hubris.

The benefits of cats were known to the farmers of the Nile River Valley prior to the time the African Desert Cat became partially domesticated around 35 centuries ago. But long before the first hieroglyphic signs had been etched in stone or painted on papyrus, Egyptian farmers provided tame and efficient mousers, ratters and snakers with supplementary food portions to keep them close by their houses and grain bins. Originally rodent warriors and house pets, cats were raised to the status of goddesses during the last half of Pharaonic history. A favorite subject of painters and sculptors, cat images appeared deep in the rock-cut tombs in the Valley of the Kings where they were painted into the post-mortem scenes of kings and nobles lounging away eternity with their families. Oddly enough, there were few male cat gods in Egypt, leading some to speculate that maybe it was the women of ancient Egypt who first invited felines to live with them inside their mudbrick houses.

§

Suddenly, and without warning, Buster saw a line of white fire streak across the body of the Great Cat and continue right to the edge of the horizon where it disappeared behind Elephant Mountain. As the line of light arced across the heavens it was accompanied by a sort of buzzing sound, leaving a phosphorescent steak that hung in the sky for a heartbeat before its photons vanished in the high altitude night. Darkness returned. Buster's eyes stared upwards, and his mouth hung open. Starstruck, he formed his mouth to make the cat sounds:

"What was that?"

It was as if the Great Cat had suddenly growled and drawn a fiery claw across the heavens in a shower of cosmic sparks. Amazed by this remarkable sight, he thought,

What does that all mean? Maybe it is some kind a sign from the Great Cat? Maybe it means something important?

Despite his immobility, the shining spectacle held his attention which was much better than dwelling on his injuries and feeling sorry for himself.

§

Cats have sensitive eyes that allow them to see things in the heavens that other animals cannot. For country cats the sun, the moon and the stars are important for situating themselves in their environment and getting in touch with their inner catness. As creatures of the night they know the moon in all its phases and welcome the waxing and waning visitor as it travels through the night-time skies. For centuries cats have collected stories and lore about eclipses, planets and the stars. Kofi had great knowledge of the heavens, and around Abenaki Falls the local cats often gazed at the heavens, identifying constellations and picking out the planets as they made their way among the permanently fixed stars. Of course country cats also knew about the 'bowl of spilled milk,' so named by a long-forgotten Neolithic cat who followed humans and their half-wild sheep and goats, furtively licking drops of milk from their poorly fired, clay-rope bowls.

One well-known episode of cat-lore is the story of the Magic Star, and with the meteor still fresh in his mind, Buster recalled the story about the heavens and celestial things. It was a story Kofi had told the Rainbow Farm cats earlier that spring while they were all lying around on the back porch. It was so fascinating that Mecki and Sparky had lain down and listened in. The wise cat recounted a story about a very special celestial event that involved a bright star appearing next to the crescent moon. A moment earlier Buster had witnessed an impressive celestial phenomenon, but he was pretty sure that the streak of light he had seen was not the Magic Star Kofi had told them about. He did remember that Kofi had said that the story of the Magic Star was very old and it came from an antique land somewhere far away. The hours passed and The Great Cat sank towards the horizon, and as Buster watched it disappear in the west more of the details of the story of the Magic Star came back to him.

§

Babylon was the great mud-brick city that rose out of the irrigated farmlands along the banks of the Euphrates River in a land the ancient Greeks called 'Mesopotamia.' The name Babylon meant the 'Gate of the Gods.' It referred to the sacred place where deities from the starry heavens would walk down the stairs of the 'ziggurat,' a great mud-brick tower situated in the centre of the city, and set foot on the land. Once on the ground they walked about among the earthbound humans. In Babylonian mythology, at the beginning of time, the gods Tiamat and Abzu, the sea waters of the Persian Gulf and sweet waters of the Tigris and Euphrates Rivers, were separated by a powerful and heroic god named Marduk. Afterwards, creator gods fashioned humans from lumps of clay mixed with the blood of Taimat's lover, the evil god Kingu. The two-legged mud lumps were called *awilu,*—'humans'—and their lot in life was to farm the earth and make fertile the river valleys of ancient Iraq. When the harvests came in, when the bread was baked and the grains were roasted, and when the beer and the palm wine flowed, the humans would burn part of their harvest as offerings to their creators. From their celestial dining rooms high above the city, the gods would smell the smoke and feast on the proffered victuals.

Kofi explained that Babylon was the most splendid city in the world, surrounded by high walls pierced by a dozen sparkling gates. Babylon was a monument to commerce and royal power; the centre of an empire that stretched across the Middle East. Every day its citizens rushed about their daily lives making pottery, weaving cloth, building furniture, grinding grain and buying and selling all manner of things. Its streets were jammed with humans and animals, and everyday flocks of sheep and goats were marched in from the countryside to be sheared and slaughtered and sold in the city's markets. Trains of donkeys and camels loaded with goods went in and out of the glazed-brick gates transporting the commerce of the world to the bazaars and sellers' stalls of the city. Cats dwelt there too, among the humans in the jumble of mud-brick houses, crooked garbage-streets, and narrow alleyways. By now accustomed to living with humans, the cats carried out their well-rehearsed task of rodent control while dodging sharp animal hooves and the unshod feet of the city's occupants. With no drains or sewers most parts of the city were filthy, and the cats shared the rough and disease-ridden living conditions with their human companions. As the cats worked mouse and rat patrol, they charmed their human companions with their beauty, their mystery and their comical antics. A few of the more fortunate cats lived in the palaces and temples or in rich merchants' houses ornamented with courtyards and fountains. Their high ceilings were crisscrossed by thick beams painted in bright primary colours, and the walls were covered in ceramic and alabaster scenes from stories about gods and goddess, kept shiny-clean by servants and slaves. As they stalked rats, mice and snakes in the vast jumbles of rooms and courtyards, the privileged cats lived in luxury, brushed and preened daily, some even adorned with jewelled collars around their necks.

In the palace, the spacious rooms hosted royal functions on a daily basis; there was always some lord or emissary visiting the king, performing obeisance while asking for royal favours. Generations of cats witnessed sumptuous banquets with royal guests reclining on finely-carved wood and ivory chairs and couches as beautiful women and handsome, dark-bearded men feasted into the small hours of the night. Since the palace dogs were always lying at the feet of their masters, palace cats rarely attempted to pick up bits of food dropped on the floor. Ducking under the table to retrieve a scrap of food could be fatal as more than one cat had learned.

But, the rooms on the outer edges of the palace, away from the throne room and the royal chambers, were the mousing domains of cats; and in those areas they watched and listened to the activities of the humans. Most of what they saw and heard was mundane and uneventful, and they often remarked to each other at the acts of affection and kindness the humans showed one another. But there were times when they cringed in horror as cruel masters beat their slaves until they lay broken on the floor in pools of their own blood. In adjacent rooms they might hear words of passion whispered between lovers tumbling above them as the always dutiful mouse-stalking cats hung about beneath their love beds. Although the dogs reigned as the canine kings of the official buildings, there was one domain of activity dogs were not privy to: the night-time deeds of the sky-watchers and celestial fortune-tellers. As nocturnal creatures this was an activity open exclusively to cats.

§

After Mushitu, the mistress of the night had pushed the fiery orb of Šamaš out of the heavens and pulled the velvet cloak of darkness around her shoulders, she commanded all the creatures of the earth to secure their flocks and go into their tents and houses to sleep. With the sun out of the way she flung her arm away from her body, releasing handfuls of night jewels and casting them into the blackness. As they flew out of her open hand, each one with millennial regularity fell into its allotted place to form the constellations of the night. Once in their proper places, the sky-watchers of Babylon positioned themselves on cushions and stools, and from the top of the great ziggurat turned their eyes towards the heavens. As the black hours dripped through their water clock they would scrutinise the heavens and remark to each other about some point of interest: the shape of the moon, the brightness of a star, or the wanderings of a particular planet. The passage of the occasional comet always drew attention as the long-tailed wisps of light flared their way through the constellations, never to be seen again during the lifetime of those who had seen and recorded them. Discussions would follow and, after hours of looking upwards, weary-eyed from watching, they would lower their heads and rub their necks as the first light of dawn chased the stars and planets into the last corners of the night. Their nightly observations were recorded on small lumps of fine river clay that fit easily into the palms of their hands. The clay was still soft and moist so the writing stylus could impress triangular signs into the clay that resembled the footprints of shorebirds scurrying across a sandy beach.

The sky-watchers were always accompanied by a few cats that climbed with them to the summit of the great heap of mud bricks called 'The Foundation of Heaven and Earth.' As night creatures they loved looking at the heavens, but many of the cats found the star-gazing activities of the humans to be very puzzling.

"Why do the humans climb to the top of this great pile of bricks and look up at the heavens?" they would ask each other.

Some of the sky-watchers showed affection towards the cats, petting them and sharing morsels of food with them. Sometimes the cats followed them to their houses, where they were welcomed as family members, and lived out their lives nightly climbing to the top of the mudbrick tower and observing the heavens with their humans, then returning home with them at dawn.

§

Life was hard down on earth, and to help their farm-hands face the hardships of back-breaking labour, floods and wars, the gods left coded messages in nature to warn the humans of evil times and impending disasters. The messages were not written on paper or inscribed in clay or stone, nor were they written in the language of the people. The gods wrote in cryptic shorthand, and tucked their messages in between planets and constellations as they swirled about the heavens. It was the special task of the sky-watchers to find these messages and read them for the king and his people.

It was the duty of the clay-made humans to make gifts of burnt food to the gods. From the summit of the ziggurat offerings of food, beverages and incense were made to the deities of the night as they floated in the black æther above the earth. On certain nights of the lunar cycle servants would carry baskets, pots and paraphernalia to the top of the tower where, under the supervision of the star-priest, they would spread them out on an altar table or place them in special cultic stands nearby. In the hushed night, as the food bowls and drink goblets were arranged and the incense ignited, the cats of Babylon would gather around their human companions to observe the proceedings and listen to the words of the star-priest.

Before reciting a prayer to the gods of the night, the star-priest had to assure the gods that he was wearing the proper clothes that he was clean and ritually pure and fit to make the offerings. Dressed in a black robe scattered with embroidered rosettes of red and gold thread, he would stand in front of the proffered victuals and, as the smoke of the burning food rose upwards, he would stretch out his hands, raise his face towards the star-dotted night and begin:

> *Stars in the heavens, I conjure you, all of you.*
> *The pure upper stars, pure lower stars, pure gods and pure goddesses,*
> *   I conjure you.*
> *My lips are clean and my hands are washed,*
> *My garment is of pure white flax and woven sheep's wool.*
> *My heart is pure, I have committed no crimes; I have broken no rules,*
> *So on this night turn your ears in my direction and hear my prayer.*

Once the gods had been reassured that the priest was ritually pure he continued.

> *The countryside is dark; the land does not utter a sound.*
> *All cattle and all sheep have been placed in their folds, and*
> *The people of the land are asleep.*
> *The doors of their houses are locked and the city gates are closed,*
> *Silence lies on the land like a blanket that covers a man on a cool night.*
> *Because this night is sacred, I have called you, the stars of the north,*
> *   of the south, of the east and of the west,*
> *You, the stars of all the regions of the sky, I have called you,*
> *The famous stars as well as you the lesser stars that sit far from the*
> *   king's table, and*
> *The distant stars that the eye does not see well.*

Hearing the sky-watcher's words and smelling the aromas carried by the swirls of smoke, the gods of the night leaned down from the heavens and consumed the proffered delicacies.

> *I call upon you shining gods of the night to surround me, and to gather near the offerings I have prepared for you.*
> *Look down from above, all of you, and see the table I have set.*
> *I have prepared for you pure and sweet incense, whose smell all the gods love.*
> *I have set a table of delicacies and many kinds of wines and sweet beers, and I have placed them next to plates full of golden wheat cakes soaked in honey.*
> *Eat, all of you, eat the pure sacrifice,*
> *Eat to your fill and drink the beer and wine, and when your hearts are light of spirit,*
> *When you are satisfied,*
> *Reveal the messages you have written in the heavens for me,*
> *So the king and the people of Babylon may know your wishes.*

Finally, when their stomachs were full, when the last of the food had been consumed by the flames and the libation jars were empty, the gods twinkled and blinked their thanks to the sky-watchers and their cats down below.

§

The Great Cat lived among the stars so the cats of Babylon had known for a long time that the heavens were important. When a sky-watcher pointed to a planet or constellation and held forth about its meaning, the cats perked up their ears or stood on their hind legs, gazing over the crenellated walls to see which wonder of the night was being discussed. When the sky-watchers noticed the seeming interest of the cats gazing upwards, most of them thought the cat's attention had just been temporarily diverted from their rodent duties.

"Don't look up at the heavens for your meals, silly cats," some would comment, smiling and shaking their heads. "Mice don't live amongst the stars and planets."

But a few of the sky-watchers suspected that maybe the cats had learned some of the secrets of the stars, and occasionally, when one of them would look over his shoulder and see a cat staring upwards he would ask himself:

Is it possible they know what we are doing here? Sometimes it seems as if they really are listening to our conversations. I wonder if they understand what we're talking about?

A few of the sky-watchers were certain the cats weren't just rodent-eaters; they believed they truly were star-cats.

They must know something. Look at the way their ears perk up when we discuss things, and look how they gaze up into the heavens. They must know what's going on up here.

After so many centuries of listening and watching, after countless nights under the heavens, having listened and followed the skyward-pointing fingers of the wise men from the East, the cats of Babylon were privy to astral knowledge that no other members of the animal kingdom knew anything about.

§

One phenomenon the cats paid particular attention to was when the crescent moon was accompanied by a bright star standing next to it. Such a conjunction, the sky-watchers said, meant that in the following days and weeks, good things would happen to the people of Babylon. They called this the *kakkab kišpi*, the 'Magic Star.' They knew that when it appeared there would be good harvests, that sheep and goats would multiply, healthy children would be born, and most importantly, there would be peace in the land. When the Magic Star appeared the cats would look on as one of the sky-watchers took a moist clay tablet in his left hand and pressed the writing instrument into the soft clay surface in a script that would baffle generations of would-be decipherers twenty-five centuries later. Once written, the event changed from something in the heavens to something recorded forever in clay. One night, a sky-watcher named Rasha observed the Magic Star and wrote:

If the moon god looks like a sparkling tiara on the first day of the month and the goddess Ištar stands by his side, this is good. Crops will be abundant and the people of the land will be happy. Public opinion will be favourable for the king my Lord and the animals of the fields will lie down in green pastures. May the gods Marduk, Ištar and Nabu bless the king my lord.

From your most humble servant, Rasha, son of the city of Babylon.

§

The star-watching tradition continued long past the time of Alexander the Great, until the city known as the 'Gate of the Gods' was abandoned and its human inhabitants moved away. As Babylon declined, one by one the sky-watchers dispersed to cities that needed their expertise, leaving the cats alone wandering the abandoned, dust-blown streets of the once-great city. For a while some of them continued climbing the ziggurat every night looking for the sky-watchers, waiting for them to join them. But they were gone. Despite their absence, as palaces and temples crumbled and the multi-coloured 'Tower of Babel' collapsed and fell into a mass of glazed shards scattered about on the ground, the star-cat tradition did not die out among the felines. In this great sky-watcher diaspora the story of the Magic Star was lost to the humans, but remained the exclusive knowledge of a handful of star-cats. With empty grain bins, dwindling food supplies and no human companions, one day a clowder of star-cats headed east, and after several generations on the road the story of the Magic Star had made its way to India. Other star-cats headed west towards the Mediterranean Sea. Later, their descendants travelled as far as Europe. A thousand years later, before the Pilgrims set foot in North America, sailors went through the streets of Le Pas-de-Calais and La Rochelle on the west coast of France, grabbing any cat they could find, throwing them into the holds of sailing ships to live among the sacks of flour, salted meat and hard bread. Their task was the same as always: eat the rodents, this time on the open seas between Europe and the New World. As the food became moldy and wormy, the cats themselves became the food of choice, and all too often every last cat on the ship was eaten by the crew. Despite the hard conditions, some sea-cats lived well, spending their time with the ship's cook and protecting the captain's pantry. The lucky ones, like the fabled *Atlantique Jacques*, made sailing ships their home and spent their lives as sailor-cats voyaging across the great oceans of the world. However, most cats hated the damp and airless confines of the holds and jumped ship, tight-rope-walking down the hemp-lines that held the ships fast to the shores along the Saint-Lawrence River. At Cap Chats, Tadoussac, Quebec City and Montreal, they found lives in New France; a place that had no mice, no rats and no cats before Europeans came to the New World. On one such voyage of discovery the cats who came with Samuel de Champlain brought the story of the Magic Star with them. Long afterwards, one of the cats who learned the story was a Siamese named Kofi, the very same cat who showed up on the front porch of the big farmhouse at Rainbow Farm one night during a thunderstorm, meowing loudly to be let in.

§

In the New World the story had become part of cat lore, and was transmitted via mime, gestures and mouth noises so most cats knew that when a bright star appeared with the crescent moon, good things would happen. It meant that barn cats that lived among dairy cattle would get an extra ration of milk or cream from grateful dairy farmers. It meant that house cats living inside the warm houses of village people would be petted and treated with extra care by their humans. Some cats, particularly mothers, believed that when the Magic Star appeared kittens living in animal shelters would be adopted and find good homes with kind humans to take care of them. Buster remembered such stories that he had heard from Kofi, and he knew that Kofi, who revered the *Buddha-cat*, was wise and had lived many adventures and knew many things. Although he never said as much to the other cats, sometimes it seemed that Kofi's life was filled with more adventures and more stories than anyone could possibly stuff into the stocking of a single lifetime. Buster was not alone in this belief. Many of the cats from Abenaki Falls believed that Kofi had already lived many lives in distant times, and to the injured Buster, peering out of his underground root-bunker, it made perfect sense that with his arcane knowledge Kofi was himself one of those antique star-cats who had climbed to the summits of the mighty ziggurats and had heard the words of the ancient sky-watchers long, long ago. On this warm summer night while Buster lay awake, in pain and immobile, the story of the Magic Star mattered a great deal because it was a promise of better things to come. There was one other thing about the story that came to him: Buster remembered that the Magic Star helped lost cats find their way home.

I wish I could see the Magic Star right now, he thought. *Seeing the Great Cat and the flashing claw in the heavens was very promising, but still the Magic Star might help me find my way home.*

§

He had to find something to eat. Under normal conditions domestic cats need to eat five or six times a day and after three (or was it four?) days with no food he was weak and languishing. At first light he clawed his way out of the root hole and forced his aching body into a standing position. He took as few steps but could not maintain his balance and had to lie down again. Once down he regretted his decision.

I shouldn't have lain down again. I don't think I can get back up.

With much effort he did manage to get back up, but he did not attempt to walk until he could maintain his balance, and deal with the pain. He took a few shaky steps and nearly collapsed again, but managed to stumble-walk on the soft earth parallel to the old stone fence. After a while he began to get used to walking with his injuries and coordinated his movements to minimise the discomfort. He was too slow to hunt mice so he made an attempt to grab a low-flying dragon fly: he missed. Later he did manage to catch a frog, which he ate hungrily despite its vile taste. It was his first food in days. The next day and the day after that, he crawled and stumbled along the ground and ate crawling insects when he could catch them and took frequent breaks under cover. As each day passed he was able to move along for short distances, but he was seriously undernourished and tired easily, and the things he managed to catch and eat provided little nourishment in the hunger-hole of his stomach.

§

Cats don't fart (or at least such gaseous activities can rarely be detected by their human companions) and there is a good reason for this. Unlike omnivore dogs, who are legendary farters, cats are obligate carnivores—strictly meat-eaters—and even though many vegetarians keep domestic cats in their homes and apartments, there is no such thing as a vegetarian cat. Feline intestinal systems evolved to digest meat, and they derive very little nutritional value from ingesting vegetal material the way ungulates like cattle and sheep do. Processing leaves or hay or grains produces biogases, and hence flatulence. *Felis domesticus* gets few if any calories from cereal-based foods and only a few meagre benefits when insects pass through their digestive system. But Buster had no choice; low calories were better than no calories. The open fields of grass and grain were teeming with mice for the taking, even with his injuries he probably was strong enough to catch a few, but there was no way he was going to risk hunting in the fields. With memories of the round-eyed night-bird still fresh in his mind, he knew he should have known better than to hunt at night out in the open. If he had stayed close to cover he could easily have avoided the owl attack, and too late he understood why Kofi and Lebeau always hunted close to the fence lines where rock piles and trees provided cover.

How stupid of me, he scolded himself. *While I was at Rainbow Farm I should have been learning these things. I guess I had it too easy there, and now I'm paying for it.*

Birds of prey were not the only danger to be faced hunting in open fields. Ground predators were everywhere and if he encountered a fox or coyote in his condition he would have no chance of escape, no matter where he was, and because he couldn't climb trees he was completely vulnerable. Knowing his condition and limitations, nightmarish scenes of escaping predators constantly ran roughshod through his brain. He was always looking, listening, and double-checking all around him for signs of danger, and he was constantly on the lookout for the next place to hide. What was that noise? Did the wind cause that branch to fall or was that a predator? Where was the nearest root-hole he could hide in? He hunted only in places with lots of cover. For days he had hoped he could catch a mouse or mole scrambling about above ground before they went into their holes, but even though he could hear them nearby they managed to escape his attempts to catch them.

I'm so slow I can't even catch a mouse. That's pathetic! At this rate I'll starve to death.

He knew he couldn't catch one of the ground squirrels chattering in the trees. There was no way he could climb anything; he could barely walk. The woods were full of all kinds of ground-dwelling birds: pheasants, grouse, partridges and turkeys. He saw them almost every day. But in his condition he was unable to move fast enough to bring one of them down. Most could just fly away before he could get close enough to grab them. However, it was summer, and the ground-dwelling birds had downy little chicks that couldn't fly. The best they could do was run along the ground and try to keep up with their family. Maybe he could get one of them.

His instincts kept telling him his wounds wouldn't heal if he didn't get some food in his stomach. He just needed one good feeding to get some of his strength back, and he would be alright for a few days. Urged on by the pit in his stomach he hobble-hunted as much as his energy would allow, but caught only insects, which didn't taste too bad if you were desperately hungry.

§

The mother mouse grasped the tiny pup in her mouth and scampered across the deep grass to her new nest. She already had a good nest where she had given birth to her ninth litter of the year, but it had been damaged by racoons trying to dig her pups out of the ground the night before. They had missed, but she knew they would be back and she had to move to a safer location. She had managed to pick up seven of her eight offspring and transport them through the grass to their new home. One more trip and she could settle into nursing her young again. She found her last pup in the darkness, picked it up between her teeth and made for daylight.

My moves are so slow I'll never catch anything, Buster lamented for the umpteenth time just as he saw a grey furry form moving through the grass a paw's distance in front of him. Without looking around or checking for dangers, like he normally did, he took one small, pain-filled leap forward, extended his claws, and came down on the mother mouse. She had not seen the big dark form moving through the grass and was caught by surprise as the heavy weight of the clumsy feline slammed her tiny body flat on the ground, emptying her lungs in one tiny puff of air. He ate his catch immediately, wasting no time slapping or batting it about. He was not aware that as he sank his teeth into his victim that the satisfying taste in his mouth came from both the mother and her pup as he introduced them to his digestive tract. The taste of mouse exploded in his mouth and his spirits soared.

I can hunt mice! I have food again! Maybe I will live a little longer. After all, he told himself, *I did see the Great Cat. That must mean something, no?*

§

A slight breeze out of the west brought a tantalising smell to his nostrils. It did not smell like frogs or insects or mice or birds. It was a big smell that filled the air. It smelled like fat and sinews, calories and protein; it smelled like meat! It was a pungent meat smell, the kind that usually repulsed cats, but attracted carrion eaters. But today that didn't matter. With starvation as his shadow, all Buster detected was the smell of meat, and he desperately wanted to eat it!

I better investigate this, he thought. *It smells really good. Maybe I can get something substantial in my stomach for a change?*

He moved ahead haltingly among the patches of dry land on the edge of the swamp that led to an area just below a gravel road. The scent grew to mouth-watering intensity, and just when he thought he might get close enough to find out what it was, he saw shadowy forms moving in the darkness. He stopped, hunkered down, and backed into a clump of tall grass. Coyotes, about a half-dozen of them, were milling around something big lying on the ground.

Maybe they made a kill, he thought. *I've got to stay hidden. There is no way I can escape these guys.* He looked about for trees, and there were plenty of them, but they were of little use. He didn't have the strength to climb even their lowest branches though his life might have depended on it.

As it turned out, a deer had been hit by a fast-moving Thunderjunker as it crossed the road a short time before. A common enough occurrence in the area, a collision between a deer and a junker travelling 70 or 80 kilometres an hour was always weighted in favour of the rolling metal box. This one struck the deer with deadly force, and as the staggering beast breathed out its last breath, its legs crumbed underneath it and its reddish brown carcass slid partway down the embankment. The once-living deer was now just 80 kilograms of edible protein: a free meal of freshly-killed venison for anyone who wanted to eat it. And eat they would. For the next few days an assortment of mammalian and insect life forms, including coyotes and aerial feeders from great vultures to tiny flies and their maggot offspring, would pay the carcass a visit and reduce it to its skeletal parts scattered about in the dirt and grass. During the off-season hunters drooled over photographs in hunting magazines of multi-pointed bucks just like this one and would have been proud to bag such a specimen. And although hunting periodicals offered pages of advice about how to bring down wild *cervidae* with a high powered rifle, none of them had articles about killing deer with Thunder-junkers. 'Junkering' a deer required no licence, and no payment of fees was necessary to turn a live deer into a fur-covered bag of bones and leave it sprawled ignobly by the side of the road.

Close by, Buster could hear the tearing of skin and flesh as the coyotes ripped off parts of one hind leg and tore a hole in the deer's thoracic cage. Then they moved off leaving most of the animal untouched. Buster pulled his way up the slope and passed within a whisker of the lifeless head and lolling tongue touching the grass before he reached the coyote-torn hole in the deer's belly. Checking for any straggling coyotes he looked into the blood-soaked opening and saw the meat. Domestic cat mouths are meant to grasp smaller animals which they can hold and crush in their jaws. Compared to dogs, cats have relatively short snouts and muzzles, while all wild canines have long snouts intended for poking deep into pack-killed carcasses, but he would have to step inside the open cavity to really get at the meat. He checked once more for predators, and then stuck his head inside the blood-damp meat chamber that arched over him. Meat was everywhere: in front of him, on both sides of his head and overhead. He sniffed the blood-protein and then thrust his muzzle into the flesh in front of his face and bit down. His mouth filled with deer flesh and he tasted meat! He ripped several chunks off and chomped down on them, swallowing them whole: his hunger would not allow him to chew them.

May the Great Cat be praised! Meat! Glorious meat! I knew there was something special about seeing the Great Cat. She sent me this deer because she knew I'm too crippled to hunt: this deer is a gift from heaven!

After several more bites he backed out and crouched down next to the carcass. Blood and meat juices were smeared all over his face, covering his milk-coloured nose and mouth. He did not wait long before he stood up, checked for predators, and then headed back into the meat chamber. This time he thrust his face even deeper into the meat wall, taking five or six big bites, pulling away chunks of red flesh and pushing them back to his carnassial teeth to be sliced up and swallowed. By the time he pulled out a third time he could feel the meat strength surging through his body. He was alive again! His inner catness revived, he was going to live! He moved off and found a crevasse to hide in while he digested. Then he slept.

§

At death, meat begins to decay immediately, releasing the compounds *cadaverine* and *putrescine*, the less-than-romantic terms referring to the stuff that makes rotting meat smell so repulsive. Under normal circumstances cats will reject foods rich in these two compounds, and although both wild and domestic cats avoid dead animals in favour of live prey, they will eat carrion as a last resort. Buster was just such a cat: a starving cat who had no choice but to sink to the level of a carrion-eater just like the vultures, coyotes and dogs, the butt of so many jokes among the cats at Rainbow Farm.

Oh I have indeed sunk low, he said to himself as he licked the blood smears from his face and used his moistened paws to clean his eyebrows.

Jokes about dogs as dumb carrion eaters are common among wild and domestic felines. Over the millennia cats have developed a snobby superiority towards scavengers, and have ridiculed carrion birds and dogs in particular, for eating dead life forms. For millions of years cats hunted exclusively live game and they had difficulty understanding why dogs and coyotes didn't just hunt down live animals and eat them while they were fresh. The Rainbow Farm cats were no different, and even though they loved their dogs, when the dogs were *charognard*—when they had the stink of dead meat on them—the cats would not go near them. It was at that moment that the cats would start telling the 'dumb scavenger' and 'rotting meat' jokes. They would run around the house, jumping on the counters, bouncing off the furniture and attacking their scratching posts with vigour. Kofi would meow at the top of his Siamese voice; Buster would chirp excitedly and break into one of the arias from the mouse hunting scene from the opera, *Manon des Souris*, while Buddy Lebeau would run around behind them making cat-laughs. Luckily for Buster none of his animal friends were here to see him thrusting his head in and out of the carcass of a dead deer in his moment of carrion humiliation. But he was beyond pride, and his hunger drove him hard.

He knew the carcass would draw scavengers, and simply lying a short distance away in the grass was not a good strategy, so he backed into the deep brush to hide for hours at a time before he made another meat run. While Buster concentrated all his efforts on getting about and finding food, Rainbow Farm faded farther away into the landscape of his memories. It was best to forget about his past. The nice people from Rainbow Farm were no longer there to pet him and compliment him on his singing abilities. His cat and dog brothers were gone as if they had never existed, and now his only friends were hunger and pain.

§

Enlivened by meat nourishment, in the morning he did a three-legged hobble back to the carcass, and throughout the day he returned several more times, sharing the kill with an assortment of crows, ravens and turkey vultures. But the most frequent visitors were the flies. Millions of flies, billions of flies buzzing and swarming over the meat as it cooked in the hot sun. After several days the meat stank something awful, and when he pulled out a chunk of flesh he saw glossy white worms wiggling in and out of the strands of meat, and they continued wiggling with vigor inside his mouth even as he swallowed them. He tried to eat a few more chunks, knowing it was his only source of nourishment, but he couldn't tolerate the sweet smell and he couldn't stand the maggots. By now the gases of decomposition had bloated the corpse of the once-handsome stag, turning it into a macabre, pig-like creature with antlers. When he first stuck his head inside the great cavern of meat it was still fresh. What a joy that had been! The deer carrion had saved his life, but now it was time to move on.

The pain in his shoulder had subsided somewhat, but he still favoured his right front leg as he walked. Limping along he made his way up the same deer path the junker-struck deer had taken in the final moments of its life. The path ran through a forest into a meadow where a mother and daughter moose grazed in grass so deep it touched their bellies. Occasionally he stepped off the path to take cover and rest. He was stronger than he had been just a few short days ago, and with his hunger appeased he hunted with a little more success. He bagged a summer dragon fly and a snake, and later in the afternoon he managed a clumsy pounce that landed him on top of a field mouse. He crushed the rodent's dark grey head between his teeth and devoured it, barely taking the time to savour it.

*Even if I'm clumsy, how wonderful it is to be able to hunt and get
something! As long as I can do this and lay low I can survive.*

The mouse was small probably a juvenile that had wandered
from the nest, but getting it had replenished a bit of his self-
confidence as well assuaged his hunger. Still, he needed a lot more
food if he was going to heal properly. He rested again and let
the throbbing in his shoulder subside. While he rested he turned
his head backwards as far as he could to see if he had re-injured
himself during his last pounce. But even though the claw-seized
puncture holes were matted with dry blood and some other dry
stuff, it didn't look as if he had reopened the wound.

I'm sore, but maybe I'm going to be alright.

At least today he had eaten a living thing that provided fresh,
maggot-free nourishment and not something that tasted like vile
frog fluids.

The threat of starvation diminished a little more each day as
he was able to hunt just enough to stay alive. His hind legs and
haunches had improved and he could feel a renewed spring in
them, but the front of his body needed a lot more time to heal.
When not hunting, he licked clear fluid from the puncture wounds
where the talons had gone deep and ripped muscles and tendons
from the bone. The spaces between his rib cage still hurt and oozed
fluids that dried, cracked, and then flaked off every few days.
Several weeks after the dead deer incident he tried his luck at tree
climbing, but when he sank his claws into the resinous exterior of a
spruce tree he was forced to let go immediately. All the strength in
his once powerful shoulders was overtaken by pain. He tried again
a few days later and this time managed to pull himself up off the
ground, but he was still very slow and the gesture wasn't worth it.
He knew that in his current condition he still wouldn't be able to
escape a predator. The best he could do was avoid them. Days and
nights passed as he wandered through forests and along the edges
of open fields, still looking for some sign of his home, or something
familiar.

*I can't believe I haven't seen anything that looks recognizable to me,
like one of the neighbouring farms or a familiar field, or the silo in Abenaki
Falls; something. I haven't seen a single object that looks like anything I
ever knew. I really am lost!*

He hid in tufts of grass, he crawled under fallen trees; he sprang for and missed targets, and ate meager bites. He tired easily and spent much of his time sleeping or staring out from under trees and rock ledges. But he had not starved, and he was alive: that was everything.

I made it through another day, he would say to himself, *I managed to provide myself with enough food to keep going and I have avoided becoming someone else's food. I just have to hang on long enough to heal, then, I'll find my way home.*

§

Buster was a different cat than the one who had been dropped off that day at *La maison des petits animaux.* He was now hunger-thin and wilderness-wise; a half-wild hunting cat, and if he could talk to his cat buddies down by the hockey pond or at the grain silo he would be able to swap stories with even the most experienced cats. He could show them the open talon holes in his back and sides, and brag how being an insector and a frogger had saved his life. He could tell them he escaped the claws of a round-eyed night bird!

I'll bet none of them could top that, he thought.

Despite his physical injuries there was this other pain, one that was not healing; the one that was not getting better even as the days passed. It hung inside his chest, a kind of physical discomfort. He didn't know where it came from but it was always inside of him. He hated to think about it, but it was always there.

Where are they? he wondered. *Why aren't they trying to find me? Maybe they really don't care about me as much as I thought. After all, they have all those other nice animals.* Still he agonised. *Why won't they take the time to look for me? I'm lost, I'm hurt, and I just want to go home.*

§

A month had passed since Buster had disappeared and Annie and Tillman had all but given up hope of ever finding him. They had systematically worked the area around the kennel and searched the roads and byways moving out from it. They spent afternoons walking roadsides, scrutinising ditches and clumps of vegetation, hoping to find him cowering under a pile of branches or in a culvert somewhere. But after a month they knew that it was more likely that they would find him dead, his grey lifeless form the victim of a car or truck. At least, they thought, if we found him dead we would know what happened to him, and we could close the book on him and move on with heavy hearts. With photographs in hand they had stopped at over a dozen farms and weekend houses in the area always asking the same question:

"Have you seen this grey and white cat?"

No one had. But if they still hadn't found him that left all kinds of possibilities: if he had been eaten by predators he would probably have disappeared without a trace. But there was a slight chance that he might still be out in the woods somewhere surviving on his own. It was well known that cats could get lost and then show up back home after living in the wild for months.

"What makes us love him so much?" Tillman asked Annie. "I mean I've had people say to me, 'Well, he's just a cat,' as if being upset about a lost cat was no big deal. One person said to me, 'Well it's not like you lost your dog.'"

"What makes dogs any more important than cats?" Annie asked.

"I don't understand that attitude any more than you do. I mean, if you love an animal, no matter what it is, a cat, a dog, a hamster or whatever, if you love that animal and it goes missing then it hurts. That's it, period. But before we give up hope we have to remember, Annie," he said trying to reassure both of them that not all was lost, "he's a cat and cats can usually survive in the wild on their own much better than dogs. Who knows, maybe he'll turn up one of these days."

Tillman had trouble believing what he had just said, but he had to say something positive.

Book V

Buster and Juliette

That must be a human house, thought Buster as he sized up the large, blue shape that emerged through the curtain of green leaves rustling in the breeze.

And the other structure on the left must be a barn, something like the one at Rainbow Farm, but much bigger.

The house was situated on the summit of a prominence. To the west was a long, gently sloping hill that descended towards Lake Memphremagog. The tree-covered summits of Elephant and Owl's Head Mountains were visible in the distance on the other side of the 50-kilometre-long body of water.

I better have a look around. This is the first human place I've seen for a while that I like, and there might be food here. That barn probably has a lot of mice I could hunt without having to expose myself out in an open field to get them. Plus, looking at the countryside from this summit might help me figure out where I am. I better check this place out.

He knew the kinds of precaution it took to approach human habitations, especially if there were dogs about. Surprising a sleeping dog was always dangerous, and a watchdog frightened, or suddenly aroused, went on the attack first if it saw an unknown intruder, so Buster had to be careful and avoid encounters with all other animals except those he ate. He spotted a pile of flat, grey stones that would make good cover; he moved cautiously towards them and hunkered down. From there he could observe the house and the barn and assess the situation before moving any closer. In the distance he could see three or maybe four horses grazing in the meadow below the blue and white barn, a large, tin-roofed structure that had been built a century before. The barn and the farm house both dated from the same period.

I don't see any dogs, but just to be sure I'll just settle in here for a while and watch things. I can't afford to make the wrong move. I'm so hungry. I hope I find something to eat soon.

He watched for a long time and noticed a porch on the back of the house he could slip under if needed, as well as a big pile of cut lumber, stacked and drying, on the left: another potential hiding place. By the time the sun had moved past the meridian he had seen no animals except the horses, so by early afternoon he ventured forth towards the barn. He had only taken a few steps when he heard a sound that made him stop and listen. Stopping was not good, so he turned, limped off to the lumber pile and slipped under it. He listened and heard the sound again, realising it was not the thumping sound of paws on the dirt or the menacing growl of a watchdog. It was a soft, crying sound, a sound conveying a mixture of stress and trepidation, and it was coming from inside the barn. In fact, it was a sound Buster had made himself many times before, when he was a nursing kitten lost in some corner of the old garage at Madame Gauthier's.

For sure that's a kitten calling for its mother. That means there must be cats here, and that's a good sign. The thought of other cats cheered him up. *If there is one kitten mewing then somewhere nearby there has to be a mother and more kittens as well. Cats don't just have one kitten, they have lots of them.*

He crouch-walked towards the barn, keeping his body as low as his bad shoulder would allow. He headed for an open, human-sized door, saw nothing menacing, and stuck his head inside. In the shadowed light of the barn interior he saw a grey and tan striped kitten standing in the middle of a large cement floor looking up at an open haymow high above. The haymow took up about half of the barn's interior and was over-arched by a tin-roofed post and beam structure.

He must have wandered off and gotten himself lost, Buster thought.

"I understand your predicament little fella," he said softly to the kitten, remembering his own youth.

To his left was a wooden stairway with a handrail on one side leading to the upper floor, but the kitten didn't seem to understand that was the way to get back to his mother.

His mother must have her nest up there, thought Buster, *and he can't figure out how to get back. I wish I could help him, but if the mother sees me for sure she'll think I'm going to harm her kitten.*

He was right. Just then Buster saw the kitten's mother coming down the stairway on his left. She had been on her way to rescue her kitten at the same time Buster stuck his head in the door. As she descended the stairway her eyes fixed on him. To the mother cat Buster was a menacing predator, closing in on her offspring. She stared holes in the grey and white cat with her no-nonsense eyes and let out a low guttural growl. Her message was clear:

Don't go near my kitten, intruder cat, or I'll tear you to pieces.

"Message received, loud and clear," Buster chirped in his friendliest tone.

Buster didn't want to fight anyone and certainly wasn't in any condition to do so, and unlike some males, he had no intention of harming her kitten. With facial gestures and body stance he signaled a non-aggressive demeanor.

"I mean your kitten no harm," he meowed.

Why would I hurt a defenceless kitten anyway? he asked himself. *I've been on the receiving end of that kind of behaviour and I'm certainly not going to do it to others.*

The mother descended the stairs, carefully placing one paw in front of the other, one deliberate step at a time. She growled her dislike again, and Buster backed away, meowing that he had no intention of making trouble. Seeing its mother, the kitten scampered towards her, its distress calls replaced by meows of joy. Glaring one more time in his direction, the mother took her eyes off the grey and white cat, and grasping her kitten by the nape, lifted it up off the floor. As she ascended the long staircase she paused and gave a single backwards glance at Buster to make sure he wasn't following her. As her eyes caught his, Buster felt something he had never felt before.

She's beautiful! he whispered to himself as he stared up at her.

With mother and kitten gone, Buster looked around the barn and decided he liked the look of things. Apart from the mother cat, he had not seen any other cats that might attack him, and best of all there were no dogs. Buster would have welcomed dogs he knew, but in his condition it was better if there weren't any around.

This might turn out to be a safe place where I can rest for a while and be safe. And if there are humans around they will be looking after their animals, and the barn is probably pretty secure against coyotes and foxes. As he looked around he thought:

I'll bet I could do some first-class mouse hunting here. He also knew that wherever there were humans, there were mice. *I don't know why that is so,* he thought, *but it's true, and being in a barn like this one is much better than being slow, weak and exposed out in the open.*

Besides, he had not seen one of his own kind for a month. He needed some cat company while he healed and the young mother cat suited him just fine. Buster repeated his most sociable and non-threatening chirping and meowing sounds, and with a pronounced limp, began climbing the stairs, but not without some difficulty. When she reached the mezzanine the mother dropped the kitten and turned her face towards Buster, and gave another menacing growl. He stopped just before the last stair.

She probably doesn't realise that I'm too weak to put up much of a fight, he thought.

He certainly didn't want to have a fight with the mother over a kitten. Quite the opposite: he liked her. He redoubled his efforts to establish a rapport with her with another friendly meow. In response the mother picked up the kitten and headed in the direction of her nest which he now saw consisted of a sturdy looking wood and cardboard box open at the top with one side cut out for access. He watched her as she hopped inside and deposited her offspring in the middle of a clowder of furry siblings. Sizing up the box Buster thought,

That looks like something humans would make.

Buster may not have had any contact with humans since his fall from the window ledge, but he could still identify human handiwork. Whatever faults they might have, the two-legged giants could make all kinds of things, like a cat box for a mother and her kittens. Looking at it, he reasoned:

If humans fabricated the box-nest then someone here likes cats enough to take care of them. This means they're feeding them and that means there will be food here.

Finally, I can get something to eat even if it's just crumbs and leftovers, he thought. *If they are nice humans they might even know the area well enough to help me find my way home. There are all kinds of possibilities here.*

Buster lay down on the wooden floor keeping well back from the nest. If he was going to make any headway with this mother cat he was going to have to put on his best charm offensive and try to win her over. And he wanted to win her over so she would let him stay, but he also just wanted to know her better. No, it was more than that. He wanted to be with her. He wanted to lick and groom her face and her thick fur coat. He was smitten!

I want her to like me. It's not just the food and the safety. I want her and I think I know how to make her like me too. I'm going to sing for her!

Cats love singing and often spend whole nights outside in the dark singing songs in cat noises. Humans think such noises are simply caterwauling, but in fact, cats invest a great deal of energy composing and singing songs to each other. Since he had first been adopted Buster had been told many times by the Rainbow Farm cats that he could sing, and he had known since kitten-hood that he could make heads turn when he opened his mouth and made cat singing noises. Even his humans had commented about how much they liked his singing.

Boy, if my singing is ever going to pay off it has to be here and now, he thought, so he stood up as straight as he could, and puffed out his chest in preparation to make cat singing noises.

Here goes!

He started by chirping and meowing a couple of verses of *La chatte estrienne*,[1] a well-known cat country-song that the females down in Abenaki Falls swore by the Great Cat was the best 'hurtin' and 'cheatin' cat song ever written. But after a couple of verses she didn't respond. She just stared back at him with a look on her face that said,

What are these noises you are making, intruder cat?

Buster stopped singing. *Why isn't this working?* he wondered. Then it came to him.

Oh no! I must have chosen the wrong kind of song, she doesn't like country music! His voice went silent as he swore a cat oath under his breath.

May the Great Cat preserve me! I should have known. She looks too classy for that country stuff. I'm such a dummy-cat sometimes! I'll give it another try.

With that he broke into the well-known aria *Mia Gatta Mio Amore*, from the opera, *Cecilia*. Ah opera! That brought an admiring

---

1   The title of this song was a play on words of the French name for the region *l'Estrie*, meaning 'the East.' For feline country-song interpreters *estrienne* was associated, homophonically, with the estrus cycle and the fact that females came into heat very often and were burdened with horny tomcats, big litters, and the hard life that comes with such activities. Feral barn cats loved the song.

look to her face. She wasn't jumping up and down, but her attitude changed, and she seemed to like the noises he was making.

This is great! I think my singing is working. I've just got to keep going and hope this opera stuff works.

She looked on with more interest now, but Buster could tell he still wasn't knocking her off her paws.

I need a clincher, something to make her sit up and take notice and see me for the nice cat I really am! And I better do something fast, because I'm starting to feel weak again.

In the opera *Cecilia*, Lorenzo, the poor but honest country cat, uses song and mime to show his love for Cecilia, the bourgeois feline from Firenze. As cats often do during intense emotional situations, Lorenzo rolls over on his back, and extends his legs and paws while singing. So, like singing cats before him, as he played the part of Lorenzo Buster rolled over on the hay strewn floor and sang to the beautiful mother cat, now his very own Cecilia.

I've done this singing rollover before in front of the village cats, but with my bad shoulder this must be the clumsiest rollover I've ever done, he said to himself as he hit the floor.

When he looked at her from upside down, his white belly exposed and his paws drawn to his breast in a gesture of adoration, he saw a sparkle in her eyes in reaction to his melodic, rolling gestures. But she was not ready to make nice just yet and when their eyes met, her smile quickly turned to an emotionally neutral straight line.

I haven't quite pulled this off, he worried.

So he did one more roll to clinch his floorshow finale. On many occasions in the past, the farm cats from Abenaki Falls had sung backup for Buster, the part where the chorus chants *mio amore, mio amore*, while the lead does the lyrics, and he had always nailed the high notes with plenty of mouth left over. But this time, as he reached the crescendo, during his second roll-over he hit his injured shoulder, and felt a sharp jolt of pain shoot down his front leg. His voice cracked, he dropped the melody, and the aria crashed to the floor in discordant pieces like shards of broken glass. In an instant he went from singer to sufferer, and his performance of a lifetime turned from triumph to flop.

The female gave a start, her head jerking back as Buster grimaced in pain, and on his second roll-over she saw the brownish, blood-caked holes on his back and shoulder. It was then she realised the ragged-looking cat-tenor, trying so hard to impress her, was doing his best to sing despite being injured. Her demeanor changed immediately.

By the Great Cat! He's not only charming and can sing, he's injured and those injuries look serious. How rude I've been, and so defensive! I haven't really looked at him for what he is. He's wonderful and he wants to make friends.

Meanwhile, Buster was mortified.

Well, I ruined that didn't I? he thought. *I was hoping to have a chance with her. Now I doubt she'll want me stay.* He sighed and looked down at the floor not knowing what to say or do. In the aftermath of his *aria interruptus*, Buster had to crouch over to hide his pain and humiliation. Then, slowly, he managed to straighten himself up, grimacing slightly, and with an apologetic smile he raised his head to meet her glance.

I better just face up to the mess I made of that song. She probably thinks I'm some hobo cat who does tricks for food. Well she'd be right, because that's exactly what I am, a starving hobo cat looking for a meal.

With a heavy mantle of embarrassment covering him, he stood unsteadily for a moment and reflected.

And to think I used to be one of the Rainbow Farm cats. I lived with my cat brothers and Mecki the famous hockey dog and I had Sparky, my very own pet dog. Now look at me: I'm nothing, I'm lost and had to eat carrion just to stay alive, and now I've shamed myself in front of this beautiful cat.

Burdened with shame, he could not maintain his smile, his mask, so he lowered his eyes and looked down at the floor.

§

"Alright Singing Cat, I forgive your intrusion into my house."

At the sound of her voice he looked up. She was smiling at him!

"Any cat that can sing and do back rolls is not a threat to me or my kittens, and I must tell you, Singing Cat, you make the most beautiful cat sounds I have ever heard in my life."

Buster smiled, somewhat awkwardly, as his heart bounced around inside his chest. At a loss for words, he managed to stutter-mutter a quiet,

"Oh, thank you, thank you very much. I'm so happy you liked my singing!"

Wow! She likes my singing! He could barely conceal his joy. Suddenly, he felt much lighter; his feelings of loss and abandonment vanished. He would have danced if his injuries hadn't been so bad. When he looked up and saw her beautiful face looking back at him, he said,

"I was doing pretty well, I guess, until I hit the wrong note, eh? I'm very sorry about that, but the pain in my shoulder just got to me. I guess I shouldn't have been clowning around so much. I just wanted you to like me."

"You needn't worry about that. I think I do like you. But first, I'm sure you're hungry, so why don't you go eat something? My food bowl is over in the corner and I'm sure it's still full from this morning. Eat all you want."

Now that I look at him he looks so skinny he must be nearly starved. I really do like him. I've never met a cat like him with so much charm, and he can sing!

"Oh yes, I'm really very hungry, thank you, thank you very much," he said, trying not to just scream out that he could eat an entire bag of cat food. She didn't need to ask him twice before Buster struggled to his paws and limped towards the food bowl over in one corner of the haymow.

She doesn't know just how hungry I am. Good thing I'd managed to catch a baby ground bird just before I came in or I wouldn't have been able to control myself, he thought.

She heard him crunching and grunting as he consumed every scrap in her bowl. He ate so much so fast he thought he would vomit, but he managed to keep it all down. Nevertheless, he was embarrassed by his hunger and his injuries and didn't want to let on how bad things really were. What he didn't realise was that she already had a pretty good idea of what kind of shape he was in. For hunting cats it was very important to be able to feed themselves and nourish their inner catness. Those were the foundations of being a cat; a cat that couldn't do that lost the respect of his fellow cats, and Buster knew that cats showed little sympathy for those in his condition. That's just how things were in the world of cats. Over the past month he had lost nearly half of his body weight, and this was the first time he had considered how he might look. Combined with his limp, he thought:

I must look awful. I've got to stop thinking of myself as I was back at Rainbow Farm and own up to what I must really look like. I must look stupid, like I have worms or fleas or something. Then a dreadful thought appeared his mind.

Oh no! I ate that dead deer. I must have carrion breath. I must smell horrible! Worse, I must stink! She probably smells the carrion all over me like when we smell Mecki and Sparky and the village dogs. This is truly embarrassing, he thought.

I must look like a fool and smell like one too.

For a moment he was forced to look away from her, but she sensed his shyness and his embarrassment, and when their eyes met again, she smiled at him. His heart melted.

She's smiling at me. I can't believe it; she's smiling at me again! Maybe I don't smell so bad after all! He gave his best smile back, shook his head to realign his thoughts and made another attempt to concentrate on what he was saying.

§

With his stomach full for the first time since the deer, only this time without the maggots, and with smiles from the beautiful female cat, Buster felt more relaxed than he had since he had been ripped from his wonderful home at Rainbow Farm. The food and all the excitement of the last while had made him tired: he yawned and felt sleepy. The female cat picked up on this and said,

"Why don't you have a little nap, Singing Cat? Now is a good time because my kittens are hungry and I must feed them. So until I know you better you just stay in front of my box where I can see you and don't try anything funny. Do you understand my message?"

"I understand perfectly, and let me assure you I mean no harm to you or your kittens," he answered with a smile covering most of his grey and white face.

The female made herself comfortable in her box-nest and took up the nursing position exposing her belly to her hungry kittens. Settled on her cushion, three little cats snuggled against her and began feeding. It was a pleasant sight and Buster remained on the floor watching them. He remembered the satisfaction of his own nursing experience snuggled against the warm and secure belly of his mother. With their little mouths just a whisper away from their mother's teats they drank their fill and fell asleep in a state of lactic bliss, their lips still white with milk drool. As he watched the mother and her kittens he forgot about the pain in his shoulder and felt relaxed and sleepy. As the afternoon sun drifted around the west side of the barn, the mother cat dropped her head and dozed with her kittens snug in their cube-shaped home. On that somnolent afternoon, the purring of the female and her kittens were the most beautiful sounds Buster had ever heard. The hypnotic effect of light and shadow filtering through apple leaves and pine boughs playing on the barn walls drew Buster into the collective cat sleep. On the day Buster met the love of his life, July slipped away into the hot and languid days of August, a time when the wheat and barley were waving in the fields and ears of maïs were being sold at local stands along the roadsides by farmwives and their children. After a tumultuous month of adventure, fear and injury, he was in the company of creatures who made the same mouth noises and who weren't trying to eat him. He relaxed in the company of his fellow cats as an invisible calmness radiated out of the kitten box and extended across the mezzanine. As they all settled into slumber, Buster experienced the first deep sleep he had permitted himself in weeks.

§

A voice like a kitten's lullaby woke Buster from his sleep.

"OK Singing Cat, time to wake up. Wake up now," she said in melodic cat noises.

Buster opened his eyes to the sound of her voice and looked around trying to recognise his surroundings. When he remembered where he was he felt good inside. It was then, just as he awoke, that he noticed something special about the female, something he hadn't detected before when there was still tension between them. In fact, it was something he had never noticed in any cat he had ever met before. While Buster had been doing everything he could to win her over she had said very little, and her mouth noises had consisted mostly of snarls and growls. But now when she made cat sounds, there was an underlying purr that continued just below the level of her sounds. It was as if there was an underground stream gurgling somewhere nearby whenever she made cat noises. It sounded like music.

How could a cat make music while making cat sounds? he wondered. The effect was enchanting and reminded him of when he rubbed against the catnip plants in Annie's herb garden. He felt a sense of euphoria.

She's intoxicating me. What kind of creature is she anyway?

§

"But tell me, Singing Cat," she said as her kittens jumped out of the box and scattered across the mezzanine floor in search of new adventures, "how did you become injured? You must have a story to tell, so why not tell me what happened to you while my kittens are up and about, and we have a few moments of quiet before they get lost again?"

With a new sense of security and well-being, and for once not having to worry about predators or food, he began telling her of his adventures.

"Of course," he said. He hesitated for a moment and then he began.

"To begin, a while back I was attacked by a round-eyed night bird, a really big one." Her reaction was one of astonishment.

"You mean one of those big aerial giants I see moving through the air outside the barn at night; the ones that prey on us cats?"

"Yes, one of those really big guys who carry off skunks and rabbits and, like you say, cats like us. To tell you the truth, I'm lucky to be alive." After his opening words the female was caught up in the story and hung on Buster's every word.

"I've never heard of any cat who survived such an attack," she said. "No one ever survives, do they?"

I think she likes me. I better make this the best story I've ever told in my life, he thought. He continued:

"You're right. Normally no one survives their attacks. I'm one of the lucky ones, I guess. I tell you that flying monster came out of nowhere and sank his claws into my back, and knocked the wind right out of me. Before I knew what was happening, he picked me right up off the ground, and began flying with me suspended underneath him. His claws were long and sharp and hurt my back.

He crushed me and I could barely breathe. I can still hear myself yowling at the top of my lungs like never before."

"Great Thundering Cats!" she exclaimed. "Then what happened? I mean how did you get away and manage to end up here?"

"I was too heavy for him. He could barely stay in the air with me suspended underneath him, and you know," he said looking up at her, "even though I was howling at the top of my lungs I knew he was struggling to stay in the air. His wings were beating so furiously I thought his bones would crack. You wanna' know something else? I don't know owl sounds, but I am sure I could hear him swearing owl oaths against me because I was so heavy!" They both laughed heartily and then he continued.

"He had me, no doubt about it, and I knew that if he ever got me to his tree-top nest he would try to do me in with his claws and beak. But you know something," his voice filling with boldness as he spoke, "if it had come to that I think I could have put up a pretty good fight and maybe even beaten him. Even in his nest. I was really strong then and uninjured, not like now, and he didn't realise how big I was when he grabbed me. It might have ended up as quite a surprise if I had eaten him and his nestlings! That would have showed him, eh?"

They laughed again, and paused then Buster continued telling his story.

Wow, she thought, *he is so brave!*

"Now, of course, I'm much weaker and my shoulder hurts me all the time and the wound hasn't healed yet."

He paused for a moment, while he contemplated his sudden outburst of feline bravado – *catchismo* – and the possibility that he really might have been able to defend himself against the owl. Then he continued:

"By the time we began to approach the trees, me hanging and wailing, and him flapping like crazy, I knew he couldn't make it over the tops of those trees. I could see the trees coming right in at us, and I kept saying right out loud to him, 'You're not going to make it, you're not going to make it,' and I knew he had to let me go. He would either drop me, or land and try to kill me on the ground. I sure wasn't afraid of the fall, at least at first, but my fall didn't turn out the way I thought it would."

"What happened when you fell?"

"When he dropped me I knew I was about as close to death as I would ever be, but when he retracted his claws and I broke free, I felt such elation I couldn't believe it! I howled like crazy in a kind of weird combination of pain and joy! It was incredible. Being dropped from that great height was liberating; it touched the very core of my inner catness," he exclaimed, his voice rising with the drama of the story, while the mother cat looked on, eyes wide, nodding her head.

"But I hadn't realised that I was partially crippled on my right side."

What a story, she thought, *and what a brave and charming young cat. And even if he's kind of skinny right now, I still think he's quite handsome.* With Buster lying down a few steps away, her eyes were on him and she purred contentedly as the grey and white cat continued with his story.

"Despite the pain and the fear and everything else that was going on, suddenly I knew I was going to get a second chance! I knew I was going to live! You cannot imagine the feeling."

He broke off again, and stared at her. He wanted to say her name, but he didn't know it. He felt clumsy; he had never been in a situation like this and didn't know what to do. They had not been properly introduced so his own name for her just came to him, and he heard something inside his head saying,

Beautiful feline creature! Kitten of all creation! Overwhelmed, he looked away from her, gathered his thoughts and continued.

"Even as I fell and the branches slapped me and punched me, I knew I was going to live. Then of course, the bad thing was I didn't hit the soft ground. I hit a rock pile! With all the forests, and fields, and the wide open spaces of soft earthy land in this part of the world, and I hit a rock pile! Can you believe it? Sacré Sehkmet!" He punctuated his story in a burst of emotion.

"I was injured and had no choice but to keep out of sight, hiding in holes in the ground and avoiding predators while living in great discomfort. I hunted when I could, but I wasn't very successful."

Is it her looking at me, or is it the story, or is it the fact that I've eaten a bowl of cat food? What's going on here? he said to himself. *I feel dizzy.*

"How did you escape and make it here?"

He felt intoxicated. He looked down at the floor and shook his head and contemplated his owl encounter and its consequences. Then, as if snapping out of a reverie he looked up at the female and said,

"After I hit the ground I was in such pain that I just hid under some tree roots for a few days, I don't really remember how long I was immobilised. But I must tell you that while I was hiding in the ground an amazing thing happened. You won't believe this but I saw the Great Cat scratch the heavens with her claws and seeing that gave me hope that I might make it through my ordeal. It really meant a lot to me, seeing the Great Cat in the heavens and fire coming out of her claws. It gave me the strength to keep going."

Her mandible dropped, exposing the pink cavern of her mouth and her white incisors.

"You saw the Great Cat scratch the heavens? That is truly unheard of. What adventures you have lived, Singing Cat!"

"Yes, and on top of that I was hungry, and it was painful just to move my legs. After a few days I started walking, and even though I could barely move, I kept walking for maybe a week with very little food. I ate mostly frogs and bugs. Sometimes I ate nothing. Then, when my energy was nearly gone, I came upon a dead deer lying by the side of the road. It was a lucky find since he had only been dead a short time and his meat was still fresh when I found him. Of course everyone else found him too, but I managed to eat chunks of meat I tore off from his insides. It gave me the meat energy I needed to stay alive. After the deer meat went bad I kept hunting, if you can call eating frogs and bugs hunting, a whole moon cycle, from crescent to crescent. My wounds healed a little. Then yesterday morning I started walking again to see if I could find anything that looked familiar and might lead me to my home. That's how I ended up here."

She shook her head in amazement still trying to fathom parts of his story.

He continued, "What I need now, if I can impose on your hospitality, is a secure place where I can just recuperate and get some decent nourishment. I'm hungry all the time and I don't think I'm healing like I should. I'm sure if I had good food this shoulder injury would heal up in no time." Sensing that security might be an issue, Buster continued,

"Believe me, I won't be any trouble to you at all. I'm not violent like some male cats, and I don't mean any harm to your kittens. In fact, I was watching you with your kittens and I already have the kinds of feelings a lot of father cats have for kittens. You know, that sensation they get when they want to help a mother raise her litter?"

She had heard of such feelings and shook her head in acknowledgement.

Oh, she thought, *he has kind feelings towards the kittens. I like that. He seems gentle and so nice. And yet he is so brave! I think I like him. Besides he's downright charming! I'm going to fatten him up!*

Buster added, "I realise I am not the kitten-maker, but I still feel that way. I don't know why, to tell you the truth, but I guess it's because my own kitten-hood wasn't a happy one so I want to be around young cats and help them get a better start in life than I had." Buster wanted to add that along with her kittens he loved her as well, but he thought better of it, and held back the full extent of his emotions; something he had never had to do before.

"Well," she said, as she looked straight at Buster as if to emphasise what she was about to say. "You're welcome to stay here as long as you don't bother my kittens and you don't get any ideas about the two of us making any more of the little critters. Understood?"

"Oh y..., y..., yes, I understand," he stuttered. And then, somewhat embarrassed, he added,

"Anyway, I have been sterilised so I can't make kittens with you or anyone else, so there is no worry there." Buster thought, *Maybe she will think I'm not a real cat, but I had to tell her so she won't worry. After all, these are special circumstances. Anyway, she can probably tell by my smell that I've been modified.*

For the second time that day Buster felt inadequate and a little shy. Not being able to make kittens had never really struck him as important before now. But then he had never been in the company of a beautiful female cat before either. He thought he noticed that the female looked somewhat relieved when she learned he was sterile, as if she had one less problem to worry about. Letting a stranger into the barn to share her food bowl was always a weighty decision for a female cat. Before Buster could respond she continued,

"I heard my humans say that they were going to get me sterilised as soon as I finish nursing my kittens which will be soon. I guess they don't want the farm to become overrun with stray males on the prowl for me all the time. But I'm not exactly sure if that is what they said or meant. You know how hard it is for us cats to understand human noises, unless maybe you don't have that problem?"

"Oh no," he said. "I understand perfectly. Humans never seem to understand what we are saying in cat noises. It's like they can't hear."

"Yes," she said, "I know exactly what you mean." They were of one mind. One of the most commonly repeated complaints among cats was trying to understand what their humans were saying to them. Try as they would, more often than not they hadn't a clue how to interpret the mouth noises humans made.

"I understand perfectly," said Buster. "My brother cats and I at Rainbow Farm....," then he broke off, realising she didn't know what he was referring to. He continued explaining:

"Rainbow Farm is where I used to live—before I got lost— anyway, we had the same problem. We were always complaining about it to each other. We rarely understood what they were saying. But it mattered little since my humans were good to us and took good care of us. I realise that more than ever now, and I miss them. I miss them very much," he repeated as he looked down in a kind of reverie thinking about his past. Once the words had left his mouth Buster realised it was the first time he had voiced his loneliness to another creature. The female purred softly and listened with her sympathetic ears pointed towards him while he spoke.

"It sounds like you live in a really nice place, ah...Singing Cat," She paused, her purring stopped and she looked at Buster feeling a little clumsy since here she was inviting a stray, half-starved, stranger cat into her barn, and she didn't even know his name. But this time Buster caught on, and interjected,

"Oh! Yes...Yes!" he stammered, not knowing the correct etiquette. "Buster! Buster is my name," he blurted out, "and I live at Rainbow Farm on Chemin de Bellevue." Then he corrected himself. "Or at least I did live there until about a month ago."

"You are well met, Buster of Rainbow Farm," she said softly. Then the purring *continuo* started up again and in her melodic cat voice she formed the sounds of her own name.

"Juliette. My name is Juliette from *La Ferme du Sommet.*"

At first when she introduced herself, Buster thought she was singing a song the way he did when he sang opera until he realized the melodious sounds she was making were actually her name.

Her very name is a song, he realized. *I'm making cat noises with a cat whose name is a song! No wonder my head is spinning and I feel so strange.*

Juliette, he said to himself. He had never heard anything so beautiful. As she spoke Buster's eyes roamed over her thick and lustrous orange and brown coat cut with vertical beige stripes. He didn't want to stop looking at her—ever. Her face, her coat, her perfect yellow eyes, her shiny-white incisors, everything about her was magnificent! He was so intoxicated that if she had told him she was a cat goddess who, by some quirk of magic, had descended from the stars and taken up residence in this humble yet seemingly sanctified barn, he would have believed her. Her very presence transformed this century-old wooden structure from a shelter for hay-eating farm animals into a consecrated place where a cat goddess lived, and where miraculous things occurred. He was unaware that striped cats that looked like Juliette were once the favoured animals of Bronze Age pharaohs who lived in splendour along the banks of the Nile River. Her origins mattered not a speck to Buster. All he knew was that when she moved, when she made cat sounds, Juliette radiated felinity.

Except for his mother and his two sisters, he had never really known that many female cats. Of course there were female cats at the animal shelter, but he wasn't there long enough to get to know any of them, and while he was there the males and females were separated until they were sterilised. Most of what Buster knew about females he learned from the farm cats in Abenaki Falls by hanging around the grain silo. They made noises together, and sometimes he sang country songs and operatic arias with them, and even groomed a few of them. But the locals knew he was sterile and never took his clumsy attempts at affection seriously. But none of them looked anything like Juliette, none of them acted like Juliette, and none of them purred when they made cat sounds like Juliette.

Juliette was cat magic! What Buster didn't realise was that even though she seemed so worldly and sophisticated, apart from the male who had impregnated her the first time she came into heat, Juliette had little experience with male cats. Things were going to change now that a half-starved male cat had shown up.

Buster and Juliette made cat sounds together for the rest of the afternoon while the kittens woke and played. Periodically they stopped talking and breathed in the day. The afternoon light and shadows continued to waltz on the barn walls until they tired and sat down somewhere over the horizon behind some trees. Juliette told Buster she called her humans Jacques and Madeleine. Names she heard them call each other as they worked around the barn or outside in the paddock. She said they were very nice people and she had lived in the barn for about a year, ever since they adopted her last summer. She had been about six months old when they brought her to the barn at *La Ferme du Sommet,* to be *la maîtresse des souris*—the mistress of mice.

§

Then, with a stern look on her face, changing to a more serious tone of voice, she said,

"There is one thing I have to warn you about: every day my humans will come to refill my food bowl. And when they come you must hide somewhere deep in the barn and not make a sound. My man human hates cats and says he will kill any new ones he sees around here, do you understand?"

"Oh yes," said Buster somewhat surprised.

Later they talked about the benefits of eating mice over cat food from a box, and like all the cats in the world, they remembered exactly what they were doing, what the weather was like, and who they were with when they got their first mouse.

"Oh how wonderful to catch a mouse and eat it," they both agreed, and laughed that 'first mouse' was every young cat's rite of passage.

"I feel sorry for those cats who live cooped up in places where they can't hunt mice," she said. Buster looked up at her and nodded emphatically in agreement.

"I can't imagine it," said Buster. "It must be awful being cut off from your inner catness like that." They pondered the thought and as their minds met their two heads shook in agreement.

What a wonderful time I'm having, thought Buster. *Here I am making cat sounds with another cat; one of my own kind. No*, he thought, *it's more than that. She is the most beautiful cat in the world, and here we are together. I had no idea anything like this even existed. This is wonderful!*

"The mice here are fat and lazy," said Juliette. "There is so much food for the horses that it spills out of the big sacks onto the ground and the mice eat until they are ready to burst. They are so fat you'll have no problems catching them, even with your limp."

Concerning the eating arrangements, she stipulated that when the food was put out, as long as she got to eat her fill first, Buster could have whatever was left over. Buster understood that she needed to eat so she could nurse her kittens and was readily agreeable. But there was so much food that after a few days she told Buster to eat all he wanted first, and just leave her a few crumbs for later. Neither of them went hungry. The barn was big and the horse feed and manure attracted large numbers of mice, but birds also flitted in and out of the big open doors during the day time, eating even the undigested seeds in the manure scattered about on the floor. There was no need to catch the birds since the mice were slow and plentiful. Juliette showed him the best spots for ambushing barn mice in the basement crawl-space. They took turns lying on a little masonry out-cropping of the old field stone foundation, and when a mouse walked by below them Buster could just reach down and grab it. After the second week he moved much faster and the pain had diminished. Ensconced in the barn Buster ate and recuperated for a full lunar cycle, staying clear of the man-human named Jacques and enjoying the rich bounty, from the dry food to licking up the remains of the milk bowl, plus the mice. The whole environment, the big barn, the plentiful food, the beautiful horses prancing about the paddock, was idyllic. Then there were the kittens, and of course the beautiful Juliette. Everything was perfect and once he learned the sounds Jacques and Madeleine made as they approached the barn it wasn't long before he knew where to hide when he heard them coming.

Life is good here and I'm getting better.

As the hot days marched across the page of August he caught so many mice he often just bit off their heads, ate their fat brains, and left their uneaten bodies lying about for the maggots. It was only a month ago with the gaunt spectre of starvation staring him in the face that he hadn't been sure he would live long enough to ever hunt again.

§

The people who lived at *La Ferme du Sommet* were not farmers. They were city people who had purchased a 19th century farm on Chemin du Lac, renovated the house, made a few repairs to the barn, and became countrified city people who kept a condo in Montreal and divided their time between the city and the country. There were other people like them in the area, *nouveaux campagnards*, people who gave up part or all of their city ways and moved to the country to be with nature. They found new friends among the locals and former city dwellers who, like them, were looking for the country life without the back-breaking plough work, the animal chores and the meteorological inconsistencies. They wanted a new kind of lifestyle with green spaces, with rolling hills and mountains in the distance, and vistas overlooking lakes and forests. As they came on the market, city couples bought worn-out family farms that could no longer compete. Although some kept animals, few of them became real farmers working the land for profit; most just wanted a chunk of land and the country lifestyle. They renovated old farm houses keeping the traditional style of architecture. Some even did the work with their own hands.

Les nouveaux campagnards were eager to jump into the country life. The musically inclined joined church choirs or fiddle bands. Some square danced, others golfed, took up sailing, calligraphy or pottery making. Most made impressive flower and vegetable gardens. Wannabe hunters purchased hunting rifles and shot guns and hunted deer and small game. Just about everyone bicycled or went on nature walks. They got together for soirées at local museums and cultural centres, and in a haze of bilingual palaver they ate in local restaurants, gave dinner parties in their homes, and celebrated birthdays together. Madame and Monsieur Dupont of *La Ferme du Sommet* were just such people.

The Duponts loved horses and kept three of them in a fenced-in area of 100 hectares of grassland interspersed with stands of trees. The enclosed grazing area was surrounded by a wooden post and board fence that bobbed up and down following the contours of the grassland towards Lake Memphremagog. Most days, Jacques Dupont, a lawyer from Montreal, would come into the barn, climb the stairway, grab two or three bales of hay, throw them down from the mezzanine onto the cement floor where Madeleine would break them open and distribute armloads of hay to the waiting horses. After several hours of riding, the Duponts returned to the well-kept barn, removed their tack, and brushed and fed their mounts.

As part of her daily tasks, Madeleine Dupont would come to the barn and put out dry cat food and some milk for Juliette, who always thanked her by purring and rubbing up against her legs. Jacques Dupont hated cats and didn't want them on the place. He would never allow a stray cat on the premise. He tolerated Juliette because his wife was adamant about having a cat, and if it were left up to him there would be no cats at all at *La Ferme*. However, his wife knew something about farms and the value of cats around grain-eating animals, and insisted on having at least one in the barn. Madeleine was a cat lover and wanted to keep many cats around, and they certainly had plenty of space in the barn, so why not? Her husband had always been against the idea.

"They breed like rabbits, for god's sake!" he claimed. "And before you know it this won't be a horse farm; it'll be a cat club overrun with fornicating felines." Madeleine riposted by reminding Jacques that he was the issue of a family of 12 children, and it wasn't only cats that bred like rabbits; his own parents were prolific breeders as well. Such reasoning, coming from his wife, who wasn't even a member of the bar, never sat well with her lawyer husband. But as she did so often, Madeleine stood her ground, arguing that cats were a necessity in an environment where grain was stored and would earn their keep many times over.

"Go ask any horse owner or anyone who keeps cattle or sheep or whatever. They all have cats. Without the cats it would cost them a fortune in lost feed grain, and you'd be knee-deep in mice and rats. Then you'd really bitch!" He didn't have a good response ready for that one and while he searched deep in the briefcase of his lawyer mind for a comeback his wife continued.

"Look Jacques, you don't have to like them," she said with an air of stubbornness she had employed with a well-honed skill developed over more than three decades of marriage.

"But I do like them and I want a cat. In fact I want cats, plural. You understand that? And that's final!" she said as she walked away.

Jacques hated to be bested by his wife, but he knew that when Madeleine put her foot down even he could not change her mind.

No use in arguing, he thought. *She's got me on this one.*

"But I don't want those damned things in the house! You understand?" he barked at his wife's back as she disappeared into the house.

She couldn't possibly be right. But she always gets her way, he thought. *That's what is so irritating about all of this. She always gets her way!*

So he acquiesced to his wife's wishes, and for now Juliette lived in the barn eating her weight in mice every month or two, and having saved the Duponts at least one 20-kilo bag of feed since she had taken up residence in the barn alongside the horses. However, both of them were in for a surprise when they rescued the young female from a neighbour a year ago. It seems they were unable to determine the sex of their new cat and were unaware that she was a female and apt to get pregnant. Some months later she came into heat and a Tom from a neighbouring farm paid her a visit, and a few months after her arrival she gave birth. The litter of three kittens came as joy for Madeleine and an unwelcome surprise for her husband.

"What did I tell you? They breed like rats! Now we're stuck with three more of the little bastards!' he bellowed at her, and putting on his tough guy voice he threatened; "I'm telling you Madeleine, if I ever see another cat on this place I swear I will get my gun and kill it! You understand?"

§

Buster stayed out of sight in the depths of the barn and ate his fill of mice and cat food. As the days passed his injuries healed and he put on weight. With all the activity in the daytime, with horses and humans going in and out distracted by their chores, the two humans rarely looked up from their tasks and with the doors closed at night no unwanted strays or predators wandered in. Juliette had made it very clear that Monsieur Dupont would not allow him to stay and that she had even heard him say in no uncertain terms that he would kill any other cats he found on the premises or if he ever caught sight of one in the barn. She told Buster that even though he could hide in the vast expanse of the barn and probably no one would ever know he was even there for many months, he was still at risk of being discovered. He should take every precaution and not be caught by surprise.

"Buster, you know that somehow humans can kill animals from far away?" she said as they hunted one day high up in the haymow. "They don't even need to be nearby to kill you. There is just a terrible noise, and then animals far away scream and howl in pain and drop dead. I have seen Jacques Dupont do this and I don't want you to be his next victim, do you understand?"

"I'll be careful, Juliette, and I will take extra precautions so he doesn't find me," Buster answered.

Although just about everyone in the country had rifles and shotguns, Tillman and Annie did not hunt and rarely had the need to discharge their firearms. They kept one shot gun and a 22-calibre rifle to get rid of the most persistent predators. But thanks to Mecki and Sparky, Rainbow Farm was a safe haven for animals, so Buster was unfamiliar with the sound of gunfire at close range. Most of the gunshots he heard came from the neighbouring farms some distance away so he knew little about guns and the human capability to kill things at a distance. Juliette knew very well what guns could do to other animals. More than once her ears had been shattered by the noise of a shot gun or rifle discharging close by. It seemed Jacques Dupont took a special interest in killing small animals even if they weren't near the barn or the horses, and on more than one occasion Juliette had seen the bloodied carcasses of foxes, racoons and coyotes he brought in from the fields. She rarely saw or interacted with Jacques Dupont and kept her distance because she knew he was an indiscriminate animal killer.

§

It was hot and Madeleine wanted to get out of the bright sun for a minute. She headed for the big open doorway of the barn, and as she walked into the cool, welcoming shade, she removed her hat and wiped her forehead with a hankie. As her eyes adjusted to the light she saw Juliette on the rough cement floor a couple of metres in front of her. Juliette was not alone. Right next to her was a large grey and white cat hunkered down waiting to pounce on a feed-bag mouse. Both cats had their backs to her so they did not hear or see Madeleine behind them. The woman remained still and watched the two cats for several minutes. Finally, Buster turned and saw the woman, and sensing trouble, he immediately loped off towards the back of the barn. Although it didn't seem to slow him down much, as the big cat ran off she noticed he had a distinct limp. She also noticed that Juliette got on well with the limping intruder, because when the female cat turned and recognised her human, instead of running to her as she normally did, she ran after her new friend.

So! She's got a boyfriend, eh? And it's clear that now he's more important than me. Madeleine smiled and thought how charming they looked. But then a worried look came over her face.

I better make sure Jacques doesn't see him.

On several occasions over the next few weeks she caught glimpses of Juliette and her grey and white beau. Sometimes the couple had the three kittens in tow behind them.

How charming. They're a real little family, she thought. *But how can I keep Jacques from finding out?* That was going to be a challenge and she didn't know how to handle it except to make sure that when he was around she would make lots of extra noises or to do more things inside the barn so the cats would know they were about. For a while that strategy worked well.

§

"Buster, Buster," sang her voice. "Come join me in the cat box. I want to have you close to me. I want you to help me groom the kittens. But most of all I want you to groom me."

Buster's heart was in his throat as he rushed to the box, and once he settled in, they passed that afternoon, and just about every afternoon that followed, cuddled close together grooming the kittens' fuzzy little bodies as well as each other. Occasionally they rolled and tumbled around inside the box, stopping only when they heard the muffled cries of one of the kittens caught somewhere in the cat scrum beneath them.

Whenever Juliette left the box to eat or take care of other needs, Buster would move in and lie down with the kittens in her spot. They were delighted to see him and made happy sounds as they piled on top of him while he groomed their little heads and faces. They chewed his ears and licked his face, and on many occasions, Buster, the surrogate father, fell asleep covered in a blanket of kittens. Although he knew he wasn't their kitten-maker, they certainly believed he was, and they loved him unconditionally. He began thinking about staying on permanently.

I like being a father cat, so maybe I should stay on and help Juliette eat the food and take care of her litter. Perhaps this barn is my new home, my new Rainbow Farm.

§

By late August Buster had regained much of his strength, his limp was barely noticeable, the healing of his wounds in his back and shoulder progressed steadily, and by his third week at *La Ferme du Sommet* he had regained much of his former mobility. He still refrained from climbing the barn beams vertically, but he did more and more horizontal beam walking. Then he started climbing all the ladders in the barn. He knew he had regained much of his strength and started to do little sprints around the inside of the barn. One day he felt well enough to climb a really long ladder that led from the ground all the way to the highest point inside the barn. Afterwards he noticed a slight discomfort, but nothing else.

Everything is working much better, he thought. *Maybe I'm going to be alright. Maybe I can be a real cat again. If only I could see that owl on the ground right now*, he thought. *I would tear him to pieces in a fight.*

While the Duponts were off riding one afternoon and had left the big doors open, Buster went outside to try some real forest hunting to see if his wounds really were healed. In no time he ran across the paddock and bounded halfway to the top of a big cedar tree. He felt great; there was no more nagging pain when he sank his claws into the stringy bark and pulled himself up. He was strong and he knew he was back to his old self.

If I wanted too, I could hunt and survive on my own; I could be a vagabond cat. But I don't really want to do that. I love the barn, I love the kittens, and I love Juliette more than anything. I want to stay with her, as cats say, 'until I close my eyes forever.'

Spending so much time in the barn, by now Buster had located a place towards the back where he could just squeeze between two planks and get outside. Jacques Dupont had not yet discovered the opening and it would probably be a while before he repaired it. So tonight, with their stomachs full and the kittens sleeping in their box, Buster and Juliette slipped through the crack into the night air. Outside, the air was calm, a few frogs were chirping, the last of the glow worms flashed their diminishing blinkers, and a small barn owl hooted a twilight serenade while a big yellow moon rose through the trees.

"Let's take a turn around the paddock and see what we find," suggested Buster.

"Let's," she said.

So off they went into the night between the fence posts and the horse tanks and up behind the barn into the nearby woods where they stopped at the edge of the duck pond. When Buster caught her moonlit reflection in the waters he looked across the mirrored water and said,

"I wish I could stay here forever."

"I know," she said. "I know."

Juliette felt the same way he did, but she did not elaborate. What could she say? Of course she wanted Buster to stay forever, but their situation couldn't last. Sooner or later Buster would either be discovered or he would decide to go in search of his home once again. Either way, she knew she would lose him, and she knew she would spend the rest of her life living on her memories of the wonderful grey and white cat who sang his way into her life as he rolled on the dusty mezzanine floor. But she was a mother cat, and like all mothers before her, she had responsibilities. She had to prepare herself for the worst. She looked back at him silently through the yellow moonlight air.

How shall I answer him? she thought. The normally velvet-voiced Juliette was at a loss to make cat sounds. Her heart was in her throat and it seemed to block the opening that normally let the noises out of her mouth. Feeling the weight of silence suspended in the air just over her head she could not come up with any words that would explain to Buster how she felt. The thought of losing Buster left her speechless. Finally, when she thought she had formulated a response the silence was pushed aside by a wisp of breeze that stirred the moonlit waters, and her sounds escaped into the night air before she could utter them.

I'll guess I'll have to explain later, after I've had time to think about what to say, she thought.

She looked up at Buster and said,

"Let's go back Buster; the kittens might need me."

Buster kept waiting for something else, but realised that she was not going to make any more sounds.

"But, uh what about....., uh... us? What about our plans?"

"We'll talk about it later Buster. We really should get back."

That was her answer? That was all she could say? I thought her inner catness… I mean, I thought her inner catness was one with mine. At that instant he thought he heard a sudden gust of wind blowing through the trees, but it was just the air rushing out of his lungs in a huge sigh. Then Buster answered,

"Yes, of course, we had better return." The night changed as a cloud covered the face of the moon and Juliette's reflection in the water faded. They walked back to the barn in silence. The following days passed mechanically as their routines repeated themselves with a steady regularity. They ate, they played with the kittens, hunted in the barn at night and slept during the day, Juliette in her nest box and Buster hidden somewhere deep in the haymow.

§

Juliette heard the crush of boots on the gravel outside. Jacques Dupont, cat-hater, was coming towards the barn.

"Buster! Buster!" Juliette shrieked out with her full voice, "He's coming! Quick! Get down from there! Hide!"

On that early September day Buster was up on one of the main rafters under the centre of the barn roof high above the floor. He moved right away and heeded her warning, but he was not fast enough, and before he could get completely down off the high beams he was discovered. He stayed put, not knowing which way to go, while Jacques Dupont looked up at him from the main floor of the barn. The man swore a human oath.

"Damn! I told Madeleine we should get that cat fixed," he bellowed as he looked up into the lattice-work of beams and struts of the roof.

"Now we are going to have every damn stray male in the county over here. Where's my shotgun when I need it?" he said looking around the barn as if the weapon might be lurking somewhere nearby; it was back at the house. Looking right up at Buster overhead he said,

"Hang on right there little fella', the two of us have a *rendezvous*."

With his eyes still fixed on Buster, he yelled out across the barnyard behind him,

"Madeleine! Get my .410 and a couple of shells. There's a predator in here and I want to kill him before he gets away."

Oh thank goodness it's a predator and not the grey and white cat, Madeline thought.

Standing on the back porch just outside the back door, Madeleine imagined her husband was referring to a coyote or a mountain lion that had managed to get into the barn and was about to eat one of the horses. She didn't know he wanted to kill the limping cat she had seen with Juliette. Had she known this she would have refused to get the gun. But at the sound of her husband's command, she grabbed two shells from the yellow cardboard box in one hand and the .410 in the other and headed for the barn. From the sound of his voice, surely there was some kind of emergency unfolding. When she reached the barn door, and before she could stick her head in and catch a glimpse of Buster high above the floor in the rafters, her husband grabbed the gun out of her hands, broke it open, and stuffed one of the reddish coloured cartridges into the breach and turned away from her.

"What is it, a coyote?" she asked.

What would a coyote be doing way up there? Maybe he's on the mezzanine, she reasoned.

He didn't answer. He just raised the gun to his shoulder and aimed at a grey form high above him. As he released the safety, Juliette screamed.

"Buster! He's going to kill you! Jump! Jump now before it's too late! Don't wait! Jump! Jump now!"

Juliette's high-pitched cat sounds rang through the rafters, and it was her sounds that distracted the fearless cat hunter just enough to take his eyes off Buster for an instant. He then had to reposition the gun and drive its wooden stock into his shoulder before firing.

The noise was deafening, not even when the night the sky broke apart and fire had rained down from the heavens was the noise so loud. The shot roared out of the barrel and the BBs buzzed through the air around Buster thudding into the beams and making tinny sounds as they tore holes in the metal roof above him.

As he fell from the cross beam, Buster's mind flashed to the last time he had been in free fall and he wondered if the results would be the same. Would he be injured again? Would the man reach him as he lay broken on the floor far below and finish him off, or would he crawl injured, wracked with pain, into some corner of the barn and expire? No! Never again! As the BBs flew by, he leapt from the haymow to the cement floor, and this time his paws, legs and shoulders took the shock the way nature had intended: there were no sharp pains and his leg and shoulder muscles felt like tightly-wound springs permitting him to react at full speed.

Once on the ground floor he had a choice to make; he could hide in the barn and risk being caught later or he could make a break for it and put some distance between him and Thunder-man. The choice was easy: he was not going to live in fear of a cat-hater. From the corner of his yellow eyes he saw the man looking around for him while he fumbled about stuffing another cartridge into the breach of the gun. He knew nothing about guns, but he knew he had to get out of the barn now! The big doors were open, sunshine and freedom were pouring through from outside. In a flash Buster was through doors and out in the yard, running full speed, but not in a straight line. He remembered the plan he had used on the first day as he approached the barn and he made a quick left detour towards the lumber pile as the gun discharged a second time, and the shot flew wide. While the man messed with his death contraption Buster cut right back across the open space and headed for the woods and the meadow where the grass and the trees swallowed him up in their green blanket. The last thing he remembered was calling out to Juliette at the top of his lungs.

§

The two of them had never considered how fast things might change. Buster had decided that when the time came he would just say goodbye and go on his way. But it was happening much faster than either one of them expected. There were things they needed to say to each other, there were noises un-vocalised. Now it was too late and what was left unsaid would remain so.

Juliette looked on as Buster ran across the yard, and the second shot was fired she feared for Buster's safety, but when she saw him hit the protection of the forest she knew he would escape. Elated that her Buster had made it to safety she was at the same time heart-struck with the realisation that whether he survived the shots or not her beautiful time with the gentle grey and white cat was over. The most wonderful thing that had ever taken place in her life was coming to an end and her singing cat who had been the light of her inner catness was disappearing in front of her eyes. In an instant he would be gone forever. He was getting away from the cat-hater, but he was also getting away from her.

Why hadn't she said something earlier? Why had she waited? She had been meaning to talk to him for the past few days, but she always had excuses: the timing or the mood had not been right. How could she explain to Buster that their inner catness was one, but they could not live together? That had been her excuse, and her mistake. She should have made her feelings clear right from the start, that night in the moonlight when she had the chance. How silly she had been. When was the right time to express such feelings? In the world of cats there is never any time to plan for such things. Now, all of the moonlight and romance had been sucked out of the situation, replaced by the blast from the .410 shotgun and the lingering acrid smell of its discharge.

I always knew someday he would leave me and go looking for his home and his humans and his brother cats and dogs. I guess that time is now.

She realised that if he didn't leave on his own then one day Jacques Dupont would discover him and either chase him away or kill him. That day had arrived unplanned and unannounced, and if she wanted Buster to know how she felt then she better do something fast or he would be gone forever. So as he raced out the door, and his form passed from the shadowed barn interior into the mid-morning sunlight, Buster heard Juliette's voice call out over the top of the slurry of oaths being expelled from the hollering mouth of Jacques Dupont, and the sound of the gun.

"Buster! Buster I love you! I love you! Come back some day Buster! Come back Buster!" she called out, her cat sounds ricocheting off the walls before they escaped through the main door.

Not able to look back, but with her words ringing in his ears, Buster ran towards the safety of the woods. He could feel his body respond to his commands to run harder and faster, to stretch out his legs and kick up the dust of the paddock as he zigzagged towards the forest, moving like feline lightning. In the same instant that he had lost his beautiful Juliette, the love of his life, he had found his fully renewed strength and knew he was ready for anything. Unable to slow down or stop, and unable to turn his head back to make sure his sounds reached her, he yelled out the sounds in front of him, over and over again.

"Good-bye Juliette! I love you! I will love you always until my eyes close forever!"

While the two cats yelled out their love for each other the man came puffing across the paddock in pursuit, but he was far behind the grey and white cat who had slipped under the wooden fence and had withdrawn into the cover of the tall grass and trees. As he disappeared, Juliette thought she heard him calling back something as his white hind paws vanished into the woods and the clarity of his cat sounds became entangled in tree branches and caught on the blades of tall grass.

"We'll meet again someday, Juliette! We'll meet again!" She was sure that was what he had said. But as of that day, Buster, the handsome and gallant grey and white cat, was gone. In an instant the love of her life had vanished into the woods in a hail of small game shot and human oaths.

Hidden in the trees but still within sight of the barn, Buster stopped to consider his situation. He knew that by night fall the barn would be sealed up tightly to keep him out. From now on he would have no way of getting back in to see her. His only other chance would be to return during the daylight hours, and look for her. That would be a risky proposition since the next time the man would be waiting for him with a loaded gun.

I'll have to see when it gets dark. He knew it would be risky, but what he feared most was never seeing Juliette again.

How awful! he thought. He didn't want to contemplate that possibility.

He had to get moving again because Jacques Dupont was still running and puffing through the grass and trees in a red-faced attempt to catch him.

How stupid this biped giant is! Buster thought as he sauntered off into the forest thick with pines and beeches.

Now that he's missed killing me with that noisy contraption does he think he can catch me with his bare hands? Does he think he can climb trees? I'm a healthy young cat and there is no way he's going to catch me!

§

Gasping and holding his sides, Jacques Dupont stopped his pursuit and leaned forward with his hands on his knees, wheezing for breath. He had lost sight of his prey. In his pursuit he had tripped over fallen logs, skinned his hands and knees, and had been forced to throw down his gun a hundred paces back. He was winded and had to stop and rest. With sweat pouring from his face and the rest of his entire body he moved towards a cedar tree while coughing up a gob of long-dormant phlegm from some dark and unused corner of his lungs. It was a reminder that he was overweight, out of shape and that his run had been overly strenuous. He was feeling faint and so he sat down heavily, leaning his back against a tree. A river of sweat was running into his eyes and the thunderous thumping of his heart pounded in his ears. His chest felt heavy, and constricted, as a wave of nausea swept over him. He put his head between his legs and vomited all over his shoes and on the ground in front of him.

I guess I ate too much for breakfast, he reasoned.

Between the waves of queasiness, and with slime drooling from his mouth, he could hear Madeleine somewhere in the distance calling after him. He didn't want her to find him. He knew he had made a fool of himself, plus he was embarrassed at being barf-sprayed and so out of breath that he could not even stand up.

When he first sat down he thought he would just take a minute to catch his breath. Then, he imagined, once he had recuperated he could amble back to the barn and continue his chores as if nothing had happened. Only now did it begin to sink in how much of a commotion he had caused. For starters, he'd lied to his wife when he should have known better. He'd never been able to pull anything over on her during thirty-five years of marriage so what made him think he could do so now? Like the Old Testament God calling out to Adam in the Garden of Eden, her voice was coming from somewhere in the trees, it was getting closer, and he could detect the unmistakable sound of justifiable anger in it.

God's scrotum! he swore. *Don't let her find me. Please!* he pleaded to some unknown force out there somewhere.

But there was no hiding from her, and he was in for it. Jacques wanted to save himself the awkwardness of being discovered both out of breath and unable to explain why he tried to kill a common domestic cat with a shotgun. What kind of man was he anyway? He couldn't even protect his barn from a house cat! He vomited again and this time most of his discharge ended up on his clothing, but it seemed to clear up his thinking and it dawned on him that there really wasn't much of a need to protect his barn from a domestic cat. Some distance away Madeleine called out.

"I see you Jacques Dupont, so don't try to hide from me behind that tree." As he once again emptied another installment of his stomach contents he knew full well that Madeleine was beyond angry.

Afraid to look in the direction of her voice he wiped his mouth and answered.

"I'm not trying to hide from you dear—*he hadn't called her "dear" in decades, not even in their most intimate moments*—I'm right here. I'm fine," he said trying to sound as if nothing had happened.

Madeleine poked her head around the tree and saw him trying to stand up with much difficulty. She was livid with anger, but waited until he was fully upright and then she ripped into her would-be cat killer husband.

"You crazy old coot!" Without even asking if he was alright she blurted out. "Do you realise what you just did?"

He cringed, but before he could say anything in his own defense she gave him a mouth blast. "You scared the horses out of their wits. They panicked and kicked down their stall doors and ran out of the barn in terror. They were so frightened they damn near trampled me. And you know what else you did? You managed to shoot a hole in the tin roof! The BBs have probably landed somewhere in Russia by now. You shot a hole in the barn roof you idiot! What the hell were you thinking? What *were* you thinking? Why didn't you just set the barn on fire for god's sake! That way you could have killed all those cats you hate, plus the horses, and if you had been lucky you could have killed me as well. Is that what you were trying to do?"

She paused and caught her breath in the process of reloading her mouth cannon in preparation for a second broadside as her husband's sinking boat fell down on its knees and heaved to the lee. He was sure he saw smoke coming from her mouth.

It must be the nausea affecting my brain, he told himself. *She's not really emitting smoke — is she?*

Madeleine moved a step closer to her husband on his hands and knees looking down at the vomit soaked patch of ground in front of him.

OK Jackie boy, thought Madeline, *I'm just getting warmed up and I feel like giving you another broadside. Are you ready for this?*

Eyes still on the ground, Jacques was now absolutely certain he smelled smoke and looked up to see if it was coming from his wife. It was. Then she gave him another mouth discharge.

"And, what were you thinking when you told me there was a predator in the barn, eh? Why did you lie to me? You knew that cat was not a predator! Why didn't you just tell me there were a bunch of lions and tigers in the barn? Or, better yet, why didn't you tell me the barn was filled with a gang of terrorists who were going to blow up the barn and then the parliament buildings!"

She sighed in exasperation as she finally noticed her husband's soiled shirt and trousers. She was tired but despite the afternoon heat and humidity she was not going to let up. She was going to put her husband in his place, knowing full well that after the anger was drained out of her it would be replaced with the all too familiar feeling of frustration, and dare she even think it, love for him. She paused for a moment and, with her hands on her hips, turned away from him looking around but seeing nothing except a blur of anger in front of her eyes. She turned once again and faced her husband.

"Then you know what you did?"

Oh my god, he shuddered, *not again. I thought maybe she was finished.* But he wasn't going to get off so easy on this one.

"Do you know what you did after you missed killing that innocent cat? You threw down your gun and ran after him. A cat! You ran after a terrified little cat! What in hell made you think you could catch him, and what were you going to do if you did catch him?"

Her anger was waning but she wasn't quite finished. She was going to get the whole thing off her chest now that it had come to a head. She had the upper hand and she didn't want to leave anything unsaid in this whole 'shooting of the cat matter.'

"The thing that makes me even angrier is that little grey cat, whoever he was, was probably a damn good cat, a cat that would have been useful around this place. Do you realise that? He could have saved us a pile of money on feed. Instead you tried to kill him!"

She omitted mentioning that on several occasions she had actually seen the cat he just tried to shoot inside the barn with Juliette and her kittens. Heck, they might as well have been the grey and white cat's kittens for all she knew. They made a lovely cat family.

Jacques Dupont could stand it no longer. He hadn't received a grilling like this since Madeleine had caught him in the bathroom at the office party with Mademoiselle Francoeur a few years back. Struggling to get up off his hands and knees he looked up at her, all sense of manly bravado drained away, replaced by the whitish-green colour of nausea. He put one hand out against a tree to steady himself.

"I know, I know. I've acted like a fool and now I will have to pay for my foolishness," he said looking at his wife. Knowing nothing good was going to come out of this, at least he felt less dizzy and didn't feel like he had to throw up any longer. Now it was time to face up to the damage he'd done to the barn roof, to his relationship with his wife, and to his self-esteem. How was he going to explain to the repair man that while he was trying to shoot a domestic cat he had blown a hole in the roof? So what ingenious bit of reasoning had persuaded him to shoot upwards at a cat while blowing a basketball-sized hole in the roof? Maybe he could say there was a huge mountain lion inside his barn and he had no choice.

Yes, that's it, he thought, *I'll tell the roofer I had trapped a mountain lion in the barn and in an act of bravery to save my wife and my horses, I misfired and blew a hole in the roof. Any decent man would have done the same.*

The problem was that no one would believe such a story and he knew it. There was no way around this and he would have to own up to his stupidity. He hated having to admit his weaknesses since he felt so emasculated afterwards.

Madeleine had her fill by now. She had vented her anger and wanted to put the whole incident behind them and go back to the house and lie down and take a nap. She extended her hand to steady her husband as they walked in silence back towards the barn to make sure the horses were alright. They couldn't face looking at each other or the damage.

"You better call the roofer first thing before it rains in and spoils all the hay," she said. Jacques nodded his head and whistled for the horses.

§

Juliette stood on the mezzanine overlooking the cement floor below and the big open barn doors leading out into the paddock. In the distance she could see a man and a woman walking slowly towards the barn. She saw nothing else. A few heartbeats earlier Buster had been there and they were talking. Now he was gone and emptiness was all around her. What happened? She sat down heavily on the thick planks of the mezzanine half-storey and stared out the door into the sunlight that poured down on the late summer earth. The day was perfect for two cats in love with plenty of mice to eat and a bunch of kittens to care for. Outside the sun moved, heating up the cicadas and as they began to sing their scratchy songs she lay down and stared at nothing. She couldn't think. The only thing she could feel was the wound that had been inflicted upon her, the hole that had been torn into her chest by some invisible weapon. At first she did not dare look down for fear she would see great drops of blood pumping from her chest onto the wooden planks beneath her paws. But then,

It must be a bloodless wound, for when she looked down she could see no blood, only the Tabby coat that covered her broken heart.

How can it be that I am feeling such pain and yet I'm not bleeding anywhere?

She stared for a long time and then she heard mewling sounds, and prodded by the hand of instinct, she raised herself heavily and turned towards the box and her kittens.

§

Buster was on the move again, far ahead of his winded pursuer and feeling his renewed strength, stretching out his legs in front and back, leaping over fallen logs and bounding through the woods the way he did before the owl attack.

Just like the good old days!

Despite the heartbreak of losing Juliette, Buster was euphoric knowing that at long last he could stand up to any adversity life threw at him. He was a healthy cat once again. A cat capable of hunting, capable of climbing trees, and right now, capable of out-running a gun-toting old human who wanted to kill him. Despite that, his inner catness was torn in two directions: one part had sunk to new depths of despair while the other was soaring like a bird in the clouds. Buster ran for a while, just for the sake of running, until he recognised the path that led from the farm house to the gravel road not far away. He slowed his pace to a walk then suddenly, in a festival of physical joy, he took off running and bounded up into a tree until he was high off the ground. He chirped with happiness, and then he thought of Juliette and decided he better get down and figure out what he was going to do.

For the rest of the day, his mood alternated between heartbreak and melancholia; from Juliette to the joy of hunting out in the open and being whole again. That afternoon he caught a bird right out of the air on the wing as it flew by low to the ground, something that required not only speed and agility, but shoulder muscles that worked properly.

Wow! I'm a 'birder' just like Buddy Lebeau!

He never ever thought he would be a birder, and now he was one. He was even better than before. With great satisfaction he munched the winged creature down in seconds. He ate everything, the beak, the intestines its light, hollow bones right down to its meatless feet. Thinking of Buddy Lebeau made him sad and he suddenly missed his cat brother very much.

I wish you were with me Buddy, I really miss you. More than ever, he wanted to find his way home.

He stayed in the area near *La Ferme du Sommet*, so he could keep an eye on things and maybe figure out a way to get back in the barn and see Juliette.

But, if I do see her, then what? She can't leave her kittens and go with me looking for Rainbow Farm.

Buster knew that Juliette would never put her kittens in danger. And if all of them, Buster, Juliette and the three kittens, did strike out on their own in search of Rainbow Farm it would be difficult, if not impossible, to keep track of them and find enough to eat. Travelling such distances at their young age would make them vulnerable to predators and starvation; they would be lucky if any of them survived more than a week. They both knew that she had to stay with them in the barn. She had her kittens and a good home. They had said their hasty, unplanned goodbyes, and with a heavy heart he told himself their time together was over.

§

That night, as the gibbous moon cleared the tree tops, Buster looked up at the bright orb floating between the planets, and with his inner catness bursting for Juliette he opened his mouth and made cat noises until his heart was empty. As the moon moved towards the meridian he sang every sad aria and heartbreak country song he could remember. When his cat sounds were used up and no more would come out of his mouth he wandered about for a while until finally he crawled under some fallen trees, and slept the sleep of the broken-hearted.

He returned to the area not far from the road where he had been hunting the day before. Although he could put her aside for short periods of time, Juliette was everywhere in his mind and he constantly saw visions of her, even as he tried to track his prey. Occasionally, he found himself engaged in long exchanges of cat sounds with her while she purred, constantly beguiling him with her music. He suffered most when he dreamt of her. After every sleep he woke with his heart aching and could only forget her temporarily through bouts of intense predation. For the next few days he hunted in the same area while keeping his distance from the Thunder-junkers and remaining vigilant of predators. He ate well, catching four or five mice and the occasional bird every day.

Just like old times, he thought with a certain satisfaction. Then Juliette's face would appear again, and he would go into a slump.

I feel awful; it's time to do some serious hunting.

§

The Great Cat

They were the biggest he'd ever seen, and the animal that made them was nearby. He had stopped in his tracks; his left paw suspended in mid-air, and hunkered down on the ground, making himself as small as possible. He knew the size of his own paw prints compared to those of his fellow cats. He knew that lynx left bigger paw prints than cats, but the prints he was looking at now were so big he could not imagine the kind of beast that had made them. Then he saw it: the earth-brown hulk of a giant feline sniffing around in the bushes just a few metres in front of him! He checked right and left for escape routes and hiding-holes or trees to climb and did a slow motion back-up into a clump of tall grass until he was completely covered.

How could I have missed seeing him? Buster thought. *He's so big, and I almost walked right into him!*

Just ahead the big cat's wide chest pushed the grass and bushes out of the way as he sniffed and snorted, drawing air into his nostrils. He nuzzled the earth then pawed it, breaking the soil.

He's looking for something, thought Buster. *I hope it isn't me.*

That was unlikely.

Why would a beast like him be interested in me? He must be looking for bigger prey. Buster never did find out what the big cat was looking for, and remained hidden while he observed the cougar sniffing about. Eventually the big cat raised his head and looked in Buster's direction, showing a good profile of his feline head and long, powerful body.

Oh no! This is it! He's going to see me!

He tightened his muscles and prepared to spring for the safety of a nearby tree. Cougars are excellent tree climbers, of course, but Buster was healthy and once in the tree he could climb to the highest branches where the big cat would not be able to reach him. He hoped!

If he comes after me maybe I can lose him in the upper branches. He's too heavy to go all the way to the top, he told himself as he stared out from his hiding place.

The cougar probably wouldn't waste his time chasing small prey like a domestic cat to the top of a tree. He was probably looking for a deer or a calf, or even a horse. Then, the big cat looked right at Buster. His large, brownish-beige face was relaxed and he had an unthreatening stance. To Buster's surprise he appeared benign, almost friendly. Then the big cat turned and slowly moved off into the woods.

Weighing up to 120 kilograms, the Eastern Mountain Lion, or cougar, had lived in the region since the end of the last Ice Age. It was hunted nearly to extinction in the north-eastern United States and Canada during the 19th and 20th centuries. Despite government bounties and high-powered rifles with telescopic sights, a few of them had managed to survive in the remotely populated areas of northern Maine and southern Quebec. In recent years their numbers began to increase when local cats began interbreeding with South American varieties that had been imported as exotic pet kittens. When the imports grew to maturity their short-sighted owners suddenly realised they were too big and too dangerous to keep around the house, so they liberated (or dumped) in the forests and left on their own. Nearly all of them died, but a few found local mates and had litters, and by the 1990s reports of cougar sightings began to circulate in the Eastern Townships. As the reports increased most people, even some of the experts, didn't believe that there were any of the big cats left. Then articles with accompanying photographs of cougar sightings began to appear in local papers and hunting magazines corroborating the sighting claims. The year before Buster saw his first cougar, Tillman Charbonneau had heard what he thought must have been a cougar making terrifying howling sounds a short distance behind the house. He never actually saw the beast but his neighbour did. A few days later, talking over the old collapsed stone fence that separated their two properties, Yves Trépanier recounted how he had seen a cougar, undoubtedly the same one Tillman heard, moving through the grassy field in broad daylight about 100 metres away from his house. Yves said he observed the beast with his binoculars for about a minute and it was a real, live cougar. Charbonneau had no reason to doubt his neighbour's story. Both men welcomed the news of the cougar's return.

Buster was both terrified and amazed that he was actually observing such a beast, and as he watched it move off into the woods it suddenly dawned on him who the big cat really was:

Great Thundering Cats! That's him! That's the Great Cat in the flesh right here on earth!

He was right. The sleek taupe-brown feline that had been standing only metres away was none other than the Great Cat: the ancient star-cat he had watched nightly until its celestial body had been consumed in the twilight and disappeared below the horizon; the very same starry creature who had scratched the heavens with his fiery claws.

At the time he remembered thinking: *Where did the Great Cat go after he disappeared below the horizon? Did he live somewhere under the earth?*

Now he understood. Once its front paws touched the ground it needed a place to land, so sometime in August the creature jumped out of the sky and landed in the forests of the Tomifobia Valley.

This is where he spends the late summer and autumn months, thought Buster. *Then, later, he jumps back up into the sky and continues his journey across the heavens.* A great mystery had been solved and Buster wished he could talk to Kofi right now and share his insights into the life and habits of the Great Cat with him.

Perhaps another time, he thought.

Buster stayed in the tall grass for a long time, held in place by the memory of the Great Cat. Then as his heartbeat slowed, Juliette's face appeared in front of him. She was back to love-haunt him, and the Great Cat was gone.

Book VI

Buster and Beagle

He had dozed only a few minutes when he heard a Thunder-junker approaching on the road not far away. Anticipating that it would pass by quickly on its way to somewhere else he paid it little attention. But when he heard it slow down and then stop he opened his eyes, lifted his head, and took notice. Checking his cover he walked a short distance and then climbed up the steep embankment to have a look. A shiny Thunder-junker was parked on the opposite side of the road. There were two younger-looking humans inside. He saw the door on the opposite side open and he could see a lady human lean down for a few seconds moving around doing something, but he couldn't tell what. Then she sat upright in her seat and looked straight ahead. At that moment the man driving the car took the steering wheel, and then the machine moved away leaving a cloud dust in the air.

I guess it was nothing, he thought as the vehicle moved off in the distance. But, as he turned to walk back to his napping spot he looked up and saw a small dog standing on the opposite side of the road. The dog looked confused and agitated. His eyes fixed intently on the back of the Thunder-junker moving rapidly down the road. The dog began to walk then run after it as the distance grew between them. Then, realising the futility of trying to catch the machine, he gave up after a few steps, and watched it grow smaller and smaller. His face was the most dejected thing Buster had ever seen.

What just happened? Buster asked himself.

Something tugged inside him and Buster wanted to cross the road and talk to the dog and find out what was going on. Why he had been left by the side of the road like that? He knew very well what it was like to be lost and dejected and in a situation where you didn't know what was going on and you couldn't figure out how you got there. If he were still back at Rainbow Farm, Buster probably would have approached the dejected dog without much hesitation, especially if his dog Sparky was with him. But now he was much more cautious, and had to be very careful since he was on his own.

How wonderful it would be to have a dog friend like Sparky or Mecki out here, he thought.

But as much as he wanted to talk to the dog, he knew that dogs were also prone to unreasonable, even crazy behaviour and might turn on a cat without warning. For a moment his head filled with thoughts of his dog friends and their crazy antics and their friendship, plus the extra security they provided just by being around. He remembered all the good times when he batted Sparky's wagging tail or his floppy ears while the big white dog played along. Then it would be the dog's turn and he would join in the fun, rolling Buster on the grass and licking him. However, he knew that if you didn't know a dog well, the way he knew Mecki and Sparky, you could not trust them, especially when you first encountered them.

OK, he thought. *Sometimes when Sparky became too excited he would chase the cats around the lawn or up into trees. But it was all in good fun and he never hurt anyone.*

Sparky was so good natured that the kids in the village called him 'Sugar Bear.' His only shortcoming was clumsiness, not meanness. The only time Sparky turned mean was when the coyotes came too close to the chicken house. Then he could be very mean, snarling and growling, his white fangs showing his blood-determination to protect his territory and all within it.

He remembered the time a man brought a smaller dog to play with Mecki and Sparky at one of the big Rainbow Farm barbeques. The guest dog, called Zippy, was a bad-tempered little nuisance and when Buster wanted to play he attacked him, and would have killed him had it not been for Mecki. The head dog of Rainbow Farm quickly stepped in and saved Buster by throwing the other dog to the ground. Mecki had a way of dealing with other animals, including those from the neighbouring farms and some of his hockey dog friends. His methods were particularly useful when Sparky became too rambunctious. He gave Sparky and the others what he referred to as a 'mini-maul' (a term Mecki said he picked up from Tillman). Even though Buster had never seen Tillman mini-maul Annie, he suspected he did so from time to time. When one of the other dogs was causing a problem, Mecki would grab them, and throw them to the ground, while stomping on them and biting them on the neck, making vicious dog noises. It wasn't a full-on attack, just a way to put things in order. That treatment usually worked, as it did in the case of the nasty little dog that was never invited back. But Mecki wasn't here now to protect him and Buster had to be careful. Even though there was nothing dangerous or menacing about his demeanour, for all he knew the brown and white dog might be really nice, or he might be a killer. Buster loved dogs and was very good at making noises that dogs understood, and he wanted very much to make dog sounds and to have a dog friend, especially now that he had lost Juliette. Instead, he remained on the opposite side of the road and watched the dog who was so distraught he did not noticed that anyone else was nearby.

§

Humans and dogs are millennial friends. Both are highly social and hunt in packs. Wolves and humans began hunting together in Palaeolithic times perhaps thirty thousand years ago. Millennia later, proto-dogs and then domestic dogs developed out of the relationship the two species had forged over the ages.

Some people believe that if abruptly thrown back into the wild and left to fend for themselves, domestic dogs will hear the call of the wild and revert back to natural hunters in some wolf-like state. Some dogs certainly can survive in nature if they are forced to, but if they were once nourished and protected by humans, it is very difficult for an abandoned dog to fend for itself in the wild. Of course some dogs will hunt down small game, but many others won't or can't, and most young carnivores need parental training before they can become proficient hunters. They may know how to retrieve a tennis ball or Frisbee, and maybe they can sit or roll over on demand, but most of them either don't know how to hunt or are not very good at it.

Homeless dogs in urban areas have an advantage because of the availability of human garbage. Humans throw away mountains of food every day which becomes available to scavenging dogs that may not have highly-developed hunting skills. Lost or abandoned dogs often can find allies in homeless people who adopt dogs for companionship and protection. Although the homeless may look like a social blight to middle-and upper-class humans, to lost dogs they are welcome friends who know the local food sources and are usually willing to share. Because of the much smaller population of humans in rural areas, food sources are scarce, meaning a lost dog, or one who didn't know his way around the Tomifobia River Valley, might wander for days before coming on a garbage can or other source of human food.

§

What happened? the dog asked himself as he swayed back and forth on his city-soft paws. Minutes before, he had been riding around in the back of a fancy human machine lying quietly in the back seat, occasionally looking out the windows as the stands of trees and open fields drifted by, without a care in the world. Now, he was here in this unfamiliar place. What went wrong? Why had they abandoned him? He remembered that earlier that day his humans would reach back and give him an extra pat on the head, more than they usually did, and they had been particularly nice to him. He did recall that the lady had been crying, but he didn't know why. The only thing that had changed recently was that he had noticed that the lady was constantly in front of her food bowl and she had gained quite a bit of weight around the middle part of her once thin body. Now that he thought about it, he remembered that his humans had been arguing quite frequently over the past few weeks. Did that have anything to do with him and his situation? The brown and white dog had never really been away from his home and his humans before. All his young life he had enjoyed the companionship of people who had loved him and had taken care of him. Now he was abandoned: what had happened? How come he was here in the middle of nowhere, in very unfamiliar surroundings while his humans had disappeared in a cloud of dust? Would they come back for him? Was this just something that the sometimes mysterious humans did with little dogs they loved? Or was it something else?

"Did I do something wrong? Did I cause a problem?" he called out to the back of the Thunder-junker as it rolled out of sight.

"I can make things right. No problem. Just tell me what to do and I'll be a good dog, I promise! I'll make it up to you, whatever it is!"

He thought the voice inside his head was awfully loud when he realised he was broadcasting his thoughts at the top of his lungs down the road into a cloud of car-dust. In the distance the silver machine reached the top of the hill and rounded the bend; then it disappeared from view. As Buster looked on undetected, the dog repeated the same statement over and over.

In a half-cry and half-howl he let out another supplication.

"I'll be a good dog. I'll do whatever you want me to just don't leave me here, OK? Don't leave me!"

Were they coming back? worried the dog. *Maybe they were just turning the car around, or maybe they were going to the shopping mall or maybe they were...... No they weren't.*

"They're not coming back, are they? No, they're not," he told himself out loud.

They were gone, and he was alone by the side of a gravel road he could not remember ever seeing before, in a place he did not recognise.

Since he stopped barking he had been holding his breath. Now he let it out from deep within, and overwhelmed with dejection, his heart fell to the bottom of his ribcage like a chunk of iron. He was so devastated he was barely able to remain conscious. With his head swirling, he fell flat on his stomach in the gravel, his paws extended in front of him. Buster was very disturbed by the whole scenario, so he turned his eyes away from the brown and white dog and withdrew a few steps from the edge of the road. His heart was barely able to deal with the loss of Juliette and the kittens, and now he was watching a poor dog who had been dumped by his humans.

This is tragic! By the Great Cat I don't think I've ever seen anything so sad! I think I need to get out of here and do some serious mouse hunting. It will be good for me to clear my head.

He headed west into the trees, and hadn't been under their cover very long when he heard barking and howling as the lost dog sent out a mournful cry. Since Buster understood dog sounds quite well he could not simply ignore them. He understood every sound the dog uttered as he begged his humans not to leave him alone. He heard the mournful wail of an animal afraid and alone with nowhere to go and no one to care for him. For a domestic animal dependant on humans it was the worst thing that could happen. With some difficulty Buster continued walking deeper into the forest while in the distance he could still hear the dog pleading:

"Come back, come back and get me. Please!"

Buster tried to block out the noise, but he couldn't. Instead of trees and shadows and grass and possible food sources, his eyes visualised images of the dog. He stopped, checked his location, looked for escape routes and then listened intently. The only thing he could hear was the dog. He couldn't concentrate and that was dangerous. He remembered that on the night he was attacked by the Horned Owl he hadn't been paying attention and that had almost cost him his life. He was not going to make the same mistake again. He would have to go back and try to figure out some way to calm the dog down. Maybe he could help him. How, he didn't know, but maybe he could say something. As he came up over the top of the bank and on to the road surface again he saw the dog sitting on his hind legs his neck stretched out and his face pointing upwards. His black-lipped mouth was open and he was howling a song of desperation with all his might,

"Come back! Come back and take me home!"

By the Great Cat, Buster thought, *the poor thing is pathetic. I've never seen an animal in such misery!*

He thought back to his own first realisation of being lost. It didn't happen right away when he first fell off the ledge of the barn because he was still in voice contact with Kofi and Buddy Lebeau. And although he was shocked to be away from his cat brothers, his humans had not just thrown him out by the side of the road with no warning. They may have put him in Bedlam Barn, but they didn't just throw him out of their Thunder-junker.

No, he said to himself, *I really didn't feel totally lost and alone until I was lying injured on the pile of stones after the round-eyed night bird attack.*

That was when everything hit home. Until then there had still been hope that he would be found and taken home to the place where people loved and cared for him. But this poor little dog, in one short, crushing moment, had to face the fact that not only was he alone in an unfamiliar place, but that he was unloved and dejected like Bernard, the unwanted lover in the opera, *Bernard Le*

Brave et la Belle Odette. Buster realised that although he had faced hardships, pain and loneliness, he was not quite on the bottom rung of the ladder of despair. At least he was surviving; he was getting food, overcoming hardships, and he still had hope that someday he would find his way home. Along the way, he had met Juliette and the kittens, and for the first time in life he knew the love of a beautiful feline dame and her kittens. These were things he could never have foreseen had he stayed at Rainbow Farm. In comparison, the situation of the brown and white dog was truly hopeless.

Several Thunder-junkers passed by, some of them coming dangerously close to the little dog who did not seem to notice them. His head was either down on the gravel sobbing or thrown back in the air making dry, croaking sounds. Occasionally they would slow down and people would peer out at him. Others seemed not to notice him; none of them stopped.

I wonder if he understands cat sounds, Buster thought. *Only one way to find out!*

Buster meowed out a big 'hello,' and the dog immediately raised his head and looked about, not registering the world around him, until his eyes blink-stumbled on to Buster. The grey and white cat called out again 'hello,' and the dog's eyes widened. He finally saw Buster, but he did not seem to understand who or what Buster was. It had been some time since Buster had made sounds that dogs understood and it took him a moment to realise that he was addressing the dog in cat noises. The dog was obviously unfamiliar with cat sounds so with his cat voice and accent Buster gave one of the universal, non-threatening dog greetings Mecki and Sparky used back at Rainbow Farm.

"Hello dog! I am a friend!" he yelled as his voice carried the greeting message across the road.

The brown and white dog had seen very few cats in his life, and he wasn't sure what cats really were or how they fit into his world. He did know that their mouth sounds were foreign to his ears and he couldn't communicate with them. But when he heard the greeting his eyes widened and his ears went up.

"Somebody is talking to me! Out here in the middle of the land of loneliness and desperation, someone, I think it's a cat, is actually talking to me. I'm not alone after all."

The city dog eyed Buster and then without looking in either direction he started to cross the road. After three steps Buster yelled out in dog sounds:

"Look out dog! Get back out of the way! Get back now!" just as a Thunder-junker roared by. The dog jumped back in time to avoid being hit by the fast-moving machine as it swerved and managed to avoid hitting him.

Wow, the dog thought, *whoever that creature is standing on the other side of the road, he makes good dog sounds and he just saved me from that machine. I wasn't even paying attention!*

The cat and the dog stared at each other briefly, neither making a sound. As the dog focused his attention on Buster he realised he was looking at a grey feline of some kind. But a special feline: one that could make dog noises.

This is amazing. He thought. *Who is this cat? What is he doing here? And where is 'here' anyway?*

The dog was severely depressed and confused. He had been dumped, nearly been run over by a Thunder-junker, and just now he had encountered a creature that looked like a cat but communicated like a dog. In his condo-sheltered life he only knew how to communicate with his humans and a couple of the neighbourhood dogs he bumped into on his walks in the park on the end of a leash. Of course there were the times when the humans gathered with their dogs and their puppy humans outdoors in the warm months and ate copious amounts of burned animal fat. Sometimes they brought their dogs with them and he had the chance to interact with them. He liked being around other dogs but such meetings were never long enough. He would just start to get to know the other dogs and then they left. That was the extent of his social life and his interactions with other animals. Now he was in the middle of nowhere looking across a dusty road at what he was pretty sure was a cat, but a very special cat.

Wow! A cat who could make dog sounds! How sophisticated! How lucky to have someone to talk to way out here in wherever I am.

It didn't take Buster long to realise that the dog didn't know anything and was totally out of his environment. He would have to take command of things, so he yelled across the road,

"Dog! Stay where you are. Don't try to cross the road, it's too dangerous. Do you understand dog?"

"Yes, I understand," said the dog, looking both directions up and down the road while marvelling at the cat's strange accent and manner of communicating. The cat seemed to know what was going on and he might be able to help out or at least help him understand what had happened.

"And dog stop howling or you'll attract coyotes. Do you understand?" The dog acquiesced to the cat's command and stopped howling. After all, the cat did speak in dog noises.

"Dog, what happened to you?" Buster called out.

Good question, thought the dog. *What did happen to me? I don't have a clue but I better say something to that cat over there.*

"My humans put me out of their machine and left me here. I don't know why they did that, and I don't know where I am. Do you know where I am?"

I'm lost and don't know myself, thought Buster, but he answered back.

"You're, you're… you're somewhere, but I'm not sure where that is."

The dog's face and eyes drooped a bit and he said,

"Where's that?"

"It's…," Buster began his answer and then, realising he didn't know where he was either, he responded:

"It's somewhere," then he added as an afterthought:

"I don't know exactly where we are. I wish I did."

"Do you live around here?" asked the dog.

Buster hesitated. He wasn't sure he actually wanted to admit to the dog that he was lost. With all he had been through and his newfound health and vitality he didn't actually feel as lost as he once did. Now he just considered himself temporarily displaced. He was sure his home was close by, and he would return to it soon. But right now he had to say something. If he just blurted out that he was lost it would seem so final, as if he were going to be lost for the rest of his life.

Oh what the heck! I might as well own up to it. After all, who is this lost dog going to tell about my predicament? Kofi? Mecki? Don't I wish!

"I'm like you, I'm lost too, and I don't know where I am."

Thinking maybe this was some kind of animal abandonment location where unsatisfied humans dumped unwanted animals, the dog asked,

"Did your humans throw you out of their machine at this same spot?"

"No my humans did not throw me away!" Buster answered impatiently. "I became lost all by myself, and I'm trying to find my way back home."

Buster changed the subject.

"What kind of dog are you anyway? I've never seen a dog that looks like you."

"I'm a Beagle," he answered. "What kind of a cat are you?" he asked Buster.

Buster had never considered the question before. He was just a cat, so he answered: "I'm just an ordinary grey and white cat."

"What's your name?" the brown and white dog asked.

"My name is Buster and I live at Rainbow Farm with two other cats and two big dogs. Dogs much bigger than you," Buster said with a sound of pride in his voice. Then, his voice took a more sombre tone as he looked down at the ground and continued:

"But I'm lost."

"Oh," said Beagle with a puzzled look on his face. "So I'm not alone in this."

"I guess not," mumbled Buster.

"Listen, Beagle dog," Buster said, with renewed determination and authority in his voice, "The best thing for you to do is to stay close to the road and wait for humans to come by. One of them will probably pick you up, give you some food, and help you find a home."

"How long will that take?" asked the dog who sensed that if Buster was lost at least he had some idea of what to do and where to go. Beagle sensed he should listen to the cat and try to learn from him.

"I don't know," said Buster, "but it might take a while so just stand there so people driving by can see you. But be careful. Don't stand in the middle of the road because you could get run over."

No sooner had Buster finished cautioning the Beagle dog about the dangers of the road than a great noise began emanating from the top of the hill half a kilometre away. Turning to his right Buster saw a massive Thunder-junker carrying a heavy load, roaring down the hill.

"Look out, eh?" he yelled across the road to the dog called Beagle as the noise increased to a roar. "This one is doubly dangerous! Hide in the ditch behind you!"

Seconds later the great rolling monster flew by, stirring up a thick cloud of dust and shooting chunks of gravel from its wheels as it sped off in the distance bound for somewhere. Once it had passed Buster said,

"Listen Beagle, I really don't know what to do, but I suggest you stay where you are for now. It will be dark in a while, so you can't stay too close to the road after dark because you might get hit. Humans can't see well at night, that's why they have those bright things on the front of their Thunder-junkers.

"Thunder-junkers? I've never heard that before, cat."

"Their rolling contraptions, like the one that just went by. We call them Thunder-junkers."

"Oh," said the dog.

"Anyway, hide in the ditch after dark until tomorrow morning. Then maybe someone will rescue you. And listen, Beagle, one more thing. There are coyotes out here at night and they may be coming around so you've got to stop howling and making noise so they don't find you. Do you understand?"

"Yes. I understand," said Beagle. Then he added, using Buster's name for the first time,

"Buster, what are coyotes?"

Great Thundering Cats! thought Buster. *This poor dog really is lost!* Buster knew the dog was confused and afraid and he didn't want to frighten him, but for his own safety he had to warn him about coyotes.

"Coyotes are kind of like wild dogs. They're mean and hunt other animals like deer and rabbits to survive. They don't live in houses and they don't have humans to take care of them."

"Oh," said Beagle. Then he added,

"What are deer Buster?"

Buster started to answer and then thought better of it.

Bastet preserve me![2] *Where to begin?*

---

2 Originally associated with lions, Bastet was the name of one of several Egyptian cat deities, known from the Middle and New Kingdoms onwards. She was considered to be friendlier than the lion goddess Sehkmet.

"I can't explain," he said, and then added, "it's country stuff. If you're from the city you won't understand. Just remember, hide somewhere tonight and stay away from the coyotes. You'll hear them howling after sundown, so there is no way you can miss them."

By now it had been a while since he had eaten and he was getting hungry. He turned to leave and go back into the woods. Beagle sat on the edge of the gravel road wagging his tail with a concerned look on his face.

"Can I come with you, Buster?" asked Beagle.

"No, you will be in the way. I have to hunt. We cats are solitary hunters and we don't like to have other creatures around when we are looking for food."

"Hunt," said the little dog. "What does that mean, Buster?"

Once again Beagle's ignorance tried Buster's patience, but he stayed calm. With concern for the Beagle dog's safety he answered,

"I have to hunt little animals to get something to eat. It's called 'hunting.'"

"You eat little animals? Why don't you eat food from a box like dogs do? Don't cats have food in boxes like dogs?"

"Yes," said Buster whose patience was by now growing thinner with each question the dog asked.

"But out here I stay alive by eating little animals. First I have to sneak up on them and catch them with my claws," he said as he held up his two front paws and brandished his front pairs of claws towards the bewildered dog. From his seated position across the road Buster was not sure that the dog could see his claws or understand his gesture, but he did it anyway.

"You eat little animals Buster?" said the dog.

"Yes, I eat them, and that's why you can't come with me. You don't know how to hunt and you will make too much noise out there. I wouldn't be able to catch anything with you stomping around in the woods behind me."

"I'll be quiet Buster. I can be very quiet. At home when my humans told me to be quiet and not bark I could stay quiet all day until they came home at night with my food." It was then that Beagle realised he was getting hungry. He continued,

"I promise I'll be quiet. You won't even know I'm there. Please Buster don't leave me here, I'm afraid to be alone." Without answering Buster turned and walked down the steep bank of the roadbed towards the woods. It was hard to leave him, and it wasn't that Buster didn't feel sorry for him. He did. In fact he needed a companion, but now was not the time. He had to survive and he knew he could only do that on his own, and not with some greenhorn dog from the city who howled noisily when things went wrong. He had to hunt now, that was his priority, and he did not want to answer any more of the city dog's questions or explain things to him. He had his own problems to deal with. But he had barely made it to the base of the bank before Beagle broke rank and headed after Buster. As he reached the other side of the road he called out,

"I'll just stay behind you and won't get in the way."

Buster turned around and with a determined look on his face he yelled at the Beagle dog who stopped in his tracks a short distance away.

"Go away Beagle, you're a dog, I don't know you and I can't trust you. Dogs attack cats like me sometimes and I can't take any chances. So don't follow me! You understand? Don't follow me!"

"OK Buster cat, but just tell me why can't you trust me? I mean I don't understand, why?" said Beagle with bewilderment.

"Follow your 'inner dogness,' Beagle! You're a dog, Beagle, and dogs and cats don't get along, so don't follow me."

Despite Buster's warning Beagle did follow several hundred metres behind and although the grey cat did his best to ignore him Beagle ventured into the woods and fields, surprised and fascinated by his new surroundings. Beagle was hungry, and by now he missed his food bowl as much as he missed his humans and his condo-home. Beagle lost sight of Buster almost immediately and was soon wandering about aimlessly. He recognised nothing as he ambled through the trees and grasses, looking all around and sniffing in every direction, taking in the multitude of sights and smells. It was all new to him. Quite by accident, he circled back to the gravel road not far from the same spot where he had been abandoned earlier. Once it began to get dark he thought,

I guess I better do as the cat said and stay here out of sight until morning. As darkness closed the day, he settled down in some bushes close to the road, which was now the only thing left in his life that was familiar to him. Huddled in a ball and unable to sleep, he trembled from fear and passed a night filled with frightening and unfamiliar sounds.

With the dog somewhere behind him Buster was able to concentrate on his hunting. He caught a couple of mice and ate them, and occasionally he napped. He hunted through much of the night and heard no more noises from the Beagle dog.

I guess he finally followed my advice and decided to lie low, thought Buster.

That night, like every other night, visions of Juliette marched through his head, cutting his sleep into tiny snippets. He remembered the honeyed sounds that came out from her deep well of purrs, which drifted across fields and forests until she appeared in front of him.

How will I ever live without her? he thought, but then he scolded himself.

No. This is about surviving and finding my way home. I will live without her and I will find my way home! That is my priority; home is my single purpose in life.

Early that morning Buster moved back in the direction of the road to check on Beagle. He was hoping the dog had been picked up by someone. But he was still there huddled under some trees. When Beagle saw Buster he jumped up wagging his tail and said,

"Buster Cat! I'm so happy to see you!" The frightened dog explained that he had passed a terrifying night. He did indeed look frightened, but Buster noticed that he was unharmed. His tail continued to wag so vigorously it made his whole body thrash back and forth.

Poor guy, he must have had an awful night, thought Buster. *From the looks of him I can imagine how scared he must have been. He is indeed lucky the coyotes didn't find him,* he thought as he looked straight at the dog, but still wary and keeping his distance. Then Beagle said,

"I saw the coyotes last night Buster: at least that's what I think they were. A whole bunch of dog-looking critters," he continued. "They looked dirty and mean and un-kempt, and like you said they're wild and don't have any humans to take care of them. I heard them howling too. Hounds of Hades!" he exclaimed, looking down at the road and shaking his head. "They scared the faeces right out of me!"

The poor dog shat himself in fright, thought Buster.

"What eerie sounds they make; all that howling and yipping and barking. I thought Cerberus and his demon-dogs had been loosed on me. Maybe that's who they really are, eh? I tell you they scared me to death. I thought they were going to find me and make a meal out of me. A whole bunch of them came across the road over there in the middle of the night," he said as he motioned with his head to the left.

"They came right towards where I was hiding and then for some reason they veered off again and never did find me. Of course if they had found me I wouldn't be here talking to you right now would I?"

Beagle stayed on his side of the road, remembering that Buster didn't want him to get too close. But as he took a closer look at Buster he furrowed his eyebrows into triple pleats of skin over the tops of his eyes and he twisted his head to the left, producing a look of deep thought, as if his mind were working out some difficult problem which involved the use of a lot of unfamiliar mathematical equations. With their exchange of glances and greetings, Beagle had suddenly become aware of something he hadn't noticed before: despite their friendly, even cordial exchange of greetings, Buster continued to keep his distance as they spoke; never approaching him. He remembered that yesterday Buster said that he couldn't trust Beagle because dogs and cats were enemies and that sometimes dogs attacked cats. He realised he had probably been too upset to understand what Buster was trying to say, too distracted to understand just how afraid of him Buster really was. And yet, Buster had said that he lived in a place where they had dogs and everyone got on well.

How could that be? he thought. He didn't really understand anything except that Buster did not trust him.

That's why he's keeping his distance, he's afraid of me!

Beagle couldn't stand it anymore and he just blurted out: "Don't be afraid of me Buster! I won't hurt you!" He took a breath and continued. "Look, Buster," the dog said with a sigh of resignation, "I'm lost; I don't have any idea where I am, and I'm hungry. In fact I'm hungrier than I've ever been in my life. You said you were lost too so we should be friends and help each other out here and take care of each other. You said you know how to hunt and I'm just hungry and I want to find something to eat so show me how to hunt," he said beseechingly.

His reasoning was sound. If they were both in the same boat then why not join forces and help each other? It made perfect sense to Beagle. But not to Buster.

"Hungry? I know you're hungry. I know that," he repeated. "That's why I'm afraid of you. Why do you think I'm keeping my distance? It wouldn't take much for you to grab me, break my neck and eat me."

Beagle gasped! He was thunderstruck! "What! You're afraid I'll eat you? That's preposterous!" Beagle tried to comprehend what he had just heard.

Buster is afraid I will eat him! Eat him? The very idea was unimaginable to the brown and white dog.

How could Buster think I would eat a live cat?

A wall of silence fell across the road between them. On one side was Buster accusing Beagle of trying to lure him close enough to eat him, and on the opposite side was Beagle, a lost dog in need of a friend. They looked at each other for a minute and then Buster shouted out.

"Look Beagle, I think your best chance to be rescued is to stay here by the road and wait for someone to pick you up. If you wait long enough maybe even the lady from the animal shelter will come by and they will find you a home. Stay here."

This didn't make a lot of sense to Beagle. He answered: "If my chances are so good then why don't you wait here with me and we can both be rescued?" Buster was caught off guard for an instant, but shot right back,

"There's something you should understand Beagle. Humans rescue dogs, but not so much cats. We cats are naturally afraid of strangers and we don't get into those strange, stinky Thunder-junkers as easily as dogs do. Besides, you dogs are friendlier and more trusting than we cats. We're loners so people don't rescue us the way they do dogs. That's just the way it is."

Beagle stood by the side of the road not knowing how to respond. He looked down the dusty road surface, not seeing the gravel and dirt only a few centimetres from his eyes.

I really don't know anything about the world and I'm so naive that I'm a danger to myself, he thought in silent introspection, shaking his head.

Here I am, lost, standing by the side of a road I've never seen before, surrounded by forests and fields. I can't see a single house, or a single thing I know or recognise, and the only humans I see go by too fast to even notice me. To top it all off the only living creature I can communicate with thinks I'm going to eat him! I just can't figure this out. I need help, I really do.

Beagle just wanted to be Buster's friend, and would do anything the cat asked of him if he could just go with him and maybe find something to eat. When he looked up the cat was gone. He had disappeared, across the road somewhere. Back to the places the cat knew well and where he felt safe. For the second time in the span of a single day, Beagle had been abandoned, and once again he was overcome with grief. He wanted to throw himself on the ground and weep.

The last Buster saw of Beagle, he was staring at the road, lost in his own thoughts, and before the dog could pull himself together and look up again, Buster had disappeared. It was not easy to abandon the brown and white dog, but befriending him was too risky.

Stranger dogs were not like Sparky and Mecki. Stranger dogs were unstable, vicious and unreliable. Don't forget that, Buster scolded the part of him that kept whispering that it would be good to befriend the dog and travel together through the woods looking for a home.

§

Buster crouched down amidst some clumps of bushes just at the edge of the spruce and cedar forest, and listened to the high-pitched sounds of the mice as they chatted away to each other. He knew one was off to his left about four or five big pounces away; too far for an immediate attack, but maybe later. There were two others much closer on the right so he turned his attention to them. He listened a while longer and then calculated that with a single high leap over the tall grass stems he could come straight down on his unsuspecting prey. The great thing about the high leap was that it was noiseless, and for a brief instant he was a hunting cat transformed into a bird of prey, falling on his prey without making a sound and barely disturbing a single blade of grass. Buster gathered his feet under his belly, making a few last-second adjustments that would afford him the proper height and distance as he leapt. Then he shot a metre high into the air like a feline ballet dancer arcing across a rustic stage in front of an audience of crickets and leafhoppers, before landing on top of an unsuspecting field mouse. He was hungry that morning and dispensed with the foreplay. He grabbed the little creature by the head, clamped his jaws down on its cranium, and consumed him. Then he spat out the bitter-tasting gall bladder, licked his lips, and walked on through the forest.

§

An animal much larger than Buster was only a few paces behind him. It had been stalking him for several minutes while Buster had been concentrating on the mouse sounds in the grass. Realising he was in mortal danger he had to take evasive action! He looked up, saw a tree and sprang towards it with full force. It would take two big leaps to reach it, and he would need every bit of his feline springing power to make it without being grabbed from behind. He could sense the open mouth and long white canines of some cat-eater just millimetres away, and in an act of mortal desperation he made two bounding jumps for the tree, caught hold of its exterior bark, and clawed his way upwards. As his claws punctured the tree bark he heard a combination of snarls and shrieks from whatever animal was after him, hoping it was not a tree climber. He hurled himself up into the first set of low lying branches dreading the deep penetration of teeth in his back as some mouth clamp closed on him, pulling him back to the ground. But he had escaped; at least temporarily, and by the time he was high off the ground he knew his attacker was not in the tree with him. Buster spun his head around and looked down, and saw his predator below him. It was a 15-kilogram lynx: a tree climber!

Why isn't he coming after me? What's going on? he thought.

He heard the hissing and growling sounds of the death-animal below him mixed with the thuds of his heart banging away against the sides of his chest. The combination of his own cries and hisses mixed with the lynx sounds of his attacker. But there were other sounds too: ones that weren't made by the lynx. Canine sounds!

Canine sounds? How could that be? Am I being stalked by a dog or that big cat creature?

The canine creature wasn't stalking him, but he was sure making lots of noise. The canine sounds were coming from a small brown and white dog planted between the lynx and the base of the tree. It was a bark Buster had heard before.

"Beagle!" Buster shouted. It was Beagle! He was standing about a metre in front of the lynx making a canine cacophony that sent the tuft-eared lynx backing away from the base of the tree and towards the cover of the forest. Beagle had the upper hand of surprise on the lynx, and kept approaching while the feline backed further away. As the lynx had been concentrating on stalking the cat in front of him, the dog had been behind, stalking him. He had never even considered that he was the 'stalkee' instead of the 'stalker,' and even though the dog wasn't huge, the lynx had lost control of the situation and was on the defensive.

Where had this dog come from anyway, thought the lynx?

The lynx did not know that the little brown and white dog with his hackles raised and barred white teeth was a rookie, a dog with no forest experience. He did not know that the canine making all the noise was a condo dog, and that until a couple of days ago he had never even seen a wild animal, let alone confronted one. Now this amateur was making violent noises directly in the face of a formidable forest carnivore. The lynx did not realise that had he stood his ground and made a few menacing gestures, the dog would have turned tail and run. But Beagle had nothing to lose by his tough-guy bluff. He was half-starved and had been frightened out of his wits on a dozen occasions since he had last seen Buster. Over the past two days and nights he had hidden in a rock cleft shaking like a leaf, trying not to give off the smell of fear that would give him away to predators. He was so frightened his hair fell out in big tufts while lean and sinewy coyotes sniffed around the hole where he cowered. More than once he thought the very next breath he took would be his last, and at any instant a gang of his blood-eating cousins would be gorging themselves on his tender condo-dog flesh.

But they did not detect Beagle's smells; they moved on. The following night he had been cowed by the big electrical storm that had roared and clapped right over his head, shooting fire from the skies and conjuring illuminated figures that came out of the cracks in the trees and rocks and moved in concert with the electric discharges. He had never actually been out-of-doors in a real thunder storm before. He could only remember hearing such things while cowering on his cushion inside his humans' dwelling while they offered words of encouragement to their poor, frightened little pet. How silly he had been then to think that inside his humans' shelter he had ever been in any real danger. Out here he was in danger! There were no walls to protect him, and no humans to come to his aid. Out here terror was the norm, the status quo; security and peace of mind were the exception. As the storm roared and cracked around him, he believed that he had gone deaf and would never hear again. It was only the next morning, when he heard some robins singing, that he realised his world had not been rendered soundless by the previous night's thunderclaps. That morning, while his stomach growled its discontent, he breathed a sigh of relief knowing that although he was two days hungry, at least he would not spend whatever time he had left on earth unable to hear the sounds of his attackers. To quell the hunger battle raging in his stomach he ate carrion. He found the remains of a mostly-eaten turkey left by the coyotes. He fell on the carcass with the kind of appetite only the starving possess. The kind of hunger that causes little dogs to eat week-old, desiccated meat and bones that had been worked over by everyone in the food chain, from foxes and vultures to maggots, and which hunger had transformed into a fine gourmet meal in an upscale doggy restaurant. It was delicious!

§

During his second night, as the sky erupted fire and thunder and he was peering out of his hole with illuminated coyotes sniffing the ground nearby, he realised:

If I'm ever going to survive out here for more than a day or two, I will have to get tough, and get tough fast. I'll either be tough or I'll be dead.

Despite the fear, the hunger and the cracked and bleeding paws, he managed to stay fairly close to Buster, keeping up the pace in the continuously changing terrain. All along he had hoped to catch up with him and try once again to convince the cat to let him travel with him. Now, still facing the lynx, Beagle hung on in his tough-dog stance, making all the noises he could possibly muster from a set of vocal cords that had been scolded to remain quiet, to not disturb people or interrupt the sounds coming from the talking box in the living room. As for his humans, the people who abandoned him, he came to the realisation that he had never really been part of their family.

May Cerberus cast them into the pit of Hades!, he snarled. *I'll make every sound I want!* And, facing the lynx, from his hound-mouth he made every sound he had been forbidden to make in his condo life. Now he made the sounds of the wild!

Once he was aware of the situation, Buster turned up his cat volume, and made as if he too were in attack mode as he worked his way tail-first down the tree to join the standoff. It wasn't long before the duet of screams, barks, and hisses overwhelmed the lynx, which opted for caution instead of *catchismo* and turned and ran into the forest. For a few seconds Buster was completely dumbfounded. Now it was his turn to be confused. It was his turn to be on the outside of events. It was his turn to acknowledge Beagle's act of heroism.

"Beagle!" he cried. "It's you!"

"Yes! Yes! It's me! It's me!" he answered, looking at Buster, his tail wagging as it never had before. Beagle had put his life on the line to save Buster and win his trust and friendship, and any fears Buster had about the dog vanished when he saw Beagle driving the lynx away toward the forest. He scampered over and threw himself against the dog's side, rubbing against him with happiness. For several minutes they bumped against each other in a display of mutual joy and relief. This was the first good thing that had happened to Beagle since he had been abandoned, and only the second since Buster had fallen from the window ledge at Bedlam Barn. From that time on theirs was a friendship forged out of hunger, fear and the need for animal companionship, and feeling Buster's grey fur rub against him, Beagle's heart grew lighter and the weight of rejection was lifted. Maybe he had lost his former life, but he had done something that was canine brave, something that only a few days earlier would have been unthinkable for a dog from the upscale *Quartier chic* district of Montreal. He had faced down a predator and passed his rite de passage with high marks.

"How long have you been following me Beagle?"

"I've been following you all along. Ever since we last parted company and you headed off into the woods a couple of days ago. I've been following you but keeping my distance so you wouldn't be distracted while you hunted. I knew that if I didn't follow you I would die by the side of the road or in the woods somewhere."

"Have you had anything to eat?" Buster inquired.

Beagle explained.

"I haven't had much, but after the coyotes left I found what they had been eating: a big dead bird of some kind. They had left some of it uneaten and I managed to clean it off down to the bones. It tasted delicious. Then I ate the bones too, and discovered that smashing bones between my teeth is a joyous experience. Before that dead bird I had never really had the chance to just sit down somewhere with a bunch of bones and gnaw away on them. It was very satisfying. I vomited up a lot of the bones, but I just ate them again and the second time they stayed down."

"You know what Buster?" he continued, tilting his head to one side. "I think I'm going to enjoy being a carnivore for the first time in my life. Anyway, the dead bird meat was dry and stringy, and it had a few of those little white, squirmy bugs on it as well so I guess it must have been pretty old. Anyway, the dead bird tasted really good. I had never eaten anything like that before, especially meat picked over by coyotes. But even with their slime and stink on it, the meat and bones and even the feathers tasted good. I haven't eaten anything since then. I wish I had some more right now." He paused, sat down on his haunches to scratch himself, and then continued.

"At first I thought it was really disgusting. The only thing I could compare it too was when I was a puppy and used to freak out my humans by vomiting my puppy chow all over the carpet. They would think I was really sick, or maybe even dying. Then, I would eat my own vomit, and look up at them and try to lick their faces. They never wanted me to do that. They seemed to think that eating recycled vomit was disgusting. But you know, I don't think they really understood. For a dog, your own vomit can be really delicious and you don't want to waste it, eh?"

Buster was having some difficulty trying to process what the dog had just said. Like Beagle's humans, for Buster the whole idea of eating one's vomit was indeed disgusting. Cats rarely eat anything that has spent any time in their own stomachs and then had been expelled, and they certainly didn't eat anything more than once. If it did come back up it stayed where it was deposited. Buster didn't know what to make of the dog's candid intestinal confession. But then, remembering his own experiences with the Rainbow Farm dogs and some of their eating habits, he gave one of his little chirps of acknowledgement and decided not to comment further on the pros and cons of vomit consumption. He changed the subject:

"OK, our first job is to find you something to eat. The next mouse I catch is yours. Maybe I can even teach you how to catch your own mousies, eh?" Beagle gave him a puzzled look, and Buster sensed his confusion so he continued trying to explain.

"Don't worry Beagle dogs do it all the time. Back at Rainbow Farm we have a dog named Sparky, and when he catches a mouse he pulls its skin off with his teeth, spits it out, and then eats the rest in one bite."

Beagle turned his head slightly as if he hadn't heard Buster correctly.

"He pulls their skin off with his teeth?"

"Yeah," said the grey and white cat. "He says that's the way he likes his mice, and he can do it really fast too. When he gets one of those little guys on the ground you should see him go!"

"Pulls their skin off?" Beagle said once again, dumbfounded by the oddities of his new and bewildering way of life.

"Why would he do that?" he said. "I mean, how do you skin a mouse?" he questioned before admitting, "Actually Buster, I'm not even sure what a mouse is." He searched his mind for an image, but came up with nothing.

Buster explained:

"Mice are little animals that are everywhere out here, and just about everyone I know eats them. I eat three or four a day: sometimes more. But I don't skin them. I just eat them whole, and they're easy to catch and they taste great! You'll see Beagle."

"OK," answered Beagle, and then after a pause, he thought to himself.

Skinning a mouse? Why would anyone do that? I wonder how they do that?

He reflected for a moment, trying to shake off his puzzlement, and shook his head causing his ears to snap and his flank muscles to vibrate the way water dogs do when they shake off excess water. Once his head cleared he looked at Buster and said,

"Alright, I'm ready to learn Buster, just show me what to do and I'll do it."

With the puppy vomit and the mouse-skinning episodes out of the way, the two of them set off through the woods in search of food. As the sun rose higher they passed the morning hours following the well-worn deer paths in the direction of several large natural clearings and farm meadows on the south side of Beaver Mountain.

Buster was a natural mouse hunter so he never went hungry, but in the beginning it was more difficult for Beagle. But, as things worked out, the dog did manage to get enough to eat most days, and over the next few weeks he learned the fine points of hunting and scavenging. With Buster sharing his knowledge of hunting the pair caught mice and rats and other ground-crawlers every day, while together they perfected their scavenging abilities among the numerous garbage cans and discarded fast food containers stacked neatly in front of houses and cottages along the lanes and narrow roads in the area. Buster wasn't big enough to turn over garbage cans by himself, but it didn't take long before Beagle became an expert 'tipper' who, with a few paw gestures, could scatter a cornucopia of dog and cat eatables on the ground in front of them. And if their pickings were sparse on some days they could always supplement their diets with both skinned and unskinned mice.

§

Beagle began to detect something partially hidden in the trees that he thought might be a human habitation. In his former condo-life he had never paid too much attention to smells other than the smell of his humans, his bed in the laundry room, and the cushion he lay on while the man and woman stared at the illuminated box-like contraption they watched intently every evening. He recalled that as they sat there staring at the box he could hear someone inside the box making human sounds attempting to communicate with them. Sometimes the voice inside the box made them laugh, sometimes the voice made them angry. Sometimes they fell asleep in front of it and they would wake up in the wee hours of the night covered in sleep. Sometimes the voice in the box commanded his humans to copulate and following the box's orders they would remove their clothes and thrash about together on the couch or on the floor while the voice in the box spoke to them.

No doubt the box is giving them procedural instructions, Beagle thought.

At the time Beagle had been curious why the box commanded them to engage in mating activities on some nights, but not others. Was there a schedule for these activities that the box demanded they follow, or was there some other reason that their couplings happened when they did? He never did figure that one out, and now that he was in the wilderness it really didn't matter. But there was a reason why he was thinking about the box now. When the box began making human noises it gave off a certain odour that he could detect. His humans did not seem to be able to smell the box odour, but dogs could, and now, as they walked through the forest, Beagle smelled the unmistakable odour of a talking box.

There must be one around somewhere close by, he thought. Since he had been in the wild he had begun detecting many different smells—smells he had never encountered before, odours that had never passed into his long nose to be sifted and analysed. Now he could smell the acrid odour of coyotes, and the lightly-scented grassy smell of deer droppings. He was surprised to discover that not only could he smell bird droppings, he could even smell their nests and their feathers; and of course, he could smell freshly-killed meat. Even though he had only been on his own for a few days, he had learned much about smells in that short time. Now he was picking up the smells of a talking box, and that meant there must be humans nearby.

It was late August, and by this time weekenders and summer vacationers were in every cottage and farm house along the narrow dirt road called Chemin Smith. And where there were humans, there was food, so every racoon, rat, and raven in the region was on the prowl for something to eat. The forest animals knew that a great banquet provided by the humans began in late May on Queen Victoria Day and lasted at least until early October. Unlike in urban areas, big metal garbage dumpsters weren't allowed so the locals used smaller plastic or metal cans, which could be tipped or jimmied by strays and forest critters and made to yield their contents. This was the good time for the animals. There was plenty of natural food growing in the fields and on the trees, and plenty of human food as well. To the animals it was clear that the humans put the food out to show their love and appreciation for the local wildlife.

"I'm a little worried about eating human food in those big cans Buster," said Beagle when they started making garbage raids.

"Don't worry Beagle. The only reason the humans put their food out by the side of the road is so we can eat it. Otherwise they would do something else with it. You know what I mean? Don't worry Beagle; they want us to have all this stuff."

"Wow, that's amazing when you think about it, eh?" said Beagle as the pair of them trotted down a gravel pathway between a collection of summer cottages.

"I smell food, Buster," Beagle said as they walked along.

"Yes, I think I'm beginning to smell it too, but I know that you usually smell things before I do. You dogs have really good noses," he commented.

"Yeah," answered Beagle, paying less attention to Buster and more attention to sniffing out the food.

In his role as leader and expert, Buster cautioned Beagle,

"There must be a garbage can around here somewhere, so keep your eyes open and stay alert. And listen, Beagle, since you're a rookie you should always remember that if one of us smells food that means every other critter in the neighbourhood smells it too, you understand? There are some pretty mean characters around here, and sooner or later they're going congregate around garbage cans. You got that?"

"Yeah, OK", answered Beagle as he slipped off to his left and ducked under the bottom branches of a tall cedar hedge. As if his nose had suddenly taken control of his limbs, Beagle followed the smells seeping through the thick green branches of the hedge from somewhere on the other side. Once he smelled food he forgot he was with a cat named Buster. Food was the only thing that mattered. Beagle looked across the inner yard of a family summer home with a nicely groomed garden with a large pool of water off to one side. There were trees and flowers everywhere.

This place looks really nice, thought Beagle.

Somewhere in the distance he could hear Buster chirping to him. He was supposed to answer back but he didn't; the smell of the food drowned out the cat sounds. His nose caught something much more interesting than cat noises. A dozen paces away was a large, heavily laden eating surface covered with plates and bowls and the metal things humans used to manipulate their food and stuff it into their mouths.

I knew back there while we were walking along I smelled a talking box somewhere and it's here; and I can hear it too.

Incredibly, way out here in the country, he recognized the voices he was hearing from the box. They were the same voices his city humans listened to as well. He started to wonder if the voice would suddenly command a pair of humans somewhere to begin mating, but he soon forgot about that since it was the food that grabbed his attention.

With no thought of Buster, he ran straight for the table. From the ground he could see it was covered with piles of food, and he was overwhelmed by the smells of sliced meat, fresh garlic bread, piping-hot pizza and what looked like a whole bird of some kind nicely browned and ready to eat.

It looks like the bird I ate that one time a while back except its brown and smells better.

It did look more appetising than the dead turkey, and the coyotes and foxes had not gotten to it yet so it had a lot more meat on it. Mouth dripping with saliva Beagle leapt up on a chair and then on to the table. He looked around in amazement at the mesa of food spread out before him. Where to begin? He lowered his head into a plate of meat slabs, clamped down on some sliced cold cuts and gulped them down.

Delicious; absolutely delicious! Hey, I didn't tell Buster about this. I better let him know where I am. I don't want to be impolite now do I? he thought, as he dipped his snout into the potato salad.

"Hey Buster, I'm over here, and the chow is great. Come and join me!" he barked.

I'm sure he won't mind if I start without him.

Buster was not the only one who heard Beagle's chow-cry. Three generations of the Stanhope family, most of them in the kitchen or in the front room seated in front of the talking box, heard him as well. Beagle's barking shifted the family's attention to the picnic table, and in an instant eight pairs of eyes were fixed on a brown and white dog standing in the middle of their table, gulping down their food.

"Hey! Hey! Get off the table you little thief!" cried grandma Stanhope.

"Kill the little bastard!" cried uncle Avunculus.

When the Stanhopes looked out the kitchen window and saw Beagle standing right in the middle of their Sunday afternoon meal gulping down chunks of food their mouths dropped, and they began screaming and waving their arms and hands while running for the back door.

"Bruno! Bruno!" yelled a young boy seeing his pizza in distress.

"Go get 'em boy. Get 'em!"

Bruno, the family's German shepherd, was supposed to be standing guard over the food, but instead had been in the kitchen begging for scraps. Jumping from beggar back into his role as guard dog Bruno shot out of the door with murder in his eyes, emitting the kinds of barks and snarls he had perfected after many years of scaring mailmen and delivery boys. The entire family joined him yelling and shouting as they ran out the door behind him. For a brief instant, before they broke through the screen door like a swarm of angry hornets, Beagle stood like a conqueror over a defeated army with one front paw planted on the roast turkey, and his head thrown back in triumph while clumps of pizza dangled from his mouth. But his moment of glory was cut short as Bruno charged out the door at full speed heading for the table. Leaping up and on to the table was not such an easy task. Bruno was a big dog, strong and powerful, but ungainly in small spaces. Fired by anger and guilt, as he leapt up on the table he had not taken into account the items on the table top. Landing in the macaroni and cheese dish, and sliding on a pile of plates, he slid across the table and fell off on the other side.

Jumping Cerberus! This is embarrassing, the big dog chided himself.

In mid-pizza gulp Beagle's ears went vertical, and his eyes grew to the size of pepperoni slices when he saw a snarling canine land on one end of the table, slide by in front of him and then, as he tried to apply the brakes, fall off the other end. Beagle took this as his cue to get out of town. He grabbed a mouthful of sausages and leapt from the table, making a run for the safety of the hedge. As he tore right through the cedars he barked,

"Run Buster, run! Buster run!"

That was all he had time to say, but it was enough to warn the Buster standing on the opposite side of the hedge. The grey and white cat came out of the scrape unharmed. He had heard the dog barking even before Beagle did and figured that Beagle had gotten himself in trouble.

Too late now, he thought, as he ran for cover.

Buster found the nearest tree and in seconds was high off the ground as the big dog shot past below not even looking up.

I love being a cat, thought Buster. *Poor Beagle is still down there on the ground trying to outrun that big dog.*

"Run Beagle, run!" he cried out into the afternoon air. "I'll find you later! Just run!"

Although he had shown himself to be exceedingly brave in his lynx confrontation, Beagle had never confronted another dog before in any kind of serious bite-'em-and-throw-'em-on-the-ground type of dogfight. Not once had he been forced to defend his humans from aggressors, or his territory against intruders. As a condo dog he had led a life as little more than a doggy-toy for his humans. Out here, when he got into trouble there was no one to protect him. As the brown and white dog tried to squeeze through the lower branches of the cedar hedge his rear end was completely exposed: his two hind legs, his tail and the little brown spot in the middle, all made a perfect target for Bruno's big teeth. As Beagle worked his way between the cedar trees, he heard a dog yelping in pain somewhere and realised it was him. Bruno had sunk his teeth into Beagle's rump. Luckily, he was able to break free and get through the hedge and out the other side. Bruno was too big to fit through, and had to make a detour around it, and that gave Beagle just enough time to get away.

Sometimes small was good, he thought as he made his escape across the road into the trees. Once he had put some distance between himself and Bruno, he noticed his rear-end hurt and when he reached back to lick himself he saw several nasty puncture holes and some tear marks in his skin.

Wow, those are big holes and they hurt. Good thing he didn't catch me or he would have torn my hinders off, he thought.

After a few minutes he stopped and licked his wounds again. *I did a really stupid thing by barking like that. If I had been smarter I could have had enough food to last me for a couple of days and some for Buster too. Instead I acted like the dumb rookie that I am. Buster must be furious with me and now I don't even know where he is. In fact, once again, I don't even know where I am.*

He continued scolding himself. *I acted like an idiot, that's for sure. Oh well, no sense just sitting here with a sore butt and beating myself up. I better start looking for Buster.*

§

"Hey! Are you OK Beagle?"

"Oh! Buster! You scared me. I thought you were that big dog. Yeah, I'm OK, just a couple of bites in my rear end. Listen I'm really sorry for doing such a dumb thing and nearly getting us both eaten like that." He wanted to continue, but Buster put up his paw and stopped him.

"Listen Beagle, let's just learn from this and move on and be smarter next time, OK? From now on we work as a team and we look out for each other. If we don't the next time one of us might really get hurt, OK?"

"Right! I hear you Buster."

Buster saw no point in dwelling on rookie's *faux pas*. He had certainly made his own mistakes and wasn't about to start criticising Beagle for his. They had to find food and survive, so they might as well get on with it. That suited Beagle just fine. He shook his ears, scratched his head and voiced his agreement.

§

At night the smells of human food were everywhere calling out to animals both large and small: *Come and get it!*

Everybody in the forest, from mice and rats to racoons, lynx, coyotes, wild dogs, country cats, and vacationing city cats, responded to the siren smell of discarded human food. Over the next few weeks, as one warm day followed another, Buster and Beagle ate well, moving from one garbage can to another while staying out of harm's way. As each day passed they learned how to identify the different types of garbage cans and were able to determine which ones were easy to break into and which ones required special entry techniques. One night they located a lidded plastic garbage can in front of a country home that was particularly promising. Though the container lid was tightly sealed a broad spectrum of smells were being broadcast from it even before they opened it. They cased the area to make sure there were no Brunos, then they walked around the container, examining it and sizing it up before carrying out their raid. Beagle placed his front feet on the on the plastic receptacle and turned it over. According to plan the lid detached and the contents spilled out scattering a vast garbage cornucopia. It was as if someone had emptied out their refrigerator and their pantry. Spilled out on the ground was a large half-eaten meat loaf, most of a chicken carcass, a whole baguette, a box of crackers, and an assortment of and meat slices the humans didn't want to be bothered with. The cat and dog dined on the chicken, split the meat, and Beagle licked up the contents of several soft drink cans.

"Hey this stuff really tastes sweet," said Beagle as he licked his lips.

"Stick your paw on this end of the bottle," suggested Buster. "It will make more of it come out." Sure enough it did, as Beagle tipped the neck of the green bottle and ended up drinking most of the Coaticook Cola, the local, fizzy favourite. He belched his satisfaction and the two of them roared with laughter.

"Don't you want some of this, Buster? It's delicious," he said. "Try some," he motioned to Buster.

"No thanks," said the cat.

"We cats can't taste sugar and so we have no attraction to sweet things, you dogs tell us taste really good. It wouldn't taste like anything special to me, so I just prefer water instead. You go ahead and drink your fill."

Beagle stopped making dog sounds. His eyes moved slightly to the left of Buster's face and focused on something behind him. Buster sensed trouble, and looking directly at Beagle he whispered,

"What is it?"

"Bandits, just behind you and over your left shoulder; don't look back," he hissed as if by turning around the mother racoon might think that the cat and dog were spoiling for a fight. The mother and her pups were just behind them and Beagle didn't want to set off some instinctual attack mechanism in the big female who might feel the need to attack in order to protect her young. Beagle assessed the situation and gave a low, but very clear command in an even and steady voice.

"Walk slowly towards me," he said barely above a whisper while keeping his eyes on the intruder. He continued:

"Check the escape routes in front of you. We have a whole family of visitors."

"How many?" inquired a worried Buster, without turning around. "Five, maybe six. It seems they want to join us for dinner without a formal invitation. They're funny that way, always showing up uninvited, and never wanting to share with anyone else. We had better vacate the premises."

Cats are no match for 'racks' and always defer to them, and Beagle was too small to fight off the big female. Racoons are intelligent and tough fighters equipped with grasping, hand-like paws, sharp claws and a mouthful of canine-like teeth. Just about every farm or ranch in the region had a story about racoons injuring dogs in fights. Buster had previously instructed Beagle about the danger racoons posed and he wanted no part of a confrontation: just a quick exit. It didn't matter anyway since they had eaten their fill and could retire for the night.

Racoons are resourceful forest dwellers who can live successfully either in the wild without ever seeing a human, or surrounded by humans in crowded cities exploiting urban food sources, and raising their families. Racoons know everything from opening garbage cans to dodging cars, bicycles and human traffic, and they do it the same way they avoid predators in the wild. Cities are full of racoons who have managed to adapt to urban situations with great success, but unlike dogs and cats, racoons do not render any services to humans. At no time in the past have they ever assisted with the hunt, or herded sheep and goats like dogs, and they never protected grain supplies from rodents the way cats have always done. They're just good at adapting to almost any environment in which they find themselves.

"Come on Buster," he said, slowly backing away. "Let's get out of here." They did just that, slipping into the cover of some nearby trees and soon they were part of the night-time decor. That night they slept well with full stomachs in a little patch of grass they had been using for nearly a week. The next day they continued their routine of hunting live game in the day-time, sometimes catching young turkeys or rabbits, sometimes getting mice, which by now Beagle had learned how to skin though he preferred to eat them with their skins still attached. At night they worked the garbage cans and food boxes along the road, and with Buster's night vision and Beagle's keen sense of smell they made a great food procurement team. For nearly the entire month of September they managed to live quite well, sharing meals and adventures and cementing their canine-feline friendship more securely each day.

That night as Buster lay in the grass listening for prey, and occasionally cat-napping, he thought about Juliette. As his eyes closed and he stepped across the chasm of consciousness into his dream world he could picture the beautiful female running through the fields between the grazing horses her coat smelling of lavender and her breath of fresh mouse. As his dreams unfurled the two cats would lick and groom themselves until they fell asleep entangled in each other's necks and legs while the kittens played in and out of the box.

§

As the first rays of sunlight touched the tops of the white pines, leaving their trunks and lower branches in the early morning shadows, brother Gregorios Kandiliotis began chanting the centuries-old words of the morning mass on this warm Sunday in late September. On this day, his brother priests in other parts of the world pronounced the same words and chanted the same liturgies, with their faces raised towards finely crafted altars within the sanctified walls of structures illuminated through clerestory windows and the lattice-work of coloured glass projecting patterns of red, blue and yellow on marble and granite floors and walls. But unlike them, the open-air plan of Brother Gregorios' 'Forest Church' had neither walls nor windows, yet its floor plan followed the traditional cruciform style of Christian architecture. Far away, his colleagues' churches received crowds of faithful worshippers for Sunday's service while during the week they dealt with the problems of the faithful and dispensed their priestly blessings. Within consecrated walls they handled the day-to-day church operations, while outside they waited at the bedsides of sick and ailing parishioners as they sweated out the pains of birth, medical procedures, and death. For those who did not survive they offered the comfort of well-rehearsed words that priests always find to explain away the deaths of the too young, or use to soothe the passing of loved ones who didn't make it through their latest surgical interventions. Brother Gregorios rarely carried out such tasks since his unofficial church was situated deep in the heart of an old-growth forest fifteen kilometres south of Smith's Landing. Unlike his colleagues, his church was not built by human hands, and because it wasn't roofed over or shaped like the traditional be-steepled structures; essentially, because everything in it was natural, some who worshipped there, believed it was created by the Christian God. For others it was the handiwork of some ill-defined spiritual force like Mother Nature. Although Brother Gregorios had never attempted to convince church authorities to officially recognise his Forest Church as a true sacred site, its location alone made it holy ground for the people who worshipped there. As far as they were concerned, the site was duly consecrated, regardless of whether some far-off church bigwigs thought so or not.

Before he found it, Brother Gregorios had thought about establishing a church in the area using one of the abandoned Protestant or Roman Catholic structures which dotted the region. But after discovering the altar stone so magnificently placed between towering rows of hemlocks and pines, he knew this would be the site of his church. In the beginning, as he chanted liturgies and recited church words he would be joined only by some of the locals. A mother deer and her fawn staring at him as he said the *Our Father*; a moose grazing on the tender shoots at the far end of the nave as he lit the censor and waved it about. Then, of course, there were always the ubiquitous winged choristers flitting about in the clerestory branches, singing their hearts out in an attempt to get God's attention. He knew the place was holy, and he knew his God was there. During that first summer Brother Gregorios would stand alone, the only human in attendance, surrounded by his congregation of tall, wooden worshippers, always eager to hear the words of his Sunday homilies as they mingled with the breezes in the upper branches. The fact that it wasn't well known to the community didn't bother him: he believed that once people heard about it they would come. He was right; by the end of that initial summer they did come.

The first attendees were mostly family members out for a visit from Montreal, or hippies and back-to-the-landers who stumbled upon the Forest Church while out walking in a marijuana haze.

Over the past decade word had spread of the wonderful natural church located somewhere off an old rutted logging road near the summit of Beaver Mountain. As its reputation spread more local people began attending. Most of them only came to services once or twice a year during the summer months when it was warm and welcoming, or in October, around Thanksgiving, as the leaves were turning and the forest was awash in colour. On those days there might be more than one hundred people sitting on rows of split-log benches. For this year's summer solstice service a crowd of two hundred showed up.

The centrepiece of Brother Gregorios' church was the altar stone: a three-metre long mass of grey granite that lay flat on the forest floor right at the transept.

It must have been God himself who placed the stone there so strategically, he thought when he first saw it. *How else could it have been placed so perfectly?*

He recognised its beauty the first time he caught sight of it 20 years earlier while out on one of his spiritual wanderings in the heavily wooded climax forest. When he saw it lying at the crossing point of two rows of trees running at right angles he felt extremely close to God and was moved to consecrate the stone in its holy setting. Such a place must be the *omphalos,* the navel of the earth, and the place where humans and gods were joined in spiritual matrimony. Moved by the sacredness of the place he knelt down and laid the bouquet of yellow and white flowers he had picked earlier that morning on the great stone. Then he took out his wine flask and poured some of the red liquid into a cup-shaped impression in the centre of the great stone. He prayed for a long time and explained to God that after years of wandering he had finally received His message to consecrate this holy ground, and he could now begin holding services among the trees in accordance with the church calendar.

The walls of the Forest Church consisted of century-old white pines and hemlocks. Its stained glass windows were fashioned by the long beams of early morning sunlight that poured through the upper branches, the kind of light that can only be produced when the sun first rises and when, for an instant, its rays pierce the low-lying air colliding with the dust particles and drops of water vapour held in suspension near the horizon. The airborne particles bend the sun's light towards the red end of the spectrum, creating the pink and orange sunrises people love to paint and photograph. On this particular morning, as Buster and Beagle looked out from the cover of some fallen trees, the sun's fiery head had just peeked around the edge of the earth, and as its orange light became caught in the high branches of the tree pillars it illuminated the billions of tiny dust motes floating about in the air, turning them into microscopic angels drifting between the boughs. The effect was like the biblical light rays children used to see in the old printed Sunday school lessons from days gone by, before God went digital.

On this particular morning about 50 people sat facing towards the east with the rising sunlight streaming in overhead. With his hands raised towards the heavens, as the light touched the tree tops, Brother Gregorios opened his mouth and the *introit* of the Sunday mass rang out through the forest carried by the man's fine baritone voice. As he stopped to take a breath, his musical words were answered by the chattering of a red squirrel from somewhere in the wooden half-circle of the apse. His voice was rich-toned and honey-coloured, much like the skin of his face set off by his black, well-trimmed beard. After the last echo of his voice had vanished into the trees he took a wooden match from the pocket of his robe, and scratched it across the surface of the altar, and a bright orange flame flared to life. When the flame had settled on the matchstick he ignited a brass censor overflowing with antique spices. As the aromas ascended he proceeded with the well-practiced movements and motions of the holy office. Occasionally he would pause and raise some sacred article he had placed on the altar, and touch it to his forehead or make the sign of the cross over it. At one point he kissed a large, heavy, bronze crucifix he held up with both of his hands before he placed it upright into a stand on the altar. Next, he picked up a sacred book of prayer whose dark exterior patina revealed that it was very ancient and had most certainly been touched by holy hands.

§

Brother Gregorios had been ordained as a priest in the church after spending years in a seminary completing his studies. If he had wished, he could have had a fine church just about anywhere in Canada, but unlike his priestly peers, he had no church and no congregation. Brother Gregorios was not a traditional priest. Pillars of cement reaching to the sky, air-choking machines, and crowds of bipedal ants negated his sense of the spiritual, amidst the bluster of the klaxon calls of progress. He was a country person, and it was in nature that he heard the call of the divine; it was in nature that he felt closest to his god. Instead of preparing Sunday sermons and teaching people how to worship the god he learned about in the seminary, he lived alone in the woods at the end of a narrow dirt road that led to the summit of Beaver Mountain on its way to the village of Saint-Felix-de-Mont-Castor, a hamlet situated a few kilometres north of the kennel where Buster's misadventures had begun months earlier.

Baptised Gregorios, he was a friendly and good-natured man who appreciated a good joke and never missed an opportunity to laugh. Years earlier he had left Montreal and moved to the Estrie region where he purchased a small house on a dirt road in the woods. Although a newcomer, he fit quite nicely in the community of grain farmers, cattle-raisers, and *nouveaux campagnards*. One day, by mistake, someone called him Brother Gregarious instead of Brother Gregorios and the name stuck. It wasn't long until just about everyone referred to him as Brother Gregarious. Those who didn't know what the word meant assumed that Gregarious was his real name and used it as they would use any other name that was somewhat out of the ordinary, like Odelion or Arlie. The renamed Brother Gregarious accepted these onomastic irregularities, and adopted his new name with a smile, and was never the worse for it. In fact, he was very comfortable in the Tomifobia River Valley, and as long as people accepted him into the community little else mattered.

Gregarious could often be seen wandering the roads and forest pathways in the area around Abenaki Falls or on the road to Beaver Mountain, or up towards Saint-Felix, dressed in a full-length black robe with a band of thick white trim along the edges. His monk's outfit was topped with a large hood that usually hung down the back between his shoulders. It only saw service in cold or windy conditions. On such days, hooded and with his walking stick in hand, Brother Gregarious appeared to be an errant medieval monk propelled into the modern world by some Gothic time machine.

On that orange and red dawn, as Brother Gregarious performed Sunday mass, Buster and Beagle looked out from their hiding place unable to fathom what the humans were up to. Like so many domestic animals that lived with humans, they knew that the tall bipeds were capable of odd forms of behaviour, but neither of them could remember their humans ever acting like the man who raised his head upwards, and sang to the treetops and the clouds while a group of his fellow humans looked on. But there was one thing both of them did understand as they watched the proceedings unfold: it was clear the man in the black robe didn't look mean. On the contrary, he looked like a very nice human.

§

Brother Gregarious pronounced his final words, waved his hands and arms about making church gestures, and then things came to an end. The people rose and exchanged words with each other and with their forest priest. It appeared that most of them knew the Forest Church and Brother Gregarious. They shook hands, slapped backs and made the mouth-noises. Finally, as the sun cleared the tree tops, the worshippers headed down the forest path. After everyone had left Gregarious began to gather up his things. He was unaware he was being watched by a grey and white cat and a brown and white Beagle dog.

"Beagle," whispered Buster, while looking just slightly over his left shoulder in Beagle's direction, but still keeping an eye on the priest.

"He looks like a really nice human," he said with the confidence of someone who had done a thorough background check.

"You should go to him and maybe he will adopt you and give you a home," he whispered. With no more knowledge about the man than Buster, Beagle nodded his head in agreement.

"I think you're right Buster," whispered Beagle, as he watched the be-robed man. "I like him and I like the way he looks. He doesn't look mean or anything like that." Then, as a kind of afterthought, he added:

"May the Cynics protect us! I sure don't want to end up with a Beagle-beater! But I think he might be nice, and I know I have to do something. I can't just stay out here in the woods eating turkeys and dumpster food for the rest of my life. And I know I wouldn't make a very good wild dog anyway. I doubt a wild dog pack would even let me join. They'd probably just eat me instead." As he spoke he continued watching the priest gather up his sacred things, placing them in a wooden box.

"But what should I do? I mean how do I go about presenting myself to him? I can't just go up and start making dog sounds and expect the guy to adopt me. Can I?"

"I don't know Beagle. I don't know what to say since I've never had to do anything like this before. But I think you should just walk over and be friendly. But you have to make your move now because it looks like he'll be leaving soon and it will be too late."

Beagle looked over at Buster and asked,

"Why don't you go over there and introduce yourself Buster? Maybe you would be better at this than me?"

Buster turned and looked at Beagle.

"I don't think so Beagle. Look, you're cute and charming. Humans love that in a dog. I think they are more likely to adopt you than me. Between the two of us you have a better chance at getting help, and maybe even adopted. If he takes you in first I'll follow you to his place, wherever that is, and maybe after a few days I can work my way into his affections and we can both find a home. That's the way I think we should do it Beagle." The dog thought for a few seconds then he answered,

"OK Buster," and with determination in his voice he said, "I'll give it a try." And with that he stepped out from their cover. Before leaving he looked at Buster and said,

"What if he only adopts me? What will you do Buster?"

"I'll keep doing what I know how to do. I'll hunt and wander the forest and keep looking for my home. If I'm lucky maybe I'll see something that will point me in the right direction. I don't know at this point Beagle. The only thing I know is that your best chance to find a home is through that man standing over there, and if he takes you in then he is also my best chance as well. You have to get him to take you at least for a few days, and maybe find you a home. I really don't know, but if he finds one for you then he might help me too."

"But what if we get separated? What if he takes me but rejects you or something like that? Then what will we do? I don't want to lose you Buster. You're my best friend and you saved my life."

Beagle's words were kind and the hand of friendship touched Buster's inner catness.

"I know Beagle. I know what you mean. You saved my life as well and you certainly are my best friend in the world too. I don't want to lose you either, especially since we've both lost so much, and if we get separated and he adopts you and not me it will be really difficult. It's lonely out here just hunting alone all the time and avoiding predators. I must say that it is exciting, a real wild cat's life, but my inner catness tells me I'm basically a domestic cat, and I would like to return to my home and my friends and my humans. I had a really good life with them and I miss it very much."

"Alright then, I guess I better get to work and find a home for at least one of us. From here on out, no matter what happens I will never forget you Buster."

"And Beagle, my friend," Buster said as he put a paw on Beagle's chest, "I will never forget you. Never."

The brown and white dog stepped out from under the pine branches and headed straight for Brother Gregarious. All the fears the two animals had about the priest accepting Beagle turned out to unfounded, because when the spirit-man saw Beagle he was immediately taken by the little dog. He knelt down to pet him and told him what a good dog he was. He even asked if he was lost and if he wanted to go home with him. Within a few minutes man and dog were walking down the gravel path that led away from the Forest Church and through the woods. As they walked Beagle ran alongside the man smiling and wagging his tail, while the man reached down and patted him on the head. Buster shadowed the pair from a short distance away and could tell Beagle was making a very good impression. He could see that the man had fallen for Beagle right away. After the man and his new dog had been walking together for a few minutes Beagle made a quick detour into the woods to let Buster know how things were going.

"It's going great Buster. I think he likes me," he said before running back to join the man.

It wasn't long before they reached Gregarious' log cabin set in a clearing not far from the Forest Church. The cabin was made of cedar logs, with the ground floor divided into three small rooms with a loft about half the size of the ground floor. It had plenty of windows and a fieldstone chimney that climbed up the back of the cabin on the north side. A steep metal roof protected it from the elements and kept it dry inside. Outside the front entrance hung a wooden sign on which someone had carved *Cabana Rusticana*. While Buster watched from a nearby clump of bushes Brother Gregarious opened the door and invited Beagle inside.

This is exciting, thought Beagle as he stepped inside of what was going to become his new home.

Brother Gregarious sensed right away that the little dog was hungry. He had no dog food so he smeared a thick layer of peanut butter on a slice of bread, and offered it to the dog. Beagle remembered peanut butter from his condo days and while he watched the man prepare it on the counter he wagged his tail vigorously as the pea-nutty aroma wafted into his eager nostrils. No sooner had the man suspended the morsel in front of his face than Beagle chomped down and devoured it in three gulps.

"Well," said Gregarious looking down at Beagle's satisfied grin. "I guess I've found myself a fellow peanut butter aficionado, eh?"

"You're sure a cute little rascal aren't you?" Seeing the dog was still hungry he said,

"Well, I guess I better make you another one." And though he did not understand a word the man said Beagle gave a big smile and wagged his tail "Yes." Beagle and Brother Gregarious spent the rest of the day out on the screened-in front porch enjoying the breeze and the forest sounds. Beagle wanted the man to know that he was a good and faithful dog who would not be any trouble so he stayed very close to him, lying at his feet on a small crocheted rag-rug while the man dozed and read his newspaper. About mid-afternoon, Beagle made signs to the man that he wanted to go outside so he sat in front of the screen door and wagged his tail and twisted his head so the man would know that he wanted out.

"Ah," he said, "the little guy probably has to pee or something so I'll let him out. I don't think he's going to run off. I think he's lost and looking for his home. He may belong to one of the people who attended the service this morning. They'll probably come looking for him sometime this afternoon. If not, I'll have to call Francine at the shelter tomorrow and see if anyone has reported him missing. Someone is probably frantically looking for him."

Brother Gregarious imagined a young boy or girl crying their eyes out as they searched frantically for their little lost dog. After his time with Buster in the woods, Beagle did not have the same fresh and shiny urban condo look he had the first day when Buster saw him being rejected by the side of the road. For the past month he had been learning to be a wild country dog, one who could catch mice and turkey chicks and eat them raw, one who could break into garbage pails for a meal; one who knew how to hide from coyotes and scare lynx away with tough-dog growl sounds. Still, he was an attractive dog, the kind humans liked for pets.

Buster kept an eye on the *Cabana Rusticana* all afternoon, pleased with the way things were going. He could tell the man was nice and figured he probably had given Beagle something to eat. When he saw the dog step off the porch and head for the cover of the trees Buster scampered through the underbrush towards him. Before Buster even reached the dog he called out:

"It looks like he gave you something to eat, eh Beagle?"

"Yeah," exclaimed the dog, turning towards the sound of Buster's voice. "My favourite: peanut butter and bread. I love that stuff and he made me two of them. Boy was I hungry! He's really nice Buster. This was a good idea; a really good idea."

"That's great news," said Buster. "I think you did well to make friends with him."

"Yes," he said emphatically, "and the best part is he doesn't seem to want to get rid of me, so I'm sticking close by. I think something good will come of this. What have you been up to Buster?"

"Oh, I caught a mouse and then I slept for much of the afternoon. I like it here around that little wooden house and think I'll hang around for a few days, but still keep out of sight. I can check up on you every day. If you don't see me I won't be too far away, just hunting. I will watch the cabin and keep an eye out for you. It's too early and too risky for me to show up on the front porch right now. If he has to deal with two animals he might get frightened and abandon both of us. We can't risk that. We have done well so far and we have to stick with our plan."

Beagle agreed that it was probably the best way to proceed, but he missed his friend just the same, and Buster missed Beagle as well. They had become such good friends, and while Beagle's situation was working out with the man, he missed his company and their adventures together.

"OK Beagle," said Buster. "The man thinks you are out peeing and you don't want him to worry so you better get back. I'll try and check with you just after sundown, OK? If we don't make contact I'll see you for your morning constitutional. The man looks like an early riser so I'm sure I'll see you around sunrise if I don't see you tonight."

"Right," said Beagle, as he did some backward scat scratches on the leafy ground before running back to the cabin.

For the next few days the dog and cat stayed near the cabin, Buster hunting in the woods and Beagle staying with the man. Brother Gregarious always closed out the season of services in the Forest Church on Thanksgiving and then he moved down the mountain about a kilometre to a small winterised home he lived in during the colder months. If the weather remained warm, as it had this fall, he would stay on until the end of October, or even into early November, just as long as the days remained sunny and golden.

While the late afternoon turned to early evening and the sun descended closer to the western horizon, Buster left the forest and headed towards the edge of a meadow for some good hunting. As he watched the day come to an end he heard the unmistakable sounds of mice not far away in the tall meadow grass. Taking his usual precautions, he moved through the grass and made a low pounce on a big, fat field mouse. He played with the little beast for a while before he ate him, and then headed through the grass to the other side of the meadow. By now the sun was low on the horizon and he would enjoy the late afternoon for a little while longer before returning to the cabin to check in with Beagle. They had been making plans on how to integrate Buster into the group, but they still weren't quite sure how to proceed.

"We better think this through a little more before we do anything," said Beagle, so they agreed to come up with a plan of action on the following day.

Book VII

The Magic Star

What a beautiful view, Buster thought as he looked out at the countryside spread out in front of him. He saw forests, open fields, houses and barns and little roads winding through the hills, connecting the dots together. He marvelled at the beautiful sight until the long early evening shadows crept across the land in preparation for nightfall. He tarried a little longer as the solar disk slipped under the horizon before heading back to *Cabana Rusticana* to check on Beagle. As the sky darkened he could just make out the semi-circular form of the crescent moon emerging from the glare of the setting sun. He watched for a few minutes more, then thought of Beagle and decided to head back and check on him. But as he got up from his perch, something else caught his eye.

Wait a minute, he said to himself. *There's something different tonight, there's something else in the sky.*

There was something he had never seen before; something new and unfamiliar. Close to the crescent moon he could see another light in the heavens. Just to the left of the slim sickle-moon was a star. It was very dim, its light nearly overpowered by the remaining light of the setting sun. Yet, the star was bright enough to see that it was very close the moon.

I wonder how that happens? he thought. *Why is it that tonight there is a star close to the crescent moon, but it was not there any other night? In fact,* he asked himself, *was it even there last night? Actually,* he thought, *I can't remember.*

As the sky became darker he could make out most of the rest of the moon disk with the side facing the setting sun brightly illuminated, while the inner portion of the lunar circle was still much darker. Concentrating on the bright star only a whisker away from the left side of the lunar orb, he suddenly burst out:

"May the Great Cat preserve me! That's the Magic Star! That's it! That's what that is! I'm sure of it! There it is! That's the Magic Star!"

At once his heart began to pound and in his mind he could hear Kofi telling the story of the Magic Star. Right away he remembered that the Magic Star was not only a portent of good fortune, it also helped travellers and shepherds find their way across the mountains and deserts of the ancient east. And he remembered one other important thing about the Magic Star: it helped lost animals find their way home. Kofi had said that the Magic Star always appeared to the west of Rainbow Farm, and that if they were ever lost and they saw the Magic Star, they should follow it and it would guide them back. Oh how Buster hoped that the story was true and that soon he really would find his way home! Thinking of Beagle he thought,

I must follow it now. "I can't stay here with you any longer Beagle," he said out loud as if his dog friend was standing next to him. "I must follow the Magic Star."

Beagle has a home now so he'll be fine. He has someone to look after him and he doesn't need me to help him survive. That means I'm free and I better go right now. I don't know how long the Magic Star will even be in the sky. I don't think it was there last night, and things change every night so I have to leave now. I can't wait a minute longer.

Buster jumped up and started running towards the *Cabana Rusticana*. He could see that a light was on and the sounds and smells of cooking came from inside. No doubt Brother Gregarious was preparing dinner for himself, and would probably share some of it with Beagle.

I don't have a minute to spare. I've got to tell Beagle now. I will have to try to signal him and let him know I'm OK before I go.

He came close to the cabin and made a few very loud cat sounds that he and Beagle had devised when they were scavenging for food. Beagle heard the cat and signaled Brother Gregarious that he needed to go out. By now familiar with the dog's requests, he let him out without any delay. Buster gave another chirping signal and Beagle ran towards him. As they spoke he lifted his leg and relieved himself on a tree.

"What's up Buster? Are you alright?"

"I'm fine Beagle, just fine. I have to tell you something."

"What? What's so important?"

"Beagle, follow me a little way will you? I want to show you something. But let's be quick about it, I don't have much time." The dog nodded and the two of them scampered off down a path through the trees a short distance away until they could see the horizon.

"Look across the valley towards the mountains. You see the moon, right?"

Beagle looked up.

"Yes, I see the moon Buster, so what?"

"Look again; do you see anything else besides the moon?"

Beagle squinted and took a good long look.

"I can't see anything but the moon Buster. Hey, what's this all about anyway, eh?"

"It's about something called the Magic Star, Beagle. Look again, and this time see if you can make out a bright star just to the left of the moon."

"I can barely see the moon Buster, it's so dim. It's not even dark yet. What *are* you trying to tell me Buster?" he asked.

"What I'm trying to tell you, to explain to you is that..."

"I see it Buster, I see it! It's a little white dot next to the moon. I guess it's very nice Buster, but why show me a little white dot in the sky?"

"Well, when that 'white dot' and the crescent moon are close together like they are tonight, they form something called the Magic Star."

"OK, Buster I get it. The two things in the sky make up the Magic Star. So is it important? I mean, what's the point?"

"Beagle, it is important for cats everywhere, because it helps lost cats find their way home. For centuries cats have followed it when they were lost. Now it's my turn. I have to follow it and I have to do it now because it will be gone before the night is half over."

Beagle didn't say anything. He just stood there looking up at the sky and as the reality of the situation began to become clearer, he realised what it meant.

"You're leaving me aren't you Buster?"

"I have to go home. You have a new friend and a new home. Now I have to find my home. Try to understand Beagle."

Beagle let out a sigh while Buster continued trying to explain why he had to go now. Once it sank in that Buster was leaving, Beagle lay down on the ground in sadness. Buster came close to him and rubbed up against him, licking his face and muzzle, but it wasn't working.

"Please understand Beagle. Please! I have to find my home. I have to find my family, my cat and dog brothers. Beagle, you are my friend and what we did together will be with both of us until we close our eyes forever. But I have to go home, Beagle. I want to go home and the Magic Star will guide me if I go tonight. I can't wait because the Magic Star won't last long. It may not even be there tomorrow night."

Beagle looked up at Buster and said:

"I know you have to go Buster. I know that, and I wish you a safe voyage to your home. I just hate to see you go. We have been such good friends."

"Yes Beagle, such good friends," Buster replied. "I will be very lonely without you, my dog friend; very lonely."

Buster was overcome with grief about leaving, as much as he was torn by the sense of urgency as the great celestial clock pulled the moon closer to the horizon. He blurted out:

"Beagle, my vagabond friend, lynx fighter *extraordinaire*, I will miss you, and I hope we meet again someday. I will miss you more than you can imagine, but now I have to follow the Magic Star before it is gone. I have to follow the Magic Star!"

Knowing the wheel of fate had turned again, Beagle stood up, raised his ears and looked at Buster saying,

"I know you have to go Buster. I know you must go now and find your home. I know that. Before you go I want you to know that my thoughts will always be with you. So, good luck my friend. Good luck." Then with a quick glance towards the horizon, realizing how precious every minute was, Beagle said,

"Go now! Go before it's too late. And may the Magic Star be with you Buster! May the Magic Star be with you and guide you home!"

Their eyes met one last time for just an instant, and then the cat turned and ran for the row of trees that ran along the edge of the wide field that spread out to the west.

"May the Magic Star be with you Buster!" Beagle called out into the twilight as he saw Buster bounding through the grass along the edge of the field.

"May the Magic Star be with you always!" he called again. And as Buster ran his friend's voice receded into the distance behind him, and without turning his head Buster called back:

"Good bye Beagle, good bye! We will meet again someday!"

Buster cried out his message as he passed trees and bushes and tufts of grass, until he had put enough distance between himself and the dog that his voice trailed off into nothing and his goodbyes were replaced by a gentle breeze drifting through the tops of the maples and beeches anchored in the line of stones that ran down the edge of the field towards the horizon where the Magic Star floated in the twilight.

§

Crossing the darkening meadow, a seemingly crazed cat ran along the edge of the field yelling out cat sounds at the top of his voice. Two rabbits listened as Buster bounded by from stone to stone a short distance away. Looking at each other, one commented:

"He's in heat and calling for his queen. Cats always do that when they are in heat," said the male rabbit as his eyes followed Buster's disappearing form. His mate nodded her head in agreement.

Now as Buster ran down the hill the Magic Star was brighter than before, out-shining everything in the sky. But though it was very bright, it was also edging closer and closer to the horizon.

I've got to get a move on. I have no time to waste!

Taking advantage of his location he recorded the lay of the land like a map across the grey matter inside his head. On it he noted the hills and the valleys, the lines of trees and stones, set off by the big lake running through the middle. He thought it was likely that Rainbow Farm was situated to the east of the big lake and to the left directly under the Magic Star.

If that's the case it must not be too far away, he calculated. He was right, it wasn't too far away, but the return trip home would not be an easy one.

Only three or four days walk from here perhaps, he figured while he stopped to catch his breath. *If I just follow the Magic Star I'll get there, I know I will!* he reassured himself.

He was off again, heading in the direction of the Magic Star. He remembered Kofi saying that the Magic Star did not appear very often and it only stayed for one or maybe two nights, then it was gone and might not come back again for a long time. He did not know if he would even see it tomorrow night, which would mean it would only be in the heavens for a few more hours before it disappeared.

He moved at a fast pace for several more hours, stopping periodically to rest. Each time he looked up he could see the moon's disk was moving closer to the horizon; soon it would be swallowed up in darkness. He ran some more then stopped again to catch his breath while looking about at the trees and the fields for a familiar landmark, anything to help him orient himself. It was difficult not to think about his dog friend as his steps carried him onwards. Right now Beagle was probably lying awake by the man's bed, thinking about their time together and feeling the hand of loneliness on his shoulders.

I can't think about that right now, he told himself. *I have to concentrate. I have to keep going and find something familiar. Something on the ground that will be here tomorrow and won't move away; something that reminds me of where the Magic Star was, and will help orient me. But what? I don't even know what I should be looking for.*

Deep darkness settled in and no matter how fast Buster ran the Magic Star continued moving closer to the horizon. The next time he looked up he gasped, caught his breath and came to a sudden stop. The outer edge of the moon had struck the tree tops on the summit of Elephant Mountain.

"No!" he cried. "You can't go down yet! You can't go down! Please Magic Star, stay in sky a little longer! Please!" Buster pleaded.

But his chirps and meows could not keep the sickle moon and its star companion from their gravitational destinies. Their one-night stand on the ecliptic was coming to an end. In a few minutes the edge of the moon flattened against the mountain, its albedo light squashed into darkness.

As it grew darker, Buster was running so fast and with such abandon that he almost ran into the fox's slim, reddish face as it popped into his field of vision. But instantly, without thinking he veered left, made one leap from a fence stone and then felt his claws sink deep into the soft bark of a fir tree. Without breaking stride he pulled himself up into its branches, and once planted firmly he looked down. Below was a fox with the look of frustration written across his face; he had missed his chance for a good meal. Buster had no fear of the fox and knew he was safe, but the fox had forced him to stop running, and he was losing valuable time.

"May the Great Cat cover you with her scat stupid fox!" Buster yelled down at him. "I'm in a hurry and I don't have time to waste with you and your futile attempts to catch me. I'm a cat and I can climb. You're a fox and you are earthbound. You know you can't catch me up here, so get lost!"

Buster looked back and forth between the fox below him and the horizon. The fox was unaware of the Magic Star disappearing on the horizon and of the cat's sense of urgency. Eyes fixed upwards from the base of the tree, the fox knew there was no sense waiting for the cat to come down; the feline could wait him out in the tree for days if necessary. He was forest-wise and knew he was wasting his time, and it wasn't long before Buster watched as the fox moved off into the tall grass. When he turned his attention again to the horizon, the crescent moon was gone! While he had been concentrating on the fox, the brighter half of the celestial omen had disappeared, leaving only a single, bright star suspended in the west. But now, its light was blinking on and off as it moved though the stands of silhouetted trees. As the earth spun into the darkness, the lone star glimmered and blinked one last time, and then it too was gone.

The fox had disappeared in one direction and the Magic Star in another. There was no sense hurrying now; the star was gone and the fox might be lurking close by, waiting for a second chance. So Buster waited in the tree while the stars wheeled overhead and droplets of cool autumn dew settled on his coat. Finally satisfied, the fox went off hunting other prey, and Buster came down from the tree and headed west again, in the direction of where the moon and star had been, staying very close to the tree line.

What do I do now? He asked himself.

He knew where the Magic Star had been earlier so even though it was gone he would keep moving in the same direction as if it were still there. If he did that for the rest of the night, it would be as if the star were still shining on the horizon and maybe with a little luck he would see a landmark or something familiar to point him in the right direction. His plan had been to sleep during the day and be on the move again the next night when the Magic Star would be visible. He could continue to follow it if it was still there.

When I see the moon or the bright star tomorrow night I'll just keep heading in that direction. At twilight the following night, even though the crescent moon had moved away from where it was towards the east, the bright star was in exactly the same place so he still had a celestial beacon to guide him, at least until the clouds rolled in and covered it up.

§

Unlike wolves or many breeds of running dogs, domestic cats are not runners. They are stalkers and pouncers, and cannot run long distances. But tonight, Buster had run more than at any time in his life, and had drained his energy to practically nothing. He needed to rest so he could be ready to continue in the morning, and morning was not far below the horizon and would be back soon.

By the Great Cat in Heaven, I'm exhausted!

Slowed to a walk, he looked around for a safe place to rest; a tree-root hole, a cleft in a rocky ledge or a pile of logs he could crawl under. As he placed one foot in front of the other the ground suddenly sloped down at a sharp angle and there was a break in the trees up ahead. He made his way across a shallow depression and his feet suddenly touched the flat gravel surface of a county road. He hadn't been expecting it, and there was nothing unusual about that since there were many gravel roads in the region. Some were wide, some were narrow, some were well maintained, while others were just tractor paths or logging roads. But this one was wider than most and well-travelled. There was something else. By now, wise in forest ways, he went through his usual security check and then took stock of where he was. He looked down at the hard gravel surface beneath his feet, he looked left then right, scanning the ditches and the trees and the lay of the land. Then his eyes opened wide.

"I've been here before," he whispered almost inaudibly, as if he were trying to keep a secret from some invisible forest creatures.

"For sure I know this road! Yes, I know this road!" he said out loud, trembling with a mixture of excitement and fatigue. Indeed, he did know it because he had been there before: it was Chemin de Bellevue. It was the road where the kennel was located; where all his troubles had started. That damned kennel; Bedlam Barn filled with animals all acting crazy with prison fear. But there was something even more important about this road.

Rainbow Farm is on this road! This is the road I live on! My home is on this road and I live near here somewhere!

Looking down and letting his eyes scan along the side of the road and then looking up towards the horizon, he said out loud with excitement,

"Yes! Yes! I live on this road! I live on this road, and all I have to do is follow it home! I live on this road!"

Only seconds before he had secretly whispered his discovery to himself, now he threw caution in the roadside ditch next to him and cried out as if making a public announcement:

"I live on this road! Do you hear me? This is the road I live on, and I don't care who hears me! I don't care if a hundred bears and coyotes and lynx can see me and hear my cat voice, I am announcing to the world that this is the road I live on and I am going to find my way home! Do you hear me, all of you who stalk me in the dark of the night hoping to make a meal out of me? This is the road I live on and I'm going to find my way home!"

The road continued in front of him, first gently downhill and then rising again until it reached the horizon where the tip of the Milky Way Galaxy came down to earth and touched it. This road led to Rainbow Farm. Tillman and Annie and all of his animal friends lived on this road. His home was somewhere just down this road. He didn't know how far away he was from his home, but he thought he might make it back there very soon, maybe even on that very day.

I should rest for a while, he thought. *No, I can't rest. I've got to get home!*

§

Earlier that evening Tillman Charbonneau paused from his work and stepped outside the front door of the house to breathe in the fresh night air and take a few minutes of pleasure from the warm fall evening. He heard the last of the robins preparing to retire for the night and saw the fluttering silhouettes of bats making their first sorties into the rose-coloured sky from under the eaves of the chicken house. Annie was out that evening and he was home with the animals and his work. As twilight settled in he thought about Buster and had an overpowering urge to call his name, as he had done many times over the past few months without ever hearing any response. He had called Buster's name in the woods around the kennel, when Buster first became lost. Later he had called his name in the fields around Rainbow Farm and in the fields of his neighbours and even in the fields of strangers who thought it a bit odd that a grown man would be so upset about the loss of a cat. As he called his name on this night he knew Buster couldn't hear him. If he was in range of his voice he would simply come home of his own accord, but he called just the same. Somehow, calling out made him feel better and helped him recover from the loss of his cat friend, the cat he had promised to care for and protect.

Charbonneau turned from the meadow and looked towards the western horizon where, just above the trees, he saw the first crescent moon. At first he saw only the very thin slice of the moon, and then noticed a bright star was very near. As his mind rambled through his amateurish knowledge of astronomy, it occurred to him that if Buster was anywhere up there on the ridge overlooking the Tomifobia Valley, say, for example, somewhere to the east of Beaver Mountain, and he saw the crescent moon he could follow it home.

Don't be silly, he chided himself. *He's a grey and white cat named Buster, he's not Galileo!* Although stories abounded about cats finding their way back home, he wasn't sure Buster was going to be one of them or if he had the same direction-finding sense as his wild cousins.

The poor little guy, he's probably so lost he has no idea where he is; if he's still alive out there some place. Once again, he reminded himself:

Cats are not astronomers or geographers. They're just little critters who eat mice and purr a lot and sometimes get lost.

He turned and saw a car coming up the long driveway. It was Annie returning from her choir practice at the church in Moulin Rouge. He greeted her as she got out of the car, pointed out the beautiful crescent moon and the planet Venus next to it. Then they went in for the night. As Annie and Tillman took one last look at the night sky, behind the house Buddy Lebeau looked up over the tops of the trees and he too saw the Magic Star. He turned to Kofi, who was lying down grooming himself on a cushion of rich, green moss, not far away.

"Kofi, look!" he said, pointing towards the heavens with his white paw extended upwards towards the western horizon.

"Look, isn't that the special star you were telling us about that one time? Isn't that it? It sure looks like something special to me. What do you think?"

Kofi got to his paws, looked up and saw the slim crescent moon and the bright star next to it. The spectacle sent thoughts and ancient memories spinning through archives of his mind.

"Yes! Yes indeed, Buddy, you are absolutely right, that is the Magic Star; and how beautiful it is! How beautiful it is, and how fortunate we are to see it on this night. I only hope Buster can see it too. Maybe, just maybe," Kofi added somewhat wistfully while his gaze remained on the heavens, "it will help him find his way back home."

"Do you really think it might help get him back, Kofi? I sure miss him."

"You know Buddy," said Kofi, "this is a good sign from the heavens and I think it will bring him home."

"Wow, really?"

§

He was exhausted, but this was not a day to sleep. This was the day to be awake, to be on the move. He walked briskly along one side of the most important road in all of catdom, his paws practically bouncing off the gravel surface. The road home! The road to Rainbow Farm. He walked with lightness while he kept trying to remember things about Rainbow Farm, about the other animals and about the nice people, Annie and Tillman. Then he realised he was hungry.

I better hunt. Let's see what's on the menu today, eh? he thought.

Take your choice, he told himself. *Mice, rats or birds or perhaps a rabbit?* As always he was on the lookout for predators: the flutter of wings, the crunching of feet on leaves, the subtle cough or growl of an unseen carnivore; he detected nothing. Experience had taught him never to walk in a straight line for more than a few paces before changing directions, veering one way or the other, or doubling back and re-tracing his steps from another angle.

Just then he heard the roar of a Thunder-junker approaching at a high speed. The vehicle was bearing down on him so he scooted quickly down the embankment and into the shallow ditch by the side of the road. As the Thunder-junker roared past, the usual shower of gravel and the stink of hydrocarbons descended on him, and then the rolling menace was gone.

When the noise abated he made his way to the top of the embankment to continue. Just as he reached the summit another vehicle was passing by, much slower and much more quietly than the first one. When he crested the edge of the road he saw a junker a short distance away. He took evasive action but as he did so he noticed that the machine had pulled off the road. He was just about to make a dash for it when the door opened and an adult human male stepped out. The human looked right at him and it appeared that he was making mouth noises towards him.

What are those noises he's making? Buster asked himself. *Why is he out of his car and coming towards me?*

Buster looked at the man a little longer trying to figure out what his noises meant. The last human he had seen was the kind and gentle Brother Gregarious, but male humans also reminded him of Jacques Dupont and suddenly blasts of sound were ringing in his ears and his heart started racing. He had to avoid humans just like he avoided all other predators. He turned and ran down the embankment and made straight for the deeper brush and trees. But he didn't run far because he longed to be with humans and was curious about this one who seemed to be paying special attention to him. He hunkered under some grassy tufts and watched the man who walked along the edge of the road cupping his hands together and making mouth noises in his direction.

Why would he do that? Why would he get out of his vehicle and start making human noises? What does this mean?

After a while the man stopped making mouth noises and returned to his car. In a while it growled to life and moved down the road.

That's odd, he thought, *very odd indeed.*

§

When Buster first disappeared, Tillman and Annie set about visiting a number of the farms in the area to let people know they were missing a cat and to inquire if they had seen a cat that looked like Buster. Like detectives, they showed people photographs of Buster in various stages of his life: lying on the grass with Kofi and Buddy, or sleeping with Sparky. But no one had seen him. People were always very friendly and wanted to help, but everyone they spoke to answered with the same tone of regret. None of them had seen a cat that looked like the one in the photographs. They left their phone number, thanked the people and then moved on. That was in June. It was now October and they had not heard a single word from any of them. On more than one occasion Annie and Tillman had questioned whether their efforts had been worth it, but despite getting no leads they agreed that it was something they had to do.

"Well," said Annie one night after she had made the rounds of the farms to the east of Chemin de Bellevue, "We will probably never hear from any of them but we have to try. If we hadn't gone to see the locals, and by chance one of them had seen Buster, they would never know he was lost and we were looking for him."

But despite having gone months with no word from anyone, things were about to change. As soon as he had seen Buster, Benoit Tremblay drove down Chemin de Bellevue and turned in at Rainbow Farm.

I better tell them right away he said to himself. *I know they were really upset when they lost their cat and they'll be glad to have news about him.*

§

"As soon as I saw him I slowed down and just let my truck coast quietly up to where he was standing. He was just standing there on the other side of the road. I came really close to him, just a couple of metres. He was a grey cat with white markings just like yours," he told Tillman and Annie who were both excited and relieved by the news.

"I got a good look at him and I'm sure it was Buster."

"Benoit, that's wonderful news!" said Annie.

"It really is," said Tillman. "It's hard to believe he's still out there after all this time."

"Benoit," said Annie, "I know you know what you are talking about, and I do not want to offend you, but because this news is so wonderful I just want to make sure. Do you mind if I go get those photos I showed you before and we just look at them again?"

"No problem Annie," he said. "I'm not offended at all. If it will make you feel better let's have a look at them. No problem."

Annie returned with a packet of animal photos, and the three of them huddled together and looked at pictures. No sooner had she showed the first photograph of Buster when Benoit responded with no hint of doubt in his voice.

"Yep, that's him, that's the cat I saw not more than ten minutes ago."

"Wow. You say you got real close to him, eh?" said Tillman.

"Oh yes," said Tremblay. "He was just on the other side of the road and I'm sure it was him. He looked just like the photographs you got in your hands right there. Same cat."

"How did he look?" Annie inquired. "I mean did he look OK or was he injured or limping or have any visible marks on him? You know," she said, "anything that would indicate he was hurt?"

"No," said Benoit without hesitation. "Nothing at all; in fact, he looked good, and I didn't see anything on him that would indicate that he was injured."

"That is amazing news," said Tillman. Annie nodded her head in agreement,

"Absolutely amazing! It's so good to know that after all these months he is making out OK. Good for him. Good for our little Buster Bear! He must be disoriented and can't figure out where he is. That's probably why he hasn't come back yet."

She looked at her husband and said, "Tillman, let's go get him and bring him home".

"Yes, I think it's best you go back right away before he goes too deep into the woods," said Benoit.

They thanked their neighbour one more time as he got back in his truck and drove down the driveway. Tillman and Annie left shortly afterwards. As they got into their truck Tillman put his arm around Annie and they looked at each other and smiled and gave each other a celebratory kiss. This was the first positive news they had about Buster since he had disappeared four months earlier. As they headed up the road they thought they might find him still standing by the side of the road, and maybe even bring him home before supper that night.

When they arrived at the spot where Tremblay said he had spotted him they saw nothing. They got out of the truck and called his name and walked along both sides of the road for a while calling him. But they saw no trace of him. Buster wouldn't be going home with them that day.

"If he's alive and hanging around here then we will eventually find him. We just have to be patient," said Tillman. Annie agreed, and with mixed feelings of happiness and disappointment they went back home.

They returned every day to the same spot for the next week, but there was no trace of the grey and white cat. Maybe some animal had finally gotten him. They began to despair once again.

§

"Buster!" Tillman Charbonneau called out the window as he pulled the truck over to the side of the road and slowed to a stop. There he was, sitting on his haunches on the opposite side of the road, his two yellow eyes looking right at the man in exactly the same spot where Benoit Tremblay said he had seen him a week earlier. The grey and white cat did not seem to recognise the truck or its human occupant. And much to the man's surprise, Buster did not suddenly run across the road chirping with happiness and start rubbing up against him as he had hoped. Instead of some happy reunion, the cat's face remained expressionless; he did not seem to recognise the man. Tillman's first thought was that the cat was not really Buster but some other cat that just looked like him. How could it be that Buster did not recognise him? Maybe it was just a Buster look-alike, some local farm cat that resembled him; after all there were probably other grey and white cats in the area. But the more he looked the more he was convinced that it was indeed Buster.

There's no doubt about it. That's Buster for sure.

Tillman decided to cross the road, intent on not scaring the cat, just picking him up and getting him into the truck, and heading for home.

"At last, there you are my little friend. The search is over. I've found you, and now it's time to take you home".

So he stepped out of the truck, closing the door quietly behind him, taking every precaution not to scare his long-lost cat. All he had to do was walk over, pick him up and the entire saga would be over. But no sooner had he stepped out onto the gravel surface than Buster turned and disappeared into the tall grasses and trees on the opposite side of the road.

"Buster! Buster come," he called with the same familiar voice and tone he had always used, the call that had always brought the cat scampering home. But Buster would not come to him. With his eyes still fixed on the wooded area across the road, a disappointed Tillman thought,

Wow I didn't expect him to run away from me. I wonder what's going through his little head. Maybe he's afraid. Maybe he doesn't recognise me, after all, he has been lost and on his own for what is it, maybe four months now?

He stood staring into the woods a little longer, making sure Buster wasn't going to suddenly change his mind and come back, but he didn't.

"Well, at least I saw him with my own eyes and there is no doubt that he's out there and he's alive; at least that's something."

Even though the cat ran away from him, seeing him again after all those months kindled hope and Tillman was now more certain than ever that they could get Buster back. But he realised it might take more time and effort than he had anticipated.

Never mind, he thought, *I actually saw him. I know he's alive and he can take care of himself. I actually saw the little rascal. Wait until I tell Annie about this little encounter.*

Not that he didn't believe Monsieur Tremblay when he said he had seen him, he most certainly did believe him. But it was just that nothing was more convincing than seeing something with your own eyes. Now he could tell Annie that their lost cat was indeed alive, and what was a little surprising, and yet reassuring, was that Buster looked like he was in good condition, just as Benoit Tremblay had said. His coat looked shiny and he moved well; he wasn't limping or hobbling about. But he now faced a new problem. Buster didn't seem to recognise his humans or remember his cat name. They always believed that the big problem would be finding him, but they had never imagined they would have trouble getting him to come to them.

We'll just call his name and he'll come running, they thought. But it wasn't that easy.

Buster wasn't the same cat they knew before. Months in the woods had made him cautious and much more independent than when he lived his carefree life at Rainbow Farm. Now he watched out for himself. There was another factor as well. People forget how much trust and courage it takes for a domestic cat to drop all of its natural defenses and approach a human. Walking up to a giant biped and rubbing up against it or allowing themselves to be picked up takes a great deal of fortitude, especially considering that domestic cats only stand about 20 centimetres high at their shoulders. Humans are ten times that height and outweigh cats ten or twenty to one. And yet they come when called. Ever since he was a kitten snatched off the ground by no-good adolescents, then with Jacques Dupont shooting at him, Buster had become very cautious about approaching two-legged giants he didn't recognise, and today his fear of humans blinded him from identifying the man who cared for him.

A week later, this time while driving with one of his friends on the same stretch of road in almost the exact same place, Tillman saw Buster again. And just like the first time, Buster was right there by the side of the road. As before, he stopped the truck, got out, and began calling the grey cat as he moved towards him. This time Buster called back! He seemed to recognise the man's voice and his call. But Buster did not come running to him. While continuing to make meow calls, he moved away from the road and went deeper into the forest just like the previous time. The man spent an hour looking for him. Finally he gave up, happy that he had seen him once again, but saddened by the fact that Buster either did not recognise him, or did not trust him enough to come to him. Why didn't he come to him? What to do? How could the man attract a little cat who was confused and afraid of him even though he seemed to recognise his voice?

Maybe Buster doesn't know me anymore, or maybe he doesn't recognise his name. Maybe he's just plain forgotten who he is.

It was sad to think that the little grey cat who used to chirp and meow in response to the man's calls and run to him now ran away from him.

I've got to be practical here, he thought. *No time for sentimentality or handwringing. I've got to figure out a way to catch him, even trap him if necessary. I've got to do whatever it takes to get him back home before winter sets in.*

The days were getting shorter, the fall equinox was a month behind them. Both the sun and the temperature were dropping lower each day. Some mornings there was frost on the ground. The sky was late fall grey, and except for the oaks and tamarisks, the deciduous leaves were all on the ground. Buster was an accomplished forest hunter with good survival skills, but once the deep snows came it would be nearly impossible for him to hunt enough food to survive. To get him back before the snows came, Tillman and Annie would have to resort to more drastic measures. Even if Buster had temporarily forgotten who he was he would remember once he got back home. Right now the main challenge was to get him in his old, familiar environment where he belonged, and Tillman Charbonneau knew just what to do.

§

Since the end of the last Ice Age and long before Europeans ever set foot in southern Quebec, indigenous peoples had been trapping beavers, foxes, rabbits and racoons in the area. By the early 1970s trapping had pretty much died out in the Tomifobia Valley and the area around Lake Memphremagog. Four hundred years after the upper classes of Paris and London had made fur both fashionable and profitable their triple-great-grandchildren brought the fur trade industry to an end as the market collapsed. No money meant no trapping, so people spent their time on their snowmobiles or ice-fishing or just stayed inside and played video games. Only a few committed hobby enthusiasts continued to set their traps, skin the animals, scrape their pelts and seek out buyers. With human predation no longer a factor animal numbers grew and the hobby trappers couldn't make a dent in their numbers.

"That's what happens when people stop trapping," said the trappers to those who complained about the ubiquitous beavers and coyotes.

Ten years earlier, with no one to set the traps, a pair of beavers moved in to one of the shallow areas along Chemin de Bellevue where a narrow stream spread out its waters, creating a marshy area before it emptied into Lake Memphremagog. The pair did what beavers do and undertook a water management project as nature had intended them to do. Before the beavers arrived, the lowlands were covered with stands of spruce and fir trees, but the beaver-waters choked their roots, the sap no longer rose in their wooden veins, and their needles turned brown and blew away in the wind. A few years later, their bark, like great wooden scabs, loosened and fell to the swampy ground, leaving a forest of denuded weathered trunks standing in the middle of a beaver swamp. When Buster crossed the big marsh and skirted around the swampy area, the weather-beaten trees stood like wooden sentinels staring down with their knotty, dark brown eyes, keeping watch for any intruders who dared enter their swampy domain.

This place gives me the creeps, I feel like a trespasser here, Buster thought as the skeletal trees scowled at him. He hurried past them as fast as he could, moving on into the friendlier grassy areas in the higher grounds farther on.

An afternoon rain had washed the skies clean of dirt, dust and pollution, and after the clouds were gone a thousand lights appeared in the firmament as the moonless night drew its cloak of darkness over the earth. In the early evening heavens, Buster could see the bright, blue-white light of Jupiter as the sparkling giant rode low in the heavens just below the Square of Pegasus, drifting silently between the starry tails of the two fish of Pisces. The temperature dropped and a thick layer of frost formed on the leaves and grasses. That night, and through the next day, Buster continued walking parallel to the road.

§

Every hunter and trapper in the county knew about wildlife-friendly traps, the kinds used to catch small animals without harming them. One of Tillman's neighbours, Winston Brown, had just such a trap that he used to catch the skunks and racoons that frequented his back porch. Brown would catch them and take them to the woods at the end of his property, and release them. Generally, they didn't come back for a couple of months, and if they did he would just repeat the trap-and-release cycle. He liked the animals, he just didn't want to share his house with them, and didn't mind trapping and releasing the same ones every few months. As he told Tillman when he came to borrow the trap,

"I figure they have as much right to be here as I do. In fact, if you think about it, they were here long before my people showed up in the valley. I just don't want them in my house and my barn, you know what I mean?"

"I hear you," said Tillman, concurring with his neighbour.

Tillman threw the wire cage trap in the back of his truck, and returned to the spot where he had last seen Buster the day before. After inspecting the lay of the land, he placed the trap near an apple tree a short walk from the road. It would be close enough to give him easy access to it, but not so far away that he would get lost in the woods looking for it. The trap was situated just far enough from the road that passersby couldn't see it. He didn't want some good-natured local person to find Buster in the trap and release him. Such a gesture of kindness might actually doom the cat to a winter of cold and starvation. And he wasn't worried about hunters messing with the trap. The ones he knew were sportsmen, not animal abusers, and none of them would waste their time or ammunition on a trapped cat. He set the trap down on the ground, lifted one of its doors and placed an open can of sardines swimming in oil inside the cage's wiry walls.

Maybe I can't attract my own cat by calling his name, he thought, *and maybe he doesn't recognise me anymore, but surely these smelly sardines will do the trick and I can finally put an end to this lost-cat saga. It really is ridiculous that I have to catch my own cat because he doesn't, or can't, recognise me. I never would have thought that it would come to this.*

When he checked on the first day the trap was undisturbed, and the oily sardines untouched. It was difficult to understand why no animal came to eat the delicious morsels of fish. Surely, an open can of sardines in oil set in the middle of the forest would send off a strong scent.

At last, I've got him! he thought, as he made his way through the bushes and small trees towards the trap. He was sure Buster would be inside. He wasn't. During the night a skunk had wandered in and helped himself to the sardines, and now the smelly little creature was trapped. To avoid being 'skunked,' Tillman went back to his truck and found an old blanket and threw it over the cage to catch any of the stinky spray the skunk might wish to offer as his way of thanking him for his freedom. The ploy worked, and while the skunk was still under cover he reached down and manipulated the release mechanism and sent the striped stinker back into the woods. After it had waddled back into the trees, he placed another can of sardines in the trap, hoping this time it would attract Buster and not the skunk.

Late that October Tillman began a twice daily run from his house to check the trap about three kilometres up Chemin de Bellevue, north of Rainbow Farm. The next day Tillman made his morning trap inspection and found the same skunk in the trap, and for the second day in a row the skunk had eaten all the sardines. Discouraged the man set the trap again. If he didn't catch Buster he might at least catch something other than the skunk. Later that day he returned just before dark and checked the trap again: it was empty and the door was still in the open position.

§

I thought I would be home by now, Buster thought. *I've been walking non-stop since I saw the Magic Star and still no Rainbow Farm. In fact, I haven't seen anything even vaguely familiar. What's going on?*

That night an invisible force made its way into his nostrils, and slithered up his nasal passages into the olfactory portion of his brain. The smell caught him by the nostrils and like a strong hand twisted his head around searching for the source of the magnificent scent.

"Oily fish, that's the smell of oily fish!" he proclaimed to the trees and the grass as if he were having a conversation with some spruce boughs, or shucks of swamp grass.

"Yes, most definitely that is the smell of oily fish!" His thoughts raced back to Rainbow Farm and the special days when Annie Perrault would come out on the back porch with a shiny, box-like thing in her hands and a trail of eager dogs and cats following her. Somehow Annie had the power to make the oily fish come out of the metal box.

It was miraculous! How did she do that? he wondered as he trailed behind her. When it was oily fish time the cats always got a taste just like the dogs and it was so wonderful, a nice change from mice, so wonderful that Buster would walk away from his food dish in a palatable trance. Now the smell of oily fish was close by!

How could that be? He thought. *It must be nearby, but I have to be careful.*

Something as good as the oily fish smell was suspect, and he knew he had to exercise extreme caution if he was going to approach it. The smell was overpowering and he was getting close now. Then he saw it. Lying on the forest floor a few paces in front of him was a box-like contraption, the kind that only humans make. Amazingly, the contraption exuded the smell of oily fish. Buster approached it and he could see through the wire mesh one of those silver-coloured metal boxes just like Annie had back at Rainbow Farm, and the silver box was wide open and stuffed full of oily fish!

May the Great Cat preserve me! He felt sniff-dizzy; something similar to ingesting quantities of high-grade catnip.

Caution, he told himself. *Caution*. But his self wasn't listening. He was now in front of the opening of the human contraption. Like the morning mist over a swamp, the aroma grabbed him, and tore the shroud of caution from his eyes. He stuck his head inside the cage and stepped forward. Then he thrust his gnashing mouth into the metal box, and chomped morsels of sardine meat as the oil ran down his cheeks and dripped onto his paws until it leaked between the wires and dripped onto the ground.

This is wonderful!

In his eagerness to eat more he moved forward to better position himself over the silver box of oily fish.

It was then he felt something under his feet move and he heard a metallic clicking sound. Bang! Bang! The doors at both ends of the trap slammed shut with stereophonic crashes! A hissing sound came ripping out of his throat. His hair stood on end and all four of his paws lifted off the floor until he struck the top of the cage and fell back to the wire floor.

"Great Thundering Cats!" *What was that? What's going on?*

Escape by the entrance: blocked. The other end was blocked tight. Buster was trapped, a prisoner inside some human-made thing. He tested the wire walls and their metallic hardness against his paws. He tried to tear through his prison bars but paws were no match for rocks dug from the earth, melted in fire, and spun into wires that become contraptions made to catch lost cats. No matter how many times he stuck his paws through the wire mesh he could not break out. Biting the wire with his teeth was futile. He could see through the wire walls, he could see the trees and the sky above where shortly before he had roamed free: free and on his way home.

Now he was a prisoner inside a wire box. He didn't know what had happened, and was confused by walls you could see through and stick your paws through but could still hold you captive. He ate the oily fish and slept the sleep of frustration. He was nervous, he was tense. And a voice inside his head kept repeating:

Get out! Get out!

§

Buster had seen them from a distance; he had smelled their great piles of scat and knew that only an extremely large beast could produce such a prodigious discharge, but he had never been close enough to hear one grunt and make nose-noises. Even in the dark its black fur looked thick, rich and lustrous reflecting in the pale night light. Looking out between the criss-crossing lines he watched as the beast moved towards his wire prison. It was big and looked powerful, perhaps powerful enough to do what Buster could not: tear open the cage. Buster could tell it was hungry. Now it was very close and he was afraid.

The Eastern black bear is one of the better adapted predators living in great forests of North America. In the autumn, a pre-hibernation male can weigh up to 400 kilograms, though most weigh less. During the summer months the average female black bear weighs between 50 and 85 kilograms, but they bulk up for hibernation and by late October this one was well over 100 kilos. Portrayed as slavering human-eaters, most Eastern black bears are shy and avoid humans. Their diet consists mainly of fruits, berries, nuts, and insect larvae, and only about 15 per cent of their food comes from meat—but that meat includes domestic cats. For the female, Buster was just so much edible protein immobilised on the forest floor, and he would be an easy prey since he couldn't get away. As the bear watched him from a few paces away Buster shook with fear; he couldn't help himself. Waves of stress swept over him.

I thought the Magic Star was a good sign and it would guide me home, now I'm trapped and about to be eaten by this black furry monster.

Bears have a sense of smell second to none. Their nasal mucosae are large, extending from nose to the mouth, making the bear's sense of smell superior to that of even a tracking Blood Hound. She was nearly a kilometre away when she picked up the smell of the fish that drew her through the woods to the trap like an olfactory magnet.

How can the smell of oily fish be coming out of this wire box with a cat inside it? she puzzled. *And why doesn't he just run away?*

The bear tapped the wire box with her brownish paw, testing it, wondering if it would bite. Buster hissed and growled at her, but she was unimpressed and not afraid of him. Then she batted the cage with more force this time and rolled the rectangular-shaped contraption over on its side, sending Buster and the tin of oily fish tumbling about inside. Realising she couldn't get at the food, she bent down and closed her big mouth over the trap, her incisors poking through the wires, just millimetres short of puncturing Buster's head. As her mouth closed around him he could see her great teeth, and despite the dark of night, he could see deep into her tongue-swollen mouth that smelled of meat and berry halitosis. With the trap in her mouth she raised her head, lifting the trap off the ground as Buster fell away from the hot bear breath to safety at the bottom of the cage.

When her tongue tasted the foul sensation of metal, not flesh, her mouth popped open letting the bitter-tasting contraption fall to earth. Once more she bent down to grasp it, and once again her mouth tasted only metal so she did not bite down. She withdrew and lay down puzzled by her situation. Food was right in front of her, she could see it and smell it but she could not put it in her mouth. She pushed the trap around on the leafy ground then knocked it sideways with her big paw. She tried to claw Buster, her curved talons as long as carpenter's nails reaching through the wires, yet he managed to squeeze out of the way and they did not reach him.

By this time Buster had stopped hissing, choosing to remain still and make himself into a small shaking lump of fur. It seemed her teeth could not bite him and her claws could not reach him so the best course of action was to stay out of her way. The bear was becoming frustrated. She pushed the cage then pulled it along the ground for some distance through newly fallen leaves and dry branches, but she still couldn't get inside it. She dragged it further through more trees and bushes, and then with mounting irritation she grasped the trap with one paw and flung it skywards sending it arcing through the air before it crashed down with such force that one of the doors bent and nearly sprang open. But in an instant the trap regained its form, the door stayed closed, and Buster remained trapped. A few seconds later he was once again airborne, this time howling and hissing from the shock as he went flying about inside the wire walls, banged by the can of oily fish and splattered by the remains of its contents. The bear was angry. She could see food right in front of her eyes and yet she could not get at it. Once again she batted the cage and rolled it, and then she pulled it past the apple trees, through some bushes and over a pile of stones. She tossed it again, and what remained in the silver sardine can spilled out on the ground. She stopped and licked up the drops of fish oil that coated the leaves and ate the scraps of meat that lay on the ground.

She had managed to get the oily fish, but the cat was still out of reach. The bear sat down and licked her paws, gave the trap several more slaps, and then turning her head in the direction of the untouchable cat one last time, she withdrew and moved on into the dark woods. It started to rain.

Things were a mess; the trap was on its side among some broken branches and a shaken Buster huddled in the cage, wet, cold and soaked in sardine oil that covered half of his body. He tried to lick it off but it was everywhere, and his tongue didn't seem big enough for the job. The smell that had originally attracted him to the trap now repulsed him, and half covered with oil he found himself disgusting. He was in one piece, he was uninjured, and the bear had not eaten him. But he was still trapped. Now that the bear was gone and his heart had stopped racing, he could hear mice and night creatures moving through the forest close by. The rain was steady now and kept up for several hours. He drifted in and out of a state of semi-conscious misery for the next few hours.

I hate being in here but I've got no choice. After the way she threw the cage around I've got to stay still and undetected. The next time that bear finds me she will break into the cage and I'll be a goner for sure.

As the night passed, Buster's capacity to tolerate confinement was weakening. Although he could see through his wire walls, they were closing in on him as surely as if they had been made of solid steel.

I can't stand being in here anymore. I think I'm going catty.

§

The hand of claustrophobia was closing its grip on his inner catness and he could no longer tolerate his situation. Rain-soaked desperation took hold of his voice and he started crying into the night. Amidst his cries the rain turned to snow. Wet lazy flakes hit the ground, the wires of the trap, and his coat before they melted. Later they froze on the wires and stuck to the ground. By morning there was a paw-deep crust of snow that covered the leafy ground, and he blended in perfectly with his surroundings. He looked out between the wires at the snow and thought:

The cold time is coming, I've got to find my way home, and now I'm stuck inside this thing. I can't take this anymore!

"Help me! Help me somebody! Come and get me out of here! Please!" his voice cried into the night.

I can't take this anymore. I've lost my inner catness. If I don't get out of here soon I'll die!

It didn't matter anymore if predators knew where he was, he just wanted out of that box before the last of his inner catness was squeezed from of him. He didn't care who heard him, or if a whole family of cat-eaters knew his whereabouts; he had to get out of that cage. He had to let the whole forest know he was in trouble; that Buster, the lost cat from Rainbow Farm, was trapped and wanted out of that damnable cage. He cried and meowed until his voice ran thin, and then he just whimpered. Worn out and voiceless he curled up in a ball while the temperature dropped and snow accumulated on top of him. He tried to think of Juliette, but claustrophobia stalked him to distraction inside his cell, and her image would not stay in front of his eyes. Even she feared the cage and refused to step inside the wire prison with him. Even she had abandoned him.

§

Just around dawn he heard something moving through the bush close by. The grey and white cat couldn't see who or what it was, but something was out there, something large and lumbering.

Oh no! The bear is back. I thought she'd gone for good.

The bear had returned for another try at the cage. It was back for a second time looking for the cat-meal that was still waiting for it. Soaked through with oil, water and fear, Buster listened to the crashing noises as the beast approached. He hunkered down as best he could inside the confines of the cage, hoping desperately that the bear would not find him a second time.

§

Due to an early appointment, Tillman Charbonneau had come that morning before sunrise and was stumbling about in the dark with a flashlight looking for his cage. He passed within an arm's-length of the trap, but he did not see it just off to his right lying in among some branches. Gripped by fear the grey and white cat did not give away his location. The man moved on, his flashlight swinging in the darkness, and then he was gone. Had Buster known it was a human, any human, let alone the nice man from Rainbow Farm, walking near his cage he would have cried out for help. But cats who want to live to hunt again don't make noises when giant bears are about. After the noise abated, Buster breathed a sigh of relief. He could hardly believe the bear had not discovered his whereabouts.

§

An hour later on that snowy morning the clouds had moved off, the sun was shining brightly, and Marc Bouchard from Smith's Landing was out early before going to work, checking to see where he should install his blind before deer season began. Like most parts of eastern Canada fall was hunting season, and by the middle of October small game hunting, along with moose and bear seasons, were in full swing. Rain or shine, hunters were out with shotguns and .22's, hunting partridges, pheasants, geese and ducks. Deer season would start in a week in early November, when they put down their shotguns for high-powered rifles or bows and arrows, or even black powder muzzle-loaders for the bigger white-tailed deer. From a distance, Buster had seen a few camouflaged hunters dressed like trees and bushes which they thought made them invisible, but such attire rarely fooled cats.

As he moved through the forest Bouchard heard the noise of a small animal in distress. He stopped and listened, going through his inventory of animal sounds, eliminating most of them until he concluded it was a domestic cat.

Probably one of the village cats wandered up here and got himself caught in a coyote trap, he thought. *I better go see what's going on. Nobody wants to waste their bait on a cat.*

As he headed towards the sounds they grew louder. When he saw the trap he realised right away it was not the type generally used by people who trapped professionally.

Why would anyone use that kind of trap out here? These things are no good in the woods: must be a kid or some kind of amateur that set it. Nobody I ever met, anyway no real trapper, would use a trap like this.

Marc Bouchard had hunted and trapped all his life and he knew from experience that the trapped cat was suffering from cage fright. In some cases, trapped animals become so traumatised they literally die of fright. He approached the trap, and in a calm, flat voice, devoid of sharp tones, he said,

"How long have you been in here, little fella?" As he got closer to the cage he continued speaking in calming tones. "Good thing you're not a skunk or I wouldn't be getting this close to you would I?"

When he knelt over the cage to brush the snow away he noticed that the cage had been overturned and figured somebody had tried to get at the trapped cat during the night. Then he saw the one end of the cage that had been partially crushed and flatted. Bouchard examined the bent wires with fresh scrape marks on them. He'd never seen anything like that before.

I'll bet a coyote did this, he thought. Then upon reflection he paused and corrected himself. *No, probably a bear tried to chew his way in here during the night. No wonder he's scared out of his wits,* he said as he turned the cage over examining it.

He continued speaking softly as he reached down and released the catch and opened the door. He noticed that despite the obvious trauma, the cat looked in good shape. He was uninjured and there were no visible marks on him.

Must be someone's pet. Probably lives close by around here somewhere.

People who had cats in the country usually expected them to go out hunting in the woods and fields, and they accepted that they might disappear for a few days at a time: nothing too unusual about that. But after spotting the empty sardine can still inside the cage he was a little puzzled.

Man oh man! Whoever this person is, they're a real greenhorn. Nobody tries to catch game with sardines!

Although he was bewildered by the odd bait arrangement, he didn't give it much more thought as he proceeded to open the trap and free the cat.

I wonder how long he's been in here, he asked himself.

"I'll just let you go little fella' and you can go back home have some food and dry off in front of a nice warm fire, eh?"

So Bouchard released the cat, not realising that the animal was disoriented and wasn't sure where he was. But right now none of that mattered to Buster. He just wanted out, and when the trap door swung open he leapt out and ran.

Thank you Great Cat! I'm finally out of that dreadful human contraption! That was as bad as the round-eyed night bird.

Buster ran a few paces but hadn't gone far before he stopped, and turned and chirped a big 'Thank you' to the man. Buster liked the companionship of humans and sensed the man was kind. Trapper Bouchard was still kneeling down and had not yet taken his tall, intimidating two-legged human stance so Buster was not overwhelmed by his size. When the man finally did get to his feet, Buster moved off into the woods.

I miss my humans, he thought. *For some reason I think that man could maybe help me find my way home; probably a silly idea. Oh well, at least I'm out of that cage and a free cat again.*

His brief brush with the human brought back the memories of his family of humans, cats and dogs. He savoured them for a moment, but he could not allow them to stay long in his mind. He had work to do and predators to avoid, so he pushed them aside and was once again a hunter, like the ancestral cats of old. The sun was out, shining brightly and the temperature was rising and the snow was melting. His horrible night was behind him and it was going to be a nice day. He felt so much better now. He could hunt in the thick beds of soft pine needles and the grassy patches; all places which contained delicious mice and birds to eat.

§

That afternoon Tillman returned to the place where he had set the trap hoping this time he would have better luck finding it. He searched in an ever widening circle from the grove of wild apple trees and finally found it a half-hour later. It was a good twenty metres from where he had originally placed it.

It's been moved. No wonder I couldn't find it, Tillman thought. I wonder how that happened.

As he knelt down and examined the cage he noticed that both its doors were open. The trap looked a little beat up and when he turned it over he saw there was a dent in it.

That's odd, he thought as he looked around on the ground. *The ground looks roughed up a bit here and there and the can is empty. I wonder what really happened here. Another one of those things I guess I'll never know.*

Because both doors were open, just as he had set it, the man assumed that no animal had been caught in the trap. But it was puzzling to see the empty sardine can some distance away.

How did that happen? he wondered again.

As Tillman picked up the trap and carried it back to the spot near the apple tree where he had first set out the trap, he thought,

I wonder if it is even worth setting this thing again. I've been checking this trap for nearly a month and so far I haven't caught anything that even remotely resembles Buster. Maybe he's too clever to get into it or maybe he's too afraid. I think I'll just give up on the trap and see if I can coax him to come straight to me the next time I see him.

He walked across the gravel road and threw the trap in the back of his pickup and headed for home.

§

"Zombie trees! Great Thundering Cats! I'm back at the zombie trees! How could that have happened? How could I be back here again?" As his heart sank, he realised something awful:

"Oh no! I've been walking the wrong way all morning!" Then he thought again, "No, it's worse, than that! I've been walking the wrong way for two days!" He looked around at the zombie trees staring down at him, and as if interrogating them, he cried out:

"By the Great Cat, how could this have happened? It must have been the oily fish."

He put his face to the ground and let the frustration of being lost once again wash over him.

How am I ever going to get back home if I keep getting lost? he admonished himself.

When he looked up again he was shocked to see that dozens of the wooden zombies were closing in on him, their dried and weathered trunks standing like elder soldiers in uniforms of cracked and tattered bark. With their wooden arms extending at different angles from their trunks, they appeared as if they were preparing to take up arms against him. Buster was afraid.

Maybe they're going to attack me, he thought. *First the trap and the bear, and now trees attacking me. What more can happen?* He looked up and saw their linear faces with knot-hole eyes and cracked-bark mouths glaring down at him. It was clear they were not happy to see him, and in unison their mouths moved and made noises saying,

"What do you want, cat? This is not your land! All who come here find only a swampy grave; is that what you want? You are lost, cat, so go home. You do not belong here, cat, go home!"

Talking trees, Buster whispered to himself, pressing the sound out between his cat-lips in a tiny hiss of frightened air.

No, this is worse than that: these guys are talking zombie trees! Thundering Cats! This place is even creepier than the last time I was here! I've got to get out of here now!

Just then, one of the trees at the head of the wooden phalanx, with a twisted branch that extended out from his trunk, making it look like he was pointing at him, looked straight at Buster, his eye knotholes bearing down on him.

"You heard them cat! Your home is not here. Turn around cat and go home!"

"Yes Sir!" Buster answered the tree sentinel. "Yes Sir! I'm turning around now. Yes Sir I'm going home!"

Buster attempted to salute the wooden warrior, but then thought better of it. Instead, he made an about-face and ran in the opposite direction as fast as he could.

That was the creepiest thing ever, he said as he bounded through the trees, putting distance between him and the wooden warriors.

And I've been going in the wrong direction all along. Now I've got to go back over territory I've already covered. At this rate it'll be mid-winter before I get home.

§

The moonlight settled on the tops of the trees, on the tips of the blades of grass in the open fields and pastures, and on the cattails and lily pads in the marshes and ponds.

I know a big change is coming. I can feel it. The nights are much longer and much colder. Some mornings there is ice in the ditches and the puddles are frozen over. There was snow that night I was in the trap. I know the cold time is coming, and I've got to get a move on.

That evening, he tried to think of home and his life with the dogs and Kofi and Lebeau and the nice people. But the memories were unclear, lost in the fog of too many events. He had trouble remembering their faces, and was afraid he was losing contact with his past life. But he had better luck remembering Juliette as she marched through his imagination and played beautiful tricks on him.

Well, maybe it is better that I do not think too much about my past because now I am a wild creature again. Still, I don't want to live out here alone, and I hope I find my way back. I wonder if they even remember me and care about me? They have probably forgotten me by now. Maybe they gave up looking for me as soon as I disappeared. I wouldn't blame them for that. It was a stupid thing I did, jumping out that window, and I've had nothing but trouble since. They probably replaced me with another cat by now.

He hated himself for being so negative. *This is no way to get home, whining and feeling sorry for your mistakes,* he chided himself.

"By the Great Cat," he shouted out the heavens. "Enough of this negativity (such a big word for a cat) I am going home, and I'm going home now!"

He began running down the side of the road as fast as he could. Winter was coming, and there really wasn't any tomorrow! Like other animals, cats knew the signs of winter, and he knew that either he found Rainbow Farm and the nice people in the next few days or he would spend the winter in awful, perhaps fatal conditions. It was either be a domestic house-dweller in front of the fire this winter, or return to the woods and fields and live the short, tough life of a hunting cat. He had made his choice. He was going to retrace his steps and follow the road home as fast as he could.

Domestic cats are not distance runners like cheetahs, or wolves. They are built for short bursts of speed and then they quickly run out of air. Their thin, narrow bodies and rib cages do not have room for big flapping lungs, the airbags of nature's distance runners like salukis and greyhounds, or even Sparky, the 'Monday dog' of Rainbow Farm. Frequently Buster had to stop and get his breath, and when he did, he just stood by the side of the road gasping and breathing.

I've got to be careful, he thought. He knew that if he was attacked by a predator while short of breath he would be at a big disadvantage so he always made sure there were trees nearby so he could make a quick escape, like the time with the fox, if he needed to.

I better get off the road for a while, he thought.

But once he had his breath, it wasn't long before he was on the move again, always ready to jump across the drainage ditch and take refuge in a tree.

Undaunted, he continued heading in a westerly direction, the right direction this time, and with every step he was a little closer to Rainbow Farm. He should have made it home in two or three days once the Magic Star had led him to Chemin de Bellevue, but things hadn't worked out that way. Now that he was finally going in the right direction he had been forced to make long detours into the woods to avoid the higher than usual number of coyotes.

§

Bedlam Barn! he whispered to himself, as though the wood and metal structure might be listening for escaped cats.

I don't believe my eyes. I never thought I would ever be glad to see this ugly place again, but there it is and I'm happy to see it.

The animal prison was just across the road, and while he took time to catch his breath he looked at the building and let the memories of his short, traumatic time there came back to him. He remembered the slime-mouthed dog, the flat-faced psycho-cat and the kennel warden. But now it was easy to push the bad memories away because Bedlam Barn was a good sign:

"I hate you Bedlam Barn," he meowed in the direction of the big structure. "But," he continued, "I am very happy to see you, because this means I'm getting closer to my home."

Close to my home, he repeated. *Home,* the very noise in cat sounds evoked happiness, and when he whispered the mouth sounds for 'Rainbow Farm' they were like a sacred mantra and conjured up visions of a warm house on a wind-swept hill on the edge of a forest: a place where all was well. If nothing else, seeing Bedlam Barn meant there would be no more traps, no more zombie trees, no more oily fish, just the road home. He watched the structure for a little while longer while he caught his breath, and then he moved on. Had Buster been able to read human symbols on the broken sign that hung by a lone hook, from a wooden pole, he would have understood that Bedlam Barn had gone out of business.

§

It can't be far now, he thought. *I should be there soon. I've just got to keep moving.*

Over the next two days Buster walked and hunted in the grass and nearby underbrush, along the edge of Chemin de Bellevue. It was on that same morning that Buster saw something puzzling. He was right by the edge of the road when another Thunder-junker came down the road, and slowed down, then, stopped completely. Tillman happened to be in the company of a friend, and both of them got out of the truck.

It's that human again. The same one I saw before, the really tall one who keeps stopping. I think I like him: maybe I have seen him before, but he's a giant! He's so tall he scares me, and there's another human with him: a human I don't recognise.

It seemed the man was not just making noises for no reason, as humans are inclined to do. Instead, he was making noises in Buster's direction. In fact...

Wait a minute. I think those noises are meant for me!

Buster listened intently, trying to decipher what the man's mouth noises meant. The man seemed to be calling out something familiar in human mouth noises. It was something Buster had heard before, and the noises made him think of Rainbow Farm. It had been so long since he had heard a human say his name that at first, he didn't recognise it when the man said it. When animals like Beagle said his name it didn't sound the same as when humans said it, and over the months his name in human mouth noises had lost its familiarity. The last non-human creature to say his name was Beagle. But Beagle said his name in dog mouth noises. When Beagle said 'Buster' in canine bark-and-growl noises it sounded much different than when a human said it, because humans don't make bark-and-growl noises like dogs.

That makes sense, he thought. Then it struck him:

Hey! Hey! The man is calling Buster! He's calling my name! Buster looked in the direction of the human, and listened.

"Buster! Buster, come!" The man called out.

There it was, and there again. There was no doubt about it: a tall man was calling his name.

That's it! Buster! That's it! That's my name! I remember now that's how humans say my name! That's me! I'm Buster, yes that's my name! He meowed back at the man as loud as he could,

"I'm Buster. I'm Buster from Rainbow Farm, and I'm here!"

He was tempted to run towards the man and see what was going on, but he knew he had to be careful because the man calling his name looked familiar, but he was accompanied by another male giant human he didn't recognise. That sent a wave of caution through him. He stopped. Maybe he was in danger?

This is confusing. I don't know what's going on here. That man looks like my human, but I can't risk getting any closer. There is another tall human over there I don't recognise. I don't know who the second giant is. I just got out of a trap, and I'm not taking any chances. I better just go and hide. And with that he ran into the woods. He wasn't about to risk another disaster. He turned and moved deep into the underbrush. But he wondered if he had made the right choice.

Maybe next time I will take the risk and be brave and go to the human who calls my name.

§

"Well, Benoit," said Tillman, "You heard him and you saw him. He was right there not ten paces from us, and yet he ran away. What do you make of it?" he asked his neighbour.

"I don't know exactly. He recognises you and he called back to you, so I think he's afraid of something. I just don't know what it is," he answered.

Both men stood at the side of the road for a while saying nothing, just staring into the forest at the spot where Buster had disappeared.

Finally Benoit said: "You know Tillman, he's probably had a few scary experiences out here on his own and he's just really being cautious. You just have to keep trying. The more often he sees you the more likely he is to come to you. So don't give up. You'll get him back before winter comes. I think he's ready to come home, you just have to be patient. I have a feeling it won't be long now."

"I hope you're right. This has been dragging on a long time, and I would like to put an end to this whole Buster saga. I need some closure here."

After a while the two men left, and as they did Buster realised he really didn't want to see them go. It was pleasant to remember how his name sounded when humans pronounced it, and although afraid, he hoped he would see the man again by himself and that he would call his name once again.

§

The next day Tillman Charbonneau had gone to Montreal and was returning home that afternoon on the local bus that motored down the autoroute towards Magog. He found his truck in the parking lot, threw his briefcase in the back seat, and drove off. He had had a long day and wanted to go home and relax with Annie. He headed south through the village, along *Rue Principale* with its restaurants and fripperies scattered along both sides of the street, and it was only a few minutes before he hit the dirt road south of Smith's Landing for the last five kilometres to Rainbow Farm. It was November, mid-afternoon, and it would be dark soon.

It was getting discouraging looking for Buster every day, and his hopes always lifted a little each time he passed down the same stretch of road where he had last seen the cat. He had given up trying to trap him because Buster was moving closer and closer to Rainbow Farm. The last time he saw Buster he was about two kilometres from home, which was very promising, but the cat still wouldn't come to him. As he drove down the dirt road his thoughts wandered to the day's activities, and once again he found himself asking the question: *Why am I doing this? I've given it a good try; I've been a responsible pet owner. Why don't I just give up?*

But there was really no mystery here. Like animal lovers from all over the world since forever, he knew the answer:

I love the little rascal, and that's the strange thing. He's just a funny-looking little bag of fur and claws and I love him. So does Annie. So do all the other animals. He's part of our family at Rainbow Farm, and the way things are going I'll probably be out here in the middle of winter with my snow shoes on still looking for him. I don't know why I love this little guy so much, but as long as I keep seeing him, and as long as other people keep seeing him, I'll keep looking for him, no matter what.

Tillman figured that for the rest of November Buster would be OK. For that matter, even December could sometimes be fairly mild in the Estrie region. But there was no doubt that the period from January to March would be brutal. The snow would be deep, and hunting would be difficult for a domestic cat whose ancestors evolved in the deserts of the Middle East with legs too short to plow through the deep snows. He was no snow leopard. And despite his thick fur coat, the cold would most likely kill him. His eyes searched the roadside once again, and he tried not to think about Buster trying to survive in winter conditions.

§

After a day of hunting in the forest Buster found himself back near the road. He heard a vehicle slowly approaching and watched as it slowed to a crawl, then stopped. A man got out.

Danger! Buster thought and ran into the underbrush near the edge of the road. But the man was calling, and the human sounds were familiar. Buster's first instinct was to not make a sound, to remain silent and undetected. He waited under cover for a while to make sure everything was secure. But he couldn't remain silent for long because he recognised the voice. It was the nice man from Rainbow Farm again. It was the same voice that had called the day before, and that same voice was calling him now.

I have to answer. I have to answer, now! He threw all caution to the wind and called out.

"I'm here! I'm here!" He chirped like crazy. *That's him! That's him! I recognise him now. That's Tillman from Rainbow Farm!* Buster thought excitedly. At the same time Tillman Charbonneau thought,

Hey, he's answering me. Maybe tonight's the night I finally get him.

The man stood very tall, and his size frightened Buster, but the cat was determined that this time he would take a chance. This time he was not going to hide, yet he didn't actually approach the man, but he kept contact by chirping while keeping his distance in the underbrush.

Should I just run out there and let him grab me? he wondered.

He was sure that was the man; but something was holding him back. Buster hesitated, but reinforced by the familiar sound of the man's voice he began to move towards the man calling him.

This is it, he thought. *Either I take a chance and go to him or I'll spend the rest of my life out here.*

Tillman could see Buster standing not far from the road chirping and meowing at him but he wasn't coming any closer.

Buster took a few tentative steps towards the road, but suddenly, before Buster could get close, the man got back in his Thunderjunker and drove away. Buster's heart sank like a stone in a pond.

Why am I such a coward? I should have gone to him instead of waiting and hiding, he scolded himself.

Because I was a coward, now I might never be rescued. I'm too cautious; I should have taken a chance! Then he thought better of it. *Of course I took a chance with the oily fish and look what happened. I don't know what to do. Giant humans frighten me,* he reflected. *But the nice man and the nice lady and all their friends always looked like giants to us cats.*

He knew more than ever that he had missed out on his chance for today, but tomorrow or the next day he would be on the lookout and he would be ready.

§

Tillman was looking forward to a nice dinner with Annie, but seeing that Buster was not running away from him he thought their chances of getting him that night were better than ever. But when he didn't come to him after a few calls he thought he should try something different. Instead of calling him alone, he decided:

I'll go get Annie and we can try together. Maybe her voice will work better than mine. Annie had only heard about the Buster sightings, but she had not actually seen him since he was first spotted over a month ago.

Before leaving he scoured the road side and found an old beer can someone had thrown out and put it by the side of the road where he had last seen Buster. When they returned the beer can would reflect in the headlights, and he would know where to start looking. Then he jumped back in his truck and drove home.

He's acting differently tonight. Tillman thought. *I think he finally recognises me. That's something I haven't seen yet. All those other times he just meowed a few times, and then ran off; tonight he's different.*

When Tillman entered the house he could smell dinner cooking, and although he was hungry he was not thinking about eating.

Without taking his coat off, he called out to Annie in the kitchen where he was sure she would be busy preparing dinner.

"I've seen Buster again," he said as he made his way to the kitchen, greeting her with a hurried kiss on the lips. He quickly explained the situation to his wife. Annie had been living with the lost Buster story for all these months, and like her husband, she too was desperate to get the cat home.

"You're right. Let's go back now," she said, as she reached over and turned the stove off and placed their dinner casserole in the oven to keep it warm. She checked the stove and oven again to make sure everything was shut off, and said,

"We'll eat when we get back. It'll keep for later. I was just outside and it's a beautiful night tonight, but we can't expect the weather to hold forever. It's going to start snowing tomorrow so we better get him tonight, before the ground is covered with snow."

She grabbed her coat while Tillman went to the back room and searched through their collection of flashlights, and found a couple of good ones with fresh batteries. Minutes later they pulled up next to the beer can marker that lay by the side of the road. They parked, and armed with two flashlights each they flashed their beams and called as they walked along the edge of the road. Annie took the left side and Tillman took the right, shining their flashlights into the ditches and the underbrush and calling out his name. They called and looked for about twenty minutes, but there was no sign of Buster. They turned around and headed back down the same stretch of road in reverse, but still, there was no sign or sound of Buster, so Annie said,

"Maybe we lost him for the night. I think we're going to have to come back tomorrow."

"Yeah, I'm afraid you're right. I thought he would be close by when we came back, but I guess he went back into the woods after I left him. Shall we try going in a little and have a look?"

"The terrain looks pretty rough, Tillman, and in the dark we're not going to get very far. You'll have to come back in the morning. I'll come with you, and we'll get an early start OK?"

"OK, but I guess you know they are announcing snow for tomorrow."

"I know. We better find him soon. I tell ya' what. It's a beautiful, clear night, why don't we go back home, grab a bite and then come back one more time?"

"Good idea," said Tillman as they headed for the truck. "I'm getting mighty hungry, and could use some chow."

§

Buster had gone back into the forest to hunt, but when he heard human noises, he looked up and listened.

Something's going on down by the road; maybe it's my humans. I better get down there right now, he said as he turned and headed in the direction of the sounds.

Just as he grabbed the door handle Tillman heard Buster calling from the woods.

"Annie, did you hear that?"

"I sure did, and I know its Buster alright. He's calling us from somewhere back in the woods." She listened intently for a minute and then said, "I think he's coming this way."

"That's great. That's the first time he's ever called to us from far away, and you're right, I think he's coming in our direction." They called his name again and again for a minute or two.

After weeks of sightings and calls, this was the first time Buster had called them first. Tillman waved his flashlight in the direction of Buster's voice and all of a sudden he saw yellow-green cat eyes reflecting back at his flashlight through the fallen trees. The cat remained in the woods a short distance from the road, and he did not run away. For about a minute Annie and Tillman continued calling and Buster continued answering.

"He knows it's us." said Annie, "and I think he wants to come to us."

"Yes, this is starting to look good for a change."

Despite his fear, Buster headed for the road. He remembered his fear of Beagle and how he didn't want to get near him. He remembered his strategy for survival: 'The more you stayed away from trouble, the less trouble you got into.' But those were different times and circumstances. This time things were different. These were his humans; these were the nice people from Rainbow Farm.

Tillman and Annie kept calling back and forth to each other narrowing down the distance between them and slowly closing in on Buster. Now Tillman could see him in the flashlight beam just off the road and down an embankment on the other side of a high metal wire fence that had been put there many years ago. He decided he would climb the fence and see if he could work his way around behind and Buster and coax him towards Annie while she stayed on the road close to the truck. He struggled over the fence and through piles of fallen trees, and all the while he continued calling.

Buster saw the man and hesitated.

Stop being a coward. Go to him. He tried to encourage himself. Just then he heard another voice.

"Buster, Buster come", called Annie.

Wait! I hear the nice lady's voice. She's over there by the road.

Then he saw her. *I see her. She's right by the road! She's right in front of me!*

As Buster took his last few steps through the trees towards the road Annie Perrault did something that the man had never done when he had attempted to coax Buster towards him: she crouched down, in effect making herself smaller, and from Buster's perspective, less threatening. She called Buster's name again, and he walked right towards her.

It's Annie! He told himself. *I know her it's the nice lady from Rainbow Farm. I'm not waiting any longer! I'm going to her right now so she can take me home!*

Having made that decision, Buster moved right through the last of the trees and into the ditch that ran parallel to the road. She was only a few steps in front of him now, calling his name.

"Come on Buster, come to mama," she said in her calm voice to the cat who was now just a couple of paces away.

That's Annie! She will not harm me. I know she will take me home with her.

"I'm coming! I'm coming so you can take me home to Rainbow Farm," he meowed as he climbed out of the shallow, gravel-lined ditch into the glaring headlight beams of the truck.

As he drew near to her a feeling of relief came over him. Suddenly her smell was in his nostrils, so familiar, as if he'd never left her. He could see her face illuminated by the headlights, and her gentle voice had a soothing effect on him. He looked up straight into her eyes, meowed and took one last step towards her as Annie leaned forward and picked him up. As her arms folded around him he looked up at her and chirped a string of 'hellos.' He was in her arms; he was safe.

Annie felt a sense of urgency to get Buster into the truck and get him home. Once back at Rainbow Farm they could examine him more closely and make sure he was all right. She could hardly believe that after all these months she was actually holding him next to her. She stood up, and then turned and walked into the glaring truck headlights. When she reached the passenger-side, she opened the door, and placed Buster on the seat.

I'll make sure he's securely in the truck and then I'll go tell Tillman, she decided.

As soon as he was inside she closed the door in case he tried to jump out. She need not have worried about that since Buster had no intention of jumping out. He just wanted to go home, and he felt so secure he never once thought about the truck as a dangerous Thunder-junker. With the cat safely inside the truck, Annie turned and took a few steps in the direction of the woods, and scarcely able to contain herself, she called out to her husband:

"Tillman, I've got him! I've got him!"

The man heard her voice, but couldn't believe his ears.

"What did she just say?" he asked himself out loud. "Did you say you've got him?" he called back in her direction.

"Yes, he's in the truck!" she yelled.

"He's in the truck?" The man was stunned!

How in hell did she get him in the truck so fast? I must have misunderstood.

Maybe she meant he was under the truck or something like that. It was hard to believe that after so long the cat was actually inside the truck.

"Did you say he's in the truck?" he called out again to Annie, who was about 50 paces away, the two of them separated by a wall of trees. He wanted to make sure that he had heard correctly, but for some reason she did not answer right away so he repeated,

"Did you just say that he was in the truck?"

"Yes," she answered, "he's in the truck!"

"Lord Thundering Jesus!" said Tillman Charbonneau, his words heard only by the trees that didn't seem terribly concerned about the cat-human drama unfolding around them.

I wonder how she got him so quickly, he thought, still astonished to hear Buster was in the truck.

Could it be true, he asked himself, *that after months of looking high and low and after dozens of sightings and weeks checking the traps every day that all of a sudden the little guy was in the truck?*

"That's fantastic!" He called out from cupped hands. "Way to go! I'm coming right over!"

Once in the truck, Buster thought, *Oh good they're going to take me home.*

But when the nice lady closed the door and left, Buster felt insecure. He had been abandoned before and he was not going to let Annie get away from him, no matter what.

Oh no! She's not going to leave me again is she? I've got to follow her, and not let her get away from me!

§

"Tillman, he's escaped! He jumped out the window!" he heard his wife call out as he was making his way towards the partially obscured headlights in the distance.

Tillman stopped in his tracks. *This is crazy. I don't understand what's going on here. Did I hear her right,* he asked himself?

"What? He's escaped?" he yelled back through cupped hands. *How could that be? Good grief!* he thought to himself. *Will we ever succeed in getting this cat back home?*

Earlier, when their flashlights started to dim, they turned the truck headlights on low beam to light the area up, and to warn the occasional passing motorist of their presence. They left the motor idling.

"No sense draining the truck battery," they agreed.

Their truck was equipped with doors that locked automatically after several minutes. It was supposed to be a safety feature, but usually it just left them stranded somewhere locked out of their truck with the motor running. To avoid this they always left a window open whenever they stepped out for a moment. But, after Annie put Buster in the truck and closed the door, she forgot about the open window on the driver's side. When Buster saw Annie leaving he wasn't going to let her get away so he just jumped out of the open window. As soon as he hit the ground, he followed close on her heels. As it turned out they were both afraid of losing each other, and when Annie heard Buster chirping behind her, she immediately stopped, knelt down and called to him. He was back in her arms in seconds. The second time she put him in the truck she made sure all the windows were closed, put her own set of keys in her pocket, and got out again. Then she called to her husband.

"It's OK. I've got him. He's back in the truck again!"

Tillman was slightly dumfounded as he came out of the bush. First she had him then she didn't. Now she had him again. The situation was confusing, but he didn't mind. As long as she had him that was all that counted. He moved quickly towards the truck and got into the driver's seat, taking care not to make any gestures that might frighten Buster. He closed the door and as Annie held him Tillman looked at Buster, petted him and said 'hello' several times before starting the engine.

"Let's just get him home before we do anything else, what do you say?" Annie agreed. "Yep, let's just get him home and sort things out once we're there," she said.

After all the excitement, the cat was remarkably calm although, truth be told, he was in a mild state of shock. As Annie held Buster in her arms, his yellow-green eyes looked about with a little apprehension at his situation. He was very happy he was at last being held by Annie, the woman all the neighbours referred to as 'the nice lady.'

Once at Rainbow Farm, Tillman went inside the house and herded all the other animals down into the basement to avoid the inevitable excitement generated when a new or strange animal comes into a place. Buster had been gone for many months and it was certain that it would take a little time for the other animals to get used to him once again. Even if they did recognise him right away, nature demanded a defensive response when strange animals appeared. That's how animals are, particularly Mecki, who couldn't remember anyone's face for more than five minutes. He even barked at overnight house guests as they descended the stairs in search of their morning coffee. The last thing Buster needed was to be frightened out of his wits as a homecoming present, and he would need a little time before he would feel secure in his old environment.

Once inside, after they had hugged him a few times they held him up and gave him the once over. The first thing they noticed was that Buster had lost weight. His flanks curved in behind his rib cage, and his usual bulkiness was gone. But other than the weight loss, he seemed fine. They placed him on the kitchen table and examined him. There were no torn ears, no missing claws, and his joints seemed to be fine. Everything bent and flexed and worked well. They detected no sores, no ticks trying to burrow their way through his skin, and no swellings, or abscesses hidden beneath his fur. Then, as the man ran his hand across his back and front shoulders he felt one, then two, then at least five nodules of healed skin. He pushed aside the fur and he and Annie saw several small scars plus four large ones the size of pencil erasers where the Horned owl's claws had punctured the cat's back. Further examination revealed a few more; the good news was they were all healed.

"This happened some time ago," said Tillman, "probably early on after he first got lost."

"Yeah, it's clear he suffered some kind of major injury," said Annie. "We can only imagine what had happened to him and how he received these wounds, but they really must have slowed him down. He could have died from injuries like these. Still, you know what?" she said, looking across the table at her husband, "in general he looks well and healthy."

"He does indeed," he concurred.

"Buster," Annie said looking at the cat, "your scars could tell us stories, I'm sure, but we'll probably never know them."

Later Tillman and Annie spent some time over a glass of wine celebrating his return and discussing how he might have come by such scars and who might have put them there.

"Maybe a coyote or a fox," suggested Annie.

"You're probably right," said Tillman. "But then who knows for sure? That will just be one of his little secrets from us, eh little guy?" he said looking at Buster. One thing seemed certain; at some point during his absence Buster had gone through an experience that left him injured, and probably nearly cost him his life. They checked the record they kept from their last visit to the veterinarian six months earlier, and as young, not fully grown adult, Buster had weighed nearly six kilograms. When they weighed him that night on the bathroom scale he was down to just under four kilos, a huge weight loss for a cat Buster's size.

"Well," said Annie, "we better get busy and fatten this little guy up."

After inspection, he ate a big bowl of dry cat food, and sniffed and explored the house by himself. An hour later they let the two dogs and Kofi and Buddy Lebeau out of the basement to get re-acquainted with their long-lost cat brother. After a cursory side-winder hackle raising by Kofi there was almost instant recognition between all three of the cats. Buddy Lebeau was overjoyed to see his brother cat once again and have him back home. The two dogs sniffed him and pushed him with their muzzles, then when Mecki finally decided he was no threat to Rainbow Farm, with his laconic sense of humour he made the dog sounds:

"What took you so long, kid?" Buster just chirped and rubbed against him.

"I'm glad to see you too, tough-guy," he said looking up at the big dog.

Sparky was overjoyed to see Buster. They licked each other and pushed each other around as a way of greeting for several minutes. Then it was Lebeau's turn, and finally, even Mecki gave the grey cat a big lick.

Later that evening, for his second helping of food, they took him to the cat feeding area up on the counter and there, just as before, was the portrait of the *Buddha-cat* looking down on the three food bowls. Buster remembered that as a young cat he thought that the *Buddha-cat* was stern and tough-looking. Now, with his forest survival experiences behind him, the Tibetan feline looked more comical than menacing.

I could handle that guy if I had to, thought Buster, *he certainly doesn't scare me like he used to*. From now on he would just be another part of the feeding station decor.

"Wow," Buster meowed as he turned his gaze away from the *Buddha-cat* to the other two cats, "This guy is uglier than ever!" Buddy and Kofi both laughed. "No wonder he has that look on his face. He's mad at his mother for giving birth to such an ugly cat!"

"Oh Buster, that's a good one!" cried Buddy Lebeau.

"That is indeed funny, Buster if I do say so myself," said the normally reverential Kofi when it came to the red and orange image.

"But you know what you guys?" he said looking at his cat brothers. "Despite that, I am really glad to see this guy's ugly face again."

"Why?" they asked.

"Because it means I'm not dreaming. It means I'm really home now."

With that, Buster and his brother cats jumped and hopped like rabbits, dancing around the feeding area in a kindred celebration of Buster's return.

Afterwards, they all went upstairs and gathered in the bed. It had been a long evening; the cats, the dogs, the humans, everyone was tired. In a few minutes the nice people had their heads propped on pillows and were reading their books and it wasn't long before Kofi and Buddy Lebeau gathered on the bed while the dogs lay down on their respective cushions on either side. Most evenings Mecki slept next to Annie, while Sparky slept next to Tillman. Buster did not get on the bed right away. It was strange and somehow didn't seem right after sleeping out of doors for so many nights. It was almost too much to digest at once, so he just lay down on the wooden floor close to them. When the lights went out, Buster was the happiest cat in the world. He looked up and saw the clear starry sky through the dormer window.

I'm home. Thank you Magic Star, I am home!

Buster slept lightly, keeping an eye open for predators. But as the hours passed, it began to sink in that there were no coyotes stalking him from the dark corners of the room, no round-eyed night bird was about to sweep out of the closet to sink its claws into his back, and no Black bear was waiting behind the bed to pounce on him. While he kept watch, Kofi and Buddy were spread out on the bed between the two snoring humans and the dreaming dogs. Later that night, when the heirloom clock struck twice Buster jumped up onto the bed and curled up with Buddy Lebeau. Then, as he did every night, he said:

Goodnight Juliette, my love. Goodnight Sommet kittens. He closed his eyes, and let the warmth and comfort of his home soothe him to sleep. As he slept clouds moved in and snow fell through the late night hours, covering the ground with white stuff.

§

Annie awoke to the sounds of Buster retching, and found him bent in half at the spine as if some piston mechanism was attempting to pump his insides out, leaving a cocktail of saliva, cat food and a knot of long white worms flailing about on the kitchen floor. Like the cats of old who boarded Champlain's ships, the worms were travellers too; they had migrated from rabbits or mice or some other animal that Buster had ingested, and set up house in his intestinal tract. Before they cleaned up the mess and washed the floor, Tillman tweezered a couple of the stomach dwellers into a plastic canister.

"I'll show these little wigglers to the vet over in Coaticook and get some pills for this."

"No wonder he's lost so much weight," said Annie, "he's got a bunch of freeloaders living in his stomach."

It is not unusual for animals living in the wild to have parasites such as fleas or worms living in or on their bodies. Humans are no exception. Roman soldiers, mummified Egyptians and African slaves in the New World have left ample evidence that humans have long served as a vector for all manner of corporeal invaders. Vermifuge drugs and better sanitary conditions have enabled many humans to divest themselves of intestinal boarders, but many other animals have not been so fortunate. Later that day, Tillman and Annie held Buster still, pried his mouth open, and stuffed a couple of worm pills down his throat. From then on the food he ate was his own and a day later the last of the worms exited his body with his scat. No longer would he need to double up his hunting efforts just to keep a bunch of hangers-on fed. By the end of his first month back home Buster had regained half a kilogram and was on his way to total weight recovery.

For the first few days after his return, Buster ate and slept and enjoyed being home. Annie and Tillman kept him in the house and they watched him carefully, making sure he did not run off, but after a week they were certain he was well oriented to his surroundings, and he began to go outside with the other cats. He didn't go far because by the time he was allowed out there were 10 centimetres of snow on the ground, so all the cats stayed close to the house, only venturing to the out-buildings for a little recreational mouse and rat hunting. Despite the snow cover and the falling temperatures, Buddy Lebeau continued to hunt, going off into the forest everyday like a miniature snow leopard, but by early January he too had given up and decided to join the other cats for the winter quiet time in front of the wood stove. Now began the lazy time for the three cats. They would eat and then return to the living room to sleep by the fire. Often it was easy to tell where Buddy was sleeping because he snored louder than any cat they had ever heard before. Later on, after their tag matches and house races they would join Annie and Tillman on the bed. After three months Tillman and Annie had to start cutting back on Buster's food portions. He now weighed in at over seven kilos, and was heavier than he had ever been in his life. With spring just around the corner, he would get lots of exercise and burn off his excess weight.

Book VIII

The Blessing of the Animals

Tillman and Annie were not regular church-goers, but ever since the arrival of Emory Braithwaite, the new pastor at the Anglican Church over in Smith's Landing, they had been taking one or two of their animals to the Blessing of the Animals ceremony held every summer in late August. Few people actually believed that some human dressed in odd clothes could actually improve their animal's lot in life. But the ceremony was fun and it brought people and their animals together in a festive atmosphere, with plenty of neighbourly camaraderie. The Blessing took place just before the out-of-towners packed up their things and headed back to Montreal, and the locals started to prepare their kids for the start of school in late August. Annie and Tillman usually took one dog on a leash, and one of the cats in a cage. Once there they might take the cat out of the cage, but with all the pets and barking the cats usually couldn't wait to get back home. The dogs had few problems and loved cavorting with the other animals while Tillman and Annie talked and joked around with friends, eating finger food and comparing their animals with someone else's. But this year they decided just to take Buster. He had never been to the ceremony so they thought it best just to take him to his first Blessing.

"I wonder if some holy water or a benediction will make him stop eating so much," Tillman joked to Annie as they coaxed Buster into his cage.

In preparation for mixing and mingling with boxers and budgies, they fitted Buster with a sturdy body harness instead of just a simple collar to be sure they could hang on to him if they decided to take him out. Not that they thought he would make a break for it or cause trouble, Buster wasn't that kind of cat. They just wanted to be sure he didn't get spooked and run off and hide someplace where they couldn't find him.

Tillman and Annie did not know that Buster had spent one of the worst days of his life trapped in a wire cage while a bear tried to break in and eat him. Reluctantly, and with a little pushing and shoving, they got him to go in.

Nor did they know that he hated Thunder-junkers.

How could they? Humans can't always know what causes fear among cats; and when it comes to trucks and cars, as long as you were sober and had your seatbelt attached, there was nothing to fear. They just assumed Buster felt the same way. After all, the dogs loved riding in the truck and they could hardly keep them out of it, and every time one of them opened the door to get in, either Mecki or Sparky was right there pushing them aside so they could leap in ahead of them. Both the dogs loved riding in the back of the pickup while they drove around their property, or if they were going over to Abenaki Falls, they would hang their heads out the passenger side window while their jowls flapped around in the wind.

"We're going to have to hide the keys from these dogs, Tillman," Annie said, "or one of these days they're going to take the truck and drive into town while we're not looking."

Buster did not mind riding in the truck if he wasn't in a cage. The night they rescued him he was fine sitting on Annie's lap as they drove him home. But in a cage and in the truck meant they were going to dump him at Bedlam Barn for the remainder of his days, and he would never see Rainbow Farm again. Now, in preparation for what was supposed to be a fun family outing he was once again in the back seat and in a cage: two of the most horrible things he could imagine.

Oh no! I'm in that contraption again. Where did they get it? I thought it stayed in the woods and it couldn't follow me. Now I'm in it once again, and to make matters worse they put me in this Thunder-junker death thing. They can't be taking me to Bedlam Barn again, can they?

"I hate this!' he howled." Don't take me to Bedlam Barn! Please!" he pleaded with Annie, who just turned around and gave him her warm smile, making human noises while patting him on the head.

"Take it easy, Sweet Cat," she said. "You're going to see a whole bunch of other animals, and have a great time. You'll see."

Buster was bewildered and looked back at Annie. *Why would they rescue me only to take me back to Bedlam Barn?*

As the truck moved down the driveway Buster meowed in desperation, but it kept on moving despite his protests. Tillman and Annie had seldom heard Buster so upset before, and they tried in vain to comfort him.

"Should we go back?" asked Annie

"I don't know," said Tillman. "He sure sounds upset. But it isn't far and maybe he'll settle down by the time we get there. I thought he would want to go. I didn't expect this."

"You're going to love seeing the other dogs and cats, Buster, just wait and see," Annie assured him. The drive over to Smith's Landing was a noisy one.

When they put the cage on the gravel surface of the parking area Buster stopped protesting, sniffed the air, and listened to the noises of other animals.

There are so many animals here, he thought. *And this isn't anything like Bedlam Barn. I have a feeling that maybe they are not all being abandoned. The animals all look so happy. Maybe this won't be as bad as I thought.*

Buster began to sense that his humans weren't going to leave him, and he could feel the party atmosphere outside the church that floated between the century-old trees and across the green lawns that stretched back to the old cemetery. The parking lot was filled with people hefting cages of exotic birds, chickens, cats and dogs out of their cars and trucks. People dragged, or were pulled along, by dogs on leashes, and even some of the cats, chickens and a few ducks were on leashes. Some people brought bigger animals: there were pigs, goats and a shiny, black and white Holstein calf. Pickups pulling four-wheel trailers disgorged horses, and as their humans led them down their ramps and onto the parking lot, the beautiful roan and pinto-coloured *chevaux* pranced about to the 'Ohhhs' and 'Ahhhs' of everyone there. The crowd favorite was called Jack; he was a big grey Percheron that worked with a lumberjack, somebody named Savard. Jack was well known to many people because he had hauled logs out of many of the forests in the county, and his owner proudly displayed his horse to the appreciative crowd. Someone sat down on the church steps and started playing a mandolin and was soon joined by a banjo and then a fiddle; bluegrass music was in the air.

When the church doors opened all of the animals were allowed inside, except for the cows and horses; they had to stay outside in the parking lot. To the sound of the old nineteenth-century pipe organ, the Reverend Emory Braithwaite, attired in the latest divinity wear, walked down the aisle and made his way to the pulpit. He knew his crowd and kept things simple and unofficial. He began by unceremoniously raising his arms in the air and giving a big:

"Hello animal lovers and welcome!" People shouted back their greetings and immediately everyone got into the spirit of the ceremony. Reverend Braithwaite was aware that although humans will sit in numbed silence through homilies that pulled convenient verses from the dusty corners of scripture and wove their words into something meaningful for parishioners, when it came to a bunch of dumb animals bereft of biblical knowledge, they would not tolerate any discourse about dogma or theological fine points. Best to cut things short and get to what the crowd really came for: the blessing part. So he said a few words about Saint Francis of Assisi, the person who came up with the idea of blessing beasts, inspired by a passage from the prophet Isaiah which spoke of wolves and lambs, leopards and baby goats all lying down together and led around by a human child.

Very nice Sunday school stuff, thought Tillman and Annie, as they looked at each other with a smile. *Nice, but not very realistic.*

By now long-time country people, they couldn't imagine coyotes lying down with little fawns in the big meadow at Rainbow Farm or cougars refraining from eating baby goats any time soon.

"Perhaps the wolves will become vegetarians," Tillman whispered as he leaned towards Annie standing between the pews near the church entrance. She dismissed his comment with a wave of her hand, and they both knew this was more about the beautiful August day and the fellowship between friends and animals, and like Christmas, the day belonged to the community's children and pet lovers. No analysis required.

Finishing his animal-love speech, Braithwaite stepped down from the pulpit, and while organ music played softly in the background, he moved down the central aisle among the two- and four-legged animals. Stopping at each one, he would ask the pet's name and say a few words about this or that little sheep, or puppy or bird, and terminate each blessing with the sign of the cross.

When he spoke and blessed, he pulled word bits from scripture, accented with snippets from Robert Frost and Khalil Gibran. Reverend Braithwaite was good at this sort of thing, and people loved it. Children smiled and parents felt pride as their particular pet received a moment of attention and a few words of poetry or scripture from the pastor.

Animals are not always proper church-goers who know the service routine and can follow it to the final amen, but most were calm and behaved quite well except for one young male Bouvier de Flandre who behaved rather badly by making a number of attempts to mount the legs of various ladies in the crowd. Someone from one of the back pews made a comment that there was always some guy like him at every party. Despite these interruptions, the rest of the animals behaved their Sunday best: there were no dog fights or cat chases, and for a moment it really did appear that lions were lying down with lambs.

The talking, barking, bleating and meowing went on for over an hour as pastor Braithwaite delivered his own brand of personalised spiritual gratification, moving from one animal to the next and allowing plenty of time for multiple photos and comments by friends and family members. Around mid-afternoon, birds, hamsters and rabbits were put back in their cages and people began to head towards the main door, carrying or trailing their animals behind them. Out in the parking lot, lumberjack Trépanier led Jack back up the ramp and into his trailer, while the calf and the other horses were put in their trailers.

Then, just as Tillman opened the cage door to put Buster back in, the cat froze in his tracks. His ears went up, turning this way and that like radar antennae searching for invisible aircraft. He had just heard something that made his heart stop: among the noises, growls and laughter he heard a familiar bark.

That's Beagle! Yes, for sure that's Beagle, I'd recognise that bark anywhere and he's right here in this very room!

Tillman had managed to get Buster's head halfway into the cage, when the cat suddenly pulled back out, snapped his body around in the direction of the bark, and then he let out a tremendous howl.

"Beagle! Beagle it's me, Buster!"

Until that moment the ceremony had proceeded about as quietly as one could expect for a bunch of pets and farm animals inside the confines of a church. It was expected that there would barking and growling, the bleating of sheep and the meows of cats. But on the whole, the animals had behaved like respectable church-goers should. All of that changed the instant Buster heard Beagle's bark. Buster let out a meow-howl that was heard clear out in the parking lot, and as far back as the cemetery tombstones at the far end of the church yard. According to one parishioner several of the dead had been awakened in their coffins. It was the same scream of delight he had emitted a year earlier when he had looked down at the base of the big fir tree and saw Beagle in a face-off with that tuft-eared lynx. It was the kind of piercing, primeval animal sound that caused pastor Braithwaite to cringe, mothers to clutch their children, and scared the bejesus out of everyone else: everyone except Beagle.

When the brown and white dog heard the cat sound he shook his long-eared head as if suddenly awakened from his afternoon nap. In a flash he knew the sound came from his long-lost friend, and one bark said it all:

"Buster!"

The cat's name was followed by a huge hound-howl that resonated up into the old wooden rafters high above the church floor and was so intense some claimed afterwards that the dog's noises caused the two wooden angels on either side of the altar to turn their heads in fright. The cacophony lasted nearly a minute as astonished bystanders looked about, wondering if someone's animal was hurt, or perhaps someone had stepped on the cat's tail, or maybe the dog's foot was caught in the floorboards. Nobody could see anything out of the ordinary—merely a cat standing in the middle of the aisle chirping and meowing and a dog at the other end of the church howling back at him. Just when people were getting really noise-nervous, Buster broke and ran through the crowd, forcing people to step aside to let him pass between their legs dragging his leash. As Buster drew near, Beagle tugged mightily at his leash, and with Brother Gregarious in tow he made his way towards his cat friend. Their reunification consisted of chirps and barks as Buster rubbed against Beagle's legs and chest and licked his face. Beagle barked a happy greeting and got down on his stomach and licked Buster's face. Then Beagle rolled over several times with a huge doggy smile plastered all over his black lips. As if trying to explain things, Beagle turned to Brother Gregarious, wagging and making little barks and whimpers. He tried to make it clear that he and Buster had survived in the woods together before they found him in his Forest Church. Brother Gregarious still looked confused, but it didn't matter too much. His dog and someone else's cat seemed to be getting on well.

"Beagle! Beagle," Buster chirped. "You're alive and well. I can't believe it! I can't believe it!" He cried out with joy as he threw himself against the dog's chest again and again.

"Buster! Buster! My long-lost friend!" Beagle responded licking the cat's face. "I thought I would never see you again!" In that instant, Beagle remembered the first time he saw Buster on the opposite side of the dusty road, so depressed and dejected he wanted to die. Now he had a wonderful new home with a new human. When their initial excitement subsided, and they had they settled down, Beagle caught Buster's eyes in his and said,

"Buster, seeing you once again gives me great joy and my heart floats among the stars in the heavens." Buster was overcome, and could hardly make any cat sounds.

"Me too, Beagle. Me too! I feel the same way."

After a brief pause Buster asked;

"Does he treat you well, Beagle?"

"Indeed, I am treated very well, Buster. Brother Gregarious is a wonderful human. We are together all the time, and I have a whole new and wonderful life with him. I don't regret anything."

Buster smiled as Beagle pointed his nose in the direction of Annie and Tillman, who were now standing close by. "So, are those your humans? They look nice."

"Yes, they are nice, and I am very happy to be back home at Rainbow Farm."

Tillman and Annie knew Brother Gregarious, so they came over and chatted for a while as Buster and Beagle played and rolled about on the church floor.

"Boy, our two little guys put on quite a show there a few minutes ago, didn't they?" Brother Gregarious said.

Tillman and Annie nodded their heads in agreement; then they all had a good laugh and continued chatting. By then, most of the finger food and soft drinks were gone and some of the people and their pets were beginning to leave the church, and the caretaker had begun his cleanup operations.

"I think we better get going, you guys, the janitor wants to clean up and go home," Annie said.

Finally, Annie and Tillman put Buster back in his cage, said their goodbyes, and headed for the door. The dog and cat knew the ways of humans and understood that they would have to part after their brief encounter.

"We have to go now Buster," said Beagle. "I hate for this to end."

"I know Beagle, but I am not sad. I saw you, I know you are well and happy, and that's what's important."

"You're right, of course Buster. It's wonderful to know that you made it back home and you're OK."

As Brother Gregarious led the dog towards the church door, Beagle stopped and turned back, and just before they parted he said,

"Buster, it was the Magic Star wasn't it? I mean, that's how you found your way back. That's what you were trying to explain to me on that last night, wasn't it?"

"Yes, Beagle," he answered. "It was indeed the Magic Star".

§

Slightly in shock, and with a tide of happiness washing over him, Buster was very happy.

I saw my friend, he thought. I saw Beagle, lynx warrior and faithful companion. I never had a better friend, he thought, and that included some really good and faithful friends like Buddy Lebeau and Kofi and Mecki. It also included Sparky, or 'Sugar Bear,' as those who loved him liked to call him.

Buster now understood that either Annie or Tillman would put him back in his cage soon, and he would be whisked away to the family Thunder-junker, and back home. He wasn't staying and he wasn't being abandoned. Just before they reached the door he gave a last glance back into the church to get one more glimpse of Beagle when, for the second time that day, his heart lurched, and nearly came to a stop. In the last instant he caught a one-second glimpse of an image that popped into his field of vision between skirts and trouser legs, leashes and cages and dog feet and cat feet. It was an image of a familiar face, someone he had not seen in a long time: standing off to one side was Madeleine Dupont, the wife of the man who had tried to kill him, the man who had chased him from the barn. Madame Dupont was talking to some people, but he could see she was holding one of Juliette's kittens, now a young adult cat, in her arms. Buster could see the resemblance and recognised her, and he remembered playing with her in the cardboard box when she was still a kitten. It was just about one year ago, and yet it seemed longer. He wanted to approach the young cat and find out if she remembered her one-time surrogate father. But, Buster thought, when he knew her she was just a kitten, barely a month or two old. She had changed and grown so much she probably wouldn't even know him, so there was no sense in saying anything, or more importantly, asking about Juliette. But... why not at least try? What could it hurt if he just inquired? So, just as they were nearing the main door, Buster looked back from inside his cage and loudly chirped the young cat's name.

"Hortense, Hortense!" his cat sounds carried across the church. Would she recognise his voice? Would she recognise the name Buster and Juliette had given her that hot August afternoon as they groomed and tumbled the kittens? It was a long shot, but he continued,

"Tell Juliette I love her and think about her all the time!" he yelled out, his words bouncing around between the walls and beams and coloured glass.

"Boy Buster, you're still going at it with all your noises today, aren't you?" commented Tillman looking down at the cage. Buster looked straight at the nice man, but he wasn't really looking or concentrating. He was listening for some kind of response, but he heard nothing. With the cat cage in one hand Tillman paused to allow Annie out the door first, then, just as the man stepped over the sill, Buster heard the young female call back to him:

"I remember you, Buster, and I will tell her. I will tell Juliette you send your love. She misses you Buster!"

She heard me! thought Buster. *She heard me, and Juliette misses me!*

It happened in an instant, and then it was over. There was no follow-up of any kind, just a few words shouted inside an old church. But for the second time that day Buster's heart rose to the sky with happiness. He had made contact. He had heard the

                    Buster and the Magic Star

magical sound of Juliette's name. As Tillman placed the cage in the back seat of the truck, Buster's head swam with the memories of that day. He didn't quite know what to make of things. He was overjoyed that he had seen Beagle safe and happy. That alone was worth the anxiety of the trip, but to see Madame Dupont there in the church with Hortense; that was truly something special. And yet...

What a day! And I thought they were going to abandon me. Great Cats, was I wrong!

Turning left up the long hill away from the church, Buster saw the countryside drifting by outside the window, but it was just a blur. Stuff was going by, but he wasn't really seeing anything. After they had driven a while, Annie turned around in her seat, looked at Buster in his cage, and said:

"Did you enjoy yourself today Buster? Did you have a good time with the other animals, eh, little guy?"

Buster gazed back at her with a blank look in his eyes. He didn't respond with any cat sounds as he usually did when dialoguing with his humans; not this time. Cat sounds just wouldn't do.

First Beagle; then Hortense, he thought. *Unbelievable! I guess it was a good thing I came after all. This will certainly be a Blessing of the Animals I'll never forget.*

§

In July, Jacques Dupont had a heart attack. It seems he was partaking in sexual activities that were beyond his cardio-vascular capacities when the event occurred. In a Montreal hotel room near his legal practice, he was about to have the most incredible orgasm of his life when he was suddenly jolted by a series of pains that tore through his body, and instead of making the sounds of coital fulfilment he made the unromantic racket unique to cardiac arrest. His brain was starved for oxygen for several minutes as he lay waiting for the ambulance crew to arrive, and just as they came through the door, things went black.

Now, deep in the bowels of a Montreal hospital, he couldn't remember falling flat on top of the woman beneath him, nor could he recall her terrified screams when the full weight of his unconscious body landed on top of her. He didn't remember her screaming and pushing him off. He didn't remember her dialling

9-1-1. Nor did he remember the wail of the ambulance sirens, the paramedics, or the ICU and the army of medical staff who worked to revive him. A month later the only memory he could draw out of his oxygen-starved brain was a murky recollection of him lifting his .410 shotgun to his shoulder, pointing it high in the air, and then firing off a round of bird-shot in the direction of a grey and white cat perched on a wooden beam high above the floor. He also had a vivid memory of the tin barn roof blowing apart, leaving a sky-blue hole peering through the structure from the outside. The frustrating thing was that he wanted to lower the gun and not fire, and he didn't want to blast a hole in the barn roof. He knew that was crazy. But the episode of aiming and firing and the appearance of blue sky on the other side of the barn roof while a grey cat plummeted to the floor repeated itself over and over again in one tiny, dark corner of his brain.

§

Driving up Chemin de la Rivière, Annie noticed a real-estate agency 'for sale' sign at the entrance to *La Ferme du Sommet*. Right next to it was another sign made with a magic marker on a piece of white cardboard:

Chatte stérilisée besoin d'un bon foyer—Fixed female cat needs good home.

Annie slowed and read both signs. She was surprised the place was for sale.

I never met these people, she thought, *but they have such a nice place up here with horses and such a beautiful view. I wonder why it's for sale? Should I stop in and ask about the cat? I better not, we have three cats already and we don't need a fourth one. But, I do wonder what happened to these people?*

An hour later, on her return trip from Smith's Landing, she saw a woman standing by the side of the road near the for sale sign picking up some things. She appeared to be doing some kind of yard work, and Annie assumed she was probably trying to make the place look its best before the real estate agent came with a prospective buyer. Annie couldn't resist, she gave a neighbourly wave and pulled over to the side of the road. She set the hand brake, got out and introduced herself. Madeleine recounted the events of the past two months, and in the space of one minute Annie had the story of why the place was for sale.

"Because of my husband's heart attack we have to move back to Montreal to be close to our children, and so as a family we can take care of him. Since from now on I'll be there most of the time, I won't be able to take care of this place all on my own. Three horses require a lot of care, and it's too much for me alone. I was lucky enough to find someone who wants our place and will care for our horses. They're city folks who want to buy our lifestyle. I don't blame them for wanting it, that's what I wanted when I came out here. It is beautiful, the horses are beautiful, the country is beautiful, and the people around here are beautiful. It's everything I ever wanted. But unfortunately, it's over for me and my husband. I'm not sure he even remembers his own name."

"That's tragic," said Annie. Then she paused and said,

"What about your cat?"

"We have a beautiful three-year-old female and her three yearlings. I found good homes for them, but I haven't found a place for Juliette, she's the mother. The new people have their own cat, plus they took one of Juliette's kittens but they don't want her. Ever since I put the place up for sale I've been worried about Juliette and what will happen to her. She isn't a city cat. She knows nothing about the city and would be completely vulnerable so I can't take her back to Montreal with me. In Montreal, I'm afraid she'd get run over in no time. She's an outdoor country cat and needs to live out here someplace. The new owners are moving in at the end of the month. I can't put her down, that's unthinkable. I can't do that. I love that cat, and I swear I'd put myself down before I would let anything happen to her. Added to all the other stuff going on with my husband, the hospital visits, the doctors, the intensive care, it's getting to be too much. Who knew it would end up like this when we got married all those years ago?"

"You don't deserve this, Madeleine."

"You're right, Annie." They had quickly moved to a first-name basis. "I don't. But we get what life gives us and we have to live with it. Maybe something will happen and I can move back out here again, I don't know. But right now I've got a sick husband, and I have to take care of him." Then she changed the subject.

"I've seen you around Annie and I know where your place is. It's the one sitting way off the road with the big field in front, isn't it? *La ferme arc-en-ciel,* right?" Annie nodded her head yes.

"It looks really nice from the road."

"It's a wonderful place," Annie said, almost feeling guilty at her good fortune with a healthy husband and a good life.

"You say you have cats?" Madeleine asked.

"Yes three of them, and two dogs," Annie paused. "Yeah, last year we lost one of our cats for five months. He escaped from *La maison des petits animaux*; you know, the kennel that closed down last year?" Madeleine nodded her head in acknowledgement.

"The little guy just wondered around in the woods all that time. In fact we spotted him a few times not too far from here. We finally managed to get him back home, but it wasn't easy."

"A lost cat, you say? What colour was he?" She paused. "I'm asking because we had a cat hanging around here for a while last summer. Could've been him."

"He's grey and white, short, thick coat; a pretty big fella' at that."

"You're kidding me! You are *kidding* me!" she repeated with added emphasis. "He was here for about a month; he took to our Juliette right away."

"You say he was here?"

"Sure sounds like him. I saw him a few times, but I didn't get too close because my husband chased him away." Madeleine didn't go into any details of how or why Buster left. "But I saw him, for sure." Seeing that Annie was brimming with interest, she continued. "He had a white belly too. In fact, the first time I saw him he had a bit of a limp, then a few weeks later, he seemed to be better."

"That sounds like our Buster alright. Just a minute," Annie said as she reached for her purse. "I've got a photo of him right here. I've been carrying it around with me ever since we lost him. It's been over a year now."

"But you say you got him back".

"Yeah," Annie answered. "He's home, safe and sound. Here," she said as she placed a colour photograph of Buster into Madeleine's hands. "Last summer I showed this photo to half the people in the county. Does that look like him?"

"That's him! That's him! He was here for sure."

"And you say he liked your female?"

"He sure did. You should have heard them carrying on. I swear they were in love. I watched them on a few occasions, but I couldn't say anything to my husband because, like I said, he hates cats."

Somewhat puzzled Annie said,

"But Buster, that's the grey and white cat's name, is fixed."

"That doesn't seem to matter. Apparently they can still really fall for each other."

"You don't say," said Annie. "Do you think I could have a look at her?"

"Of course. Follow me, she's in the barn."

§

"Tillman! Tillman! Come here! We have a new member of the family."

"We do? What do you mean?"

"Come and meet Juliette."

Uh oh, sounds like she's gone out and adopted another cat. Are we ready for another one? I better go see what's going on, he thought as he headed down the stairs from his second-floor study.

"But Annie," he called out as he grabbed the hand rail, "we already have three cats, aren't we at our limit?"

"I'm told that she and Buster are in love, Tillman," she said, appealing to her husband's sense of romance as he reached the stair landing.

"What? Where did you get her?"

"La Ferme du Sommet."

"Hey, didn't that guy just have a heart attack or something?"

"Yes he did, and now he's back in Montreal and his wife can't take care of the place, so she has to sell and give Juliette away. That's why she's up for adoption. Come have a look at her. She's beautiful."

"She sure is. Our boys are going to love her. She'll get plenty of attention from all of them."

§

Buster was dreaming. He was sure of it when he saw her in the living room about an hour after Annie brought her home.

This can't be real. It can't be. How would Juliette get here? She lives far away at La Ferme du Sommet. *How can she be here?*

She was lying on the couch next to Annie, who was doing her best to keep her calm and make her feel comfortable. Juliette was still confused and a little frightened by all the recent changes in her life. She had been taken from her beautiful home in the big barn among the horses to a strange new place. Even though she sensed no threat, she wanted to go back home to her barn. This new place had strange smells and strange sounds. There were canines around here; she could smell them. She had never really been around dogs before, if that's what they were. But were they dogs or coyotes?

Maybe these people kept coyotes instead of dogs, she thought. Humans do odd things.

When she was much younger an old female told her that some humans kept coyotes instead of dogs. Juliette hated dogs. She always had since she was a kitten and had been chased by them. The idea of a cat-friendly dog was unknown to her. For the last hour she had wanted to bolt and hide somewhere, but this big house was full of dangerous smells and unknown places. The only reason she stayed on the couch was because the female human had one hand restraining her just enough so she couldn't jump off and run for cover somewhere.

Then, right in front of her, they introduced a grey and white cat, a stranger. She arched her back even as the lady held her fast on the couch.

Who's this guy? she wondered. *Do I have to fight him? Wait, maybe this isn't so bad. At least they have a cat, one of my own kind, and he doesn't look mean. That's a good sign.* She kept her hackles up and her back arched while she surveyed the grey and white intruder. Then her body language and facial expressions began to change.

He looks familiar, he's making nice-cat sounds at me. What's going on here? she thought. Her eyes became much, much larger.

He looks very, very familiar, she told herself as her hackles went horizontal and her back flattened out. Then, she began purring.

Buster had no problem recognizing her. He knew right away it was Juliette in front of his eyes, but he thought she was a part of one of his frequent visions he had while dreaming. But he wasn't dreaming now, so she had to be an apparition that had somehow escaped and was now sitting with Annie on the living room couch. It was a little frightening.

How can I be dreaming this, it's so real? he asked himself. *I'm not sure, but I think I know how to find out. I think I know exactly what to do.*

With that, Buster began to chirp and meow the sounds of *Mia Gatta, Mio Amore*, directly at Juliette, just as he had done the first time he met her. As cat sounds poured from his mouth, Annie's eyes almost popped out of her head, and she gasped when she saw Buster throw himself on the floor in front of the new cat.

"Tillman, do you see what I see?" she cried. The man looked on with his mouth open at the cat-music spectacle, filled with wailing and howling cat sounds emitting from Buster, and directed right at the new female. Unlike their first encounter in the barn when Buster had rolled on the floor in front of Juliette but missed the high notes, this time he hit every note perfectly, enrapturing Juliette and overwhelming the two humans. As Annie and Tillman held their ears and the dogs barked from down in the basement, Juliette jumped off the couch and ran to Buster. For the next few minutes they carried on an intense feline greeting ritual of rubbing and licking and rolling around together. By the end of it Juliette had found her lost love and a new home. As they tumbled on the floor together, Annie looked up at her husband and said,

"I don't think she's going to be running off anytime soon, do you, Tillman?"

"Not a chance," he said.

§

Epilogue

In March of the following spring, Buster and the other cats, now including Juliette, were back outside at the first sign of warm weather. Buddy Lebeau and Kofi loved Juliette and they were all eager to show her around her new home. As the days grew warmer in the spring sun the four of them explored the garage, the garden shed and the chicken house, and frolicked about in the areas of grass exposed between the patches of melting snow.

By this time Buster was a mature cat, much different than the one who had escaped from the kennel that hot June night nearly two years before. He was a strong, healthy cat, muscular and wise in the ways of the woods and hunting. He was a cat who had lived in the wild world of aerial and earthbound predators. As soon as the spring thaw ended, the three males were eager to take their new cat sister down the path to Tomifobia Pond and continue on all the way over to Abenaki Falls. Once there, Buster was fearless and tough. Even Goliath kept a respectful distance. Juliette was an instant hit with the other cats and with her three new cat brothers to protect her, no one bothered her. But most of the time, as summer approached, and the world turned from white to green, Buster stayed close to Juliette near the house and the rose and herb gardens, the miniature Edens Annie created every spring and summer. His happiest times were the daily outings when Annie and Tillman and all the animals went for walks in the woods. When their humans called them, Mecki and Sparky, and the four cats gathered behind the house and headed down the moss-covered path that made its way beneath the overhanging canopy of maples and beeches. Once in the forest, the dogs would bolt deeper into the woods in search of some new smell and then return for the little treats the humans pulled from their pockets. Moving through the forest the cats would jump from one stump or fallen tree to another, and then sit patiently to receive a reward for their precocious antics. Afterwards they continued their jumping game to the next long-ago fallen tree, its moss covered trunk slowly rotting away on the forest floor.

Author's Note

Although fictional, the Buster story is based on a number of real events and animal characters. Buster really was lost in the woods for a period of five months several years ago, and Buster's cat and dog brothers, Kofi, and Buddy Lebeau, along with Mecki and Sparky, are all real animals who live in a rural environment in southern Quebec, and whose lives and characteristics have been incorporated into the story.

The Magic Star is a well-known astronomical phenomenon that occurs when the planet Venus crosses the ecliptic and appears very close to the first lunar crescent.

Most of the historical characters mentioned in the story are well known to the public. All other human characters in the story are fictitious.

Cats like Mushi, with solid colour coats lacked the necessary camouflage to be proficient hunters in the wild, and his uniform colour was in part, responsible for his need to be near a human settlement to get enough to eat.

Latin and Greek were used, or inspired a number of names and terms, such as the name Buster. However, Middle Eastern personal and place names were either taken from, or inspired by, Akkadian, the ancient language of the Babylonians and Assyrians. There are several different versions of the Prayers to the Gods of the Night, known to Assyriologists. A number of liberties were taken with the version used in this story, as well as with the astrological report from the hand of the fictitious scribe Rasha used to describe the Magic Star. Although celestial objects were considered to be omens in Mesopotamia, they did not possess magical powers in the modern sense of the word. Nor is there a word that can be securely translated as 'magic' in the Akkadian language. I opted for *kišpum* because it was often associated with sacrifices made at the dark of the moon.

Ancient Egyptian names are unchanged. However, the etymology linking the modern name Kofi with the name of the

Fourth Dynasty king Khufu, although somewhat homophonic, is fictional.

Recent genetic and archaeological research indicates that both dogs and cats played a key role in the agricultural revolution and subsequently the development of civilization. Until recently it was believed that cats were originally tamed and domesticated in ancient Egypt during the second millennium BC. Although it is true that cats played an important role in Egyptian life, genetic evidence indicates that wild Desert Cats (*Felis silvestris libyca*, and several other subspecies) began their close interaction with humans more than 10,000 years ago in Syria-Palestine, early in the Neolithic Revolution. I have retained the capitalised spelling of Desert Cats throughout when referring to the direct ancestor of modern-day domestic cats (*Felis silvestris catus*).

Animal-human burials that include dogs, foxes and cats are known from the Neolithic period. The discovery of a cat-human burial in a Neolithic context on the Island of Cyprus, which had no cats until humans introduced them there, indicates that cats were so important that someone made the effort 95 centuries ago, to transport them by boat across at least 100 kilometres of open water, most likely for the purpose of protecting their grain supplies from rodents.

§

Acknowledgements

A number of friends and colleagues were instrumental in helping me complete this story. My thanks go first of all to Tim Doherty of *VisImage*, Sherbrooke, Quebec, who did the set up and cover for the paper and online versions of the book. To Julie Frédette and Helga Loverseed who helped edit the manuscript and to Nicole Fontaine who read several versions of the story and made many valuable comments, suggestions and corrections. Further thanks go to my colleagues Professor Douglas Frayne, of the Department of Near and Middle Eastern Studies at the University of Toronto, for linguistic assistance; and to Professor Sumio Fugii of the School of Human Sciences, Kanazawa University, Kyoto, Japan, for sharing unpublished information concerning feline history and cat domestication in the Pre-pottery Neolithic period in Jordan. A very special thanks goes to my wife Karina, my most patient critic and commentator.

§